THE WATCHERS

The Trekana – Book 1

A Novel by
JO SISK-PURVIS

THE WATCHERS
The Trekana – Book 1
Copyright © 2022 by Jo Sisk-Purvis

FIRST EDITION SOFTCOVER
ISBN: 1622530357
ISBN-13: 978-1-62253-035-9

Editor: Anita Lock
Cover Artist: Kris Norris
"Moons" Illustrator: Wednesday Purvis
Interior Designer: Lane Diamond

EVOLVED PUBLISHING™

www.EvolvedPub.com
Evolved Publishing LLC
Butler, Wisconsin, USA

Printed in Book Antiqua font.

BOOKS BY JO SISK-PURVIS

THE TREKANA
Book 1: *The Watchers*
Book 2: *The Knowers* [Late 2023]
Book 3: *The Trekana* [Late 2024]

DEDICATION

For Pat and Mike Sisk,
who taught me that love is the most powerful force of all.

PART ONE – WATCH

The path to peace is never passive. It is steep and winding and relentless, and even the most faithful student of the A'lodi may be tempted to take an easier road. But keep faith, for every living being possesses only one undeniable power—the power to control their own thoughts and actions.

~ The Book of the A'lodi

CHAPTER 1

Lulla loni
Lulla laiki rohn
Lulla loni

"Argh!" My fingers tangled like the washed-up seagrass piled on the sand, and I struck an angry, sour chord on the strings of my *lele*.

My baby brother Konu looked up from the hole he was digging in the sand. "Laysi owie?"

I had to smile at his sincere little face. "No, just frustrated."

"Fuhtated." He frowned, then went back to his digging.

I resisted the urge to play the passage a twelfth time since I'd been playing it perfectly for weeks. Now on the morning of the biggest and most significant performance of my life, it flitted away from me like the golden gull in Uma's folktales.

"The problem isn't in your fingers, Alesea. It's in your mind." That was my mother's favorite advice for elusive fingerings, cooking disasters, and even messy rooms. Stop practicing, and meditate.

Fine. I set my *lele* in its case and closed my eyes, shifting into my meditation posture. *Breathe. One, two –*

"Laysi! Big boats!" Konu was back to his typical style of speech, made entirely of exclamations. "Laysi, Laysi!"

"Shh, Konu, I need to focus."

"Mmm mmm mmm."

Konu's excited humming built my curiosity, and I opened one eye to peek at whatever he was seeing. He was right. I leaped to my feet and gaped toward the horizon over the glittering, morning-blue sea.

There *were* big boats—huge boats, like nothing I'd ever seen. Something—excitement or fear or both—choked up my throat. "C'mon,

Konu." I fastened my *lele* case, swung it over my shoulder, scooped my baby brother onto my hip, and ran for the forest.

The ships grew impossibly large, dwarfing our little fishing boats tied to a nearby dock. Men swarmed the decks, throwing out anchors in the middle of the harbor, while others swung from the rigging to lower sails that billowed with more cloth than I'd ever seen in my life. I caught glimpses of brightly-colored tunics and long black braids against the white. The word *Paav* decorated sails and hulls in fancy script. What could it mean?

The scene unfolded with an eerie silence, even though the ships had come so close that I should have heard the sailors' shouts as they climbed the masts and threw ropes to secure the sails. I stopped breathing when a man leaned over the deck of the closest ship—gazing, it seemed, straight at our hiding place. His eyes were huge, his head strangely narrow, but it wasn't until he turned away and revealed the dark stain from hairline to shoulder that I remembered. I'd seen a head like that once before on a shipwrecked foreigner.

That foreigner had been a Watcher from distant Mata, and the stain was an intricate tattoo that emphasized his missing ears.

These sailors weren't being silent for stealth but because they had no voices, just eagle-sharp eyes and a reputation for secrecy.

I squeezed Konu tight and ran for the village.

***

"Itu!" I plopped Konu down on the soft earth next to our garden and listened to the blood pound in my ears. "Itu, where's Mama?"

My older brother frowned at me as if I'd dropped from the sky and spoken the wrong language. He closed the book he'd been drawing in and swung his gangly brown legs over the side of his hammock. "Alesea, where've you been? Mama's already gone to Kokka to rehearse."

Of course. Half the adults from our island of Akila were already at the Great Hall of Kokka, preparing for tonight's Solstice celebration, where I would make my professional debut. A hint of those nerves returned to my stomach.

"I made you this for luck." Itu pulled a loose paper out of his sketchbook and handed it to me.

"Oh, Itu!" It was beautiful, maybe one of his best drawings: a sketch of me, sitting in our family's garden playing my *lele*, and Konu dancing in the flowers. "It's amazing."

"Itu, come see big boats!" Konu clung to my leg.

"Boats, huh?" Itu grinned. "I think it's nice to have a break from boats on a holiday. All the fish we need for Solstice are already in the Great Hall kitchens."

I pulled my attention away from the gift, remembering why we'd come in such a rush. "No, Itu. There *are* big boats, huge ones—full of Matan Watchers."

"What? Are you sure?"

I nodded. "Taller than I've ever seen. They anchored at the edge of the harbor. The Watchers could already be coming ashore."

Itu's eyes excitedly glowed as he giggled like a boy Konu's age. His reaction brought the fear back into my belly, where it flopped around like a half-dead fish.

"Itu! Don't you think—"

"Let's go tell Uma, so that we can welcome them. Come on!"

"Wait, I...."

Itu had already run off toward the village square, so I followed him, Konu at my heels yelling, "tag." At least he was enjoying himself.

We didn't have to run far. Itu had already found Uma, our village's head elder, sitting on her favorite bench in the flower garden, positioned nearly at the end of the village square.

I bowed my head in the proper gesture of respect for a wise woman, trying to catch my breath.

"Watchers, Uma! On tall ships, in our harbor!" Now Itu talked like Konu—all exclamations.

"I found them!" Konu grabbed Uma's generous leg in a hug.

"I see." Laughter played in the crinkles around the old woman's eyes. "Now tell me everything you saw, Alesea."

Uma's laugh lines smoothed to wide-eyed astonishment as I described the boats and the people on them. When I finished, she looked nearly as excited as Itu. "Perhaps they've come to trade, or they are explorers."

"Three ships with... what... hundreds of people? What do we even have to trade?"

"Must be your seagrass mats, sis."

I glared at Itu's tease. Why couldn't they sense the danger I was feeling clear down to my bones? "What if they want to live here, or... or steal from us, Uma?"

Uma gazed into the distance as if she could see clear through the trees to the harbor. "We will give them a proper friendly greeting, of course." She smiled. "And on the Solstice, too, a fortuitous date."

"But Uma—"

"It's not like you to be so suspicious, Alesea. Why would you feel that way?"

"Because—"

"We have no reason to assume bad intentions. Remember, '*Not even the foreigner from a most distant land is truly a stranger, for the spark of A'lodi resides in every human soul.*'"

There was nothing more to say to an elder who quoted from the *Book of the* A'lodi. My gut twisted into a painful knot.

"Alesea." Uma's voice was as hard as dried clay. "It is the only way."

***

An hour later, I trailed behind a small procession to the fishing harbor because no one had said I could come along, but no one had said I couldn't, either. At first, I held Konu's hand, then carried him when he started to drag.

The elders sang as we walked as if we were heading toward the shallow water rafts that would carry us to the Solstice feast that afternoon. Konu sang into my ear with gibberish words. Despite my nerves, I couldn't keep silent, and my voice rose on the high harmony:

> *Mother wind and Father sea*
> *Fairest Lords of fairer land,*
> *Greet the Sun with song and feast*
> *That she may keep the Light at hand.*

Itu gave me an approving glance over his shoulder.

"Ah, Maia!" Papi, the oldest of the wise elders, sighed. He must have seen at least eighty years, yet had a spry gait and bright eyes. "Your gift blesses us all."

I smiled, unsure if I should correct him, but Itu did it for me. "It's Alesea, Papi. Maia's daughter, remember?"

Papi waited for me to catch up to his side and touched my arm, his hand wrinkled as a *capeo* leaf. "Why yes, it is, with a voice as pure and sweet as your mama's and those same wise brown eyes. When did you grow so tall, girl?"

I ignored Itu's snort—we both knew I was smaller than some of the eleven-year-olds still in First School—and bowed my head to the elder. "Thank you, Papi."

Uma's resonant voice called us to a halt. "They're here."

We stood where the wide path from the village opened onto the sandy beach, and, as usual, I could hardly see, stuck behind a wall of tall adults.

"Itu!"

He didn't respond to my whisper. Instead, his eyes fixed on the giant ships.

I pushed in front of him, poking him in the stomach as I passed. "Big, huh?"

Itu whistled softly through his teeth in reply.

Narrow-headed men climbed onto our docks from the rafts and small boats they'd used to cross our harbor. Their tunics were bright as Uma's flower garden, in colors more vivid than the Village Islands' most expensive dyes. They wore flowing white pants and braids in their long, dark hair, and were utterly silent.

Uma turned to face us. "I will speak for all of us, for now. Keep your mouths closed."

I thought her unusually rude until Papi covered his mouth with his hand, and I realized she'd meant it literally—keep our mouths closed. I remembered then that our open mouths disgusted last summer's shipwrecked Matan, Sinon. He'd even eaten with his lips pulled over his teeth, never letting us see inside. The Island Watchers seemed just as confused by his behavior as we were—they opened their mouths just like anybody else.

Some of the other elders covered their mouths as Uma led us onto the soft sand to meet the first group of strangers walking up from the docks.

"Konu, play the quiet game, okay?" I hid my whisper with his head. "For real, until we go back into the woods."

He clasped a chubby hand over his mouth in response.

I tweaked his nose, but I didn't cover my face. Why should I worry about offending these people, who'd come to our home uninvited? Shouldn't they be worried about offending us?

Uma spread her arms wide in the universal gesture of greeting, then bowed deeply toward the five men approaching our group.

Their tattoos were repulsive—geometrical patterns that made them look like a bunch of two-legged snakes. I wished they would cover those before they met me.

I fought the childish urge to stick out my tongue, then nearly lost my balance, dizzy with a rush of angry emotions that seemed to bombard me from all directions. I steadied myself with long breaths, and Konu patted my shoulder, his lips squeezed shut tight.

A red-clad man in the center of the Watchers bowed his head ever so slightly, and the realization hit me with a shock that he was the same man from last summer, Sinon—now well-dressed and puffed up with pride. His fingers flew like twigs in a storm as he signed to Uma. Though I'd learned Watcher-speak in First School, like any Double, I could only pick out a few words in the flurry: *friend, visit, talk, Mata.*

Uma, though, betrayed no confusion. When Sinon signaled an end to his speech by resting both hands on his belly, she bowed again and responded. She signed slower, more straightforward, and communicated in ways I understood better, as fluid as the dance of fish around my ankles in the shallows. *Welcome back. Home,* A'lodi, *feast, join us. Gratitude.*

Gratitude? That had to be a joke because I was sure Sinon had been sneering through his closed mouth. He radiated pride and superiority. Even the other Watchers kept a few feet away from him as his hands flew back into action. I suddenly wished I hadn't come with Konu.

As if he heard my thoughts, Konu struggled to get down with one hand still clasped over his mouth. I let him slide to the ground and reached for his other hand to avoid wrestling, but he slipped out of my grasp and took off toward the Watchers.

"Konu, no!" I lunged for him.

Sinon froze, all five Watchers stared at me, and I realized what I'd done. I'd opened my mouth—wide, right next to the Wise Elder of our village. My face burned as I dropped my head in a bow. Fortunately, I remembered the Watcher-speak for "forgive me."

I raised my head, but no one looked at me anymore. Konu had gone right up to Sinon. He used his free hand to wave up at the tall man, who gave him a closed-mouth smile that looked more frightening than the sneer.

I gasped as a flash of light spread down Sinon's body, from his thin lips to his stomach, just as the emotion of desire hit me like a tsunami. Somehow, I knew it had come from the direction of Sinon. Had I read his ugly mind? I had to get my brother away from him.

I wanted to scream out that he couldn't have Konu and make these men leave my home, but Uma stared at me, eyes firm with a warning to stay silent. Surely, she could see the Watcher glowing.

Uma raised her eyebrows. I kept my mouth clamped shut like an obedient child, but my mind raged on for Sinon to leave my brother alone.

Sinon lurched backward as if my thought had been a thrown weapon. His four companions all leaped to steady him, even though he'd regained his balance almost immediately. He picked up a shell near his foot, frowned at it as if it was the cause of his stumble, and hurled it toward the ocean. The glow was gone.

Konu skipped back to me.

I picked him up and squeezed him too hard, relief flooding my heart. I'd seen enough. I pushed past Itu to take my little brother back to the village.

CHAPTER 2

By the time Konu and I headed for the shallow harbor, I hadn't seen the elders or Itu again. We stood, waiting for a raft to the island of Kokka and the Solstice feast, dressed in matching yellow outfits and representing the sun. Konu's was a simple tunic with pants; mine was similar but with fancy embroidery around the edges. I'd braided and twisted my coal-black hair into the most elegant style I could manage. Someone called from behind.

"Alesea!"

I turned to see my best friend, Sarai, jogging down the path to catch up with me.

"Rye!" Konu scuttled back up the hill to throw himself into her arms. "I yellow!"

Sarai wore a blue tunic to represent the ocean, her braided black hair like mine. The similarity ended there—everybody agreed Sarai was one of the most beautiful girls in the Village Islands.

I was next to hug her, standing on my toes to squeeze her shoulders. "I thought you were already on Kokka! Did you hear about our *visitors*?" I spat out the last word as if it were a sour berry.

"What? No, I was on Kokka all morning. Mama forgot some spices, so I came back for them." She gestured to the bag slung over her shoulder.

I hooked her arm into mine as we walked the rest of the way to the docks.

"Tell me."

I told Sarai about the terrible Watchers in their impossibly tall ships. I told her about Sinon, the sneering man in red, and how eerie the silence was around him and his companions. "But then I embarrassed myself,

Uma, and everybody else, because Konu went up to them, and I shouted for him to come back."

Sarai's laugh burst out like a spray of flower petals. "And did the poor Watcher die of disgust, seeing your horrible opened mouth?" She opened her mouth wide and crossed her eyes.

I stuck out my tongue at her, causing her to gasp and cover her eyes in mock horror. Sarai could make the worst moment feel like a party.

"I wish. I left with Konu. I didn't want to see any more of their lies."

"Lies? How do you know?"

"I don't know, I just.... I just have a feeling." I couldn't tell her about the strange light and emotions, or she'd think I'd gone mad.

"Well, I've learned to trust your feelings, certainly more than some foreign Watcher's sign-speak."

"Thanks." My feelings usually involved things like who liked Sarai's pudding cake the best or which boy had his eye on her. This time, they spoke of impending disaster I'd never had reason to imagine. I squeezed my eyes shut and hoped to the *A'lodi* I was wrong.

***

Our raftsman, Roni, lifted Konu aboard first, then gave me a sympathetic grin when I stumbled as I stepped onto the raft's polished wood. Not much older than me, Roni was a friend of Itu's who used to bring me handfuls of sweet wild berries every time he came to our house. He was an Island Watcher, with ears that looked like a Double's, not any foreign "pureblood."

His mouth opened when he smiled, like any Islander. He blushed when I met his eyes, then stared at beautiful Sarai for longer than was proper as more villagers piled onto his raft.

"He's staring." I didn't move my lips. Most of the Island Watchers could understand Double-speak by watching our mouths.

"Shush!" Sarai kept her mouth still, too. Her perfect copper cheeks faintly flushed as she gave Roni a shy smile.

"Konu! Don't dangle your feet in the water. You'll get your special pants all wet."

Konu pouted, but he pulled his legs onto the raft and sat cross-legged at the edge. "I want to!"

"Look, KoKo." I distracted him by pointing at our destination. Summer Solstice was no time for Konu to get into one of his toddler moods. "It's so clear you can see the Great Hall."

"Oh. So perfect."

I sighed along with Sarai because she was right: It was perfect. The Shallows, the sound between Akila and Kokka, was named that because you could practically walk between the two islands at low tide. Today, the water was so transparent you could see fish flitting about the sandy bottom. There was no sign of the fog that so often blanketed the north shore of Kokka. Instead, we had an excellent view of their matching Shallow Harbor and the stone road twisting steeply up to the heart of Port Kokka, the largest village in the Islands. Uma had said the whole island had over thirty thousand people now, a number so impossibly large, I couldn't even imagine it—and in just a few hours, I would be performing for many of them.

Sarai and I sat cross-legged next to Konu, leaving the benches for the older villagers. Soon the raft was full, so Roni untied it from the dock. I held my *lele* in my lap, protecting it from splashes and stumbling feet, then turned my face toward the sun, letting the gentle rocking of the raft and the salty summer breeze calm my nerves.

"Watchers from Mata, I heard. Coming to our feast!"

The woman next to him, one of our village healers, snorted at the man's excited whisper.

I glanced back to see them shielding their mouths with their hands, probably to keep Roni from seeing, not that he was paying attention.

Sweat collected on his forehead, dripping into his eyes as he rowed hard. His eyes were on Kokka—and occasionally me and Sarai.

"They think they're better than anyone else," the healer said to her companion. "I hear they control Mata now."

"Control? I thought half the houses were headed by Doubles!"

"Do you know Ren?" Her supposed hushed voice was undoubtedly loud enough that every listening ear on the raft caught her response. "He heard it from traders in Ana. Just got back yesterday."

"But... how?"

"Force, he said. They've taken over their farms and indentured the workers. The Listeners have gone into hiding, and some of the Doubles, too."

Force?

A collective gasp betrayed all the eavesdroppers aboard the raft. Sarai and I looked at each other with wide eyes. Violence was a thing of the past, or so we had been taught in our history books. We'd lived in peace for at least five hundred years, ever since the *A'lodi* spread into the world after the horrible devastation of the Great War.

Konu trailed a finger in the clear water, oblivious.

I turned to address the healer directly. "So, why do you think the Watchers are here? And why does Uma think they won't hurt us?"

The woman frowned, the wrinkles in her forehead growing deeper. "Uma would never go against the A'lodi, that's why."

The man beside her added, "And the A'lodi teaches that any visitor must be treated as an honored guest, as precious as one's own child."

"Even if they want to hurt us."

"Even if they want to hurt us." Sarai echoed my conclusion in a whisper, and I was sorry I had said the words out loud.

Now the sun felt too bright, too hot. I shaded my face and looked back toward Akila. The south forest of my home island was as dark as the thoughts swarming in my mind.

***

Konu weaved among our legs, babbling and laughing, as we walked up Kokka's stone path to the Great Hall. I scooped him up to keep him from joining a game of chase with the dozens of children running about in every direction. People laughed and sang, others already sloshed from the Solstice wine. Artists and craftspeople sold their creations at little tables, and there was even a booth full of colorful clothing and rare spices from faraway Ana. I gazed longingly at my favorite table—that of the luthier who'd made the precious *lele* I'd received for my Coming-of-Age day that Spring—even though my mother was expecting me in the Great Hall.

Sarai and I said our temporary goodbyes before I headed for the broad front steps of the Great Hall with Konu and Sarai, the kitchens in the back. Her mother, the best cook in the Islands, headed up the preparations for the Solstice feast. My own mother was the most famous musician.

"Mama!" Konu wriggled from my arms as soon as I'd opened the heavy wooden door to the main hall.

I always felt disoriented by the size of the place, which could swallow up my whole village. My eyes widened at the room's transformation. A thousand yellow Solstice ribbons hung from the high ceiling, flowers decorated every table, and rose petals adorned the front of the stage, where my mother and the other musicians would perform.

Where *I* would perform.

"Ah, Konu." My mother's famous voice filled the entire hall, even before she began singing. She swung him up in an embrace, and he giggled wildly. "You finally made it. Alesea, how does it look?"

"Beautiful, Mama. Sorry I wasn't here sooner to help." I approached the stage, heart fluttering as I imagined myself upon it in front of the largest audience the Islands ever saw.

"How are you feeling?"

"Nervous and excited. Also worried." There was no point in lying to Mama.

"Perhaps you should go out in the market to get your mind off things."

I shook my head. "Too noisy, and I might run into... Mama, do you know about the Watchers?"

Mama cocked her head. "*The* Watchers? I know Roni and Ashu—"

"From Mata. In the Akila harbor, with Sinon from last summer."

"What?" Surprise filled her eyes, highlighted with ocean blue for her performance.

I recounted the morning's events for the second time in an hour. I cast my eyes down as I told my mother of my shameful mistake, but she only let out an anxious laugh.

"Ah, Alesea. You always wind up in the thick of things, don't you?"

"I don't mean to. It just... happens."

Mama sat on a chair on the stage and picked up her *lele*. She absently tuned it as she spoke. "And it will happen more after tonight, little flower. Once they hear you sing, the people will be so hungry for more they will invite you permanently into the thick of things. Like me."

My insides felt heavy. It was proper and exciting for me to join Mama at the first Feast after my Coming-of-Age. Still, I hadn't thought much about all I could lose—quiet hours teaching Konu to climb trees in the forest, sunny mornings splashing about in the shallows, long afternoons practicing my *lele* all alone in my secret forest clearing. Were those moments now things of the past? Mama lifted my chin with one slender finger, and the weight in my chest lifted.

"Don't worry, my flower. You won't have to do anything you don't want to, not for now."

I couldn't shake the feeling that she was dreadfully wrong.

CHAPTER 3

An hour later, the Great Hall doors opened to anyone who had paid the season's Community Contribution. Hundreds of people from all the Village Islands burst into the enormous room, light-heartedly jostling one another in a contest for the best seats.

I sat back in my own chair at the performers' table near the stage, closed my eyes, and pretended I could still hear the ceaseless pounding of the ocean's waves. I only opened them when Mama said my name and placed my first-ever glass of Sol wine on the table — the real thing, not the colored juice given to children. The burgundy liquid didn't fill more than an inch of the tall glass, but it was an honor, anyway. I took a tiny sip and nearly spat it right back out, shocked by the bitter taste and wondering what possessed me to want to wait sixteen years in anticipation for this moment.

Mama smiled. "You'll get used to it, but not too quickly, I hope."

Across from me, the portly, bearded *lele* player gulped from his full glass. "That you will, dearie, especially in your mother's line of work."

"Oh, please," Mama smiled despite her exasperated voice. "It's just you who wants me to drink too much Sol wine, Ben."

Silence blanketed the room back to front as Medor, the head elder of Kokka, entered, followed by a small crowd of men and women in long elder robes. Medor managed a stately march through the dense crowd even as he stepped over feet jutting out into the aisle and dodged running children. The other elders walked with considerably less grace but more friendliness as they greeted people and patted the errant children on their heads. I grinned to see Uma leading the small group of Akilan elders among the delegations from the other islands.

Exclamations of surprise rang through the room after the last of the elders passed through the great doors. Those elders should have been the end of the procession, but one more group followed on their heels. Wearing colorful robes and long black braids, with tattoos on their heads and necks, a dozen men entered the hall in a solemn, single file. Their eyes remained fixed on the stage, mouths closed and unsmiling.

The nerves I'd barely kept under control flared to the surface—the last thing I needed, and not here, not now, and especially not for my first song.

Sinon led them all. He wore a long robe of blood red, the same shade as the tunic he'd been wearing on my island.

My heart pounded with each of his steps, and the urgency to protect my baby brother from Sinon's strange desire overcame me—that flash of emotion as tangible as the awkwardly long nose on his face.

Konu stayed in Mama's lap as Sinon stared straight ahead at the back of the last Island elder.

Then, Sinon's eyes shifted slightly and met mine.

My fear returned with a vengeance, eating up my insides and rising into my throat. It wasn't fair! Who did these people think they were, taking over our feast, our celebration, our lives? I pushed the fear down and replaced it with burning defiance.

Sinon averted his eyes, but his high brown cheekbones flushed to the shade of the *kreo* wood that grew only on Akila. Perhaps this man was made of wood, come to join his own.

The absurd thought pushed an unexpected snort of laughter out of my nose, which I covered with a cough.

Mama raised an eyebrow in my direction but didn't comment.

The Watchers followed the elders to tables on the opposite side of the stage from the performers. Medor stood on the stage, waiting for the last of the guests to be seated.

The final Matan was the only woman in their group. Unlike the men, she wore a white band of cloth over her hair, hiding whether or not she had ears. Her clothes were a cheerful yellow, like mine, but her pale face was a mask of misery. Instead of joining her group at the tables, she stepped onto the stage and stood a few paces from Medor.

Did I imagine the look of loathing she shot him before she turned to the audience?

"Welcome to Kokka on the holiest evening of our celestial year!"

The woman faced the Watchers, her hands flitting about animatedly translating Medor's announcement. That explained her role—she was their translator and a Double like me.

"In the name of the *A'lodi*, which binds us together, please extend a warm welcome to our honored guests from Mata."

While a smattering of applause broke out across the room, other Islanders, taken aback by our sudden "honored guests," shifted uncomfortably in their seats.

Medor glanced at the Watchers and cleared his throat. "To greet the Solstice with the first cycle of songs of the *A'lodi*, representing the sun, please welcome Maia of Akila."

Much louder applause filled the Great Hall as my mother made her way to the stage. She and Medor gave each other a formal bow, then Medor joined the other elders as Mama touched up the tuning on her *lele*.

Then she began to sing, and I felt like myself for the first time that day.

Mama's voice poured out like medicine, soaking into my concealed sore and empty places until I floated on the gentle waves of the shallows, face to the sun. All seemed well with the world. Around the hall, people smiled and sighed, taking each other's hands.

The cycle ended much too soon, and unfamiliar anxiety overwhelmed me. A plethora of "what ifs" ran through my head, wondering if everyone would expect me to be as talented as my mother, my voice would crack, and I'd forget the *lele* countermelodies.

"Have another sip of your Sol wine, Laysi." Somehow, Mama had returned to her seat while my panic rose.

I blinked at her since developing a taste for Sol wine was the last thing on my mind. "But it's so... uh...."

She smiled. "It will help with your nerves."

I tried to smile back. "Am I that obvious?"

"Only to me."

I did as Mama suggested and finished off the small bit of wine in my glass. I did feel more relaxed—and a little dizzy—as a hundred waiters clad in white delivered the first course of the Feast. Even so, I couldn't bring myself to eat more than a bite of the steamed sea vegetables or a spoonful of the exquisite shellfish chowder.

All too soon, the waiters came back to clear our places. Medor returned to the stage, and my heart pounded a little harder with each of his dreadfully formal steps. He again cleared his throat, and silence as thick as my uneaten soup fell over the hall.

"The second song cycle of the *A'lodi* represents the moons. This cycle is traditionally performed by the youngest singer of the musician's guild. This year, Maia of Akila's own daughter, Alesea of Akila, will make her debut Festival performance."

The applause that greeted Medor's announcement was deafening—even louder than Mama's—which did nothing to calm my nerves.

Mama put her hands on my shoulders—as if to transfer her ease in performing to me—and whispered, "Be blessed." She then gave me a gentle nudge toward the stage.

I concentrated hard, reminding myself about the moons and that I was calm as a half-moon in the night sky.

It took a million years to reach the performer's stool at center stage. I focused on every step, unreasonably scared I might trip and fall and humiliate myself and Mama. Finally, I reached my *lele*, picked it up, and checked the tuning, my back still to the audience. The *kreo* wood felt warm and reassuring under my hands, and suddenly, I knew I would perform well. I turned toward the audience, propped my right foot up on the stool instead of sitting, and plucked the haunting opening melody of the Moon cycle.

The hall fell dead silent. I waited extra long for the last note of the introduction to fade, just as Mama had taught me, then sang the long, lonely opening note of the cycle.

The entire first song was wordless, representing the sadness of the young First Moon, Luna, alone and small in the night sky. As my voice rose and echoed through the rafters of the Great Hall, I heard the sorrow of a thousand generations reflecting on me. I nearly choked in despair on the last note. I closed my eyes and paused for the customary applause. After an uncomfortable silence, I forced myself to open my eyes to prepare for the opening *lele* run of the Song of the Second Moon, but I froze before my fingers met the strings.

Tears glistened on the cheeks of nearly everyone at the front tables, including Mama, who never cried—not even at her own mother's funeral. Only the Watchers stared straight ahead, unmoved. Their translator gazed at me, her face transformed with sadness.

And every single body in the room glowed with that strange light I'd witnessed in Sinon that morning, totally unnerving me.

I cleared my mind with a deep breath, then began the song of Phoemek, the playful Second Moon. *Joy*, I thought. *Konu. Itu. Sarai.* I projected the feeling into every note, this time watching the audience as I sang. Many picked up their napkins to wipe their tears. Before long, most were smiling at me with a sort of awed expression, their glow fading until I was sure it had been a trick of the candlelight.

I launched into the lyrics of the final song without a pause, which had the most challenging *lele* part in the cycle, as I wove the melodies of the first two songs together with a third melody in the vocal line, my fingering flawless as if blessed by sweet Phoemek herself. I allowed myself to smile as I finished the triumphant lyrics:

Forever sing your joyful tunes,
Mother and daughter, the blessed moons.

When I let go of the last note, the silence was so powerful it felt as if my eardrums would burst. Then, my people stood as one body to applaud, hoot, and call my name—not Mama's, mine. I blinked back tears, filling with gratitude and love as I gave bow after bow.

It was the happiest moment of my entire life.

CHAPTER 4

I finally made my way off the stage and back to the performers' table just as the white-clad waiters brought out the second course of the feast. The murmur of conversation resumed around the hall, except at our table. Everyone seated there, including Konu and my own mother, stared at me as if fascinated with my every movement.

I plopped down in my chair. My embarrassment morphed into sudden ravenousness when I focused on the mouth-watering selection of food in front of me and stuffed a piece of Sol bread in my mouth. I struggled to chew it when I realized everyone still had their eyes on me.

"What?" I sprayed a few crumbs out of my mouth and back onto my plate and blushed. I swallowed a bit painfully. "Why are you staring?"

Konu broke the awkward silence when he hopped from Mama's lap, ran around the table, and gave me a sticky hug around the neck. I reciprocated, grateful for the distraction from all the gawking.

"Laysi sad?"

"No, Konu. Laysi happy. Why do you think I'm sad?"

Konu pulled away and peered at me with his big brown eyes. "Mama cryin'."

I peered over his shoulder at Mama, who smiled as she leaned in toward Rekan, a harpist designated to play for the dance, as he whispered something in her ear. I turned him around to face her. "Look, Konu! Mama's happy. See?"

Konu giggled and ran off, leaving me to munch on my Sol bread.

"You've got your mother's gift, haven't you?" Ben's rumbling voice carried across the table effortlessly, even as the Great Hall grew noisier by the second. "Maybe even more so."

I shook my head, though my heart swelled with pride. "I just do what Mama taught me. She's the best."

Mama and Rekan stopped whispering and turned to Ben, whose brown nose had grown reddish from the Sol wine.

"No, it's more than that. You've got the Knowing about you, and that's it."

My spine tingled with an unwelcome shiver because it was a terrible thing to say. Centuries ago, Knowers had disappeared, hunted down after they committed the most horrible crimes of the Great War — using their telepathic powers to destroy their enemies' minds.

"Ben! Don't fill the girl's head with your stories." Anger flashed from Mama's eyes. "She's done her own work to get here. She's dedicated her life to being such a beautiful singer and *lele* player — better than me at fifteen."

"What?" Surely Mama was only trying to distract Ben from his dangerous, drunken thoughts. "I can't be."

Rekan laughed and turned to Mama. "Does she really not know?"

"Rekan." Mama's response came off like a warning. Regardless, I had to ask before Mama scared the men away entirely.

"What do you mean, the Knowing? Knowers don't exist anymore."

"Oh, no!" Ben shot his two cents back at me before Mama could stop him. "Knowers are real. They're jus' too frightened to admit it. Never'd use it in public, would they?"

"So is it possible that—"

"No!" For me to argue against Mama's irrefutable comment would have been plain stupidity, so I let it drop. "Let's eat. Laysi, you most certainly deserve another sip of Sol wine. I'm so proud of you."

Everyone mumbled their agreement as Ben poured too much wine into my glass. I didn't really want it, but all the same, it was an honor.

***

Like previous years, dancing at the Feast began once the last of the twilight had melted away into the sea. At first, it was delightful. A flutist from Kokka joined Ben and Rekan, and I wouldn't have been surprised to see the *kreo* carvings of past elders start tapping their wooden feet to the lively tunes.

As the revelry intensified, people surrounded me unexpectedly, asking to dance with me — people I didn't know who asked me too many questions about my music, family, and *lele*. Some said kind words but leered at my face and body as if they might devour me instead of dance. Others flashed with light, which gave me a headache. I could've sworn one man made the sign against evil when I met his eyes.

Knower.

The whispers came from everywhere but never to my face.

Sweat dripped from my forehead, and I thought I might suffocate. I searched for someone familiar as I shook off the hands of strangers with less and less grace.

"Laysi!" I shoved away the owner of a hand who exclaimed my name. "What's wrong?"

Relief filled me when I looked upon the concerned face of Brahn, my oldest brother. He was twenty-four—married with a little one on the way—and calm as the Shallows on a windless day.

"I just... I need to get out, Brahn."

He put a strong arm around my shoulders and steered me through the crowd to a relatively empty corner of the room. "Are you all right? You were amazing, you know. I've never heard anything like it."

Knower.

I didn't know if it was a real whisper or only in my mind. I could barely manage a smile for my brother. "Thanks, Brahn. But now, I just want to go home."

"Yeah, the crowd is huge this year. Want me to find Mother? I think she went off somewhere with Konu."

"No. I'll just go to the docks. Surely, I'm not the only one ready to go."

Brahn screwed his face as if to argue. "All right, Laysi. I'll tell her for you. Do you want me to come?"

I shook my head emphatically. "No, no. Stay and have fun." I eyed Brahn's heavily pregnant wife Lori, who'd spotted us from a distance as she pushed through a group of dancers to reunite with Brahn. "Well, I bet you won't feel like partying for a while in another couple of months."I offered him a half-hearted grin just as she approached us.

Brahn smirked back, looking relieved as Lori approached, and the two embraced. He quickly filled her in on my intention to leave and nodded to me approvingly. "Okay, then. Let's get you out of here."

I grabbed my packed *lele* from the stage, and Brahn and Lori shielded me from the rowdy crowd to the market square outside. I bade them farewell and made my way to the docks by the light of the two moons.

***

Roni sat alone, dangling his feet from the side of the dock, fidgeting enough to set a sparkling series of concentric circles dancing across the Shallows. I was surprised no other villagers had been waiting for rafts, but the hour was still early for the Solstice Feast.

"Roni." I forgot and called him, yet my movement alerted him to my presence anyway, and he jerked his head in my direction, his eyes wide with alarm. I signed in Watcher-speak.

Sorry.

Roni shook his head slightly as his eyes grew wider.

What's wrong? I furrowed my brows, wishing I understood more nuances of his language.

Footfalls erupted behind me. I spun, but it was too late. Too late to run, too late to even scream. Sinon grabbed me by the neck and clasped his hand over my mouth. I struggled and tried to bite him, but I could barely breathe, let alone open my mouth.

"He says that if you shout, he will kill you." The familiar low, scratchy, and oddly accented voice of a woman caught my attention, but from my view, I could not see her. "He means it."

Kill me! I thought I might pass out. Bile rose in my throat. I nodded as best as I could.

Sinon released me, and I sucked in the sweet air. Before I could form another thought, he yanked my arms nearly out of their sockets to tie my wrists together so tight behind my back that the tips of my fingers started tingling. My eyes smarted with tears as I glared at Roni, who had stood up and watched us, still with that stupid, alarmed look on his face like he knew what would happen.

Relief hit me when Sinon jostled the rope enough to release the tension around my wrists and then prodded me toward the end of the dock. I dutifully stepped off the pier onto Roni's weathered raft, terrified that I'd anger him further or that he'd kill me if I ran. My *lele* bag flew past me and landed on the raft's floor with a painful clang. I racked my brains, trying to remember when they took that off my shoulder.

"Sit." The woman's command tore my eyes away from my *lele* to face my captors. My eyes widened when I immediately recognized her as the translator from the Feast. The woman lifted her yellow robe and sat across from me on one of the benches.

Sinon stood, staring at me as Roni boarded the raft, while I refused to meet his eyes.

"What do you want from me?"

"Just do what he says." The translator kept her head down.

Sinon had to have moved quickly, slapping her and then resuming his stiff stance because it took me a bit to realize just what had transpired. The translator's eyes brimmed with tears, but she made no sound. Even in the moonlight, I could see the handprint blooming on her cheek.

My terror transformed into pure rage. I rose to my feet awkwardly, conscious of how clumsy my balance had become with my hands tied, and glared at the vile man. I spoke in my language because he didn't deserve the honor of me talking to him in his.

"She didn't do anything!" I didn't care that he couldn't hear me shout but instead hoped my spit reached his face as I screamed the words. "She answered my question! What is wrong with you?"

Everyone on the raft lit up with that strange light radiating from their chests.

Sinon didn't seem to notice the light. He remained calm except for his eyes, which narrowed, and one twitched with each of my words. There was a soft *snick* as I watched my captor pull a long knife from deep inside his robes and finger it for a moment. He used his other hand to sign to the woman.

"He says you will regret disrespecting your elders. If you disrespect him again or speak at all, he will kill you, but first you will have to... You will have to watch me die." She didn't, or couldn't, hide the trembling fear in her voice.

I stumbled back to my seat, my bravery evaporating with the mist over the shallows. The light also disappeared and left spots in my vision. Even though Roni must have sensed Sinon's knife and the women's emotionally-charged response, he never turned around to watch.

***

It felt like it took hours to reach the Shallow Harbor of Akila. I asked no questions and shouted no accusations as Sinon jerked me to my feet and dragged me to the road that led to the village. He pushed the translator in front of us and signed *follow* to Roni.

We stopped at the first pair of *kreo* trees that bordered the path beyond the rocky beach. Sinon reached back with his free hand, and Roni handed him a black canvas satchel.

Stand at tree Sinon signed slowly, as if I were an errant toddler.

I could be as stubborn as any toddler. I might be scared, but I wasn't going to make it easy for him. I walked to the *kreo* tree, leaned my head against the warm, smooth bark, took in its familiar, earthy smell, and mentally asked it to give me strength. If only my hands were free, I could be in its branches far from the Watchers' reach before they knew what was happening.

Instead, Sinon jerked my shoulder backward and spun me around before slamming my back against the tree with one hand and signing *stupid girl* with the other. He pulled a coil of rope from the satchel and tied me to the tree. The translator, whose hands were behind her back, watched her toes where they peeked out from her long yellow robes. Roni stared at Sinon. I wondered if his face would be frozen in that stupid, surprised expression forever as he stepped forward and gave Sinon a deep bow after he finished binding me to the tree.

Speak? Roni signed and ended with open palms to signify a question. Sinon replied with *quickly*.

Roni's next signs were too rapid for me to translate fully, but I caught the gist of it. *Girl, good, not dangerous, let go soon.*

Sinon signed slowly, maybe for my benefit. *Remember my promise to you. The girl is dangerous. I know you can feel it. You are lucky she was the first to arrive.* A sneer replaced his usual blank expression, and Roni flinched. *Thank you for your help.*

My thoughts ran wild, wondering if he promised Roni to go to Mata or join his ship's crew, how much my "dangerous" life was worth, and what would happen to my family, Sarai, and Uma.

My captor reached into the satchel again and pulled out a long rag. He handed it to the translator. *You do it.* His hands jerked sharply, signing the simple words—a threat.

With fear in her eyes, she took the cloth and walked toward me. She stretched the rag to its full length and gently pushed the middle through my lips into my mouth. It was rough, salty, and horrible, but her hands were kind. When she leaned forward to tie it behind my head, she whispered in my ear without moving her lips and barely breathing.

"Wait till morning."

Something dropped down my back, falling through the small space I'd managed to open to keep from crushing my arms. I instinctively grabbed it with half-numb fingers. The woman finished her knot as if nothing had happened.

She stepped away, and Sinon pulled on my gag, which held firmly. He gave me one last glare, then gestured for his two companions to follow him back to the docks.

I held the object in my hand, moving it with excruciating slowness to avoid dropping it out of my stiff fingers while feeling its physical properties—a hard and slightly curved surface, with one side smooth and the other covered in narrow ridges.

It was a seashell and sharp as a knife.

CHAPTER 5

Wait till morning. Wait till morning.

I repeated the words like a mantra to still my heart and slow my breath, but I felt deserted by my years of faithful *A'lodi* meditation practice. I tried not to panic at the pain shooting up my arms from my numbing fingers and struggled to ignore the bugs that flitted about my face and stung my bare skin as I was helpless to swat them away. I relaxed into the tree, listening to the insects singing far away in the treetops, and hummed the most calming melody I knew through the gag in my mouth. It was a lullaby Mama used to sing to me, and now I sang to Konu every night.

> *The stars watch over the night moons,*
> *The moons watch over the sea.*
> *The sea guards our beautiful island,*
> *The island, it grows* kreo *trees.*
> *The trees tower gently above us,*
> *Filling us with A'lodi,*
> *And I will protect you, my baby,*
> *With the island, the moons, and the sea.*

As my fingers lost sensation, I panicked that I'd dropped my shell, but when I pushed, I could feel its edge, wedged between my hands and the tree. For the first time since Sinon left me, I heard something besides the sounds of my abandoned island—voices, lots of them. Voices raised in laughter, some sounding a little drunk, others annoyed. Voices of people who had no idea what was to come.

Footsteps crunched in the dead *kreo* leaves as an entire group of Watchers led by Sinon, with the translator on his heels, swept past me. They paused just beyond my tree, waiting in the shadows.

I wondered what they would do to the rest of the villagers. Tie them all to trees?

It didn't make any sense. I groaned, then screamed a warning, but the sound muffled by the gag probably didn't even reach the ears of the translator, now hidden by the crowd of Watchers.

I listened helplessly as the villagers stomped off the rafts onto the docks like a herd of hungry *brahmi.*

"Safe rowing." The few who shouted amidst the laughter signaled the routine departure of rafts followed by fetching another load of Akilans. I recognized one of the voices as Itu's, and I felt so lightheaded I thought I might faint, which would have been a blessing.

Since Itu and a gaggle of his fisherman friends were the first to appear climbing the path to the village, it was Itu who first saw me tied to the tree.

"Laysi?" He squinted and shook his head as if afraid of imagining things.

Someone moved so silently behind me that I didn't know he was there until I felt the cold metal against my exposed throat.

My brother lunged toward me. "Alesea! What—"

"Stop! Please!"

At the translator's command, Itu froze, and Sinon stepped onto the path to face him. I squeaked with every breath as the knife pressed against my throat.

"What are you doing?" Itu's demand led a crowd of villagers to immediately gather around him, fear and confusion reflecting on their faces in the moonlight.

Sinon's back was to me as he signed, but the translator spoke for him. "He says that the girl will not be hurt if you cooperate and that if you go with him, she will be released."

"Release her now, and *we* will not hurt *you.*" Itu's response cut through a rising chorus of jeers from the other villagers.

Sinon turned his head and nodded sharply to the person holding me. Pain jolted down my neck as the pressure from the knife increased and broke my skin.

"Unnnnngh," I moaned through the gag. I struggled not to vomit. My thoughts ran wild again, wondering if he would kill me in front of my brother.

"Stop!" The crowd grew immediately silent with Itu's shout. For a moment, my ragged breaths were louder than the ringing in my ears, and I couldn't entirely control the choked sobs. "What do you want from us?"

"Simply walk back to the village with us, and you will not be harmed. We will give you further instructions then."

"And my sister?" I'm sure Itu still sounded fearless to his friends, but I could hear the quiver of terror in his voice when he raised the question to the translator.

There was a long pause, and then the translator spoke oddly again with no movement from her lips. "Don't tell him she's your sister. Make him think she's not important." It took me a moment to realize she was not translating into Watcher-speak. I feared Sinon would slap her, but he didn't, as if he never noticed what she said.

I watched through blurry eyes as my brother and dozens more villagers followed the Watchers beyond my tree and toward the village. More Watchers scattered throughout the group to prevent escape. The line passed so close to me that I could smell the Sol wine on their breaths and hear their whispered words of encouragement and strength, even though no one dared to engage the man with the knife. How could they? The Islands had forbidden fighting for centuries and only permitted using knives for scaling fish or cooking. They would only get themselves killed if they did otherwise.

All too soon, they were gone. The knife slid away from my throat, and I was again left alone, with only the *kreo* tree and my secret seashell to give me hope, but only momentarily.

The scene played out six times that terrible night with the arrival of rafts followed by a Watcher in blue holding his knife to my throat— sometimes threatening, other times breaking the skin until blood dribbled down my front— before he led the villagers away.

Sarai, who was in the second group, looked as if she might scream. My attempt to reassure her through my gag succeeded when her countenance shifted, and she whispered to me as she passed my tree. "Oh, Alesea, *A'lodi* be with you."

And also with you, I thought, wondering if she was heading toward even greater danger.

The last group of villagers came with the first light, purple bruises appearing in the sky where the moons had kept me company for so much of the night. The musicians always stayed the longest at the festivals, and sure enough, Mama showed up with Konu, thankfully asleep on her shoulder, so he didn't see me tied to the tree. Mama's face looked as if someone had ripped her heart from her chest when she stopped before me to whisper in my ear. "Be strong, my flower." The words barely made their way out before a Watcher shoved her along with the rest of the group. Konu stirred and mumbled, but his eyes never opened. Most of the Akilan elders were at the back of the group, but I never saw Uma or Papi. Maybe at least they and the villagers too drunk to leave Kokka that night would be safe.

A final line of Watchers passed my tree close behind the elders. Each of them held a knife to an oarsman's back. I knew most of the oarsmen, all of whom lived on Akila. Some were Watchers like Roni. *No, better than Roni*, I thought bitterly, watching their distressed and angry faces as their captors marched them away. I counted nineteen rowers, which meant every public raft—ten smaller ones like Roni's, and five larger ones that took two oarsmen each—had docked at Akila. *How long will it take for Kokka to realize something is wrong?*

I faded in and out of consciousness, lightheaded from fear, exhaustion, and pain, until my ears caught the faint *crunch* of a single person approaching my tree. The Watcher in blue, his robes dull in the early light, gripped the knife that had cut my throat as he slowly came to my tree and crouched before me as if hunting a flighty beast.

"What do you want with me?" My question came out as little more than a croak, muffled into nonsense by my foul gag. Although he couldn't hear me, he flinched, waving the knife in a strange dance.

"Go away!" My attempt to shout muffled again. Rage filled my bones, pushing away the fear and despair until I was on fire with it. Even the Watcher seemed to glow with it.

The knife faltered, and the man took a step back.

"Leave me alone!"

My muffled shriek exploded into a million shooting stars.

CHAPTER 6

I awoke to a cheerfully blue sky and the happy chirps and squawks of rested birds, like thousands of mornings past on my little island, but everything was wrong.

My head pounded, my throat ached, and dark spots danced in my field of vision, making me dizzy and nauseous. Memories flooded my mind like a sudden thunderstorm. For a moment, I fought panic and struggled to breathe. *How long have I been unconscious? Where is everybody?*

A breeze rustled the *kreo* leaves above me, and an object glinted on the path in the flickering sunlight: the knife held to my throat and meant to kill me.

My rambling thoughts madly swirled, wondering if someone had escaped to save me after I passed out, but that didn't explain my present captivity to the tree.

Knower. The whispers from the Solstice dance seemed to echo around me, caught in the wind, in the leaves.

Hundreds of years ago, Knowers had ended the Great War by joining forces and fighting with their minds. The results were unspeakably awful—histories told of worse damage over those few months than the previous twenty years of widespread war. Entire cities went mad. Parents killed children, children killed each other, and soldiers changed sides mid-battle. In the face of that horror, all other factions agreed to work together to exterminate the Knowers, destroy their weapons, and sign treaties to end violence forever while adopting *A'lodi* practices worldwide.

I wasn't a Knower. I couldn't be.

Enough. I couldn't waste any more time figuring this out, not while my people were in such peril. I had to find them. I had to escape.

"Wait till morning." The translator's words swirled as I found the seashell still locked between my hand and the tree trunk. The hardest part of breaking free was manipulating the shell with my stiff, numb fingers, but once I had it at the right angle, the rope was no match for its sharp edge. My hands freed quickly, and I nearly dropped the shell in surprise when they sprung apart.

My whole body ached, made worse by nicking myself more than once as I sawed at the ropes around my chest. When I finally freed my upper body, the rope fell to the ground, and I untied my gag.

Every step jolted my head as I approached the fallen knife. I reached toward it gingerly, as if it might spring to life and kill me after all. I shook my head, attempting to knock out my illogical thoughts because knives were for gutting fish and cutting rope, not for use against other humans.

I tossed it into the dead leaves and left it there.

My joints screamed in pain as I crept into the forest until I completely concealed myself—even from a Watcher's eyesight, which was said to be twice as sharp as a Double's. I collapsed onto the ground and pressed my forehead into a mossy patch to stop its pounding. Images of Konu, Mama, Itu, and Brahn—captured or worse—accompanied each throb. I fought off the sobs that would only increase the pain. I'd never felt so helpless, so useless.

A loud squawk startled me into a frantic crawl, but it was just a big *duomo* hen, another wonder of my little island. She cocked her fat chicken-like head and rustled bright green tail feathers.

The hen bustled away as I pushed myself to my feet. I was hungry and thirsty. My throat and ribs ached with every breath, and my red and swollen fingers throbbed violently. Fortunately, the shallow slashes on my neck scabbed over, and I could still walk. I would live, and there was no time to waste.

I used glimpses of the sun as my guide and headed north toward my home, sticking to the forest for safety. It was slow going at first, but the deeper into the forest I traveled, the taller the *kreo* trees—leaving little sunlight to support tangled underbrush and a mossy carpet under my bare feet. I'd been exploring this part of the forest since I was old enough to toddle after Itu on his adventures.

I knew I was getting close to the village when I started to recognize individual trees—the one with the low branches like a spiral staircase and another with a circle of *kreo* saplings surrounding it like children in a classroom. I wiped the sweat off my hands onto my now-filthy tunic, then climbed the staircase tree slowly, trying not to shake the branches.

I perched about twenty feet up, where an oddly shaped branch turned the waxy green leaves into a window frame. I could see through the window the outskirts of the village, including a tiny segment of the main road.

I waited and watched, but the only signs of life were a few chickens in the backyard. I scrambled down the tree, much less carefully than I'd climbed, and made my way to the closest well, where I gulped down nearly a whole bucketful of water and dumped another over my filthy head.

I climbed twice, high enough to see no one in the village either time, trying to figure out where everyone could have gone.

Though I trembled with exhaustion and fear, I finally crept into town and ducked behind houses until I reached my own. I didn't dare enter the front door but peered inside my bedroom window since it faced the back.

Everything was as I'd left it, except for no Mama, no Konu, nobody.

Our island included a dense forest, which I couldn't imagine the Matans slashing through, yet it was small but wide from east to west. I could easily walk on the road from the open sea to the Shallows in an hour, but for safety, I chose to circle the village and head through the woods toward the North Harbor, where the tall ships had come to dock.

Back among the trees, my thoughts grew slow and foggy, my eyelids tried to close, and I stumbled painfully over every root and rock as I willed myself to take one step at a time. I just couldn't let exhaustion and hunger win over my fear for my family.

Bang! Sounds of thumping, clanging, and metal hitting metal jolted me out of my stupor. A new surge of fear powered my muscles as I climbed up yet another tree until I could see the harbor.

Hundreds of men I had never seen before— nearly as many as the entire population of Akila—wore swinging black braids and bright clothes. Tattoos covered their heads from side to side. I watched in horror as they swarmed the docks and lugged crates, axes, and large equipment from the two tall ships docked in the harbor, which pushed our fishing boats all askew.

My eyes, growing blurrier from fatigue, reduced my vision to a mess of unnatural colors. I spotted a person who looked out of place with his shorter, single braid and brown tunic. I squinted to make out his features as he turned to deliver a box to the end of a dock.

Roni. The traitor.

I looked out to sea, sick to my stomach, and a new shock of alarm assaulted my body. I climbed another three branches, then two more, hoping to find it was just a trick of the light.

It wasn't.

The third tall ship was gone.

Fear and grief paralyzed me, high in that *kreo* tree. I knew from the bottom of my soul that my people had left the dock on that enormous ship.

My mind, though, refused to believe it: *Konu couldn't be gone. How could he sleep without his special blanket, the one I'd wrapped him in the day he was born? Did Itu have his sketchbook? Lori couldn't have her baby on a ship! Brahn had just finished carving a cradle. They had everything arranged – the midwife, the naming ceremony... Mama can't go through the agony of thinking I'm dead, not after mourning my father for so many years after he died when I was a baby.*

I had a reason for every villager on our island. Still, with each name, the absence of the third ship pressed into my conscience a little more until I had to admit that I was alone— more alone than I'd ever been in my entire life with no one left here—not one soul I loved or even knew.

I whispered my sorrow. "Roni is still here," but my anger answered with *Roni betrayed us. He is dead to me.*

I lay hugging my branch with my bottom shoved against the tree trunk for stability, scared to attract attention by climbing down my tree and afraid I would have no strength to escape anyone who saw me. I watched until the silent snake-men completed unloading dozens of crates onto the shore and disappeared into their ships in the fading daylight.

CHAPTER 7

I still fought off shudders of terror as the First Moon rose into the darkening sky, but I couldn't stay on my branch forever. I imagined the tree gifting me some of its calm, its roots reaching deep into the sandy soil, supporting it through season after season and never having cause to fear or grieve.

Breathe, the tree murmured in my imagination. *Be strong.*

I climbed down a branch, then two, until my view widened to see the docks.

No one.

I nearly lost my balance as one set of footsteps passed beneath my tree, crunching unevenly in the sticks and leaves. I couldn't see a thing below me, so I waited until the steps faded to nothing before climbing down the rest of the way and stealing toward the village, daring to use the path in the darkness with only the rising of one moon.

A strange sound drifted toward me when I was halfway to the village. At first, I thought it was coughing, then grunting. It grew in volume, followed by a crash like a body falling into dead leaves. I tiptoed closer, and the sound suddenly became clear.

Sobbing. The person was taking great gulps of air that came out in horrible rasping breaths as if trying to suffocate to make it stop.

He lay half off the path, face in the dirt. He hadn't yet noticed me, but I knew who it was by the bare feet, dark clothes, and hair pulled back in a single braid.

Roni.

I had half a mind to keep walking, but maybe Roni knew something about where my family had gone. I kicked his shin.

He jerked his knees under himself and rolled over, pulling himself away from me into the woods like a wounded animal.

"Roni!" I whispered, forgetting he couldn't hear me.

Something about my posture or maybe my opened mouth caused Roni to freeze and then collapse on his back with one more sob. I could barely see his hands in the dim moonlight, signing the same word repeatedly as he sucked in shuddering breaths.

Sorry. Sorry. Sorry.

I squatted down, torn between fury and pity, and extended my swollen hand to the boy who had been my brother's friend. I grabbed and pulled his arm to make him notice.

Roni's eyelids fluttered as if he might pass out. I forced him into a sitting position and reached out with my other hand to grab his shoulder, which slipped away, sticky and wet with blood.

"You're hurt! Come on." I signed *help* twice, right in front of his eyes.

Roni didn't respond, but he let me put my arms around his middle and heave him upward. He leaned heavily on my shoulders as we made our silent, slow way to the village.

It was no use trying to be stealthy while supporting Roni. His breaths came in noisy gasps, and judging by the increased weight on my back, he would be unable—or at least unwilling—to walk alone, much less navigate the forest in the dark. We stayed on the path the remainder of the way to my house without encountering another soul.

I kicked open my front door with the last of my body strength, dragged Roni to my bedroom in the back of the house, and paused only to shut the door behind us. I pulled the shade over my window, hoping the thin seagrass mat would be enough, and lit an oil lamp as Roni collapsed onto my bed.

The color had drained from Roni's face, usually dark as *kreo* wood. I hoped the flame played tricks since he looked near death. I tried to peel away his blood-soaked tunic sleeve but, in the end, ripped it through to find the injury, a deep cut at the shoulder and a second that went across his chest to his belly.

I hated blood and didn't particularly like dealing with Konu's over-scratched bug bites.

My mother's voice whispered in my head: *"We must help those who need us, no matter what. If not, our souls will grow tinier than even an ant's."*

He betrayed us, Mama. Nausea quickly overtook my thought, which I swallowed and ran to my mother's room for rags and ointment.

I washed the wound as best I could, and relief came when my initial impression was correct—it was only deep at the shoulder, far from any internal organs, and the bleeding had almost stopped. Roni had fallen asleep or maybe passed out. I rubbed on half of Mama's bottle of ointment and wrapped his shoulder with a clean rag. I fetched water, trickled some down his throat, and patiently watched until he swallowed and gulped down the rest. I didn't know anything else to do but blow out the lamp and wait.

I found Konu's favorite soft blanket in Mama's room and hugged it, inhaling my precious baby brother's sweet scent.

"I will find you, Konu. Mama and our brothers, too," I whispered, too spent for more tears.

I huddled on my mother's bed, too fearful to rest until the Second Moon was high in the sky. Enough moonlight flowed through Mama's window for me to see all the things she and Konu had left behind. I picked up an empty canvas knapsack from her chair. I couldn't leave everything here for the Matans to loot.

The bag was heavier than I expected. I reached the bottom and pulled out a thick brown package stuffed with stiff papers. My fingers discovered a series of raised bumps as they brushed the edge of one that didn't quite fit with the others.

It was Listener-script, something I'd only seen in examples at First School. Listeners, the race blessed with the most sensitive hearing but no sight, punched tiny holes in the thick paper to make a language they could read with their fingers. I untied the package's rough cord, and several dozen pages spilled out onto the bed.

I hadn't even known Mama could read Listener-script. Perhaps the pages belonged to someone else. However, as I flipped through them in the silvery moonlight, I stopped at a single word scribed in black ink in the corner of one page: *Alok*.

Alok—A name I'd heard only a handful of times as an answer to my innocent childhood questions. The name of my father, a Listener luthier who had died shortly after my birth in a fishing accident and left my mother bereft for years until a brief relationship with a fellow musician brought us Konu.

I clumsily tied the pages back together and dropped them into the bag, adding Konu's blanket on top. There would be time to wonder about my father later. Now, the family I knew and loved needed me, and I couldn't wait another minute for a traitor's injury to heal. I crossed the narrow hallway to my room and avoided looking at Roni until I gathered two changes of clothes and the canteen I would need on long days in the forest.

I finally turned to Roni, his eyes open and milky in the moonlight and staring at the ceiling. Regret wrenched my gut. Perhaps his injuries had been worse than I thought, and he'd died. Then he let out a long, trembling breath, and I saw the tears streaking down his face.

In the pale light, I noticed his color returning to normal. I approached him slowly before signing.

Better?

Yes. I thought you died.

Why would you care?

Roni squeezed his eyes shut, but it didn't stop the tears. *I never thought they would hurt anyone. They weren't supposed to.*

What difference did it make? I nudged his foot until he opened his eyes. *Where did they go?*

I don't know. Determination hardened Roni's features as he pushed himself with his uninjured arm to a sitting position. *I'm going to find them.*

Stop! You're hurt. I shook my head, frustrated at my limited Watcher-speak. *Tell me everything.*

Roni fired off a lengthy statement I didn't understand. His flitting hands reminded me of Sinon's. My anger flared, and my vision blurred as those same spots appeared like they had on the beach when Sinon tied me to the tree.

"Wait," I growled, not even bothering to sign in that foul language. I grabbed paper and a pen from my desk and thrust the items into his lap.

Roni painstakingly scratched the pen on the page, his writing hand on his injured side, which he avoided moving as he wrote. Sweat trickled down his forehead.

I tried not to care, yet wondered how much it hurt him to write what he could so easily sign in his language.

Finally, he sat the pen down and pushed the paper toward me, which I read quickly:

> Sinon said they were here to trade for kreo wood. All I had to
> do was let him use my raft and tell him names to help with the deal.
> He promised I could go with them and live with Watchers like me.

His writing became sloppier, the strokes heavier, for the final sentences:

> He lied. He said they wouldn't hurt anybody. I asked him why
> and he stabbed me and left me for dead. He stabs badly.

I had so many questions, but writing them all was too much. So, I wrote just one:

Why didn't they take me?

Roni read my words with half a smile as I placed the journal back in his lap. This time, he wrote quickly:

Because they're afraid of you. Your power. Sinon sent someone to kill you.

I signed in his face: *What?*

Even the man in blue dropped his knife and ran away when I passed out. They weren't afraid of the power of island politics. They were afraid of *me*. They should have left the elders behind—or even Mama, who was famous enough for her disappearance to be noticed beyond our small island—if the Watchers were worried about power.

Roni shook his head, signing: *Music. Knowing. Power.*

Right now, I felt powerless as a day-old chick. *Help me.*

Roni grabbed the paper. I moved next to him and read as he scribbled:

I'll take you to Kokka. We'll talk to elders and look for Akilans. Sasha, the translator, told me they're selling the ones they captured as servants, and the Matans here will harvest the kreo trees.

Even I knew people captured and sold slaves, not servants. I choked back another flood of emotions as I signed, *Yes. Let's go.* Roni's response confirmed I could trust him again, even if I were still furious.

Now.

CHAPTER 8

We left through the side door and my family's garden. There was still no sign of life in the village, so we risked a stop at Roni's house. I waited in the tiny but tidy entryway as he bustled through his little home, collecting items into a gray cloth bag. I had known where Roni lived—our island was small enough that I could name at least one occupant of every house—but never visited. I didn't know if he lived alone, though it was highly possible since only one pair of shoes sat next to the door.

Roni returned to me with a long bag and a genuine smile.

"Is that..." I sputtered, staring at the shaped leather bag, "my *lele!*" I frantically untied the bag and took it out, searching for damage. I could hardly believe it, but other than being horribly out of tune, it was healthy as the day I'd received it.

Thank you.

Roni looked away from my eyes. *You're welcome.*

I thought about hiding the *lele* in my house but couldn't stand the idea of a Matan Watcher touching it, plus everything else I loved was gone with that ship. I twisted the case's carrying strap together with that of my knapsack and hung both across my back.

Roni and I snuck to the village square in a last attempt to search for anyone left behind. Instead, we found the translator, Sasha, lying on her back, arms spread wide, in a dark puddle that reflected red in the moonlight. Even from a distance, I could tell there was no life behind her wide-open, dull-gazing eyes.

Dead. Killed. Murdered. My mind whirled before going blank.

Roni ran, then stumbled toward her body. He threw himself to one knee, nearly pitching forward onto the dead woman, as he grabbed her wrist, then felt her neck and heart. He left her arms crossed on her chest, then fell back to sit on the cobblestone, head in his hands.

I approached slowly, planning to close the poor woman's eyes and pull Roni away. Instead, my eyes fixed on the growing pool of blood that made crooked streams of moonlit red, filling the cracks between the cobblestones that Konu had just recently jumped over and traced with chalk. Without warning, the sickening, metallic smell overwhelmed me, and I barely managed to stagger a few steps away from the scene of the first Akilan murder in centuries before vomiting at the edge of the decorative fountain. I collapsed sobbing, not even knowing if I wept for the woman who had saved my life only to die so far from home, my lost family and friends, or my ruined world.

After a few shuddering breaths and much too overcome to object, a warm arm settled around my shoulders and squeezed me tight. Roni held onto me as I cried, even though this was all his fault. He waited until my sobs dwindled, and I could open my eyes without feeling like the weight of the humid air and empty village crushing me.

She saved me. I struggled to sign but somehow communicated.

Me too. Roni handed me a blood-stained paper, the top bearing the seal of the Akilan elders and covered in hasty scrawl from Sasha, who must have gone into the Common House to find it:

> *Roni, don't go with them. Liars. Save the girl. My husband*
> *Juhani in Mata will help you. Fisher district, 3 Thera St. Apts. Tell*
> *him and Yalene I love them forever. A'lodi be with you.*

They killed her I signed stupidly. *They kill people.* I wanted to scream at Roni and the horrible people who'd murdered Sasha. *She has a family, and they killed her. Now they have my family.*

Of course, Roni watched my outburst in silence. *We should go now.*

But her body...

What can we do?

We were in no condition to cremate her and throw her ashes into the sea, so instead, I stood tall and sang the traditional funeral song for a wise woman.

Roni stood respectfully with his palms together, thumbs on his forehead, even though he couldn't hear me, and his right arm shook as blood seeped through his bandages and shirt. I wished I could translate the song for him, but I didn't know half the words in Watcher-speak. Instead, I finished and signed *peace and* A'lodi *for her.*

I closed her eyes and signed *peace* one more time. It wasn't much, but I hoped it would be enough for her to rest with the *A'lodi.*

***

We left the path for the forest and headed toward Shallow Harbor. As we grew closer and noticed that nothing remained except for abandoned rafts floating at the dock like a mass of driftwood, we threw caution to the wind.

Once the two of us boarded, Roni skillfully navigated his raft around the ghostly fleet but grimaced with every stroke of the oar. I feared he would worsen his wound before even passing the docks.

I stood up from my bench and tapped Roni on his uninjured shoulder.

Me.

He shook his head and gave too strong of a stroke as if to prove himself. Instead, he made a strangled sound with his grimace, and beads of sweat glistened on his forehead. I grabbed the oar before he could do anything stupider.

Roni gave me a sheepish look. *Teach?*

I nodded as he guided my hands to the correct position on the oar and used his left hand to row a few strokes until I understood the pattern. Finally, I shooed him away, and he sat on the bench I'd first claimed.

Roni's oar was too big for me. Before the lights of Kokka seemed any closer, my arms trembled with fatigue. It didn't help that my hands still ached and throbbed from being tied up, and I hadn't had any sleep or a meal since before the Feast.

Konu. Mama. Itu. Brahn. Lori. Sarai.

I inwardly chanted their names with every stroke, imagining their faces, even daring to picture my triumphant rescue and return to our island, where everything would be as it had been before.

I don't know how long it took to get to Kokka, but it felt as if the journey lasted close to forever. Roni, who had been snoring softly since early in the journey, leaped to attention when I finally rammed the raft straight into the pile of one of the Kokkan docks.

I handed him the oar and tried to sign *sorry*, but I'd used every last ounce of strength and sheer willpower to make it to Kokka. My arms and numb hands hung uselessly by my sides as I stumbled off the raft, nearly falling into the Shallows, and tumbled headlong onto the dock. The maritime structure shook as Roni stepped on it and sat my knapsack and *lele* next to my face. I wondered if I would even be able to lift my belongings.

"Ho, there! A raft this early? What's happened?"

I turned on my side, unable to push myself up with my arms, and looked for the source of the friendly male voice. Though the sky flushed with the pink of first dawn, I couldn't make out anything beyond the end of the dock but a looming dark shape.

On the other hand, Roni had the sharp vision of a Watcher. He gesticulated wildly with his good hand, but I couldn't catch one word as I struggled to sit up.

"Slow down there, boy! I haven't got the best Watcher-speak."

Another silence as Roni continued signing.

"What? Your village, gone?" The man stepped onto the dock. He was middle-aged, with a dark, full beard and laughing eyes. He wore the simple off-white garb of a fisherman. "Girl, please tell me my Watcher-speak is worse than I thought."

I shook my head and spoke with a hoarse voice. "The Watchers from Mata... They took them all — all but Roni and me."

The man's eyes widened. "Wait, I know you! You're the girl who sang — you're Maia's daughter!"

"And she's gone, too. Please, help us." I choked back yet another sob. "They've been taken for slaves!"

"Slaves? I can't imagine it's as bad as all that. Come, girl, you're delirious. I'm Pedi, and I'll help you to a bed."

The man only spoke, but like all the island Watchers, Roni was good at lip-reading. He nodded. *Tell him more.*

I told the short version — the part that made me feel like this was all my fault somehow. I skipped the agonizing raft load after raft load of people I loved most who disappeared from the island because they wouldn't let the Watchers kill me. After all, if I hadn't performed so well at the Feast, I'd at least be with them on that tall ship, planning our escape.

Pedi finally looked genuinely concerned. "We should go to the elders. They'll know what to do. Come on! I'll walk you to Medor's house."

I coaxed enough strength from my arms to pick up my bag and *lele* and followed the man up the path with Roni at my heels.

CHAPTER 9

The first rays of sunlight sparkling off Kokka's Great Hall somehow made it look even more imposing than usual. Its massive white columns and golden door taunted me with happy memories. Turning my thoughts to our next task didn't help—Medor was the head elder of Kokka, known to be selfish, stingy, and generally the opposite of the teachings of the *A'lodi*. I started to grow nauseated despite my hunger.

Pedi led us past the giant building onto the road that led to the city. Unlike Akila, it was a short walk, and the main square and elders' homes were closest to the Shallows. We headed for the most prominent house, the one with a dozen glaring glass windows and columns that gave the impression of the Great Hall in miniature. Papi had often complained about the ostentatious Kokkan elders, and now I understood why.

The door even had a brass knocker, a perfect reflection of wealth on our metal-poor islands. Pedi lifted it and gave three sharp raps. A moment later, the heavy door creaked open, and an elderly man with an equally creaky voice stuck his head out the door and spoke.

"Pedi?"

His hair, unbraided and disheveled as if he'd just gotten out of bed, was nearly completely white. He squinted at our guide through sleepy eyelids before his gaze fell on Roni and me. His forehead wrinkled, maybe in confusion or just appalled by our filthy clothes and faces.

The man's beady eyes snapped back to Pedi as he nodded and gave a respectful bow.

"I am very sorry to wake you, Bibi, but these two visitors from Akila bear heavy news, and they need to see Medor right away."

"Heavy news? So soon after the Feast? Is it about the Watchers? Have they—" Bibi's eyes opened wide as he chattered.

- 42 -

"Please, Bibi. Medor." Pedi bobbed his head politely, but his tone was sharp.

"Of course." The door slammed shut.

Pedi turned to me and said, "Bibi is Medor's attendant and the biggest gossip on the Islands. I thought it better to save your news for the elder."

I didn't think so because I wanted our news shouted from the rooftops. We needed to drum up a mob of islanders to take to the water and find that ship. *Then, we'll rescue my village and throw the Watchers overboard, one by one –*

"Pedir!" Medor threw open the door, cutting off my thought.

Even though I'd only seen him leading the Kokkan elders at Feasts, he was nearly as dignified in his nightclothes.

Pedi bowed deeply. "Medor. I am sorry to wake you, but these two Akilans have urgent news."

"Come in, then." He beckoned for us to follow.

I gawked at the expansive *kreo* wood entrance made of material much too precious for a mere house. Fragile pottery and knickknacks lined countless shelves, and four austere chairs sat snobbily in the middle of the room as if daring someone as unworthy and dirty as me to sit in one.

I sat in one anyway, waiting just long enough for Medor to sit first, as is proper when meeting with an elder. Roni squeezed my shoulder, communicating strength or maybe a warning. He sat on the edge of his chair next to me as if he might spring up at any time. Pedi sighed as he hefted his weight into the last open chair and flinched when it creaked slightly.

I struggled with maintaining politeness, waiting for Medor to address me, even as he took an unreasonably long time to straighten his sleeves and fold his hands elegantly over his lap. Finally, he spoke to Pedi.

"Bibi was in quite a state to wake me up, Pedir. I hope this is truly important."

"Oh, yes," said Pedi. "Ask the girl."

Medor slowly turned his head to gaze at me. His patronizing countenance made me want to stick out my tongue, but instead, I bowed my head.

"Maia's daughter, is it?"

"Yes, sir." I couldn't bring myself to use the more affectionate honorific, *Papan*.

"Out of respect for your mother, I will choose to ignore the state in which you arrived at my home. Please do explain."

My face burned, and I took a long breath to control myself. From the corner of my eye, I spied Bibi hovering behind a doorway.

"Sir." I wrestled with keeping my voice calm as I looked straight into the elder's eyes. "The Watchers have stolen my entire village."

Medor cocked his head as if I were a little girl telling stories. "Your village? Akila? What on earth is there for them to steal?"

I wanted to stand up and hurl his stupid, uncomfortable chair at him. "The people, sir. They have taken all the people except me. And Roni. One ship left with them while the other two were still docked at the North Harbor last night. Their translator, the Double, told us they were taken to Mata. To be sold as slaves." My voice broke on the last words when grief threatened to overtake my anger as I remembered Itu's joke that they might be there for my seagrass mats.

Medor looked as appalled as if I had thrown the chair. "That's impossible! There is no slavery in Mata, nor anywhere else. And that's a Watcher right next to you. Why is he here if what you say is true? What kind of trick is this?"

A growl rose in my chest, and Medor flinched, but Roni broke in before I could do anything too stupid. He threw his good arm in front, so no one could miss his speech, which was far too fast for me to translate. The elder scowled but seemed to follow whatever Roni was saying as he began barking out orders.

"Pedir, find a few men to take a raft to Akila. I want a full report on the state of the village. Be sure you take a good Watcher-speaker in case you meet any of our guests."

Pedi's chair gave way as he snapped to attention and leaped to his feet. "Yes, Papan."

I watched Pedi until the door shut behind him, then glared at Medor. He stared at me like I was a dangerous wild animal that suddenly appeared in his entrance room.

"I'm half-tempted to think you're just eager for more attention, girl," he said, looking far too calm for the news we'd just brought. "Maybe all that applause after your careless display got to your head."

That was too much. *How could he?* I ignored the glow growing around everyone's chest as I stood, and with tears welling up, spat my words directly at the elder.

"I spent the entire night after all that applause, sir, tied to a tree, watching all the people I care about being stolen by people we welcomed to our islands." I was crying now, but I wouldn't stop. Medor's blank expression infuriated me more than his patronizing one. "They almost killed Roni. They stabbed him, and they murdered their translator! How can you not believe us?"

While Medor's nose twitched oddly—the only sign he heard me at all—his chilling voice presented a more accurate picture. "Why would I believe you, girl, when I've just found out your village has been hiding you, lying about you for years? And then had the nerve to reveal you in front of our Matan guests? Are you trying to start a war? Think what happened to your father, girl, and leave my house. Now."

"Are you insane? War? No one hid me. The Feast planning committee placed me on the schedule to sing practically the day I was born."

"And the more you walk around looking and talking like that," Medor said with a dangerous calm, "the more people will believe you are controlling their thoughts about you, compelling them to believe impossible things like your entire village being kidnapped."

Yellow light flared in the corners of my vision. "I have never done such a thing. What makes you think—" Roni interrupted by placing his good arm around my shoulder. I hadn't even noticed him standing. He steered me toward the door and jerked his head, nodding toward Medor on the way out.

I caught a flash of Bibi's white hair from the open doorway and hoped he was as big of a gossip as Pedi claimed. We needed all the help we could get.

CHAPTER 10

I left so heatedly I should have breathed fire, enough to burn down Medor's ridiculous house. I vented as soon as the ostentatious door closed behind us, not caring if I woke the whole village and that Roni might not understand me.

"How could he not believe us? Look at your shoulder! And why would we lie?" My toe caught the edge of a pavement stone, and before I could react, my knees, palms, and forehead smacked the uncaring road.

Roni, who was at my side, lifted me to my feet with his good arm before my mind registered what had happened. His deep brown eyes filled with concern as he touched my hurt forehead and recoiled when I winced.

Sorry. He slung his shoulder bag to the ground, rifled through it, and returned with a clean white cloth.

Thank you. I took the cloth. There was blood, but not much. I blotted a few times, then checked my skinned hands and knees. Fortunately, the cuts weren't deep, even though the skin pulled tight from the swelling on my hands.

What should we do? Roni signed.

I stifled an angry sob, wishing I could speak with Roni like a normal Islander. I had nobody to talk to, nobody to go to for help.

I wondered if Medor would come to his senses after Pedi confirmed I was telling the truth, but until then, the Kokkan elder council wouldn't go against their leader. Rumors said the whole council was as crooked as the trail leading up Kokka's dormant volcano, so trying to talk to another one of them would probably only make things worse. Besides, after what Medor said, I wasn't sure anyone would believe me anyway. Not if they'd already decided I was a dangerous Knower. Plus, what did he mean about what happened to my father?

I looked up at Roni, still staring at me for an answer. *We need friends and somewhere to think.*

I have an idea. Roni started down the road, and I trudged behind him a step, limping slightly from my newly bruised knee. We passed the giant houses and entered a more modest neighborhood with small cottages and the occasional shop opening up for the day. Any Kokkans along the way gave us a wide berth as if we might be dangerous, and maybe we were.

I already chastised myself for my outburst at the elder, no matter how much he deserved it. Mama would be ashamed and say I was too hot-tempered to set a good example for Konu and disrespectful to a grown-up—a head elder, at that.

However, that didn't matter right now. I might never see Mama again. Or Konu, or Itu, or Brahn. The weight that grew in my chest over the past two days became too heavy to bear. I lagged behind Roni more and more slowly until he finally turned and waited for me next to the peeling, blue-painted door of a tiny, boxy house.

We're here. I will talk.

He pulled a lever next to the door. I didn't hear a bell. Instead, the door opened a crack.

Roni signed something to the person hidden behind it, and it opened further. He waved for me to follow.

The house was so different from Medor's that it hardly seemed right to use the same word to describe the building. The entire thing was one room, no bigger than Medor's entrance area, with scattered sleeping mats—three occupied—off to one side. An art studio and workspace, crowded with two desks, an easel, stacks of books, and half a dozen colorful, frameless paintings pinned to the wall, filled the space immediately in front of me. I spotted the tall, slender woman around Brahn's age who'd let us in, working in the back kitchen. Steam rose from a pot on the wood stove, and the scent of brewing *caoro* beans filled the house.

Were you in a fight, Roni? Why are you here so early? The woman was clearly fluent in Watcher-speak. She tossed sleek braids with a flick of her head behind her shoulders, then peered into the pot, satisfied. The woman fixed her large dark eyes on me for a long moment.

"Hello."

She didn't respond to my greeting. Instead, she signed furiously at Roni, far too quickly for me to follow.

I dropped my head, embarrassed, then turned it to look around the small house for a place to sit before my legs gave out entirely. My eyes fell on a canvas flag in the space by the front door, usually reserved for a bell. A string stretched from the flag and over the top of the door, like a doorbell for Watchers. I slammed my hand on my mouth.

"This *is* a Watcher house!"

No one seemed to notice my muffled exclamation as I tugged at the back of Roni's tunic. He spun, surprised. His body blocked the woman's view as I signed close to my body: *Not here, not more Watchers!* That day, I would have bathed in the village square fountain rather than stay with more Watchers.

I am a Watcher.

I forgot to sign, startled by Roni's reply. "But... you're..." *Different*, I finished with my hands. *Akilan.*

Something closed off in Roni's eyes. He looked at my mouth instead of my eyes, and I cursed my stupid, impulsive heart, even if I was right.

Roni signed harshly, his hands like the knives Itu used to gut his daily catch. *Then go, if you think...* His Watcher-speak became too rapid for me to follow, and I realized how much he'd been slowing down to communicate with me. He turned his back on me before I had a chance to respond.

I stumbled backward and huddled against a cushion on the wall by the door. Two of the three mat sleepers—one with only nubs where his ears should have been—moved to a sitting position and stared at me. I didn't care as tears of anger, loss, and humiliation flowed. I buried my head in my knees, finally allowing the fatigue to wash over me, hoping I'd wake to find that the last two days had been nothing but a nightmare.

***

A rough hand on my shoulder shook me awake. I wiped sleep and sweat from my eyelashes and gazed at the owner of the hand—the woman who'd let us in the house. The air was stifling, and not a single window was open to let in the island breezes.

Visitor.

I pointed at myself, confused, wondering where Roni had gone and if he'd abandoned me here.

She shook her head and gave me a piercing look. *Visitor for you.*

I sat up fast. Roni snored faintly, lying on a sleeping mat, and no one else was in the room.

Outside, she signed.

Sorry. I noticed the woman's impatience and quickly changed the gesture to *thank you.*

My body ached in a thousand places, my hands worst of all, as I stretched out my stiff limbs, stood, and wondered if it was Medor or maybe a group of Kokkans ready to rescue my people. I opened the front door and dared to let a little hope seep into the cracks of my soul.

Uma and Papi stood there, small and fretful. I shrieked.

"Uma! Papi!" I forgot all decorum and threw myself into Uma's arms. The elder cried out in joy.

"Oh, Alesea, you're safe."

Papi gave my back a gentle pat as I peeled myself off of Uma, her face already turning to its usual knowing yet kind expression, a slight redness in her bright eyes as the only sign of her sadness.

"Uma, Papi, did Medor tell you? Will we rescue them? Can we go right now?" I couldn't make myself slow down.

Uma shook her head. "No, Alesea. Medor's servant, Bibi, told us what had happened. We spent the night with friends, and this morning we wondered why the rafts hadn't returned, but..." Her voice quivered as she trailed off.

Papi took over, though his voice trembled more than Uma's. "It wasn't hard to find you. Half the city watched and wondered why you and Roni walked through Kokka in such a state. Some recognized you from the Festival and Roni from his raft."

"So, when are we going after them?" I didn't really care how the elders had found me because I was thrilled to see them. Now, it was time to rescue my family.

"We're not, Alesea." Uma hung her head as if she were the child addressing an elder. "Well, they're not. That's why we came here." *May we please come in,* she signed into the house behind me. *Not long.*

I turned to see the tall woman gesturing for the elders to follow her. Once everyone was in the house, she bowed to Uma and Papi, glared at me, then went over to sit at a desk full of books.

I struggled not to speak first, to be a respectful child like I'd failed to do with Medor. I burned with impatience, but for once, I managed it.

"Alesea," Uma said, "According to Bibi, the Kokkan elders took Pedir off the mission and sent a diplomatic team."

"What does that mean?"

"No one is going after our villagers," Papi said when Uma didn't answer. "They're too scared they'll be next."

"What?" Papi's dark face blurred in front of me. "How could... but..."

"Sit down, girl," he grunted, and I did, on the floor.

"Medor thinks he can make a deal with these Matans," Uma said. "They call themselves the Paav. Medor and the others will help them steal everything they can from Akila and teach them our secrets in exchange for Kokka's safety and a trade agreement." She spat out the last words as if she couldn't get them out of her mouth fast enough. "The Kokkan elders have already issued an announcement that the Akilans accepted the Paav offer to relocate their village to the 'great city' of Mata in exchange for the *kreo*—"

"It's not true, Uma," I blurted out. "I was there! They threatened me! They—"

Uma spoke over my raving. "I know, child. The Matans called you a Demon of the Islands, and they are terrified of you."

"What? They're the ones killing people!"

Papi shook his head, fury in his narrowed eyes. "It makes a convenient excuse that the Akilans were eager to escape a demon."

"How could anybody believe that?"

"Fear leads to hate, and there is no legend more feared by the Matan Watchers than that of the Knowers," Uma said.

"But I'm not even—"

Uma held up a finger to silence me. "The story has already spread around Kokka that the Paav slew the demon, yet her body disappeared along with the body of an unfaithful Akilan Watcher."

I leaned into Roni and shook him lightly, hoping he'd awake and hear what Uma had to say but to no avail. Uma continued, unfazed that he was sound asleep.

"Anyone who claims to have seen you this morning was told they saw a ghost, or worse."

I felt anger rising within me again, and this time, it threatened to boil over. I sputtered, too furious to form words, and that strange glow came over everyone in the house—Uma, Papi, the Watcher woman, and even Roni as he snored.

"Breathe, Alesea. I fear they will feel your emotions, even outside this house," Uma murmured. "Your mother suspected your Knowing for some time, but no one could have predicted how strongly it would come on and how quickly."

"We've seen nothing like it before," Papi agreed. "It's even rarer in the Islands than on the continent."

"So what do I do about it? I thought Knowing had been gone for centuries!" My voice quickly rose in pitch and much against my will. "I don't know how to control it. I don't know anything! Why didn't anybody tell me?"

Papi flinched, and I didn't know if it was at my tone or because he could telepathically feel my rage as I muttered under my breath.

"Maybe I am a demon."

"You are no demon. Your Knowing suddenly came on when your mother thought she had years to seek guidance for you. Knowing is not evil, Alesea, no more than a fishing knife is evil. It's all in how you use it. But it can be easier to believe it doesn't exist at all than to live with the paradox."

The last thing I needed right now was a paradox. "Uma, why did Mama never tell me? And now she's... now she's..."

"Be strong, little flower." Uma used my mother's nickname for me in her command, which shattered my heart. She leaned down and placed a finger under my chin, lifting my face toward her. "There may be hope, yet."

I could barely whisper my response. "What hope? If no one will help me?"

Uma raised her eyebrows. "Is Roni no one?"

"Roni's a Watcher! He betrayed us once already, and now he's mad at me for some reason." My eyes wandered to the sleeping mats, where Roni was no longer glowing or asleep but sitting up, watching my lips move.

This time, Uma's voice was firm. "Roni knows how to sail, having traveled beyond Kokka, and knows touch-speak. You..."

I looked at my lap, embarrassed, picturing Roni on the *kreo* forest floor, begging to die for his betrayal. A mix of anger and sadness rose in my throat, which I struggled to shove back down, and signed *sorry* toward Roni. It was the best I could do since I wasn't ready to mean it. Not yet.

Roni nodded once and looked away just as I addressed my concerns to Papi.

"So, what do we need to do? How can we save them?"

Papi's eyes clouded with sadness. "Alesea, you and Roni are all we have left. Perhaps, we should be joyful you have not been taken. Settle on one of the other Village Islands, and —"

"No!" My snapped response startled us all. I flailed my way to my feet, trying to look strong but probably giving the opposite impression. "Demon or not, I'm going to get them back. Even if I have to... to *swim* to Mata!"

I sounded ridiculous, but Uma grinned. "That's my girl."

Papi snorted, but he didn't argue.

Uma translated for Roni as she spoke, and as much as I hated Watcher-speak in that moment, I envied her easy fluency. "Medor has already begun sending messengers to the rest of the villages to tell them his version of what happened to Akila and lies about you."

Papi interrupted with a disgusted grumble. Uma glared before she continued.

"But there is one island that may still help you, and wiser than all of us, and with an active trade agreement with Ana, so there are plenty of ships going to and fro."

A tiny spark of hope lit the emptiness inside me. "Kuul." It was the monastery island of the Listeners and a pilgrimage site for *A'lodi* devotees in their eighteenth year.

Roni didn't look surprised—he was nodding, though his face was grim. I wondered what a Watcher could know about Kuul. Did Watchers go on pilgrimages?

Uma nodded, too, but her forehead creased with worry. "Papi and I are too old to go with you. We'd surely drag you down, but the Listeners are wise, and they will appreciate your gifts, Alesea. I am sure they will help you. They have heard of you already from your mother."

Papi shifted uncomfortably, clearly wanting to argue. I stepped toward him and took his warm, papery hands in my smaller, swollen ones. "It's all right, Papi. I'm going to Kuul, and then I'm going to save them. All of them." The courage I heard in my voice surprised me. "Even if I have to chase them all the way to Mata, I will bring them home."

CHAPTER 11

I spent the next few hours trying to rest in the stuffy house, but instead, I jumped at every voice on the street, reliving the horrible events of the last days over and over in my mind. Uma and Papi returned to their Kokkan host's house to avoid making Medor suspicious. The willowy Watcher woman still worked at her desk, alternating reading with furious scribbling in a notebook. Roni told me in slow Watcher-speak that one of his friends had gone to arrange for a boat to get us to Kuul.

I pulled out the mysterious packet of pages I'd found in my mother's bag and examined them one by one, but it was no use. Unlike Watcher-speak, I'd received no lessons in Listener-script in First School, and the only thing I recognized was *Alok* in the corner of several pages and *Maia* on another.

Roni must have felt just as listless. I could tell he was only pretending to sleep on his mat, but I didn't trust my temper enough to have a conversation. *What would we discuss, anyway?* We needed a plan, but I didn't even know how to start. I'd never been as far as Kuul, didn't know anyone who'd been as far as Mata, and knew little about boats beyond rafts and tiny fishing boats like Itu's.

I longed to escape the suffocating room, but we had to wait until night to escape undetected. I'd never felt so helpless.

A half dozen Watchers trickled through the front door as the dusty light wore into shadows. They signed to each other with tiny gestures and threw suspicious glances my way. Although, an older woman brought me a bowl of hot fish soup, and a bearded man handed me a chunk of bread. *Thank you,* I signed to them all, still feeling claustrophobic and completely alone, especially when Roni didn't look at me — not even once—until darkness fell and all the other Watchers lay on their stiff mats by the light of a single candle.

That's when he rose from the chair he'd taken during our humble dinner, slung his knapsack over his uninjured shoulder, and picked up another larger seagrass bag his friends had packed. The rest must have done Roni some good. His movements were already more effortless than they'd been that morning.

Come. Roni turned his back on me and slipped out the rear door of the house with a welcome breath of cool air. I blew out the flickering candle and followed, my knapsack and *lele* on my back.

The island breeze lifted the sweat from my brow and the tightness from my chest. Roni navigated the forest like a fox, which struck me as an odd skill for someone who couldn't hear. I felt clumsy in comparison and blind to the branches before they smacked my face as I struggled to match his pace.

When Roni finally stopped, I nearly slammed into his back. He scanned the darkness as I listened to the ocean waves crashing nearby. He nodded, apparently satisfied with himself, and continued forward.

We left the trees and scaled a small dune. All at once, the moons' light revealed the south side of Kokka, the southern border of all the Village Islands. The open ocean, usually comforting, was an endless and impassable void that filled me with dread as it pounded relentlessly at the rocks on the beach.

Roni kept moving, and I had to focus on my balance, steadying myself as we scrambled over slippery rocks in the dark. Soon, I saw the outline of a small sailboat resting on the beach, then gasped to see the silhouette of a man next to it. If I could see him, Roni had to have spotted him ages ago, but to my surprise, he sped up to reach the stranger.

I noticed the man gesticulating but couldn't quite decipher his hand motions in the dark. Roni seemed to have no trouble. The two engaged in a brief conversation before Roni signed *thank you, my brother*, then jabbed backward with his elbow and hit me in the chest, which made me yelp loudly.

"Ouch!"

Thank you, Roni repeated to the man. That I understood.

Thank you, I signed twice, belatedly translating the few words I'd seen before I realized the man to be the Watcher friend who had somehow procured us a boat. I bowed deeply to him as if to an elder, but when I raised my head, he had disappeared into the night.

Time to go, Roni signed.

***

My sheer determination—not enough to compensate for my small size and inexperience—offered little help to push the boat into the waves. I kept hopping up to check on my *lele*, tucked in the bow. Roni shot me many annoyed looks and gestured for me to get in the boat before we were even clear of the breakers. I followed his command and tried to help with an oar, but I was too inept to make a difference.

Finally, Roni hefted himself into the boat and held his injured arm for a moment before standing to raise the sails. To keep out of his way, I huddled in the back of the boat with my *lele* and soaked knapsack. I had never learned to sail since I never ventured beyond the little sailboards children played with in the shallows that were no more than toys. Even on this small vessel, the sails and lines were nothing but a dimly lit maze to me.

So, I sat until dawn, watching the moons' journeys. I tried to think of everything I knew about Kuul. My father lived there when my mother first met him after a performance at the monastery, but the small amount of information wasn't enough to occupy me for a dozen swells. A Listener and master luthier—Alok fell in love with Mama over the songs of our islands.

"*Think what happened to your father,*" Medor had said.

It had to be more than a fishing boat accident. Was Alok a Knower?

After years of avoiding the subject that made my mother so sad, I had a million questions about the man whose blood ran through my veins. These pages that bore his name had to contain something that would help me.

We'd rounded the deserted eastern tip of Kokka by the time the sun peeked over the watery horizon. Roni gripped the mast, sweat glistening on his extended arm in the golden sunlight. He held his injured arm close to his side.

I rifled through my bag and found a packet of dry *cao* nuts. Roni turned as I rocked the boat, stumbling forward to stand on shaky legs.

His nostrils flared, but his expression was otherwise neutral. I held out the nuts, which he took with his good hand.

Help?

Roni shook his head, then pointed at the deck where the seagrass bag sat. *Food. Water.*

I scrambled to pull a canteen out of the bag, offering it first to Roni, then taking a long drink myself. I gulped the musty water, not wondering until I finished if he intended it for himself or me.

I had to tap Roni's arm to get his attention again. *How long to...* I paused, not knowing how to sign "Kuul." *Listeners*, I finished.

Day.

It was a long, long day, with nothing but the occasional fish leaping from the endless sea and my dangerous thoughts to keep me busy. Though my hands were still stiff and swollen, I caught two fish with a moldy line I'd found on the deck—something I had learned from Itu during our lazy times together off the coast of Akila.

Itu. Just thinking his name was like having that knife at my throat.

Roni avoided me as much as he could on such a small boat. It wasn't that hard since he only had to turn his back. I couldn't understand why he was so angry at me. Since we stayed at the Watchers' house, I could practically feel the fury rising off him like mist from the sea. My anger rose with his dodgy attitude because he had no right to act like this. Watchers had stolen my people, tried to kill me—and Roni, for that matter—and now they would destroy Akila. Their vile act validated my hatred toward Watchers. If I were Roni, I would wish to be anything but a Watcher.

Roni acted like I'd hurt him rather than the other way around. I was letting him help me, despite what he'd done. My thoughts ran wild: *So what if I'd said a few stupid words at the Watchers' house? I was the one who was all alone, who had her family stolen. Besides, a lot of it was his fault. How could he have been so gullible?*

The more I stewed, the angrier I became. I stared at Roni's back, hating him more as the hours passed. I wished I had another way, any other way, to get to Kuul.

The sun over the open ocean was relentless. The wind shifted every time I placed myself in the shade of the main sail, and Roni adjusted it until I burned once again. I imagined he was doing it on purpose, though even in my anger, I had to admit that thought was unfair. I'd been on enough boats to know that.

My hands throbbed worse than before after I reeled in the second fish. They had swollen to nearly twice their usual size since my tree-tying incident. My skin was numb, and my fingertips tingled oddly. I didn't realize the fishing line had dug through the tight skin across the palm of my right hand until I saw my blood dripping onto the deck.

I swallowed the growing lump in my throat as I grabbed the only dry cloth from my bag—Konu's special blanket—and wrapped my hand tight. It should have been the least of my worries, but the idea that I couldn't play my *lele* in my condition sent me over the edge into a few dry-eyed sobs as I watched Konu's blanket turn red with my blood.

Roni, of course, didn't notice. He kept his back to me, through countless hours of the monotonous ocean and as the first hazy edge of the legendary mountain of Kuul appeared like a mirage on the horizon, oddly orange in the late afternoon sun. I watched the mountain grow and loom in front of us like the entrance to a magical kingdom and squeezed my hand until blood soaked through the last clean bit of the double-wrapped cloth. My skin was so hot in the sun, even as it dipped low in the sky behind me, that I was beyond sweating. A voice like Mama's in my head told me to drink more water, but the seagrass bag across the deck seemed impossibly far away, and the small boat started lurching in the higher waves as we approached the shore. My stomach heaved along with the water. The best I could do was curl up in a ball against the wall of the boat.

A distant part of me registered the abrupt bump of our hull hitting a dock and nearby voices murmuring and then yelling.

"Quiet, Roni!" I realized how foolish it was to speak out loud to a Watcher as Roni began shaking my shoulder.

Roni, his face blurry and unreadable, towered above me when I finally managed to peel open my eyes. He placed my *lele* on my stomach and picked up my knapsack, his pack, and the seagrass bag. I rolled onto my knees, managed to stand without dropping my *lele*, and picked up the pair of fish I'd wrapped in a piece of greasy paper I'd found on the deck. I dropped the packet twice before balancing it on my bound hand.

My skin still burned, though the sun was nearly set. I thought I must be sunburned. Then again, Islanders rarely get sunburned, though I'd seen a light-skinned Anak trader's face grow pink, then red and blistered, after just a day at the Kokkan market. Fog filled my head, and I could barely remember how to place one foot in front of the other. I stumbled off the boat onto the dock and into a crowd of people.

"Welcome! We were not expecting visitors on this day." The old woman's rich, melodic voice felt like a fire in the hearth during a winter sea storm.

I bowed my head, not trusting my balance to bend at the waist in a more formal gesture. When I opened my mouth to speak, no sound emerged. Instead, I produced a strange dry cough. Shock filled me to see so much blood as I reached to cover my mouth, and the bloody baby blanket fell from my hand and dropped at my feet. It continued spreading until my whole world morphed into that bright red stain. Hands gripped my back too late as I felt myself free-falling into nothing.

PART TWO – LISTEN

A Listener is blessed with the language of the sun, the moons, the planet and all the life upon it, and the heart of a philosopher. The Listener may have been given the least winding path to the A'lodi, but she must not be fooled by this. Compassion, understanding, and teaching must be an equal part of the Listener's journey.

~ The Book of the A'lodi

CHAPTER 12

Na-nu la, Keh-la la, Na-nu la ley...

The nonsense song worked its way into my consciousness like the gentle sensation of my mother stroking my hair. My face lay on something soft. As I came to, pain overcame the pleasant feelings. Some were sharp and stinging, some achy and throbbing, from my hands to my head to my soul.

I opened my eyes. A fire flickered nearby, and someone's dark, wrinkled hand lay near my face.

I tried to roll onto my back, then groaned as pain shot down one arm and to the tips of my fingers. I collapsed back into the pillow, and the humming halted, followed by a murmur.

"Stay still, stay still." Her hand rested on my forehead as she leaned down to look into my eyes, except she wasn't looking.

A Listener. Her eyes were small and milky white, blank circles that sunk into a face like old leather. She sniffed several times before sitting back up.

"The infection is almost gone. You are a lucky one." She returned her hand to her lap. "Or lucky in your body, I suppose. Your friend has told us your story. You have had most unfortunate times of late."

It took three breaths before I could part my lips to speak. "Roni?" I croaked, barely audible even to myself. "Is he... how did..."

"Your friend is fluent in touch-speak. He was quite concerned for your health, though he is obviously racked with conflicting feelings towards you and his home."

What? I didn't have time for Roni's conflicted feelings. *Maybe if he had looked at me during our trip to Kuul, I wouldn't be so sick, and if he hadn't helped the Matan Watchers, maybe we would —*

"And you? Your feelings are a thousand times more active than our volcano, are they not? So much has happened to you in such a short time. You are lost, betrayed, confused."

I almost laughed, but it turned into a painful cough. "Are you..." I gasped, "some kind of fortune teller?"

The old woman cackled with delight. "Aren't we all?"

Her laughter faded into more silence, broken only by the crackling of the fire. I tried again when I realized she wouldn't give me a real answer.

"What happened to me? How long have I been here?"

"Oh, my dear girl. You were horribly sick for three days, infected with your grief, powerful anger, and a contaminated fishing line, I believe."

"My hands!" I remembered my injury as I cried out with another jab of pain that stopped me from rolling over.

"They are not well. Perhaps with time."

"Oh." The woman's gentleness momentarily caught my emotions off guard, and they broke free into sniffles and gulps. I burst out crying, and every sob tore from my body like an animal struggling to escape a cage.

The woman patted my hair and resumed her haunting song, voice rasping like something ancient. I controlled my breath enough to speak.

"Will you help me?"

"I am already helping you."

I counted my breaths to three and tried again. "Will you help me find my family? My friends?"

"Ah!"

The old woman's sigh perfectly blended in with the fire's popping and rustling. I counted my breaths to ten.

"First, you must heal yourself."

Her response startled me into another cough. "How long will that take? How... how bad is it?"

"Even if I could truly listen into your mind and soul, my dear, only you can answer that question."

"What? I thought it was an infection." I managed to sit up, though I nearly gave up along the way. I was in an open-air room like those common in South Village. A cool breeze soothed my face and fluttered the curtain in front of me, revealing a rocky path lit by the light of dusk or maybe dawn. The sound of the ocean was close, and a child shrieked with laughter not too far from that.

"Easy now! Breathe."

"I have to find them. And I have to leave now!" My head began spinning into near-blackness, but I refused to lay back down.

"If you are well enough, the next Anak traders are likely three or four weeks away. Perhaps you can beg passage onto their ship."

"Ana." Ana was the largest city I'd heard of outside of Mata. A trader had once told me it wasn't even halfway to the continent, but it seemed impossibly far away. "Then... then I have to go to Mata."

"Ah." The woman again fell into silence.

"Ah?" I succumbed to the dizziness and lay back on the bed.

"Three to four weeks is barely enough time to improve your Watcher-speak, much less clear your heart and tame your emotions. Drink this, then go to sleep, and if you are strong enough, we can begin work in the morning."

She leaned below me, making a strange clicking sound with her tongue, and lifted a small clay pot. She helped prop me up to drink its contents. It might have been Sarai's mother's *brahmi* soup, but for the bitter, medicinal aftertaste.

Warmth spread through my aching body, and I slept.

***

I dreamed I was playing with Konu in the Shallows. He splashed and laughed as I chased him, but the harder I tried to catch him, the heavier my legs became as if I were slogging through deep mud instead of clear, warm water. Joy turned to panic as I lost sight of him, and I woke to his distant laughter.

Closer by, someone really was laughing. My eyes popped open, then squinted in the bright sunlight coming through the half-opened curtains. The old woman from before was now conversing with a little boy beside my bed. He had short hair and a ridge where a Double's eyes would have been. He gave another giggle before running from the room and clicking his tongue. I wondered how he ran so quickly and dodged obstacles without vision.

"Hello."

"Oh, good morning, Alesea. How are you feeling?"

"Better, I think." I tried sitting up, and this time my body cooperated despite my bandaged hands, wrapped from the tips of my fingers to my wrists. The world remained stable around me as I swung my feet over the edge of the bed, and my stomach rumbled with hunger instead of nausea.

"Thank you for taking care of me." I bowed my head to her, then realized my mistake and instead placed my hands on her shoulders in the proper gesture of respect for a Listener elder — a memory dredged up from a First School lesson. "I'm sorry, I don't know your name."

"I am Sofi, and caring for you honors the *A'lodi* in us both." She stood and made a popping sound with her lips. "If you feel strong enough, we can take our breakfast in the garden."

"I am, thank you." As I stood, I found I was wearing an unfamiliar off-white robe held closed by a series of ties around my belly and chest. I tightened them, hoping there weren't too many sighted people around.

Sofi hummed and clicked her tongue as we exited the simple shelter. The garden was right outside — two stone paths twisted in figure-eight patterns among lush fruit trees, trellised vines, and giant flowers. A large, lidded basket sat next to three wooden chairs inside one of the eights.

"Sit." She gestured toward a chair.

"How... How do you know where the chair is?"

Sofi chuckled. "There are those who would like you to believe Listeners harness dark powers." She sat in another chair, opened the basket, and pulled out a loaf of bread. She tore it into three chunks and handed one to me, followed by a piece of hard cheese.

"But you don't."

She answered me with a series of tongue clicks.

"The clicks?"

"With the ears of a Listener, sound can tell us anything. For example." She clicked twice and clapped. "You are holding your bread in front of your face. And your companion approaches from behind."

I turned, startled, to see Roni only a few feet away on the path. He kept his eyes on Sofi, and when he reached her, he took her free hand and did something with his fingers on her palm. Sofi returned the gesture before Roni took the third chair and hunk of bread. He used his injured right arm, which no longer had visible bandages.

I was too busy stuffing bread into my mouth to ask any of my million questions. Cheese followed, then I took a swig from the communal water skin Sofi had sat next to the basket. Still, my stomach growled.

Sofi laughed. "Your belly sounds as empty as an orphaned baby whale's."

I flushed but couldn't apologize because she had more to say.

"Have another piece. There's more in the basket, but do slow down because your stomach may have forgotten how to deal with a proper meal."

I rummaged in the basket but kept my eye on Sofi as she took Roni's hand and drew more messages with her fingers. I wondered how Roni knew touch-speak. I'd almost finished my second piece of bread when Sofi made an announcement.

"So, dear ones, we have broken bread, and it is time we clear the air. You face a near-impossible task, but a sliver of hope is found in combining your talents."

Roni grimaced.

"What did *I* do? He sold out my entire village!"

Roni must have read my lips since he nearly glared a hole through my face.

Sofi's forehead crinkled. "I assume you know the story of Creation?" She signed on Roni's hand.

"Why?"

Sofi smiled at me. "Tell me."

"The creation story?"

"Yes, please."

I was so annoyed that I recited the old story as quickly as possible while Sofi translated for Roni.

"Before people, there was an argument between Thera, the goddess of the sun, and Luna, the goddess of the first moon, about what their creation should value most. They couldn't agree, so out of spite, Thera divided the land and created her own, unique race, the Watchers, who could use her light to see and rule the world with the *A'lodi* to give them knowledge and strength. Luna created the Listeners to appreciate the soft sounds of the night and use the *A'lodi* to become one with nature. Sad at her sisters' war, the goddess of the Second Moon, Phoemek, worked with the earth goddess, Donya, to create the Knowers to find the heart of the *A'lodi*, and eventually created peace among the races. At first, it worked, and the races met and created Doubles. But the Knowers..." I stopped. I never expected this part of the story to become personal.

"Go on."

"The Knowers were too powerful and betrayed them all. The Watchers, Listeners, and Doubles set aside their differences to defeat them in the Great War. And with the goddess' help, the *A'lodi* again spread through the world."

Sofi continued to sign on Roni's hand for a moment, then cocked her ear towards me. "And is it true?"

"It's... I don't know. It's a story."

Sofi's voice grew deep and serious. "But do you believe it?"

I contemplated whether I did believe. It was so long ago, and the gods never interfered in our lives or, at least, not anymore. Now, the Watchers were attacking us again, and I wasn't sure I should trust the rest of the story.

"I don't know." My voice was hesitant.

"Roni." Sofi's voice lost its edge, and she was again the caring grandmother figure. "Tell us the Watcher's story of creation."

When Sofi finished signing on his hand, Roni looked alarmed and drew on hers.

"Same, he says. But no." She signed on his hand some more.

Roni glanced my way, then traced more signs. She translated for me, slowly speaking as if spelling out many words.

"This is the creation story of the Watchers. It starts like yours, with the war between Luna and Thera. But Luna was devious. With Phoemek's help, she created the Listeners so that no one would value Thera's light, and the people would feel safer with the moons at night than in the bright sunlight. Thera was sad to know that the people did not love her, so she created the Watchers as her companions. Some of them betrayed her, having children with Listeners so they would have both senses, but those who were true to her were the most blessed. Donya, the earth-goddess, was jealous of both, so she used the stuff of demons to create the Knowers, who—"

Roni dropped his hand and shook his head.

"What is it?" I demanded. I'd never heard this story before, but it explained a lot. How Watchers thought they owned the world, for instance.

"A story, only a story." Sofi exuded confidence in her answer.

"Then which one is true?"

"Hmm."

I questioned whether or not she was playing games with us while I ate an entire third piece of bread, and Roni stared intensely at a purple-flowered vine. My stomach was nearly full, and this was feeling like a waste of time—a philosophy lesson when lives were at stake. "So, the creation stories are different to make different people look better, but what does that have to do with rescuing my family?"

"Everything." Sofi lifted her ancient face toward the sun she couldn't see.

I wasn't in the mood for puzzles. "Everything. Will it help me get to Mata?"

Sofi reached out and grabbed my arm, all mirth erased from her face. "No. Roni will help you get to Mata."

I could've sworn she was staring at me. She didn't make a single click.

Finally, she released her grip, and I could breathe again. "Let me tell you another story." She took Roni's hand to translate.

"Thousands of years before the first humans, the fish grew tired of the sea and longed to feel the sun on their scales. Through the generations, they sprouted legs and grew lungs and walked ashore, all over the world."

I turned my surprised snort of laughter into a cough and hoped she didn't notice. Roni still stared at the flowers, his expression blank.

"Over time, the fish people grew and changed to fit their new homes. In the northern areas, they faced silent predators, colder weather, and storms that required sturdy shelters. Their weak sense of hearing was of little use, but those who could spot enemies, locate the purple berries in a patch of poisonous red ones, or fell the thickest tree without hurting anyone, lived to have children. Children with even sharper eyes than their parents, and stronger."

"Watchers." I glanced again at Roni, who scrunched his forehead as if he couldn't believe the words Sofi pressed into his palm. At least, we had that in common.

Sofi nodded. "Yes, but those who emerged from the ocean in the Southern islands found themselves in a virtual paradise. Few predators, warm weather, and abundant food year-round, except their eyes, made for dark water, were blinded by the brilliant sun. Over time, the islands favored those who could sit on the rocks at midday until small fish nibbled their fingers without being driven to the trees for shade. Those who could hear the rustle of the *brahmi* in the forest. Those who could best hear had the most children, and those children created song and story and the contemplative practice of the *A'lodi*."

"And the Doubles?" I wondered whether Sofi was making this story up on the spot.

"That is where the stories converge. Most certainly, the Doubles are simply the result of Watchers discovering the Listeners and the two races mating. Though I suppose it is possible you are but another type of land fish."

One corner of Sofi's mouth twitched, perhaps with a smile, but since my frame of reference was so shattered, I had no idea if she was joking. Before I could sort anything out, Roni flipped his hand over and signed to Sofi.

"Ah, the gods." Sofi took a long breath. "It is true my story does not involve the gods."

"So where does the *A'lodi* come from in a story with no gods?"

Sofi turned and, without hesitation or a single tongue click, touched her finger to my chest. "That answer is always the same, Alesea. The *A'lodi* comes from inside you and every other living thing, which is where it has always come from."

"And the Knowers?"

"This story does not tell. Perhaps some things are meant to be a mystery."

I closed my eyes and sucked in the floral-scented air through my teeth. I needed a plan because Mama and my brothers were waiting for me.

I tried to redirect the conversation as calmly as I could manage. "So, if I can get along with Roni, will you help us devise a plan?"

Sofi laughed as if I'd made a wonderful joke. "Your impatience colors every word, dear." She tilted her head toward Roni and grabbed his hand, the smile dropping from her lips. "You will rescue no one if you can't rescue yourselves. Your stories are so strong within you, Alesea, that you blame Roni for the violence of others. And you, Roni, do you not blame Alesea for the oppression of your people in the Islands?"

"Oppression?" I couldn't believe it. There hadn't been a violent crime on our islands for a hundred years, not until the Watchers came. The biggest conflict I'd heard about was whether to allow the poor at the Great Feasts.

Roni drew his lips into a thin line and looked straight down at his bare feet.

"We live in peace!" I watched Roni, even though he could only hear me through Sofi. "Or we did, until the Watchers..."

I stopped short. *The Watchers.* Not Roni nor Roni's friends who'd helped us escape from Kokka. I'd been blaming Roni for something that wasn't his fault. Not mostly, anyway. I stared at Roni until he met my gaze. Then, I found myself unable to hold it. I was ashamed, just a little, of how angry I felt when I saw his non-functional ears. "What do we do, then?"

"You will practice Watcher-speak, Alesea. You will also learn some touch-speak. It will be useful for you and Roni to have a more private means of communication."

My stomach filled with dread as I watched her fingers translate on Roni's hand. Watcher-speak was bad enough, but touch-speak was the most intimate language. Roni looked as dubious as I felt when Sofi finished.

I dug my toes in the sandy dirt as Sofi signed on Roni's hand some more. It seemed rude for them to talk in front of me without me knowing what they were saying.

Finally, Sofi dropped Roni's hand and spoke to me. "You, Alesea, must spend time in meditation learning to control your emotions. The Knowing has been unleashed in you, and there are few who trust that rare gift."

"Why now? Why didn't it show up sooner?" Roni sat without being part of the conversation, frowning, but I didn't care.

"Your father's Knowing appeared when he was a teenager, as well. And it is known that a traumatic event can trigger a... quicker awakening."

"Wait, so my father *was* a Knower? You knew him?"

"Yes, of course. He lived here for a few years as an initiate before he met your mother, but his thoughts were more on crafting instruments than becoming an *A'lodi* monk. He came back after you were born, seeking answers because he worried for you, your mother, and brothers."

"Worried for me? I was only a baby when he died!"

Sofi turned to face me, unfazed by my scoff, and I again had the uncanny sensation she was somehow seeing me in a realm beyond eyesight. "He worried for you every moment since your conception, Alesea. Knowing is a great blessing, but our people have learned to treat it as a curse, even to pretend it's only a legend from the dark past."

The bitterness in my voice took me by surprise. "Then why did he have children?"

Sofi sighed. "The world is more complex than you imagine, Alesea. Alok hopes that with proper guidance, you will be able to live among the people who rejected him."

"Hopes?" I kicked at the dirt hard enough to send a clump flying into the air. "From his place in the Beyond? How is that supposed to help?"

Sofi lowered her head, and her nostrils flared.

"What is it?" I switched to a gentler tone, wondering if I'd finally gone too far in my rudeness to the elder.

"Your father is not dead, Alesea. He seeks answers, even now, in the farthest reaches of the continent."

My gut roiled as if trying to digest this revelation. Somewhere impossibly far away, a father I'd never met was alive, searching for answers for me—answers that would allow me to continue to live with my people. A possibility that no longer existed, and he didn't even know it.

CHAPTER 13

I hated Watcher-speak. I couldn't sign the simplest sentence without picturing Sinon in his blood-red robe. My motions grew angry, rigid, and clumsy, and not entirely because of my injured hands.

My sessions with Roni were the worst. I tried to think of him as an Islander, as a friend, but my mind sabotaged me with memories of that horrible night in Akila. Roni grew impatient with me, too. He stopped trying to hide his frustrated grimace at my poor memory of the language, sometimes even rolling his eyes.

When Roni was off doing *A'lodi*-knows-what at the harbor, a gentle Double named Tika took over my lessons. Her skin, blacker and shinier than crow's feathers, with spiraling white arm tattoos that marked her as a sighted monastic, fascinated me. Though she was a Double, she spoke little, forcing me to use Watcher-speak for every communication. At least with Tika, it was easier to forget why I had to practice the language.

I found out the real reason why she'd been assigned to help me on my second day with Tika.

I am looking for my family. I practiced signing phrase after phrase, which could help me on my voyage. *They were brought here on a Paav ship by people who...* "Ugh!" I said aloud, burning with frustration. "I can't remember any of the words."

The strangest sensation came over me. It was as if a wet blanket smothered the fire of my anger and left me in an unwilling state of calm. I wanted to cry out, but my body refused. "What's happening?" My voice cracked.

Tika gazed at me with eyes that seemed decades older than her body. "I needed you to feel what it is like when your emotions run wild."

"You're a Knower." It should have come out as a shout, but somehow the words mellowed into a bland statement. "And you're doing... that... to me?"

The calm lifted, and emotions came crashing into my body — anger and excitement, frustration and confusion.

"Now breathe. Repeat your mantra."

"A'lodi sahm." I closed my eyes, repeating the words. Then, in my head: A'lodi sahm. A'lodi sahm.

"Much better!" Sofi told me you were strong. I could barely manage to turn back your emotions. What frightens me is that you did not intentionally share them, correct?"

My eyes popped open. "Intentionally? Of course not. How do you do it?"

To my irritation, Tika returned to Watcher-speak. *I will teach you what I know, but I fear it is not much. There are very few Knowers now, and none of us has the power of the Ancients. I could affect you in that way only because your emotions were so obvious.*

"What can you —"

"No." *Sign.*

I clumsily signed *What can you normally do?*

I can help one who is distressed feel peace. And I can excite the young children to get them to exercise. I am good at reading others' emotions and... She signed a word I didn't recognize.

"What?"

"Their motivation," she said before signing it again.

Is it true that a powerful Knower can control other people?

I thought a flash of anger crossed Tika's face, but her features returned to their usual serene state, so I quickly wondered if I'd imagined it.

That is what the histories say. But the histories... she signed another unfamiliar word, saying out loud, "The histories vilify Knowers," *perhaps because there are no strong ones left to defend themselves.*

When the Matan Watcher in blue tried to slit my throat, I exploded with rage, then woke up to find myself alive and the knife discarded in the grass. I could only imagine what else could have happened, which was something I couldn't tell Tika.

So there are none left that strong? You're sure?

I certainly hope not. Tika signed so violently her papers blew off the table and settled on the floor.

***

Sofi changed my bandages for two nights, and I squeezed my eyes shut both times to avoid seeing the damage to my bare hands. I asked if she would translate the papers with my father's name on them to distract me, but she gave me an inarguable "no," saying they were letters of a personal nature and not my business.

On the third evening of my "education," Sofi brought an unfamiliar Listener to the open shelter that had become my guest quarters on Kuul. The tall man had no eyes, only a slight horizontal bony ridge protruding between his nose and forehead. The two laughed and talked as they approached my shelter but fell silent when he reached the edge of my opened curtain. Sofi spoke first.

"Alesea, this is Yori. He took care of you when you arrived and would like to check your hands."

I managed to squeak "all right."

Yori approached me with two clicks and took my hands in his. He hummed as he unwrapped the bandages. His deft movements, unaided by sight, fascinated me to the point that I forgot to look away.

My left hand was first, and the unwinding cloth revealed unnaturally pale skin, wrinkled up to the middle joint of my fingers, which contrasted with the still-puffy brown tips. When Yori gently balled my fingers into a loose fist in his large hand and straightened and stretched each one, the pain was nothing more than a dull ache.

"We can leave that one uncovered."

Yori's heartening news so moved me that I watched as he unwrapped my right hand. I shouldn't have. My right fingers were swollen and red as uncooked sausages. Worse was the angry red line across my palm, skin puckered despite the salve smeared across it. Yori didn't even try to make a fist out of it. He bent my fingers ever so slightly and stopped at my gasp of pain before running a finger along the cut, which I couldn't feel. I would have rather felt more pain.

Sofi frowned. "What now?"

Yori sighed. "Healing slower than I'd like. The damage to the tendons—"

He stopped when Sofi cleared her throat. "Time, Yori. She just needs time."

Now that I'd looked, I wanted to know everything. "The damage to the tendons what, *Papan*?"

Sofi gave a series of clicks, and Yori hesitated. I hadn't realized they also used the clicks for communication. *Great.* Another language I didn't know.

Yori frowned like Sofi. "The damage to your tendons may be more serious than I thought, but you are young. Likely, even this damage will heal with time, as Sofi suggests." He pulled a bottle out of his side bag and again took my right hand.

"Oww!" The clear drops stung worse than a snake bite. Yori's fingers held tight around my wrist to keep me from jerking away.

"I am sorry, child. It is often easier if I do not warn of the pain. You were asleep the last time."

I nodded, then, glancing at his eyeless ridge, I uttered a "Thank you."

Yori instructed Sofi about changing my bandages as he rewrapped my right hand. This time, he left my swollen fingers uncovered. I stretched my left-hand fingers and tried a few finger signs I couldn't do with the bandages. I pushed thoughts of my *lele* to the back of my mind and reminded myself I was one step closer to my family's return.

***

Once I could use my left hand, I began learning touch-speak. Sofi insisted that I work only with Roni, even though she could have taught me herself.

"You don't have enough time as it is. Roni is the only one you need to communicate with, so you are best suited to practice together." That was her reasoning.

I grumbled bitterly, but I heard the sense in her argument.

It was horrible because having to touch Roni with things so awkward between us was bad enough. His long, gentle fingers tickled my palm, and the constant urge to laugh made me angrier than anything. I practiced day and night regardless, touch-speaking into my soft cot until my thoughts dissolved into nightmares.

Though my signs were clumsy, my ability to read Roni's and Tika's at full speed grew. As we practiced, Tika walked with me around the monastery. I eavesdropped on the day-to-day conversations of the Double initiates, many of whom used Watcher-speak to protect the silence of the sacred spaces. Or at least that's what Tika told me. Most conversations I saw involved complaining about impossible assignments given by a Listener teacher or noting the most attractive students and whether they were choosing to take vows of chastity.

Sometimes Tika bombarded me with an unexpected emotion as a reminder of my growing sense. *A'lodi sahm,* I repeated over and over, striving to close my mind to her emotions and suppress my own. It was the best I could do.

Two weeks into my stay on Kuul, Sofi found Roni and me practicing touch-speak. She sounded more distressed than I'd heard her.

"Alesea, one of our initiates returned today from a visit to Kokka. Translate for Roni."

I flailed about with Watcher-speak until my mind adjusted to switching languages again. "Go on."

Sofi's thin black eyebrows dipped over her glassy eyes. "The Kokkan elders have signed a treaty with the Paav, and they have agreed to recognize Akila as a Matan colony in exchange for the safety of Kokka."

The now-familiar rage rose as I translated. I couldn't control it and sign at the same time, and by Sofi's flared nostrils, I guessed she was feeling it, too.

I had to finger-spell the word "colony." Roni's eyebrows threatened to leap from his reddening face as the meaning became clear.

An unexpected wave of affection for Roni distracted me from my anger. For the first time in days, he looked directly into my eyes, his angry gaze softening as Sofi continued.

"I'm sad to say there is even worse news for the two of you."

"What? How can it be worse?" I tore my eyes from Roni's.

"The Paav were concerned with your escape." Sofi paused as if weighing her next words. "The Kokkan elder council has declared the two of you fugitives, offering a generous reward for your capture."

And our crime? Roni signed for me to translate, his hands nearly as forceful as mine had become.

"Treason."

I had no translation for the word because it was something from storybooks—a crime from ancient lands, with kings, dungeons, war, bandits, and murder. Treason wasn't even defined in the Village Islands, as far as I knew.

I finger-spelled the word for Roni.

His response began with an unfamiliar sign I presumed to be "treason." *It doesn't exist in the Village Islands!* I spoke his words to Sofi.

"It does now." Sofi's reply sent shivers down my spine.

***

Now that we were fellow fugitives, Roni and I found new solidarity. Like it or not, we would be stuck together for months or more as the only flotsam left from the shipwreck that was Akila. Practicing my slow but improving Watcher-speak, I told Roni stories about my brothers' antics. I told him about tagging along to performances on other islands as my mother's apprentice and my mild rebellion against countless assigned hours of A'lodi meditation, in which I practiced from the swaying tops of kreo trees or floating on a little raft in the Shallows, instead of in the meditasi.

Roni told me about his childhood and what it was like living as an Island Watcher, outnumbered by Doubles and Listeners fifty to one. When he was fourteen, the same Watchers who'd helped us escape Kokka took him in after his mother, a Double, had died. He'd lived in that tiny house for months, learning about Watcher culture and customs and fitting in better than he ever had on Akila, making me feel even more ashamed at how rude I'd been to them. I contemplated why he hadn't told me those people were practically his adoptive family. Once he was old enough to run his own raft, Roni chose to live on Akila. He loved our island and the house his mother had left him and hated Kokka's crowds and dirty streets. Only recently had he been thinking of leaving the Islands altogether.

Our touch-speak was much more limited, but we'd adjusted our signs and invented new ones that allowed us to almost completely conceal our communication by holding hands, my healed left hand in Roni's right. *Danger,* I practiced scratching onto his palm. *Don't look* he signed into mine.

Roni told me that his hours-long absences were for hands-on training with a Double monk who'd once worked as a deckhand. Roni could sail, but he'd never worked on a larger trading ship, and he needed to seem experienced if we were to pose as shipwrecked traders. His frustration at working the complicated sails made me feel a little better about my language troubles.

Now, I faced another challenge. The more Sofi—and now also Tika, who had been on the same trade ship as Roni's mentor—regaled me with facts about the trade economy, the more I was sure I would blow our cover before we were out of sight of Kuul.

I'll never remember all this! I vented to Roni one evening. *I'm failing before I've even started!*

Roni looked down at his bare feet for a moment. *It's a lot for both of us.*

You're doing just fine. I signed down low, so he couldn't avoid seeing me. *But no one will ever believe I'm a trader! Unless...* I stopped, an idea forming in my mind—a disgusting idea, but one that might work.

Roni looked at me again. *Unless what?*

The sailors are likely to all be Doubles, right? Tika had told me the Anak sailors, who made up most of the trade ship crews that came as far as Kuul, had become suspicious of Watchers as the Paav became more controlling of the trade routes. They'd stopped hiring them, for the most part.

Yes.

I need to pretend to be a Watcher, then.

The corner of Roni's mouth quirked up. *Is he laughing at me?*

I continued with my train of thought. *Doubles won't notice my Watcher-speak is bad, and if we're both Watchers, they won't suspect we're the fugitives. If they think we're from the Islands, they won't think we're with the Paav.*

Roni nodded. *You're right! That's actually a good idea. We'll practically be invisible – Doubles usually prefer to act like Watchers aren't there rather than sign.*

I didn't know what to say because I knew I was one of those people.

But trade ships rarely take on passengers who can't pay their way. I don't think you have time to learn to sail, too.

A'lodi sahm, I thought, trying not to project my frustration onto Roni. *Then how will I get on that ship?*

Roni's face flushed bizarrely, and his eyes darted away from mine.

What? I thrust my hands in front of his face.

If you were... he paused as if gathering strength. *If you pretended to be... my–* and he signed a word I didn't know.

Finger-spell, please.

He signed meekly in small letters. *Fiancée.*

I wished I hadn't asked.

Nonetheless, there was sense to the idea. If Roni could get a job as a sailor, how could they deny passage to his fiancée, if we claimed to be moving to Ana? *It makes sense*, I finally signed, then brightened with a new idea. *I could offer to make seagrass mats on the voyage! I know they're nothing special, but Mama said –* I slowed as my eyes began to sting with tears. *Mama said she heard they were popular on Ana.*

Roni smiled a *real* smile, and laid one hand on my shoulder. *We're going to do this* he signed with the other.

I could only nod.

CHAPTER 14

"Alesea! Alesea!" Clicks and claps punctuated the small boy's shouts as he ran up the path from the beach.

I dropped Roni's hand to the ground and leaped to my feet. "What is it, Tuk?"

"The traders! I heard them coming."

Roni took off down the path before I'd finished translating. As the owner of the sharpest eyes currently on Kuul, he could most easily assess the new arrivals at a distance, but my instructions were simple as could be: hide. I would do it to show my respect for Sofi and all her help. For now.

"Thank you, Tuk." I patted him on the head. *A'lodi be with you.* I sang the traditional blessing to my little friend, though my voice shook.

Tuk grinned and squeezed me around the middle. "You'll come back with all of them. You have to."

***

The monastery quarters were a cluster of enclosed wooden huts on the far side of the *A'lodi* garden. The largest and barest of the huts were the bunkhouses for new initiates. Spare beds had been set aside for Roni and me in the male and female huts, and we'd stashed clothes there to go with our cover. Mine weren't much different from my usual attire—a sleeveless off-white tunic and dark brown linen pants—but Tika had assured me they'd make me look more like a girl from South Village.

I didn't see or hear another soul in the residential area of the monastery. I threw on the clothes and stuffed my old outfit under the cot, then gave into my restless worries and paced.

When I was about to scream with impatience, the sound of quick footsteps in the gravel drifted through the open window and startled me down to the floor, out of sight. I snuck to a spot in the wall where time and insects had bored a hole through the wood and peered out.

Roni jogged alone toward the male initiate sleeping quarters.

All stealth forgotten, I burst out the door. *What happened?*

Roni jumped. *Go back inside!* He spun on his heel and entered the men's hut.

I sputtered with anger at Roni for snapping and my impulsive acting as I slammed the rickety door shut. I turned so sharply my hair smacked me in the face, which made me realize I hadn't put it up like I was supposed to. We hadn't even started, and I couldn't remember such a simple thing. No wonder Roni treated me like a child. No wonder everyone did.

My bandaged right hand made a braid impossible, but I could pull my tangled hair into a single tie as I calmed my breathing. Danger or not, I couldn't stay in the hut alone for another minute. I swung open the door and nearly ran straight into Roni, who held his fist up to knock but then quickly switched to signing.

Sorry, I panicked.

What happened?

Go inside.

I backed up.

Roni followed me in and shut the door. *They have a Matan Watcher on their ship. One of the Paav. I don't know why, because the elders made me hide after I told them. The rest are Doubles like we expected.*

No! I squeezed my eyes shut for a moment, fighting off the first pangs of a new headache. *Tika said the Matan Watchers never come to Kuul. You must have seen it wrong!*

He shook his head. *He was there. Sofi said there's another ship due in two weeks. It would be safer to try then.*

My frustrated tears blurred Roni's face. *My family has been gone for a month. We must go now, right now.*

Yes, Roni signed, to my relief. *You're right. Before anyone tries to stop us. I'll go right now and introduce myself as a trader, but first, I have to change.* He looked down at his hands as he signed, *From now on, you're my fiancee. Right?*

A rock settled into my stomach. *And a Watcher.*

And a Watcher.

I turned away, but Roni caught my shoulder and signed again. *The ship—it's named the* Phoemek. *Maybe it's a sign.*

Phoemek, the joyful second moon. I tried to smile. *It must be.*

Roni had more to sign—a confession. *Alesea, I never thought they would hurt anybody. It was so stupid of me. But I wanted to trust them.*

I didn't have to ask who "they" were. *I know. I believe you.*

To my surprise, I realized it was true.

***

I gathered my few remaining belongings and put them in the plain canvas bag Tika had left me. With a pang in my heart, I glanced at my *lele* propped in the corner. There was no way I could bring it, disguised as a Watcher and hiding from those who sought an undersized girl musician. I tore my eyes away and quietly prayed that I would hold it again someday.

Roni had been waiting for me in the courtyard, and I was shocked by his transformation from a rugged Island boy to a worldly young man. He wore a Matan green tunic over the canvas sailing pants popular with traders and leather sandals. A thin yellow scarf tied over his ears marked him as a Watcher, rarely seen in the Islands but common among traders and snobbish Watchers embarrassed to show their useless ears. A few wayward black curls protruding above the scarf made him look mysterious and sophisticated rather than childish.

He handed me a matching scarf to tie over my ears and signed before taking over for my clumsy hands and knotting the scarf behind my neck.

Keep your mouth closed.

I scowled as I jerked my head in a single nod. I reminded myself for the millionth time that it wasn't Roni's fault.

To the harbor?

Roni didn't see me. He fumbled through his bag, finally pulled out a ragged, off-white cloth and held it out toward me. I took it, confused, and wondered what other shameful body parts I needed to hide.

The second my fingers touched the cool, soft cloth, I realized what it was. Konu's baby blanket—somehow rescued from the trash heap and washed of my blood.

I threw my arms around my brother's childhood friend. He stiffened, then returned the embrace as I sniffled into his fancy tunic. A memory surfaced like a long-submerged branch rising from the sea:

I'm on a child's paddleboard in the Shallows. My older brothers Itu and Brahn are with me because I'm not yet a strong swimmer, but they're distracted because they've found a school of tiny fish and followed them nearly to shore.

"Itu, Itu!" I call, tired of being so small and slow. "Look what I can do!"

I stand up on my board, as I've done so many times before, but Itu's not looking. I stamp my foot in frustration, and before I know what's happening, the board flips and throws me into the Shallows. Something catches my hair, and I can't tell which way is up.

Someone leaps in the water as I struggle, arms wrap around my middle, and lift me until my head is above water. I hear my brothers' shouts as I breathe in the sweet air.

"Alesea! What did you do?" Airborne droplets sparkle with rainbows as Brahn splashes toward me like an angry sea elephant. He grabs me around the waist and sits me on my board. "How could you be so stupid!"

I refuse to cry as I turn to my rescuer. Eight-year-old Roni, shirtless, silent, and sleek as a fish, stares at me with gentle eyes dark as a moonless sky.

Then as if he really is some sort of fish-human, he dives into the water and swims away without even a splash.

I squeezed Roni hard. He was no stand-in for the Matan invaders, an arrogant Watcher I could hate in their stead. He was an Akilan, a friend, the kind boy who'd saved a little girl's life and never adequately thanked for it.

So, here I was, punishing him for weeks for a crime he never committed, and even so, he rescued the only thing I had left of my baby brother. I couldn't bear to let go because I would have to look in those honest eyes and admit how horrible I had been and probably still was.

Instead, I let go with my left arm and pulled his hand into mine.

I didn't know any touch-speak for what I needed to say. However, I did know how to form letters, so I awkwardly spelled into Roni's hand, my face still buried in his tunic.

I'm so sorry.

Roni flipped my hand as if to respond, then his body jerked and went rigid as a tree trunk. His fingernail scratched my palm three quick times.

Danger.

I would have spun around, but Roni clutched me with one arm and pushed my head up with the other until I could see his alarmed face. Then, he leaned down close. Too close and with his eyes shut.

He kissed me.

I was too shocked even to register what his lips felt like on mine. He kept kissing me and kissing me. His face still pressed so hard to mine that

I could barely breathe as he grabbed my hand and squeezed it between us.

Spelling two short words on my palm took an eternity. *Trust me.*

Roni jumped and jerked his head up as if startled. He began to sign furiously in Watcher-speak with his free hand, holding me tight against him with the other. Feet crunched in the gravel, coming closer, and someone coughed.

"Oh, what's this?" The man's voice rumbled with laughter. "Young lovers in the monastery? Have things changed so much?"

"Please tell our guests that the monastery center is sacred ground, and we would appreciate them taking their... activities elsewhere." The voice belonged to Sofi, who stood behind the man who chuckled. Silence followed, presumably while someone translated into Watcher-speak. Roni hung his head and released his grip on my back.

I turned slowly, keeping my head bowed like Roni. At the last second, I realized a Watcher in my position wouldn't have heard Sofi's words, so I cocked my head up at Roni, who fortunately remembered the same thing. His face flushed with the proper level of embarrassment, though not for the reasons the visitors would think as he signed, *I am sorry, dearest.* He managed a rueful, closed-mouth grin. *You told me we should take a walk. Next time, I will pay attention.*

I tried to look appropriately bashful and contrite as I turned the rest of the way toward the newcomers. Two men stood with Sofi. One bore long braids and Matan Watcher tattoos, stretching from earless head to below the neckline of his purple tunic. The other was stocky and dressed in the rougher clothes of one who lived at sea—stained linen shirt and loose pants, black hair in a single braid tossed over his shoulder and decorated with gull feathers.

Amusement danced in the sailor's eyes as he grinned at me. "Oh, you can't begrudge young love a few moments alone, *Maman.*"

Remembering to keep my mouth shut and not betray my understanding of the Double's words, I signed, *Please tell the elder I am very sorry.*

I imagined the Matan Watcher's eyes boring directly into my soul as the sailor translated. I could never keep up this disguise under his stare. It was a terrible idea to try. I bowed my head and refused to meet his eyes as I pondered how I could have ever compared Roni to these creatures.

Sofi cleared her throat. "It is, of course, difficult for me to communicate with these two. It seems the man lost his ship after picking up his betrothed from her home island, and they ended up floating here on little more than a canoe, sunburned and injured."

I struggled to keep my face blank and thanked the stars that Sofi was playing along, despite us disobeying her orders.

"What a terrible ordeal." The sailor translated with his hands as he continued, watching Roni. "I am called Flick. We will only be on Kuul for two days, and then we will begin the return voyage to Ana." He glanced at the Watcher, who gazed at Flick's hands with a distasteful glare. "I would be happy to deliver a message. I assume you are based in Ana?"

Roni nodded as he signed. *I appreciate your kindness.* He bowed his head, with his lips flattened to a straight line as if he carefully chose his next words. *But I was hoping you could use an extra deckhand.*

Flick raised his hands to answer, but the Matan came to life and batted them away before taking a step toward Roni.

What is your name?

A pause before he spelled *Ronan*, a name sign slightly more elaborate than the one I knew. I wondered if it was an alias or if Roni was simply a nickname.

Where are you from?

Roni stiffened but did not step back. *Ana.*

What district?

Cloth, he answered without hesitation.

Family?

Ryston, Roni spelled.

How long have you been away from Ana?

Flick stepped forward, angry, but Roni held up a hand to stop him. *Over a year*, he signed. *Why do you ask these questions?*

The Watcher's nostrils flared. *I represent the Paavden house of Mata, which has responded to reports of unrest in the Village Islands. Everyone aboard this ship must be approved by me.*

The tension between Flick and the Watcher was palpable. "You've missed a lot in a year." A deep growl accompanied Flick's comment as he signed different words: *Things have changed.*

It does seem so, Roni signed. He ignored the Watcher and turned to Flick. *I lost everything with my ship, but I am a hard worker and can repay you further when we reach Ana.*

Flick grinned. *Everything but the most important, you mean.* He gestured to me.

My heart beat so loudly I was sure the Watcher would find me out. I bowed my head, silently counting my breaths for emotional control, and pressed against Roni, hoping I looked embarrassed.

Sofi cleared her throat. With so much of our conversation in Watcher-speak, I wondered how much she knew of what had just transpired. "Shall we continue our tour?"

Flick invited us to walk with the small group, and Sofi agreed. As we plodded up a steep path beyond the monastery, Flick kept a hand on the elder's back though she scarcely needed the support. Despite his obvious distaste for the Matan Watcher, he strove to keep the tone light. I found myself liking him quite a lot.

Flick gasped when we rounded a curve to find the path growing even more treacherously steep. "*Maman*, these sea legs have not been asked to climb such a slope in years! Please, take pity on a tired sailor."

Sofi chuckled. "I hear straight through your words, Flick. You think I am no longer up to walking the mountain path. No need to worry about me, so please stop that ridiculous puffing." She clicked several times as if to emphasize her point.

Flick gave a hearty laugh. "Well, I certainly am working up quite an appetite, and the last time I was here, I believe you fed me nothing but seagrass."

Sofi sighed dramatically. "Ah, dear Flick. You would eat our entire herd of *brahmi* if I allowed you to sate your appetite."

I found myself smiling as the two laughed their way up the mountain, so it was fortunate that Roni stumbled on a rock and caught himself on my shoulder before I did anything stupid.

Are you okay? I signed.

Roni nodded, and we continued up the path, my face hard as a stone.

CHAPTER 15

The view from the top of Kuul's dormant volcano was worth the effort. The lush island stretched below us, cradled by the deep blue ocean striped with sparkling green currents and foam. The sandy beach, harbor, and monastery only made up a tiny part of the island, much larger than I'd realized. Though much of the land was densely forested, clusters of houses appeared throughout, and I made out a larger village on the opposite shore from the monastery.

Sofi sat on a boulder, face held toward the sun, as the rest of us gawked at the view.

"It gets me every time, *Maman*," said Flick.

Roni put his arm over my shoulders, playing the loving fiancée.

Even the tattooed Watcher signed *it is beautiful* to Flick, his sour expression softening as he gazed at Kuul.

"It is beautiful, says our Matan friend," Flick repeated, turning his back to the Watcher. "So you'd better be careful welcoming any Matan ships to your harbor."

Danger pounded in my skull, but Sofi didn't react. The Watcher, whose name I still didn't know, could not have known what Flick had said, but clearly, Flick was wary of his intentions. I longed for more information, but I knew I had to be careful as I wondered if Akila was only one of many conquests.

***

Upon our return, Roni spent the afternoon helping to unload goods from Flick's vessel, a standard trade ship of the type that occasionally stopped in the Akilan harbor before making its way to the much larger

- 84 -

market of Kokka. A few initiates came out to gape at the spectacle, but none of the children were there, probably warned to stay away because they'd give away my Watcher disguise. Or perhaps it was me who couldn't be trusted.

"Could you ask the young Watcher girl to accompany me back to the monastery?" Sofi's voice approached behind as Roni hefted a crate into a wheelbarrow on the dock.

I waited until someone tapped my shoulder, remembering not to react. I turned to see Tika sign *please go with Sofi*.

I nodded and took the elder's elbow as we silently walked onto the wooded path, through the open-air huts and *A'lodi* garden, into the heart of the monastery. She clicked, stopping at one of the enclosed huts identical to at least a dozen others, and led me through the door.

It was nearly as bare as the initiate's quarters, with a single cot in the corner, an altar and meditation cushion by the wood stove, a full bookshelf, and two sturdy chairs. Sofi took one chair, and I sat on the other before she candidly spoke for the first time during the ruse.

"You have gotten yourself into deep trouble, Alesea."

I kept my voice low. "I know. I had to."

"Did you?" Her kind voice was harsher than I'd heard. "Flick privately told me that the Matan Watcher is looking for dissidents— anyone who might spread the truth about Akila instead of their manufactured story. How long can you keep up your Watcher disguise in front of one trained to see through it?"

"I don't know." My voice shook. "I will do my best."

"That is not enough! You will stay away from the Matan at all costs." Sofi's voice rose in agitation—something I'd never seen in her. "Either pretend to or really be seasick. Always stay among others, so he cannot safely corner you."

"I will." I didn't know what else to say as she rattled off commands.

"And the Knowing... You must not give yourself away. It will be difficult enough to hide your ability to hear, but you *must* conceal the Knowing. You must find time to practice and meditate, no matter what else happens around you."

I nodded, then remembered she couldn't see me. "Yes. I will. I promise."

Sofi lapsed into silence or perhaps meditation. I shifted in my seat and spoke quietly.

"Sofi."

"Yes, Alesea."

"I can... I can *do* things to people with my Knowing. Like in the old stories."

"Such as?"

"Such as making the man who came to kill me while I was tied to a tree drop his knife and run somehow."

Sofi thought for a long time. "I'm not surprised. Tika has been amazed — frightened, even — by your powerful sense."

"Oh."

"What worries me is that the Knowing sense usually starts very small — like an offshoot of normal empathy — and grows for years until the Knower is like Tika. Mature Knowers have the power to sense others' emotions, but they can only influence what's already there, and they certainly can't cause others to act against their will."

"What about my father?"

"Your father is no more powerful than Tika, or at least he wasn't when he was here on Kuul, but he made the mistake of thinking the best of people. Alok was positive he could remove the stigma of Knowing if people understood what Knowing really was. So he offered his services as a Knower to the Kokkan elders."

"Services?"

"Helping to soothe a grieving mother or to keep tempers from flaring during a council meeting. Small things like that."

"That sounds wonderful."

"Some thought it was. But old prejudices reared their ugly heads, and the elders rejected Alok and revealed to the public that he was a Knower instead of taking up his offer. People were terrified, and some even thought he should be put to death."

"Put to death? No one's been put to death since the Knowers at the end of the Great War!" I gripped the arm of my chair until my still-healing hand sent arrows of pain up my arm.

"Exactly, and that is why Knowers conceal themselves and why you must be so careful. I doubt the Kokkan council would have really put your father to death, but would they in Ana? Mata?"

The question hung in the air like a poisonous cloud. I wondered if Sofi could feel my fear. *A'lodi sahm*, I tried, but I still felt like I couldn't breathe.

Finally, Sofi spoke again. "Some will not fear you, Alesea, at least not in that way. There are others who will look at you as a savior. Perhaps *their* savior, and that could be just as dangerous as naming you their enemy."

A bitter laugh escaped my throat. "I'm no savior. I'm afraid of myself."

"Well, that is quite wise at this point. You understand the importance of keeping your Knowing hidden, no matter how difficult." Sofi stood and gestured toward her door. "Now. Come, and I will show you where the tallest seagrass grows on this side of the island. Roni told me you would offer to make mats to help pay your way."

I followed, nearly feeling the Matan Watcher's knife stuck inside me after all.

***

On our last night in Kuul, Abel, the Matan Watcher, loosened up with a few glasses of wine and interrogated us in a slightly friendlier manner than when we'd met. He sat across from Roni and me and asked us questions about our childhood, our families, and Roni's career as a trader. I did my best to act shy and sign little, which I hoped was a believable behavior for an unintelligent Island girl finding herself dining with traders and foreigners.

"Leesa," Flick called across the table on the second night, waving to catch my eye and translating above his hunk of stewed fish. "Have you collected enough material for your mats?"

Leesa was my Watcher name. I'd chosen it over Sofi's objections—it reminded me of Konu's nickname for me, but it was also the ancient Island word for "freedom."

I kept my eyes wide and innocent as Roni signed to me. *I asked Flick about your seagrass mats and bags. He will accept your work in exchange for your place on the* Phoemek.

Yes, I have. Sofi's spot for collecting seagrass had provided enough material for weeks of work, especially since my injured hand would slow me down. I smiled at the captain. *Thank you.*

Abel stared at me through narrowed eyes, then hit Flick's arm to get his attention. *We did not discuss bringing the woman. A foreign sailor is enough risk, is he not?*

Flick snorted and again spoke as he signed. "Risk? Do you think she'll hang you with a seagrass rope? Have pity on the poor boy! He's desperate to make her his wife!"

I suppressed a shiver, and Abel looked as disturbed as I felt at the idea of a wedding but changed the subject.

What do you know of Akila?

My mouth dropped open. Fortunately, I quickly recovered my senses enough to pretend I had choked on a bit of fish and coughed into my napkin. Roni looked on with concern, such a devoted fiancé, and patted my back.

Excuse me I signed when I'd regained control. *I heard the village left for Mata. That they signed a...* I realized too late I didn't know the Watcher-speak for "treaty." I looked at Roni, who signed an unfamiliar word to finish my sentence. Unintelligent, indeed.

And do you believe it? Abel continued when I turned from Roni.

Yes. I hated myself for answering too quickly. *The elders said so in South Village.*

Abel nodded and gulped his wine. His eyes never left me.

Flick cleared the last bit of sauce from his plate with a scrap of bread. "Pack your bags and sleep well. We leave at dawn."

CHAPTER 16

I didn't get to say goodbye to Sofi. Tika woke me just before dawn and gave me a quick embrace before tying my Watcher scarf and pushing me out the door to rush to the docks with Roni, who'd emerged from the men's quarters. All our possessions fit into our single bags.

The first sliver of sunlight washed the sea in sparkling silver. Flick's boat swarmed with sailors, their laughter ringing as far as the dunes. I imagined they were excited to return to Ana, their home, though the voyage would take weeks.

At the dock, Flick chatted animatedly with Sofi and an unfamiliar initiate. A deckhand stood next to him, holding a beautiful little wooden table. Sofi smiled and rubbed the polished top of the table before the initiate took it. A gift, perhaps.

"Ho!" Flick spotted Roni and me and raised his arm in a friendly wave. *All hands on deck,* he signed. Roni nodded and glanced at me before jogging to the gangway.

Flick turned to the stocky, dark-skinned deckhand with a full black beard holding the table. "Mir, show Leesa to her quarters."

Mir grunted, then signed *Come with me* in my general direction. Sofi's back was to me as she spoke with the initiate. I swallowed the lump in my throat because I could not use my voice to get her attention. The proper way for a Watcher to approach an elder from behind was yet another thing I didn't know, so I followed Mir up the gangway.

***

My "quarters" turned out to be a net hammock in an empty corner of the cargo hold of the *Phoemek*. The only thing distinguishing my hammock from six others was the thin curtain that hung around it, roughly nailed to the wall on one side and the ceiling on the other.

This is it, Mir signed, then glared at me as if he expected me to object.

Thank you, I signed and sat my bag under the hammock.

He lifted a bulky arm to point at a stack of blankets on top of a crate. *It will be colder soon at night. Blankets are there. Your materials are in those crates.*

I nodded and tried to smile at the gruff man. *Thank you.*

Stay out of the way. Make your mats. He climbed the short staircase to the main deck without looking back.

I sat on the hammock, afraid to disobey his command, and let the boat's gentle rocking lull me into something like calmness. Men shouted, and things banged on the deck, but like a real Watcher, I didn't flinch. *A'lodi sahm.* Sails flapped, and the boat lurched forward. Wind from a tiny opened window near the low ceiling whipped my curtain.

I did startle when someone came running down the stairs. The vibration of heavy footsteps gave me a Watcher's excuse to pull aside my curtain and see who it was.

Roni's anxious face turned to relief when he saw me. I wondered again how I could've thought he was anything like the Matans.

Are you okay?

I nodded but added *I didn't say goodbye.*

You'll be back. Roni appeared genuinely convinced. *Come up. It's a great view.*

A series of waves tossing the boat made me stumble as I followed Roni up the steps into the bright morning sunlight. My breath caught in my throat at seeing beautiful Kuul, already too far away to make out who stood on the shoreline. I touched Roni's arm.

I didn't really see it before.

I know. I'm sorry.

I leaned my head on Roni's shoulder, grateful for our cover story for the first time, and watched the land disappear into the ocean's vastness.

***

It didn't take long for me to find out how little some of the crew wanted Roni and me on their ship. They talked freely as long as we weren't watching their mouths, so I heard it all.

"First, this Matan idiot who expects to be treated like a king, now castaways?"

"The girl doesn't even seem all there. Have you seen how slowly she talks?"

"Poor boy had to go all the way to the Islands for a bride. Probably the only one who would have him."

They hate us, I told Roni one lazy afternoon when he'd finished his shift, I'd made things out of seagrass until my fingers blistered, and we found ourselves alone on a bench near the back side of the deck.

Roni searched my face. *They didn't think Flick should take us, you know that. They don't trust Watchers.*

They can't feel that way about all Watchers!

Roni's eyebrows went so lopsided at my statement that I almost laughed before the horrible untruth of it hit me in the stomach.

They *did* feel that way about all Watchers.

I had, too. Maybe I still did, except for Roni.

Something brushed my bare arm, and I nearly jumped off the bench. Abel had passed far too close to me as he approached the railing, where he now stood gazing out at sea. Roni and I gave each other an uncomfortable glance. Had he seen our conversation? I tried to remember if I'd possibly said anything that could reveal my true identity or Roni's.

Finally, Abel turned to face us. His eyes were narrowed and cold. *A beautiful spot for a lovers' meeting.*

Roni gave a close-mouthed grin, probably meant to look sheepish, nodded, and put his arm around my shoulders.

You're right, Abel continued. *They hate you. They are angry that the new government requires my presence on their ship, though I offer them more protection than they know. Yet, they hate us.* His nostrils flared as he stared straight at me, and I shifted uneasily on the bench that now felt hard as stone. He continued, *which is why we, the most blessed, must keep them under control.*

My eyes narrowed against my will, and I fought to widen them as I forced an answer. *Of course.* I felt seasick for the first time since boarding the *Phoemek. Excuse me. I don't feel well.*

I stood and turned away from Abel.

A horrible crash sounded behind me, and I spun around.

Abel's thin lips spread into a close-mouthed sneer. His foot rested on the remains of a crushed, empty wooden crate. *You're a Double.*

The blood rushed from my face. With shaking hands, I signed *I felt it.* I ran to the railing and vomited over the side of the ship.

Roni rubbed my back as I repeatedly heaved and patiently waited until all that came out was dry heaves. He led me back to the bench before facing the amused Matan.

How dare you accuse my betrothed? See what distress you have caused her! Roni signed angrily, his face flushing as my usually stoic friend openly scowled at Abel.

Have I? Abel replied smugly. *Or have I hit too close to the truth? The girl is hiding something. From me, maybe from you. Or are you in on it?*

Loathing toward the man filled me as I turned away from him to see Flick standing with two sailors whose names I didn't know. His face was furious as he roared his words, simultaneously translating to Watcher-speak. "You have no right to intimidate my crew! You are not in charge of this ship or the people on it. Am I clear?"

I turned to see Abel respond, more self-satisfied than contrite, drawing himself taller before replying calmly. *I most certainly have authority if it turns out you are giving passage to a fugitive. Or if a Knower has taken over your minds.*

I stumbled back as the boat lurched on a steep wave, feeling like someone had punched me in the stomach. A fugitive? Had I failed so badly that he already suspected I was the runaway girl charged with treason by the Kokkan elders? He must have heard about me when the *Phoemek* stopped in Kokka, and now he'd found me out. I was through, and so was my family.

Roni stepped in front of me while I panicked, so I couldn't see what he said to the group. Whatever it was, it made Flick laugh out loud.

"The boy is right! The girl is meek as a chick. Besides, word on Kokka is that the Akilan Double drowned trying to escape."

Meek as a chick. I never thought I'd feel relief at being described so. I inched to one side to see around Roni, kept my head bowed slightly, and willed myself to seem small and innocent. *A'lodi sahm,* I repeated over and over in my head.

"Anyway," Flick continued when the Matan's hands remained still, "What's so dangerous about refusing to leave her home? The only reason I can think of you'd be so scared of that Double–" One of Flick's companions grabbed his arm, eyes wide with a warning, but Flick shrugged him away. "Is if your story about Akila is a lie."

Abel's hands flew into action. Not all his words were familiar, but the context was clear. *Is that an accusation? Because if it is, you too are charged with treason, and I become the captain of the* Phoemek *until we reach Ana, where proper legal action can take place.*

Flick's sailors stiffened, but Flick just laughed. "You know as well as I that speculation is not treason. I wondered why a group of powerful men were so afraid of a little girl. Perhaps the rumors of her secret powers are true." Flick glanced at me, eyes full of amusement and curiosity, then returned his attention to the Matan. "I'd love to meet such a girl. But I assure you, she is not aboard the *Phoemek*."

Abel stalked past the three sailors and down the stairs with a fiery glare. Flick dismissed his companions and gestured for me to join him at the railing. *A moment*, he signed to Roni. *Keep watch.*

Roni nodded and sat on the bench with his back to us and a full view of the ship when Flick spoke in a low voice.

"Look out to sea."

Something like a flock of sparrows took off inside me, and I felt ready to leap from the deck into the ocean.

"Stars and moons, girl, you have got to learn better control. Look out to sea."

Terrified, I did so. What did Flick know? Was he about to reveal my identity?

"Calm down! My sailors are already agitated enough at having Watchers aboard, and I think half the nerves are coming from you. Sofi told me who you are."

"What?" Since it came out as a whisper, I wasn't sure my voice still worked. How many days since I'd used it?

"As a young man, I spent a year on Kuul. I was called to a deeper practice of the *A'lodi*, but the call of the sea turned out to be stronger. When my older brother died of a fever, I gave in and took over the *Phoemek*."

I felt like I had just seen a different person from the loud and carefree sailor I'd already grown fond of when I turned to Flick.

"Look out to sea!" He never cast his eyes at me with his warning.

"Sorry." My response was barely a whisper.

"When you pulled your stunt despite our Matan... friend," he spat the last word, "Sofi told me everything and left the choice to me whether to take you. She knew what I would be risking."

"Thank you. Truly." I couldn't believe my ears as my words insufficiently expressed my gratitude.

Flick sighed. "I don't know what's happening to the world. Somehow these people rose to power, and no one noticed until they were on our ships and invading your Islands. I fear what we'll find in Ana after three months away."

My eyes prickled, and I blinked hard as I controlled my emotions. "Do you think I'll ever find my family?"

Flick didn't answer for a long moment. "We've lived in peace for five centuries. Violent crime was a thing of the past, even in Mata. Now I don't know what to think. But I hope so, Alesea. By the stars, I do."

We stood in silence until Roni returned and put his arm around me. A warning. Feet approached our corner of the deck.

"Captain!" someone called. "Wind's changing!"

"To them, you're still a Watcher." Flick laid his hand on mine for a moment, and then he was gone.

CHAPTER 17

We nearly made it to Ana without further confrontation. I avoided everyone but Roni as much as possible and spent most of my waking hours weaving seagrass. My right hand moved easier with every mat as the pain reduced to a dull throb. My grief settled into something like an ulcer — always lurking but erupting painfully at unexpected moments.

I meditated for hours each day, far more than I'd ever practiced. Roni kept increasingly busy as the water grew choppier, and we ran into spotty thunderstorms and heavy winds.

I was safe from Abel in my tiny living space since his quarters were in another part of the ship. A few sailors, including Roni, took shifts sleeping in the hammocks beyond my thin curtain, but they paid me no mind.

We were only a few days from Ana when I awoke before dawn to shouts and the ship bucking and tossing like an enraged *brahmi* bull. I was nearly thrown from my hammock as water gushed through my window, and I struggled to my feet. I slammed it shut and latched it, panicking that I might drown in this hold and never see the sun, moons, or my family again.

I fell to my knees with the next lurch of the ship and was alternately pressed to the floor and lifted as we went over a series of enormous waves. I struggled to crawl up the stairs far enough to push open the hatch. Angry rain pelted on my face, blinding me in the barely-there morning light.

My ears told me that the crew moved in all directions around the deck, and as my vision cleared, I could see them fighting the waves, pulling themselves by ropes and railings and each other. Suddenly, I realized the panic I felt was not entirely my own as it rolled over me, strong as the storm's waves, from twenty human sources on the deck.

I closed my eyes, overwhelmed but fascinated. So many people felt the same emotion in so many ways. I gasped as the image of a woman holding a little girl flashed in my mind, then a picture of the sunny shore of an island I didn't recognize.

In their moment of fear, I saw their thoughts.

A scream jolted me back to the ship. "Ronan! Get down! Get down now!"

Roni!

Where was he? He couldn't hear their shouts. I pulled myself up another step and peered at the sails on the second mast, all but one tied down. I wriggled the rest of the way up the stairs, fell on my bottom, and slid across the deck until I caught myself on a coiled rope.

Two sailors clung to the rail, looking up and shouting. I followed their gaze to the top of the second mast.

A flash of green moved against the white sail that caught gusts and sent us nearly horizontal with the worst of them.

I clutched the rope harder as a terrible gust powered directly into the sail, and I barely had the strength to keep myself from flying into the sea. I grabbed at another splintery rope as it swung past me. Everything was the dark ocean for a moment, and I was sure I would die. I squeezed my eyes shut and held my breath as if that would help, and after what felt like an hour, the ship lurched upright, and I still held the ropes, imagining the number of people thrown overboard if Roni hadn't taken that sail down to save us.

That thought lasted less than a minute when a horrible cracking sound came from the second mast. Time slowed as I watched Roni hang from the top like the last leaf on a dying tree while the wood splintered and tore.

I let go of one rope, waving my arm hard as if my warning could somehow help, and screamed, forgetting everything but my friend. "Roni! Roni! No!"

The last bit of wood gave way, and the mast crashed across the deck, sending Roni hurtling toward the stern. I groped, stumbled, and crawled my way across the deck. I couldn't stop screaming. People yelled everywhere, and someone grabbed my arm, but in the chaos of the torrential rain, I got away. Twice I got tangled in the fallen sail, and I tore like a crazed animal until I could continue to Roni. A lurch sent me skidding the rest of the way to the stern, where I smacked into something soft.

"Roni!" I was now in tears. The fallen mast pinned Roni to the deck, and he lay crumpled and still as death. I began yelling since I couldn't identify any of the figures blurred by the pelting rain.

"Help! Help!"

Three of the crew pulled themselves toward Roni, one on hands and knees, and helped me heft the broken mast off his body. I pulled myself to his chest and laid my head on his heart.

It was far too noisy for me to hear Roni's heart beat, but when I finally lifted my head, his eyelids fluttered, and he let out a choked sigh.

"He's alive!" I waved my arms as I yelled at the sailors, hoping my voice carried over the deafening noise of storm and ocean. "Help me!"

They somehow lifted Roni, even as the ship lurched to and fro, and though they slid and stumbled, they pressed forward toward the main cabin. I struggled to keep up. *Be okay, Roni. You have to be okay.*

The ship bounced, and I fell again, slipping sideways and landing hard on my hip. Not more than three feet away, a man huddled against the rail.

Abel.

Though his body projected fear, his face twisted into a knowing smirk. *I knew you were the traitor,* he signed. *The filthy Knower – .* He stopped signing to grab the rail when the ship tossed, but the smirk was still there.

"Help!" My screams at the men and woman who carried Roni had zero effect since none glanced back.

There's no escape now, Knower, Abel signed as the ship steadied.

I got to my feet, crouching, keeping my eyes on Abel. Once I had my balance, I spun around and bolted.

Abel grabbed my braid, and pain shot through my neck as my head snapped back. He squeezed my arm and pulled me around to face him.

You're under arrest he signed one-handed.

I tried to jerk away, but the vile man only squeezed tighter. "Help! Help me!"

No one responded to my shriek.

Abel slapped my face toward the roiling sea, slammed me against the railing, and held me there. I struggled and yelled until he pressed my throat against the top rail.

I was going to die. Mama and my brothers were lost. Roni was alone, hurt.

No! I filled with rage even as my thoughts grew fuzzy.

A roar of anger—mine—broke through the fog as I pushed against Abel and threw him backward. I gulped sweet air, the ocean, the boat, and the world spinning around me.

- 97 -

Abel crouched on the deck, holding his head, blood pouring from his nose.

It happened again. *I did that.*

Demon, Abel signed, and took a lurching step towards me.

"No!" My rage had barely settled, and aiming it toward him was easy.

This time, he fell away from me, squeezing his eyes shut in a horrible wince. He stumbled sideways and ran into the railing, then scrabbled at it as if to climb over, a rabbit desperate to escape a hungry fox.

"Stop it!" I lunged forward and grabbed at him. I caught his leg and braced my feet against the rail.

His eyes opened, and I glimpsed feral panic before he wrenched himself out of my grasp and fell into the bluish-black ocean.

He disappeared so quickly it was as if he had never been. His purple cloak floated in the yellow-white foam like a dead fish until the next wave also took that.

I don't know how long I stood there in shock, but it was long enough for the rain to let up and the ocean's anger to calm. With that cloak, my rage had sunk into the waves, and I thought I might never feel again.

I seriously considered that that might be best for everyone.

A rough, dark hand settled on my shoulder. Flick turned me around and peered into my face.

"You all right, girl?"

"I killed Abel." I could barely force out the words.

"Did you?" The captain gazed past me, eyes scanning the sea as if he might find him there. "Well, the good moons know we're in a blaze of trouble now, you and I."

"I'm sorry." What else was there to say? I had killed a man on Flick's ship. The ultimate act against the *A'lodi*, not to mention the ship's captain. I was cursed. I *was* a curse.

"Come on, the storm is breaking, and Ronan needs you." Flick gently pushed me, and we walked together to his cabin.

***

Roni was in the captain's quarters, laid out on an actual bed. The three crew members who'd carried him grumbled to one another as they crowded around it.

"How's he look?" Flick asked as I ran to Roni's side, stumbling into Mir as the boat bucked and fell.

Mir steadied me with a gentle hand. "He's breathing, but fast."

Roni's face was a strange color—his dark brown skin looked paler than usual, with a bluish tinge. His nostrils flared with each breath, eyes rapidly moving behind closed eyelids. I took his frigid hand and squeezed it. No reaction.

I looked to Mir, who seemed to be in charge of the rescue effort. "Do you think he'll be okay?"

The other two sailors burst into muffled conversation, but Mir registered his surprise with a single, extended blink. "So, you're a Double, now? I thought I was imaginin' things from the storm." He pulled up one side of Roni's soaking wet tunic, which had been ripped in half, to reveal an angry diagonal line of dark red bruises across Roni's torso. "Not bleedin'. Probably broken ribs. The way he's breathin', a punctured lung. Not much to do but wait."

Broken ribs. People survived that and more. "Why won't he wake up?"

Mir shrugged. "Sometimes the pain does that. But I imagine he got quite a bump to his head too."

When I was little, someone dared a teenage boy on Akila to jump off a cliff into the sea, and he hit his head on a rock just under the water's surface. He recovered but remained forever as a young child, a live cautionary tale for wayward children.

Fortunately, Roni hadn't fallen that far, and he'd hit his head on wood, not stone. He would be all right. He had to be. I sat on the edge of the bed with Roni's hand in my lap, determined to stay there until he woke up. The two sailors on the other side of the bed turned to go.

"I'm sorry, lass, and you to be wed on Ana."

Flick snorted at Mir's comment, and I managed a half-hearted glare before addressing Mir. "We're not actually... together. That was just a disguise."

Mir, taken aback, glanced between Flick and me. "What's this, now?"

Flick sighed. "There's much to explain. Now that the storm is past let's set things aright. Then, I'm calling Council."

"Council!" Mir's eyes widened.

"Aye." Flick ducked out the cabin doorway, gesturing for Mir to follow.

Mir emitted a low growl. "What have you gotten us into?"

CHAPTER 18

I sat alone by Roni's side for hours as the crew repaired the *Phoemek*, except when Mir brought me a handful of fish jerky and some water. I knew I should help, especially since they were short a deckhand — or maybe more than one. I had no idea, nor did I ask, about the amount of possible loss. My mind filled with visions of Abel when I turned my thoughts to anything but Roni: the terror in his eyes as if chased by his worst nightmare, his once-ostentatious purple cloak, blood-spattered and floating in the sea. *Murderer.*

A'lodi sahm, I repeated over and over as I jumped at every twitch of Roni's eyebrows and every pause in his breath. I meditated, prayed to my ancestors, and examined every part of Roni's body I could see — twenty times over, never finding anything new except for the bruises that turned dark purple and spread.

Roni's condition hadn't changed by the afternoon, and I could no longer stop my thoughts from wandering: *What would Flick tell his crew at this council? Would I be punished, killed? And if Flick defended me, would he be overthrown somehow?* I only had my word to prove I hadn't meant to murder Abel.

I'd been taught since infancy that taking another human's life was the ultimate crime, no matter the reason. Stories told of the tormenting of souls for eternity, never reborn or released, forced to relive their horrible deeds until the end of time. I seriously contemplated whether there was no difference between taking someone's life and saving one's own.

Not according to the *A'lodi.*

Abel would have killed me or, at least, tied me up and thrown me to the Matan Watchers. There would be no one left to go after my stolen people with Roni so severely injured. Another thought crossed my mind, wondering if it was possible that killing Abel saved the lives of my family and friends.

I knew my rising anxiety couldn't be good for Roni, and he seemed stable, at least for now. So when I heard the long trumpet of a conch shell and the stamping of feet toward the ladder to the lower deck, I squeezed his hand and snuck out the captain's door to my quarters.

***

As I expected, no one was in the small hold with the spare hammocks. I checked my bundle of possessions and found a pile of rags to mop up the largest puddle left from the previous night's terror. I pulled the shameful Watcher's cloth off my head. I wouldn't need it anymore, thank the moons.

Spending so much time alone in my quarters during my brief stint as a Watcher had one benefit—out of boredom, I'd explored every nook and cranny of the space. Now, I knew precisely where to squeeze between crates to find the thinnest board, complete with knothole, between my room and the main quarters of the lower deck. I lowered myself to sit next to it and pressed my ear to the wall. I couldn't translate the blurred gibberish of men's and women's voices speaking over one another.

"You still haven't told us where he is, Captain." I jumped at the shout, a rumbly baritone voice emerging above the racket.

The noise settled, and a man cleared his throat. Flick. "Lost in the storm, Uri. A'lodi knows it was a bad one, and the fool didn't have the sense to stay below."

"But he was still there when the other Watcher fell," Uri insisted. "And that was the last of the bad swells."

"What are you saying, Uri?" I flinched at the danger in Flick's tone. Even through the wall, I felt his fusion of pride, anger, and almost-hidden anxiety.

"They'll never believe us!" His emotions were as distinct as Flick's—frustration and a slippery form of panic. "They'll throw us all off the ship, take our goods—"

"Silence!" Flick interrupted Uri. "No one is taking my ship, our goods, or anything else! The Paav have gone too far!"

There were murmurs of agreement, but the feelings of doubt kept growing.

"This is bigger than you know, bigger than a single lost Paav official. After I speak, I will grant any who asks for an early release from their contract when we reach Ana, but first, you must swear secrecy on the matter I'm about to discuss."

Sounds of disbelief and emotions more robust than the sounds increased—frustration, awe, confusion, excitement.

"Secrecy?" A woman's voice cut through the cacophony as she posed her question to Flick. "How can we swear that without knowing what your 'matter' even is?"

"Because if you cannot all—every one of you—make that oath, I will keep silent, respectfully discharge all of you from my service in Ana, and continue to Mata with a new crew."

Fear and curiosity loomed, and vengeful eagerness from somewhere on the ship. My overloaded heart pounded fast.

"I will pass this roster for your blood oath."

Blood oath? Sailors shuffled and muttered, but no individual comments surfaced as the crew presumably passed the roster around.

"You've all marked it. Sealed in blood." Flick grumbled the final pronouncement.

"Sealed in blood!" The sailors' chant sent chills down my spine.

"Some of you already know that our female guest is no Watcher. Nor Ronan's betrothed. Her true name is Alesea of Akila."

I felt the air knock out of me like someone punched me in the chest, and my shock amplified two dozen times over that of the sailors.

"Treachery!" one shouted.

"The fugitive?" called another.

Uri's voice rose above the rest. "The Kokkans themselves said that girl is a demon of the Islands. A Knower resurrected from the Purge!"

Shock and fear swelled from all directions.

"A Knower, on our ship!"

"She'll control us all!"

"Sailors! Come to order." Flick's roar did nothing to control the din. I had to do something.

I scrambled to my feet and ran up the stairs. I kept slipping on the still-drenched deck, but the emotions hitting me from below—growing stronger every second—propelled me forward until I reached the ladder that led down to Flick and his sailors.

The room silenced as soon as my foot hit the top rung. I could feel their eyes on my legs, then my back, emotions frozen in surprise and suspicion as I slowly climbed down. The only sounds were the boat's creaks and wails as if the *Phoemek* insisted on giving its own opinion.

I reached the bottom and turned to face them, at least thirty people. They stared at me, some eyes wide and fearful, others squinted and angry. One young man with multiple braids and curious eyes looked at me with a strange half-smile. I held his gaze for courage.

"I am not a demon." My voice came out as a pathetic squeak, barely audible.

Around the room, sailors grumbled and eyes shifted, tension rising, except for the man whose eyes stayed locked on mine.

I am a performer, I remembered. *This is just another performance.* I gathered my breath and projected as my mother had taught me. "I am not a demon." My voice echoed from the far wall, and all eyes snapped toward my face. I lifted my chin and rose as tall as my small frame would allow.

"I am Alesea of Akila, and the Paav kidnapped all the people of my island." I took a breath and willed my heart to slow. More than anything, I knew I must remain calm. "The men who took my people claim to have made a treaty, but that is a lie. One by one, they stole my friends and family and tried to kill Roni and me. The Double translator told us our people were to be sold as slaves before the Paav murdered her."

"Ha!" The voice I recognized as Uri's came from a short, burly man with a single braid, who looked like he'd been marinated in the sea and left to dry like an old piece of leather. "How did you escape, then? If you aren't a demon like they say?"

A few men mumbled their agreement, or at least their doubt.

"There are no demons!" I called over them. *Calm down, calm down,* Sofi's voice whispered in my head.

There was no way I could hide from them, not for long, and I didn't have the necessary control to do that. I started up again quietly.

"It is true, however," the sailors silenced to hear me, "that the Paav are afraid of a Knower."

The level of fear in the room rose, threatening to ignite. Flick, standing at the far side of the room, gave me a warning glare.

I again fixed my eyes on that one calm sailor. Not one emotion came from him, like an island of serenity amid a hostile room. "Knowers are not dangerous now, and that danger has been gone for centuries if ever it even existed."

"How do ya' know so much about 'em?" raised a different voice.

My mind battled itself: *Would they accept me, kill me, or worse?* I went with my gut.

"Because I am the Knower." I ignored the gasps of shock and horror, the rising murmurs of dissent. My calm sailor did not flinch.

"She's not dangerous." Flick spoke above the rumble, walking through the crowd of his crew to join me. "Sofi of Kuul, the holiest person I know, charged me with keeping her safe aboard my ship. Alesea is of the *A'lodi*."

"And Ronan?" The calm young man spoke for the first time, his eyes still holding mine and voice much deeper than I expected, steady, like a singer's voice. "Is he also a demon in hiding?" He smirked, perhaps to show his disbelief in demons.

Flick answered before I could. "Ronan really is a Watcher, but from Akila, not Ana."

"It's true. He's not a Knower, and he doesn't have any connection with the Matan Watchers who stole Akila. He's my friend, and he has lost as much as I have."

The mood in the room calmed with my comments, though a simmering anger still came from the direction of Uri as another voice brought up another concern.

"So, what do we do when we get to Ana, and we've lost our Paav overseer?"

"The Paav stationed in Ana will likely assume the worst," said Flick, " but this is much bigger than the *Phoemek*. These Paav are threatening to end five hundred years of peace and freedom. They're taking over the trade routes, taking slaves, stealing resources. What will they do next?"

"Get rid of 'em all! That's what we need to do," one called.

"We aren't the ones to do that, but we can do something. I am offering Alesea and Ronan passage the rest of the way to Mata."

My ears rang painfully at the racket that ensued. I absorbed as much shock, anger, and excitement as possible, then focused on my breathing to block out some of the emotions. Flick continued, yelling above the near-riot.

"You have sworn secrecy through a blood oath! You are free to leave us in Ana, but if you betray the *Phoemek*, you will live a lifetime of cursed guilt. If you stay," Flick paused as the crew calmed before lowering his voice, "I cannot guarantee your safety or even your income. We may be unable to sell our goods without producing Abel, but you will have done an honorable thing, standing up against those who threaten our peace and our way of life. I expect your decisions by midday tomorrow when we will likely sight land. Now back to your posts."

I stood to the side to avoid being bowled over by all the sailors making their way to the ladder. Most of them avoided looking at me, but one woman briefly laid her hand on my shoulder, and the young man with all the braids held my gaze, searching my eyes for... something. Then he was gone, too.

Finally, it was just Flick and me. "Thank you." My inadequate little words could not have meant much.

"Hrmph." I watched as he climbed the ladder.

***

I gave everyone time to start working before I came back on deck. I felt so drained from the events of the last hours that I wasn't sure I had any more strength for confrontations. However, when I emerged into the cheerfully sunny afternoon, I found myself face-to-face with Uri, the most hostile of Flick's sailors.

"I don' care what the Cap'n says. Yer a demon, I know it, and somehows, ya' threw Abel overboard."

"I'm not a—" My words cut off as he grabbed my throat and squeezed, not enough to stop me from breathing but enough to send pain shooting down my neck and into my chest.

"You'll get off this boat in Ana or pay the cost." Hatred filled his every word.

I couldn't control it any longer. Anger flooded my heart and mind.

Uri jerked his arm away from me like a viper had bitten him. "You *are* a demon! Who're you after, evil one?"

He lunged forward to grab my throat again, and this time, with murder in his eyes. I ducked and bolted away from him toward the Captain's quarters.

***

I ignored Uri's bellowing and the shouts of nearby sailors as I fled toward Roni. Once inside the little room, I slammed the door shut and locked the strong bolt at the top. Only then did I turn to face my friend, afraid of what I might find.

Roni's eyes were opened, moving to find me.

Roni, I signed. *Are you awake?*

Yes, he signed weakly with one hand, then began coughing. It was a terrible sound, like choking. I stared helplessly until he finally finished. *The storm.* He slowly formed the words with his hands. *What happened?*

I told him about the mast breaking, about me screaming and blowing our cover. He repeatedly blinked as I described my encounter with Abel, but I only picked up a little fear, not the horror I felt myself. Finally, I recounted the events of the council and Uri's threats. His eyes drooped as I finished, then closed.

I wondered if his mild reaction to Abel's death had been because it didn't horrify him or because he was losing consciousness. I told Roni that I'd murdered Abel to save myself. What difference did it make that I'd tried to pull him back up? If I hadn't attacked him with my Knowing, he wouldn't have gone over in the first place.

The A'lodi *is in us all,* Uma's voice whispered in my mind. "*To harm another is to harm yourself thrice over.*"

At least I didn't have to hide who I was anymore, even if the person I'd become was a stranger.

CHAPTER 19

"Alesea!" Flick pounded on the door, sending my heart through my throat and another wave of emotions flying around the cabin.

"Coming." I glanced at Roni, who still slept, then opened the door.

"Locking me out of my own cabin, girl? What's next? You'll be asking me for your own dining room?"

"It's your crew!" I slammed the door behind Flick and slid the bolt locked as he watched, bemused. "Uri tried to strangle me right after the council!"

Flick's face, twice illuminated by moons and candlelight, turned from dark red to an alarming purple as I recounted my encounter with Uri.

"Good gods, girl, you *must* learn to control your emotions!" Flick snapped when I'd finished. "The men are afraid enough as it is!"

"But... but... he was going to *kill* me!"

Flick closed his eyes and inhaled as if gathering the patience needed to deal with a toddler tantrum. "And I suppose it's a good thing you threw your anger around like a raving seaspout, because at least you're still alive?"

A coughing fit from Roni interrupted my chance to reply. I stroked his forehead as he wheezed and hacked, leaving a fine spray of blood droplets on the sheet.

"What if he dies?" My voice broke. "What if we saved him, and he dies anyway?"

Flick's eyes softened, and he put a hand on my shoulder. "He won't. Not on your watch. Look after him, and I'll find a healer soon as we dock at Ana in the morning."

All I could do was nod and angrily swat at the tears leaking down my cheeks.

***

At dawn, I watched through the Captain's scratched window as the coast of Ana grew from a blurry green lump on the horizon to a bustling city that made Port Kokka look like a tiny village. Sandy beaches stretched east of the harbor, tall white structures with red roofs gleaming beyond the short dunes. The buildings to the west and inland were mostly dull brown and stacked up the steep hills like Konu's toy blocks. A smoky haze ringed the highest portions of the city.

A cheer on the deck and the hull bumping on the dock signaled our safe arrival at Port Ana. Safe for the time being, anyway.

Shortly after landfall, Mir knocked on the cabin door. "Captain's filling out the manifest. Dock inspector will be in soon. I'm to give ya' this."

He held out a bundle of purple and white cloth.

"Is that... Abel's clothes?" I asked weakly.

"Aye, the bastard. Flick said to put 'em on Ronan. He's already forged a letter from Abel with his seal, and he's tellin' 'em Abel's caught the sea plague."

I glanced between Roni and Mir. Roni's eyes were open, but no one had been translating.

"He doesn't look anything like Abel." I took the clothes and tossed them on Roni's feet. "And what if they want to talk to him?"

Mir snorted. "Not much chance 'o that. Anak and Matans alike're terrified of the sea plague. Think it's the curse o' the Doubles." He laughed, then stopped short at the expression on my face. "Anyway, he'll be in bed. They can peek in the door if they want. I'll put a poultice on his head, hide his ears. Here." He handed me an inked pen.

"What's this for?"

Mir scowled. "Tattoos. Do yer best."

It made me sick to my stomach, but I nodded. Roni stared, uncomprehending.

"Could you dress him? We're not, you know..."

Mir blinked once. "Aye. Turn around, then." Shouts rang out across the deck. "Sit down while yer at it."

When Mir finished helping Roni change, he showed me a hiding spot in the Captain's wardrobe to use when I heard the signal: Mir calling, "Cabin's sealed."

"What if they find me?" I tried to keep the fear out of my voice and mind since it wouldn't do to rile up one of Flick's loyal sailors.

Mir shook his head. "They won't. But keep that mind o' yours quiet when they come."

***

We didn't have to wait long. The ink I sloppily applied to Roni's neck barely had time to dry before I heard Mir's warning shout. I stuffed myself into the wardrobe and hid under piles of the Captain's clothing.

Silence, then banging, over and over and over, and close enough to rattle the thin doors of my wardrobe.

Breathe. Breathe.

Then, nothing. I held my breath, my heart pounding faster and faster.

The door to the wardrobe flung open, and light poured in, blinding me. I flung my arms over my head as if somehow that would help, but no one attacked. It was Flick who entered.

"Safe for now, and lucky thing they didn't come in, girl, 'cause those ink marks look more like he got attacked by an octopus than tattooed."

I tentatively lifted my head. "What was all the banging?"

"They suspected something. Think they were tryin' to figure out if he was a Double. Gave my heart a turn, that's for sure."

"No kidding." I extracted myself from my hiding place to find a middle-aged woman in a humble brown dress standing in the cabin's doorway.

"This is Tyra, a healer."

"Oh!" I bowed to her after Flick introduced me, nearly losing my balance from the head rush I got from standing up too quickly.

Flick grabbed my elbow to steady me. "You can trust Tyra. She has even less love for the Matan Watchers than most traders."

Tyra's nostrils flared. "You could say that." Her voice was low and quivery, and with her words, grief flowed from her mind like a cloud of smoke. I wanted to ask what the Matans had done to her, but I knew I had no right.

Instead, I took my curiosity and stowed it in my mind. I looked at Tyra's face, just below her eyes, and pictured my question pushing away her grief cloud.

"My daughter disappeared two moons ago." Her sudden candidness startled me.

"I'm so sorry." I could only murmur as I tried suppressing my feeling of surprising accomplishment.

"She disappeared with a group from the Anak main orphanage, where she was visiting a friend. Gone without a trace, the same day the Paav ship left for home."

"That's terrible," I whispered. "That's who took my family too."

Tyra nodded and wiped a tear from her eye. She cleared her throat and looked at Roni. "Broken rib, you say?"

Flick answered. "Had a bad fall. Very bad. He's been coughing up blood, short of breath."

Tyra sat her bag on the foot of Roni's bed and approached his side, but as she reached toward his tunic, she hissed and drew back as if burned.

"A Watcher!" she snapped.

"Yes, but of Akila, the stolen village. Not Matan, and definitely not Paav. Look." Flick removed the poultice from Roni's forehead to reveal the smeared top of the fake tattoos and Roni's ears. Roni was asleep, breathing fast, eyes fluttering behind his lids as they did after his accident.

Tyra spun on her heel to face Flick. "I don't heal Watchers. What're you playing at, Flick?"

"He's a victim too, Tyra. He's trying to—"

"Goodbye," she snapped, throwing her bag onto her shoulder.

Her snapped remark made Flick sigh as he mumbled to himself but made no move to stop Tyra. Roni coughed without waking.

"Wait!" I leaped to block the doorway and caught Tyra's arm. Tyra paused, though she looked ready to knock me out of the way. The image of a little girl—six or seven—with tangled hair and smiling dark eyes flitted through my mind, followed by more overwhelming grief. I softened my tone of voice.

"Please, he's not one of them. He's helped me, and he's helping me find my family. The Paav wronged him, too."

"He's a Watcher." Her anger crashed into my mind like wild surf, and I struggled to receive it, afraid to project my feelings and scare her off entirely.

"Please. I'll... I'll look for your daughter. We both will." My voice caught in my throat at the promise I had no idea I could keep, but I could tell it was working. "Please."

I experienced a new feeling, barely discernible within Tyra's great sorrow. *Hope.*

Though she still scowled, Tyra gave a single sharp nod and stomped to Roni's side. "Fine." I winced as she roughly pulled Abel's tunic up

Roni's torso, but Roni didn't stir. *Hang on, Roni,* I thought, hoping my message would somehow make it through.

"His lung is punctured," Tyra said in a flat voice. "I'll need to drain it."

Flick shuffled his feet, looking sick. "I'll, er, get Mir. He's more experienced in these things."

I swallowed hard as Flick rushed from the cabin. "What does that mean, exactly? Can I help?"

"Stay out of the way is all." Tyra pulled a bottle, towel, and a metal tool that looked like an awl out of her bag. "Might be messy."

It was messy, horrifyingly so. Tyra turned Roni on his side, and I sat against his back, unable to hold his hand. Though Mir held a soaked cloth over Roni's nose that he claimed would keep him unconscious, the series of unearthly sounds coming from Roni's throat as Tyra poked and prodded him nearly sent me running. Tyra grunted, followed by a splatter of liquid, and Roni's body jerked against me, almost knocking me off the bed. Then it was over.

"Keep it clean," Tyra instructed, and I hoped she was talking to Mir because I couldn't bring myself to look at whatever "it" was. "He should stay on his side for two days and limit activity for a full moon cycle."

Tyra shuffled to the foot of the bed, where I could see her face. She was wiping her bloody hands with a wet towel. "My daughter's name is Tam. She's seven and small for her age. She doesn't like to talk to people she doesn't know." Tyra glared at me as if that were my fault, but I could feel the sorrow hidden behind the veil of anger.

"I'll find her," I nearly choked on the promise I couldn't make. "I'll do everything I can."

Tyra nodded once. She tossed the dirty towel on the floor, picked up her bag, and left.

***

A few hours later, Flick brought me dinner and told me nearly two dozen sailors, who had been with him for five years or more, had committed to our mission. The interference of the Paav in the sailors' trade made the sailors angry. Some feared for their relatives in Mata, and others knew people like Tyra whose loved ones had disappeared with a Paav ship. Flick stood to leave his cabin.

"I'll sleep below. At least, till we leave day after tomorrow. I'd promised 'em three days in Ana, and now they only have one to keep you safe."

I felt guilty. Flick gave up his cabin, and now, he and his sailors planned to give up two days on land. I wondered how many had families in Ana.

"Wait." I wanted to tell him how I felt, somehow make up for everything he'd sacrificed, but how could I? He stared at me, expression unreadable but projecting such a complex mix of emotions I didn't have the energy to sort through them.

"Thanks," I said meekly.

He nodded sharply and left.

I felt anxious and trapped and couldn't sit still. Losing control of my nerves couldn't be helpful for Roni, either. I needed to run, scream, or get out of this cabin that seemed to be growing smaller by the minute. So when the sun finally crept below the horizon, and I heard someone running across the deck, calling "Captain!" in little more than a whisper, I slipped out the door, crouching so no one on the docks could see me, and followed.

CHAPTER 20

It was that calm sailor with all the braids — the one who'd held my eyes when I burst into Flick's Council. He didn't seem so placid now, though I still couldn't feel any emotions coming off him, probably because mine were so strong.

"Lin?" The captain's familiar grunt came from the stern of the *Phoemek*. I remember seeing him sitting on the same little bench I used whenever I was on lookout duty.

I crept as close as possible without being seen and hid behind a pile of coiled ropes. Lin was breathing hard.

"Captain, my friends saw the ship we're after."

"Sit down, boy." Flick's voice was low. "They're suspicious of everything, those Paav watching us."

There was a pause, presumably as Lin sat. When he spoke again, he sounded calmer. "They said it was less than a moon or maybe three weeks ago. They said they had cargo that would make them all rich, but they wouldn't speak of selling any in Ana. They wouldn't even hint at what the cargo was."

"People, then. The Akilans." Anger rolled off Flick in waves. "So, it's true. They're planning to sell them as slaves." Flick's tone never waivered as he shifted from reconnaissance to typical sailor talk. "Mind that guard over there, don't look. Tell me a joke."

"A joke? I don't—"

Flick laughed and laughed as if Lin had said something hilarious, and Lin joined in. It was surreal hearing the joyful laughter while feeling Flick's revulsion at their real conversation.

My knees were aching from my position, but I didn't dare move a muscle as they fell into silence.

"Go on," Flick finally said.

"They said the leader, tall and wearing red, like Alesea mentioned, brought a young boy with him. Maybe three years old. An orphan, he said, from the islands."

Konu. It had to be. He was the one Sinon had projected that strange desire toward, and he was the only Akilan boy of that age right now. I felt I might vomit and hoped Flick's burst of surprise and confusion covered my fear and disgust.

"There's more," Lin said, and I could tell from how his voice projected that he had turned toward my hiding place. *Had he sensed me?* He kept talking with a slightly muffled voice as he turned back to Flick. "He left the boy here with an inspector who lives in the apartments next to the docks."

Flick sighed. "Don't even think about a rescue on Ana, not for one child. We'll never make it out of here."

A'lodi sahm, A'lodi sahm. I closed my eyes and focused on my breathing to keep from shouting. Nothing was too dangerous if it meant saving Konu. Nothing.

"What if I take my friends and find where he's staying? No one would make the connection."

"No!" Flick's response to Lin jolted me, but then he paused for what seemed like forever. "No, Lin. I forbid it if you are to stay on this crew."

Now it was Lin who sighed. Regardless, every emotion I felt from the pair belonged to Flick. "Will you at least tell the girl?" Lin asked.

Yes. I silently thanked the sailor because I knew he had been on my side since that awful council.

"No, and neither will you," Flick growled. "She's too impulsive, and she'll do something stupid."

"Fine." Lin's tone was barely civil, and before I could react, he stomped toward me.

I shrunk back, but it was too late, and the moon was too bright. Lin walked past my hiding place and turned to meet my eyes as if he knew I was there.

Don't tell, I thought, *please don't tell Flick.* What would the captain do if he found out I'd been spying?

Lin nodded once as if he'd heard me and walked away.

I crept back into the cabin as soon as he was off the ship. Flick was right—I *would* do something stupid. How could I stay here, crammed in a tiny cabin, when my baby brother was so close I could nearly touch him?

***

An hour later, the second moon was high and bright, and Flick had come to check on Roni before he went below for the night. I snuck out, keeping low to the ground, hoping no one watching the *Phoemek* would notice the cabin door open a second time. I crawled to the stern that held ladder rails attached to the hull and, trembling with anticipation, peeked over the railing toward the still-empty dock, climbed over the rail, swung to the other side, and groped around with my bare foot for one of the rungs until I found one.

I'd made it down two steps when a jolt of pain from my still-healing hand shot up my arm. My foot slipped on the wet surface of the third rung, and I fell into the sea.

The chilly water stole my breath, and for a moment, I could think of nothing more appealing than giving into its watery embrace, sinking into its depths to rest forever and forget all I had lost.

My bottom hit the sand, and I came to my senses. *Konu.* I pushed off with my feet and gulped air from the surface before gliding underwater with my quietest stroke. Hopefully, anyone who'd heard my ungraceful splash would assume it was only a sea creature.

The route I'd planned around the docks stretched much longer than I'd expected, only having viewed it from the comfort of the cabin. It was good to know that I was a strong swimmer, even after weeks out of the water, but my arms ached before I'd passed the smallest collection of fishing boats at the east end of the docks. Each pump of my legs seemed to propel me a shorter and shorter distance. My lungs felt like they would burst like Roni's when I finally reached a small wooded area separating the harbor from the beaches. I cut my shins, scrambling on the rocks near shore before I emerged among the trees, dripping and cold.

As I made my way toward the road, I could barely keep my balance as the ground seemed to buck and sway. I sent a silent request through the *A'lodi* to regain my land legs quickly because I had no time to waste. I wrung out the front of my tunic and peeked around a tree to spy on the empty road a few yards away.

There was a row of inns and restaurants along the road to my right, probably for tourists visiting the wide sandy beaches, which meant I would have to double back toward the docks to find the Paav apartments. I'd already braided my hair in an approximation of the Anak style, so I only had to pull the despicable, sopping wet Watcher-cloth out of my pocket and tie it over my ears to complete my costume.

I stuck to the shadows along the roadside, hoping anyone who saw me would think I was a fisher girl out for an early start or one of the urchins I'd heard of who lived on the streets in big cities. It was too dark for anyone to notice the trail of seawater behind me. At least, that's what I told myself.

When the road forked, I took the right side. That should be close enough to find the apartments but far enough to avoid any inspectors watching the docks.

My adrenaline soared as a man and woman approached me until they huddled together and kept to the other side of the road. As far as I could tell, they paid me no notice. Perhaps dripping waifs walking down the street in the middle of the night were a common sight in Ana, or maybe they were conducting their own nefarious business.

Finding the apartments was one thing that was easier than expected. Just past the fishing boat docks, which I glimpsed between the houses and shops, sat a large, block-like building that bore the Paav name over its highest sparkling glass window, bright against the dark bricks in the moonlight. A solid wooden door faced the road. Next to the door was a small candlelit booth that housed someone sitting and looking half-asleep.

A guard, I assumed, which would make it far too dangerous to sneak into the building that way.

Before I could formulate a plan, the door squeaked open, spilling lamplight onto the paved sidewalk below. I slipped back into the shadows and hid behind a shrub.

A tattooed man in yellow robes stood in the light, holding the door open. He signed to the person in the booth, who had snapped to attention. *Early* was the only word I could make out.

A woman stepped out behind the man, who let the door shut with a bang. She wore similar yellow clothing with a long skirt instead of pants and a cloth very similar to mine wrapped around her head, hiding whether she had ears. *Thank you,* she signed toward the booth and followed the man up the road toward the city center.

I kept my position behind the bush until the stars faded and the sky tinged with pink. Konu was sure to come out. *He had to!* Several more Watchers in bright colors, including some older children, left the building, but no one near Konu's size. Worse, my shrub would no longer cover me as the sky lightened.

Flick must be up by now. My mind raced: *Had anyone noticed I was missing? If so, what would they think? Would they come looking for me, or would Flick and his sailors be relieved to have gotten rid of me?*

I pushed away the anxious thoughts. At least I was finally dry, and in the growing light, my clothes didn't seem overly stained or damaged. I adjusted the scarf over my ears and straightened my braids. I stood and panned the area to ensure no one watched me before casually walking back to the road, where I shuffled past the Paav building, head down.

A few people passed me in either direction, ignoring me entirely. Some wore colorful robes; others wore plainer linen like mine. When the area near me cleared, I looked up at the next building.

It was identical to the one I'd been watching for the last hour, and beyond that, I saw another—a total of three buildings full of Watchers.

Something zoomed past me, and I nearly screamed. A boy on a bicycle, a vehicle I had heard of but never had seen. Another flew past before I could move.

A girl about my age gave me a suspicious look and swerved away from me on the road. I counted and took deep breaths, struggling to control my fear and frustration as I wondered if she felt my Knowing or if I just looked strange. I didn't want to find out.

I picked up my pace and passed the third building, watching for bicycles. The buildings beyond appeared to be warehouses and shops, thank the moons. Even so, I couldn't think of any way to keep watch on all three Paav buildings, with the street increasing in crowds and the guards in the booths growing more awake. Any place I could find to hide from them would be visible to someone else, and since I didn't have any money, I couldn't sit in a café, spend very long in any shops, or go in them at all—they looked too fancy for my simple attire and bare feet.

Spending so much willpower controlling my frustration made me reckless. I turned into an alley next to a warehouse and cut through to the street right in front of the docks.

I needn't have worried. The street and docks were lively with morning activity—sailors and dockhands moving crates in and out of the warehouses, urchins begging for coins, groups of Doubles walking and laughing, and Watchers signing to each other on the docks. No one even bothered to look at me. Regardless, I made the most disheartening discovery yet. I'd been at the back door of the apartment buildings all night. The front of each had a grand entrance of tile and brick, guards on either side of the decorated double doors. I would've known that if I had even thought to scope them out from the *Phoemek*.

I couldn't believe I'd been such an idiot since my hope of chancing upon Konu shrunk by the second. I didn't even know how I would return to the ship.

Breathe. I kept my head down, risking occasional glances at the children in the groups of Watchers until I saw the *Phoemek* at the dock. It sat well past the Paav apartments, halfway to the beaches. The distance I'd struggled to swim last night now looked pathetically small—and completely exposed.

I kept walking past a tall ship almost as large as the one that had stolen my family away, fearing someone would get suspicious of me pacing in front of the fancy Paav apartments. Beyond the apartments, I found a small garden park with wooden swings hanging from the trees. A few children— Doubles and Watchers—played chase and hide-and-seek together, and there was an empty bench in the far corner shaded by overgrown shrubs.

I sat on the bench, completely drained of energy. I'd been so sure I could find Konu that nothing else had mattered to me. Instead, I both failed and endangered everyone trying to help me. I'd abandoned Roni and risked Flick's livelihood. Now stuck in Ana with the only routes back to the *Phoemek* visible in the daylight, I was doubtful I'd make it back alone. How could I have possibly managed it with Konu?

I wallowed in despair and barely noticed the ball land beside my bench until a large, sandaled foot startled me. I jumped as the man reached down to fetch the ball and jumped too.

Very sorry, he signed. He wore dark blue, and his Matan tattoos were simpler than most—a few interlocked shapes. His face almost looked kind when his lips curved upward into a small smile.

I nodded, hoping he would go away quickly.

Are you all right? he signed instead.

I nodded again. *Yes, thank you.*

He gave me a long look of concern, then turned and tossed the ball to a small child who missed and laughed out loud as he chased it.

My heart froze in my chest. I would know that sweet laugh anywhere.

Konu wore a tiny, dark blue Matan outfit matching the man's, though his feet were bare like mine. His hair had grown longer and wild. I couldn't breathe as he grabbed the ball and heaved it toward the man, giggling.

I wanted to wave, scream, leap up and grab him, and swim back to Akila if I had to.

My rational mind knew I wouldn't make it out of the park with Konu. As I became aware of a nearby group of children openly gaping in my direction, I realized I might not make it out of the park if I didn't control my emotions.

I kept my eyes on Konu and counted my breaths over and over and over. *Konu is safe. Konu is safe,* I told myself, trying to feel thankful and nothing else. Finally, I trusted myself to look around and found that the children had dispersed, some to the swings and others to play tag.

Konu and the Paav man continued to toss the ball, Konu having to run after it each time. I was at the wrong angle to see what the man signed whenever they paused, but Konu, who periodically laughed, watched him intently—a signal that he had been learning Watcher-speak. I wondered if he even remembered how to talk.

After a few more minutes, the man signed again, and Konu ran toward him and hugged his legs.

Jealousy flared in my chest, and I again fought the urge to reveal myself to my brother, except what I saw next sparked rage as uncontrollable as a drought-year wildfire. Konu smiled and looked up at the man's face and signed *Daddy.*

CHAPTER 21

"No, Konu!" The wild scream tore from my throat as I jumped to my feet, all stealth forgotten.

Konu froze. The ball flew past him, unnoticed, as he stared at me, a glint of recognition beautiful as the first sunbeam after a hurricane, followed by a shriek.

"Laysi!" He ran toward me.

"Konu, oh, Konu." He was in my arms as I sobbed. His sweet smell, his too-tight hug even tighter now, the warmth of his forehead on my cheek.

"Where Laysi go?" Konu's muffled little voice as he pressed his face into mine warmed me.

"Oh, Konu, I didn't go—I didn't mean to—"

Then the air shifted, and the hurricane returned. The spectacle of my brother and me drew people all around. The man in blue towered over us, and the bench blocked me from behind, cornering us.

I squeezed Konu as if that could protect him. I made out a few of the Watcher's frantic signs through my tear-blurred vision. *Stop! He's my son!* Somehow he projected anguish as if he believed his poisonous lie, as if he had raised Konu himself. *Let him go!*

"He's not your son!" I shouted, and a few more park goers stopped in their tracks, some flinching backward. It gave me an idea.

I kept my grip on Konu, stood straight, and faced the liar. "He's *not yours,*" I threw out all the anger and hurt I could muster.

Konu started crying and struggling in my arms, and I held on even tighter.

Someone shouted nearby as others fled the park, but the man claiming to be Konu's father did not back away. He only wrenched up his face as tears flowed freely from his piercing blue eyes and took another step toward us.

The sight mesmerized me for a moment. I couldn't help but gawk at such a strange color—blue eyes.

"Papa!" Konu cried, then pushed away from me with all the strength in his little arms. The emotions coming from Konu were a new sensation yet as familiar as the sea.

Terror.

Konu was scared of *me*, not the Watcher he'd called Daddy or all the people surrounding us. He wanted me to let go of him, and he wanted to be safe.

I wasn't safe.

I stumbled from rage to confusion. Konu twisted out of my arms, and the man in blue swept him up and ran away from me toward the crowds in the street, Konu's little tear-streaked face telling me I was the monster, and the Watcher had saved him.

***

I barely remember how I made it back to the *Phoemek*. I ran, fell, crawled, and ran again, shooting out my fear and anger like wild arrows. Hands grabbed at my tunic, but the rage arrows drove them away and allowed me to carry on—my feet bleeding, clothing shredded, screaming like something out of a tale meant to frighten children into staying in their beds at night.

I looked back once to see dozens of men, women, and children crowded onto the street, watching me flee and making signs against evil. A child burst into tears, and I turned around just in time to collide with a sizeable Paav man full of fear and anger. Triumph joined the mix as he gripped me by my arms.

"Let me go!" As I screamed, I let loose a full quiver's worth of mind arrows. The man let go as if I'd kicked him in the groin, doubling over and retching.

No one else dared to get in my way. "Flick!" I roared, flying toward the dock, a nightmare coming to life.

"Wha—" Flick looked up from his conversation with two Watchers a short path down the dock. They spun around quick as lightning and pulled swords from their flowing robes.

Swords, sleek, long, deadly, and banned five hundred years ago, pointed at me.

I flung my emotions, and the men flinched, but their arms held firm, blocking my one clear path to the *Phoemek*. Flick seemed frozen in place, mouth gaping.

I leaped into the sea and glided underwater to the far end of the ship, searching for the ladder I'd climbed down the night before. Sounds of clashing steel joined shouting as I struggled to pull myself out of the water. My arms trembled, and I slipped back into the ocean twice before finally getting my feet on the bottom rung. I dragged myself up the ladder and collapsed on the deck. Someone screamed nearby.

"Flick!"

I forced myself to sit up, muscles crying out in protest but obeying the fierce energy surging through my heart and pounding head.

A sailor ran across the deck with an armful of long metal objects.

They couldn't be swords. Not my sailors, not on the Phoemek. *Besides, they were too thick and dull,* but she threw one to Mir, and with a metallic *swish* Mir pulled out one of the horrible lethal things and tossed aside the larger piece of metal. *Scabbard*, a distant memory of a children's tale told me from the back of my mind.

Both sailors ran for the dock toward their captain.

I dragged myself across the deck, terrified to show my face, terrified for the sailors whose lives I'd endangered.

I didn't deserve the safety of hiding, not after what I'd done. I struggled to my feet and crouched just high enough to see over the railing.

Paav swarmed like colorful termites on the dock, most of them wielding awful weapons of various lengths, but some held onto the ropes tying the *Phoemek* to the dock to prevent us from leaving. Flick fought off two men—all of the Paav on the dock were men—as he backed toward the gangplank, where Mir and the sailor who'd brought the stack of swords fought off another group trying to board the ship. I threw more of my invisible arrows at the Paav men fighting Flick and Mir, but they fell short, as far as I could tell, as they outnumbered and surrounded my sailors. Soon, they'd be dead, and it would be all my fault.

The gangplank swayed dangerously as the dock side of the *Phoemek* dipped low from the pressure on the ropes. I barely caught myself on the side railing, and Mir regained his balance in the nick of time before nearly falling into the water. When he turned back, there was a bloody slash across his cheek.

I had to do something more because if anyone died on either side, I might as well be the one wielding the sword. I gulped down my rising

THE WATCHERS

panic and felt for the minds of the Watchers, which was as easy as hearing a melody at a festival. Their anger rushed over me like a tidal wave. They felt cheated, robbed, and scared.

I sensed one of the men fighting Flick was a Double, though he wore Paav robes. His anger felt especially righteous. *Why was he fighting for them?* I shook away that thought. These Paav had plenty of fear in their minds, so maybe I could turn it against them and make them feel it even more.

"Konu." Whispering his name was the spark I needed to ignite my rage into a near-physical thing. I reached for the Paav and poured my emotions into the mix on the dock. Together, our minds magnified to something unimaginably horrible and almost palpable. Swords faltered, duels slowed, and a few men on both sides of the fight raised hands to their heads.

Then, I started throwing it at them, like some awful parody of a child's dodge-the-ball game. I worked intentionally and methodically, taking out as many Paav minds as possible to help our crew escape.

The boat lurched upright as the ropes fell slack. Men stumbled back from the *Phoemek,* and two Paav swordsmen on the gangplank fell into the water, which allowed our sailors to run for the ship.

I aimed another fear weapon at the Double attacking Flick. He dropped his sword and fell to his knees, blood trickling from his nose as if hit by Flick's sword. Two more of our crew ran past him for the gangplank, and one was Lin.

Before the Paav could regain their senses, Flick sliced through the ropes with his bloodied sword. He leaped up the gangplank, roaring "go" as he reached the deck, and his sword clattered to the floor. Flick swung the gangplank up and away from the dock as if it was part of a toy ship.

We were twenty feet from the dock by the time the echo from Flick's shout died away. Men scattered on it like fallen leaves, stunned, not even helping the two men struggling to pull themselves out of the ocean.

The Double with the bloody nose shouted like a madman. "Sorcery! Demons! Knowers!"

One of the Watchers who'd been holding onto the ropes stood straight up, spat into the water, and with large gestures, signed *Knowers,* followed by the sign against demons.

What had I done?

The boat bumped over a wave, and I sat down hard, my tailbone smacking into the floor. My whole head shrieked with pain. It didn't help that my face felt on fire from my nose to the tips of my ears. I barely pulled myself up in time to vomit over the side of the ship, each heave more excruciating than the last.

Finally, it was over. The sailors shouted, flung ropes, and climbed masts. No one looked in my direction. I crept to the cabin and collapsed on the floor next to the bed, dizzy and throbbing with pain.

Fingers touched my hair, then settled on my head. Roni was awake, his ever-calm face pale but scrunched with concern. He took his hand away and signed, *What happened?*

I could barely stand to see him looking at me. I didn't deserve his concern, not now that I was worse than the Paav. Worse than anyone in the world.

They were fighting I managed to sign. *With...* I had to finger spell *swords. I helped somehow with my Knowing. And I nearly got our crew killed anyway.*

You did what you needed to do. You let us get away. It's not your fault.

But it was *my fault. It was all my fault. It was all because...* A new wave of guilt overwhelmed me as I remembered I hadn't even considered what would happen to Roni if I didn't return. *I'm sorry,* I repeated. *I'm stupid. I'll never–*

What did you do?

Konu is there, on Ana. I found him. I held him. My closed eyes leaked tears as my body tried to cry, too sapped of energy. I couldn't form the words to tell Roni what had happened, nor could I face that wrenching failure so soon again. *I left him,* I managed, before I dissolved into sobs and buried my face in the blankets.

Roni pulled my hand out from under my face and squeezed it, and I clutched his like a piece of flotsam in a shipwreck.

Eventually, my exhaustion took over, and I drifted into a dreamless sleep. When I woke, it was to the dark of night and the gentle lap of water against the hull of the *Phoemek*.

For now, we were safe.

Except from me.

PART THREE – KNOW

A Knower is blessed with the language of the mind and the deepest knowledge of the soul. But if the Knower's search for truth is unbalanced, the paths of the mind become the bars of a prison. The A'lodi resides in the soul.

~ The Book of the A'lodi

CHAPTER 22

I had been dozing when Flick burst into his cabin in a cloud of anger so thick I could nearly see it.

"What in the demons' names were you thinking, girl?" His harsh whisper was more frightening than a scream. I thought it better not to mention that he wouldn't wake Roni by yelling.

"You risked everything! You're lucky to be still alive. You're lucky any of us are still alive!" He stared at me through wild eyes.

"I'm sorry," I mumbled.

"You're *sorry*? You risk my whole life and livelihood, Roni's, my crew's, and yours, and all you can say is you're *sorry*?" Spittle flew from his mouth and stuck to his beard.

"I *am* sorry. I was stupid. Selfish."

"That you were. Now, we're short at least a dozen sailors left in Ana, too."

A dozen sailors. Left without employment, stranded. Yet instead of remorse, I felt jealousy because they were on the same island as Konu. I was angry that Flick hadn't told me about Konu and mad at him for being able to say "I told you so" to Lin. Impulsive, indeed.

I swallowed and tried to control my voice. "My brother is everything to me. I couldn't just leave, knowing he was there."

"How did you know, anyway?" He glared at me through slitted eyes. "Lin told you, didn't he? So I can't trust him, either, stars above."

"No! He didn't tell me," I said. "I... I snuck out and overheard him telling you. I'm sorry."

"What a fool's mission!" Flick's voice rose with every statement until he was yelling. "Didn't you hear me tell Lin we couldn't interfere? You'd sacrifice the whole rest of your village—"

"I know!" I shouted over him. "I know. I'm sorry, I'm sorry. And I scared... I failed..." I gulped sobs, overcome yet again, and hated myself even more because Flick was right and I was wrong. I struggled in vain to keep the bed from shaking and hurting Roni and finally made myself roll off it into the chair. Roni woke up anyway.

I could no longer sense anyone's emotions but my own, yet I told myself Flick's face softened as he watched me. That was until he snapped at me.

"What'd you find out?"

I took some deep breaths, and the intense emotions stuffing the little room felt a little less like drowning and more like being under too many blankets. Roni watched my lips, and I hoped his lip-reading was good enough to understand me. I could hardly bear to tell it in one language.

"Konu is living with a Paav man. He has blue eyes. Blue! He's... Konu..."

"Is Konu hurt? Being tortured?"

I shook my head. "He's safe. I think he's been adopted." The word tasted sour in my mouth.

Flick blew out his breath in a huff. "Safe. And I suppose you tried to grab him."

I didn't recognize my bitter laugh. "When he called that man 'Daddy.' I was so stupid. And..."

"What?"

"Konu was afraid of me. He doesn't know me as a Knower. He wanted to go back to that man."

Now Flick's face finally softened, at least a little. "At least you're brave." He grunted. "Stupid, impulsive, and downright idiotic, but brave."

I had nothing to say to that.

"What my men want to know is how we got away from those Paav. We were outnumbered, outflanked... and they just, well, stopped. Let us go. What did you do?"

"I hurt them. I hurt them with my mind. I don't know how badly."

Flick shook his head to my quiet admission. "Gods above, girl, what *are* you?" He stomped away and slammed the door shut before I could answer.

I wished I knew.

***

I should've offered to help on deck immediately, especially now that we were so shorthanded, but I couldn't bear the thought of looking more sailors in the face. So I laid my back at Roni's to clear my mind and listen to the sea splashing against the hull.

Then, I saw my brother Itu waving his arms in Watcher-speak. He appeared so unexpectedly yet distinctly in my mind that my eyes startled open, and then he disappeared. I unnervingly closed them because I had to try again since I'd already failed one brother.

To my shock, Itu reappeared, and he seemed to be speaking, shouting even, but in my mind, I heard nothing, which filled me with a wave of strange anger. My gaze froze on his face, so I could only catch glimpses of the words formed by his hands — *a child, not a Watcher, don't you dare...*

Roni stirred and coughed, and the vision disappeared.

A shiver ran through me, realizing my ability to see into Roni's mind, his thoughts. An argument with Itu, maybe real or a dream, and silent because it was Roni's vision, not mine.

I pressed my back against Roni's and felt for his mind. It was almost a physical sensation of pulling toward him as light burst through my head and my mind filled with images.

I'd done it.

Sifting through Roni's thoughts and memories was like nothing I'd ever experienced. Closest to me, like open pages of a book, were images of Flick, Mir, me, the *Phoemek*. The closer I got to any image, the more emotions I felt. Flick inspired friendship and loyalty; Mir humor and a slight wariness. Something made me draw back before I reached my image, so instead, I explored the more shadowy edges of Roni's mind, which turned out to be the distant past.

There was the woman from the Watchers' house on Kokka, hands covered with colorful paint and arm around an unfamiliar man. She laughed and signed rapidly with her free hand, which filled me with contentment.

I steered away from the many memories of my family, afraid of what I would find, unwilling to dwell on those whose loss pained me so much more than a broken rib. I dug deeper and found a man who looked much like Roni, only older. A woman I vaguely recognized stood next to him, crying and pleading. Neither signed in Watcher-speak, but their lips spoke precisely, enhanced, I supposed, by Roni's excellent lip-reading ability.

"He is not my son," the man said. "My family is only Doubles, as far as..." He turned to the woman, and the rest of his sentence remained hidden. Anguish overcame me.

"He's your son!" pleaded the crying woman. "He needs a father. He's just a little boy!"

"No Watcher is my son," the man replied, staring straight at me. Straight at Roni.

"Then you are not my husband," said the woman.

After a long look at his wife, Roni's father spun and walked out of the memory. The woman, Roni's mother, knelt and held out her arms, signing, My boy.

I opened my eyes, too overwhelmed to continue. What kind of monster had I become? Roni never did anything wrong to make his people—even his father!—reject him. The world, however, was right to reject Knowers who prodded into their private memories and manipulated strangers. No wonder Islanders raised their children to believe we didn't exist. The alternative was just too terrifying.

***

Later that morning, I swallowed my fear and went to find Flick to give me a job. My headache eased, and my skin longed to feel the sun. And I couldn't stand another minute stuck in the tiny cabin while Roni slept, and I fought my urge to spy on more of his dreams and memories.

I stuck to the railing and pretended to be fascinated by the open ocean while painfully aware of all the curious—and suspicious—eyes following my movements. When I accidentally met a sailor's gaze, she quickly looked away.

Mir emerged, sporting a large bandage on his cheek that sent yet another pang of guilt through my middle, but he smiled when he saw me. "Alesea."

I gratefully bowed to him as if a child to an elder.

The big man guffawed as if I'd told him a bawdy joke. "That's the first and last time ya' need to give me that sort 'o greeting," he roared. "Save it for yer grandpa." He gave me a friendly pat on the back with one enormous hand, nearly knocking me to the deck before he bent and whispered in my ear as I lurched to the railing. "And stay calm."

Stay calm. I wanted to scream, but I smiled sweetly and nodded while my mind raged. Would the world be afraid of me for the rest of my life? Would I?

I found Flick at the wheel. "How can I help?"

He fumbled with a compartment next to it, then thrust a spyglass into my hands without sparing me a glance. "Keep watch behind us. Sit in the stern and scan in all directions. Let me know if you see anybody at all."

I murmured "thank you" and headed toward the stern just as Flick called after me.

"Do you read Listener-script?"

I turned back, startled. "What? No. Why?" I followed his gaze and saw the edge of one of my father's letters sticking out of the seagrass bag slung over my shoulder. "Oh. I wish I did. They're from my father."

"Sofi said he sailed north months ago. Are they about the Paav or Mata? Anything that could help us?"

"Maybe. I don't know."

"Let me see."

I didn't want to let go of the letters — all I had right now of my mother — but I didn't want to do anything else to offend Flick, either. I pulled the stack from my bag and handed it to him. He ran his fingers over the writing on the top page. "Ah, same dialect as Kuul."

A nervous feeling entered my throat. "Wait, you can read it?"

Flick nodded, fingers flying over the page as I'd seen Sofi's do with her *A'lodi* texts. "I can read through them if you let me hang onto them for a while."

"Yes. Thank you."

"All right, then." Flick stuffed the letters in a bag next to his foot and turned back to the wheel before he dismissed me, and I made my way to the stern with the spyglass.

I sat on the little bench for the rest of that day, only leaving once to check on Roni and remind him to stay on his side. I pretended not to hear the murmurs of my name or see the hostile stares in my direction. When the sun finally dropped below the horizon, I put together a simple dinner for myself and Roni and went straight back to the cabin.

I lit a candle on Flick's desk, and Roni opened his eyes. Memories of stolen dreams flickered through my mind, and I fumbled with his cup of broth, nearly spilling it.

How are you feeling? I signed after I'd sat everything down.

Roni barely moved his arm, but his hand signed, *Alive.*

Hungry?

He jerked his head forward in a nod and started to roll on his back.

"No!" I grabbed his shoulder to stop him.

Pain stabbed my middle, knocking the wind out of me. I let go of Roni and fell backward into Flick's wardrobe. He watched me through widened eyes as I flailed around for whatever had attacked me.

However, the pain disappeared with not a trace.

Oh, no. *I felt your pain, didn't I?*

To my surprise, Roni smiled while slowly signing *You'd do well in theatre* with his available arm.

I pulled myself up to kneel next to the bed and wondered how he could joke about something as serious as that. *It surprised me.*

He just grinned.

Despite all that had happened in Ana, I felt a bubble of hope. *You must be feeling better if you feel like teasing me.*

You must – A violent, wheezing cough overcame Roni, and I stood there useless, afraid to touch him again and do anything that might make him worse. I found a handkerchief on Flick's desk and held it to his mouth. This time, at least, there was no blood.

I'm okay. Broth?

With an extra pillow stuffed under his head, Roni managed to feed himself with the spoon while I held the bowl. I carefully kept my hands on the far side of the bowl to avoid even the lightest brush of Roni's skin.

My eyes prickled as I longed for Itu or Sarai, someone I could really talk to in my language. Someone I wasn't afraid to touch.

Roni dropped the spoon into the empty cup. *You're afraid* he signed one-handed. He remained propped with the extra pillow and almost looked like his usual self.

Of course, I am. I sat the cup on Flick's desk and tried to smile.

Of yourself.

Roni's inquisitive expression blurred through my tears. *I can't control it*, I signed clumsily in the only way I knew how. *Everyone can feel it.* I wiped at my eyes with the back of my hand, my thoughts growing uglier by the second. *I'm a monster.*

Roni took my wrist with surprising strength. I yelped and jerked away.

Touch me, Alesea he signed fervently. *It's okay. I'm not hurting so much now.*

He thought I was afraid of feeling his pain again. He would hate me if he knew my real fear.

It's okay, he repeated and reached toward me with his free arm.

I couldn't force myself to meet his eyes as I took his hand, bracing myself for the pain.

It didn't come. Instead, a calm flooded me. Tension released from my neck and shoulders, and I'd barely even registered the headache until the moment melted it away. Was he —

You're not a monster.

I gasped and let go. "What... how..." I sputtered.

Roni smiled, looking unreasonably delighted. *You understood me*, he signed.

"You're a Knower!" I blurted out my revelation, forgetting to sign.

He shook his head, reading my lips, and retook my hand.

This time, a nervous eagerness joined the calm feeling. *I'm not a Knower. It's because of you. You can do this.*

It's impossible to explain Roni's thought voice. It wasn't Watcher-speak, but it wasn't like talking, either. It was simply there.

How did you know? I thought in my spoken language, hoping Roni would understand me like I understood him.

He did. *I thought we might be able to talk this way, ever since...*

An image of myself filled my mind:

> *I was in the garden on Kuul, my face contorted with anger and stubbornness. My eyes rudely rolled when Roni reached for my hand and spelled a word on my palm. Anger flowed from me into Roni like hot waves. Along with the rage came despair, confusion, and grief, yet Roni held all of them.*

The memory disappeared and Roni's calm thought voice replaced it. *I don't think you even noticed. You were so upset.*

Guilt poured through me and my connection to Roni. *I was horrible to you. How can you even stand me?* I told him as another vision flitted by of me tied up, huddled on Roni's raft in the dark and feeling Roni's horrible regret.

Because I understood why you felt that way. Because I deserved it.

You didn't. But thank you.

We held hands for a while without exchanging any words. I reveled in the feelings of friendship and strength.

I wasn't alone after all.

I'm sorry I'm so terrible at Watcher-speak, I finally thought.

Roni snorted with laughter. *You aren't that bad, but I like talking to you this way better.*

Me too.

Roni held my hand as he drifted off to sleep, and the pain returned. He must have been hiding it from me somehow. Instead of flinching away, I let it settle in my middle. Perhaps I could hold it for him like he had held my anger and grief before I knew how powerful it could be. With each of Roni's breaths came a sharp jab in my chest, and I used my breath to wait it out. Sure enough, his breathing settled into a quieter, deeper pattern.

Roni's eyelids began to twitch, and dream visions floated through my mind. I tried to ignore them, remembering the promise I'd made just that morning. I kept my eyes opened, focused on Roni's face. It worked until the vision I saw was of me on stage with my *lele* in the Great Hall of Kokka.

I told myself that Roni wouldn't mind as I closed my eyes.

I was singing the lament of the First Moon. Though Roni was standing at the far back of the enormous room, through his sharp eyes I could see the shape of my mouth and each movement of my fingers on the lele strings. The sadness of the moon swelled up in my mind, more powerful than a song should ever be. My eyes filled with tears.

Not my eyes. Roni's, in his dream-memory.

Roni could hear my music, after all.

However, the song of the Second Moon did not fill Roni with joy as it should have. He fought off the happy emotions with a more solid feeling of despair and something else harder to identify. Hopelessness? Longing?

The tap on my shoulder was so real that I jumped, but it was only someone getting Roni's attention in the dream-vision. He tore his eyes from my face to find a green-clad Matan Watcher with cold, round eyes. He beckoned for Roni to follow.

I breathed so hard I couldn't possibly be helping with Roni's pain anymore, so I let go of his hand. Already, I'd broken my promise and seen too much.

Was it a memory or just a dream? Were the feelings real ones or just something silly conjured up by Roni's sleeping brain the way I dreamed of living under the ocean or having a sister?

Roni's eyes kept twitching. I stood and paced the tiny room, more confused than ever.

CHAPTER 23

I couldn't ignore the crew on the way to Mata, and I wouldn't. So I forced myself to eat the next day's dinner of freshly caught fish and still-soft bread with the sailors. Other than a few sidelong glances, they ignored me. Soon, the food was gone, and the bitter ale flowed freely. I declined Mir's drink offer because the smell alone was enough to turn my stomach sideways.

"Men!" Flick called over the sailor's gruff racket with the filling of the last mug. "Now that we're clear of Ana and no Paav in sight—"

Two men spit over the railing.

"It's time to come up with a plan," Flick finished.

"Aye!" The sailors' unanimous agreement combined with some suspicious-bordering-on-loathsome looks toward me. I took calm breaths and ducked my head in the most unthreatening way possible.

"So let's lay out the details we have," said Flick. "The Akilans were taken two double moons ago by a group of Paav led by a man named Sinon."

Lin spoke next. He'd cleaned himself up, and his hair was now in at least a dozen neat braids. "In two double moons they could already be spread all over Mata. Where do we even start?"

"And *The Phoemek* can't dock anywhere near the city. Even if we beat the messengers there, they won't be far behind us."

Flick nodded to the woman who'd spoken. "Aye. We'll stay west. I know Fa'ad a little, and the villages there are far enough from the border to be safe."

"And we'll just leave the ship there?"

Flick only shrugged at Mir.

"Then, we'll go to Mata city." Lin gave a humorless laugh. "On foot. And the twelve of us will find the entire village of Akila and our own missing relatives, free them from the Paav or whoever has them now, and then, what, swim away?"

No one laughed, and I wanted someone to laugh.

Instead, Flick cleared his throat and addressed the sailor. "I didn't say it would be easy, Lin."

"Or successful?"

I swallowed the lump in my throat at Lin's remark before I countered. "Fa'ad seems a long way from Mata. Who do we know that can help us on the continent?"

A dozen heads swiveled in my direction. Along with the attention came whiffs of emotions — fear, doubt, regret.

Flick answered first, though he didn't look at me. "I've visited the Listener monastery just outside of Mata City, and we may find help there. Anyone else?"

A grizzled, older sailor took up Flick's challenge. "I fished around the Fa'ad villages for a summer when I was younger. Good people. Good fishin'."

"Do you still know anyone there?" The old sailor shook his head at my query while everyone else looked around uncomfortably.

"The Paav translator." Again, all eyes jumped to me. I fleetingly wished for a *lele*. If only I were singing, not speaking to a bunch of sailors who already thought I was something terrible. I raised my voice to cover its trembling. "She was a Double, and they killed her. She left me... Roni... a note. She said her husband would help us. He lives... I can't remember, but Roni still has the note."

"Well, that's something, and we have you."

Someone snorted at Flick's response, then covered it with a cough. A wave of disbelief hit my mind.

"Yes. What exactly can you do?" asked a long-bearded man.

Flick gave me a hopeful smile.

I couldn't meet his eyes. "It's so new. I don't really know."

"You called her a secret weapon, Flick?"

"Weapon?" I glared at the sailor and then the captain and stood up from the crate serving as my seat, painfully aware that my stance barely raised me any taller than many of the seated men. "I shouldn't be able to use my Knowing as a weapon. That power disappeared with the Purge. And I don't believe in hurting other people."

"Girl, nobody *wants* to harm, not unless they're wrong 'bout the head. But you're a weapon, whether you want to be or not." Mir looked around at the crew. "Did you all *feel* her yesterday?"

No one smiled with Mir. Instead, some stared at me, others gazed angrily at Flick, and the long-bearded one made the Islanders' sign against bad luck.

Anger and desperation surged in my mind, and for a moment, I lost control.

Every sailor on the deck flinched backward as if they were part of a choreographed dance.

I fled to the cabin before they could see me burst into tears.

***

Sing for them, Roni said in his thought-speak the following day after I'd told him how much the sailors hated me.

Why?

They need to trust you, that's all. I think singing will help.

What song would make them trust me, then?

I'm the last person you should ask, he said. *I don't even know what it sounds like.*

But you do know what — Too late, I realized he hadn't intentionally shared that memory with me, and I couldn't stop it from flitting through my mind.

Roni's internal flinch felt like cold water dousing my insides. *When did you see that?*

I didn't mean to — I started, but Roni's other stolen thoughts and dreams surfaced even as I tried to suppress them. I let go of his hand, but it was too late.

I felt sick as I watched Roni lying there, eyes closed, unreadable. I didn't dare reach out with my Knowing. How could he trust me now?

I guess I have no secrets anymore, he finally signed, opening his eyes.

I'm so sorry. I tried to project emotions with my signing. *I didn't mean to. You were asleep, and it just... happened. The sailors are right to be afraid of me.*

Roni just stared.

Aren't they?

Maybe. But that's not necessarily a bad thing. I was even a little afraid of you the first time I felt you sing, and it was months before that... that memory you saw.

What? When?

Roni signed *I'm tired* again and then closed his eyes.

***

The next evening, I watched the sunset off the bow. Flick cleared his throat from behind me. "I've looked through the letters."

I whirled toward him and, quickly collecting the stack in his hand, stowed the letters safely back in the bag I always carried.

"And?"

"Most of them are, well, love letters. They seem a bit... private."

I wasn't sure if I felt ashamed at taking the letters or angry at my mother for telling me my father was dead when she had been receiving his love letters all along. "I'm sorry. I shouldn't have—"

"But there are a few things you should know. Your father thinks there are still Knowers—pure Knowers—north of Mata."

"Pure Knowers? Really?" This was widely believed to be a thing of myth. Then again, until recently, I'd thought that part-Knowers like me were a thing of legend too.

"It sounds like your father has always struggled to control his Knowing ever since it grew strong after your older brother was born, and I think you know that's why he felt he had to leave you." Flick's voice was full of sympathy.

"He shouldn't have left." I didn't want sympathy. I wanted my family.

Flick gave a noncommittal grunt. "Your mother did keep visiting him in hiding that included a visit that, er, made Konu."

Konu. His musician father was *my* father, and Itu's, and Brahn's.

When I said nothing, Flick continued. "So apparently, your mother began to suspect you'd inherited his gift a few months before your debut at the Solstice feast. That's when he left Kuul to find the Knowers. He couldn't stand the thought of your life being... well, like his."

My head spun with questions. "Wouldn't it have helped me more to *know* my father? He could have taught me, and we could have learned from each other. Mama lied to me all my life, and I never even got to *meet* him!"

Flick stared over my head out to sea, looking uncomfortable. "Actually, well, you have met him. He wrote about it, and it's part of why he was so worried."

"Wait, what? I have met him?"

"He made your *lele.*"

Kalo. The Listener assistant of the famous Kokkan luthier. How had I never noticed how close his name was to that of my father's, Alok? Then again, why would I? My father had been long dead.

I racked my brain for every memory of Kalo and came up with just one. He was in the corner of the luthier's workshop playing my *lele* when I came to pick it up. I sat and listened for a long time, admiring the resonance of the amazing instrument that was about to be mine. But I remembered little of Kalo himself. He had eyes, but he kept them closed. His long fingers were graceful and swift on the *lele* strings, like mine. His hair was sleek, straight, and pulled back with a single tie. His clothes were simple, of undyed linen. He listened as I tried out my beautiful new instrument for the first time, but he didn't say a word.

Now my *lele* was an ocean away on Kuul, and a pile of letters and that single memory were all I had of my father.

After Flick walked away, I was about to return to Roni when a sound I hadn't heard in a lifetime plink-plink-plinked its way into my consciousness.

Someone had been tuning a *lele*. A real *lele*, here on the *Phoemek*.

It knocked the wind out of me. For a few precious seconds, it was as if the last horrible months had never happened and I was on my way to Kokka, and Mama, Konu, Itu, and Brahn would be waiting for me there.

Then my throat swelled with the memories, and I was back on the *Phoemek*. The *lele* player launched into an unfamiliar melody, though the instrument still wasn't properly tuned.

Once I could breathe, I followed the sound to the other end of the deck. Flick, Mir, and two other sailors formed a rowdy audience around Lin, who was playing the *lele*. He laughed and swung his braids out of the way of the *lele*'s neck, and I winced at his sour chord.

Lin's eyes met mine, and the smile left his face as if I'd criticized him out loud. "Flick says you're a musician. Better than me." I couldn't feel his emotions or read his dark eyes.

"I sing." I held up my scarred hand. "I haven't played, not since..." I let my arm drop.

Flick broke the tension with a half-laugh, half-cough. "What about it, Lin? Give the girl a turn?"

Lin gave his captain a tight-lipped smile. "I'm nothing if not a gentleman." He held out the *lele* without looking at me.

"Thank you." I tried to breathe my emotions away.

I took a moment to retune the *lele*, reveling in its familiarity and ignoring the sailors around me. The *lele* wasn't horrible, but it had the rough look and feel of an apprentice-made instrument. I could feel Lin's glare as I struggled with a stuck peg, but I tried not to care. *An out-of-tune instrument will ruin even the most perfectly executed performance.* I could almost hear Mama whispering it in my ear.

My hands were stiff, and it took too long for my right hand to respond to my commands, the tendons aching as I tried out once-familiar strums. So, I picked a slow, easy tune by my standards.

I closed my eyes and let the music take over my mind. For a few blessed moments, I wasn't on the *Phoemek* anymore. The pain melted away, and I was just Alesea, the girl who spent her days weaving songs and seagrass mats among the *kreo* trees.

When the last note of the old tune faded into the wind, I opened my eyes to a smattering of applause. Flick and Mir grinned openly, and the other sailors—including a few who hadn't been there when I started—clapped politely. Lin, too, though his face remained expressionless. I held the *lele* toward him.

He shook his head. "You play it better. Give 'em another."

"My hand hurts. You play."

Another long, intense look from those deep brown eyes. Strange that I couldn't read any of the emotions behind it. Finally, he took the *lele*, careful not to touch my hand.

"Play one she can sing, Lin." Flick glanced at me, then added, "If she wants." It still sounded like an order.

I nodded, though I didn't want to. Something was strange about Lin beyond his stares and his... well, his good looks. I wasn't used to not being able to read people, even when I was younger, and Knowing was just a story. While everyone else was slightly lit with the glow I'd come to associate with my Knowing, Lin remained dark as the night.

"'The Death of Puika'." Do you know it?"

I nodded to Lin, a knot forming in my middle. I groped for another option, something happy. Something hopeful. Something to make these men trust me, to know I could use my unwanted power for good. "'Lila'. 'Lila and the Moons.'"

Lin frowned at my suggestion, but it was too late. The other sailors were already murmuring their approval as he muttered that he knew it.

He struck the opening chords with none of the ornaments I would've added. Still, there was a stark beauty to it. His face softened as he watched his left hand fingering the progression until it looked like a face I wanted to get to know, to understand the mystery of his invisible emotions.

The song of Lila told the ancient story of the girl who loved the moons so much she flew on a magical bird to visit them, where the gentle First Moon granted her wish to become a star. It was a song of happiness, dreams fulfilled, and the polar opposite of "Puika."

My voice emerged clear and true, despite the moons that had passed since I'd last sung. As I relived Lila's story, the emotions in the lyrics became almost tangible things—thoughts I could shape and control. I reached for hope and sent a thread of it spinning through my song, braiding in joy and love as much as possible.

Hardened sailors' faces turned gentle, and their middles glowed brighter. Some gaped, others smiled. Tears formed in the corners of their eyes. Flick wiped at his face with the back of a hand.

Only Lin, focused on the *lele*, seemed unmoved.

I finished to raucous applause and shouts, with demands to sing another. Mir called out, "'Phoemek!'"

With an eye-roll, Lin opened with the introduction to the "Dance of Phoemek." I stopped trying to puzzle out my mysteriously grumpy accompanist and directed Phoemek's gleeful song to the other sailors of her namesake.

I sang their requests for what felt like hours, Lin grudgingly playing along. I knew all but a few of the songs they requested—it seemed most of the sailors had spent time in the Village Islands, even if they were from Ana. Maybe the songs of my people were Ana's songs too. There was so much I didn't know.

Both moons were high, the ocean magical with their silver beams, when Lin pulled out a ratty cloth *lele* bag. "It's late." His rough voice made it seem as if he'd been the one singing for hours.

Disappointment wafted off the other sailors. Regardless, they gathered mugs and wished each other a good night.

I waited until Lin met my eyes and said, "thank you."

A deep sorrow crossed his face, and he turned away.

CHAPTER 24

Three weeks passed in a monotonous cycle of keeping watch, talking with Roni, singing for the sailors after dinner until my throat wore raw, then restless sleep back in my old hammock. By day, the crew treated me like a *laurok* snake—a holy creature to be treasured that could kill you with its venom at any moment, but at night, they begged me to sing so they could drink in every note like sweet wine.

Lin started changing, little by little. He would glance at me but always look away if I met his eyes. It became a bit of a game, trying to get him to look at me while we performed together. I was sure I'd seen a fleeting smile a time or two, like a peek of sunshine on the grayest day.

Moods grew sour as our food turned to bland porridge and jerky, and the ale ran low. The sailors reminded me with every glare that it was all my fault we didn't have our cook or enough food as they struggled to chew tough, dried meat or crunch stale bread. Even worse were the increasingly wandering eyes during my evening entertainment that examined my body with a hunger that had nothing to do with our food stores. The two female sailors still with the crew were older and tougher than most of the men; I was something new, young, and fresh.

As long as bulky Mir sat near me, no sailor dared do more than ogle, but one night, Mir had late watch while Flick fussed and grumbled over his navigational tools in a cloud of aggravation that kept us all on the far side of the deck. The women were on duty, and the men demanded the "Love Song of Druids," which I reluctantly complied with but wished Lin would stop the looking-not-looking game so I could beg his help in saying no. Sure enough, as I began the plaintive calls of the introduction, the grizzled sailor called Mo took Mir's usual seat. He leaned close enough for his sour breath to turn my stomach.

Ironic as it was, I projected anger at the man while singing the beautiful minor melody. He recoiled, then laughed, while I sang.

"Ah, the kitten has claws, eh?"

I squirmed away, voice faltering, as he breathed into my ear.

Lin looked straight at us. I was so surprised to see his eyes that I forgot Mo.

Mo didn't forget me. "But kittens are easily tamed," One damp hand crept onto my thigh as he whispered.

Before I could react, Mo yelped and fell backward. I hadn't even seen Lin stand up, but there he was, *lele* in one hand as he shook out the other from punching Mo in the face.

It was as if the rest of the deck had frozen in the moonlight — the still-seated sailors with wide-open mouths, mugs halfway to drinking, and Lin glaring down at Mo where he lay on the deck, nose bleeding.

Then, Lin stepped back and struck a chord with his bloodied hand as he sat down. "Shall we continue?"

I nodded, wide-eyed, and joined Lin in the chorus with his eyes back on the *lele*. Mo eventually brushed himself off, wiped his bloody nose, wandered away, and everyone acted as if it had never happened.

***

Twenty-two long days into our voyage from Ana, Roni sat in bed and stretched both arms high.

"Roni!" I shrieked with joy before grabbing his hand. *You can lift your arm!*

He grinned and twisted his body, only slightly wincing when he stretched to the left. *I'd like to stand up.*

Hurrah! I pulled the covers off his feet and supported him as he swung his legs off the side of the bed.

My legs are so weak. He projected embarrassment.

You'll be yourself in no time. I'm sure of it.

He took a deep breath and pushed himself to a standing position, one arm around my shoulders for support.

You did it! I felt like cheering.

I want to walk on the deck.

I opened the cabin door and led him through. His knee shook against my leg, but he stood straight, and I didn't sense much pain.

"Ronan!"

Roni smiled at Mir's shout of excitement as we continued our slow walk around the deck. Sailors stopped their work to greet him, and it felt good not to be the center of their attention for a change.

From that day forth, Roni took his meals on the deck and sat by my side for every evening performance. All it took was a glare from Roni to make the sailors avert their eyes from my body, and Lin could scowl— even if it weren't often now—at his *lele* in peace.

Sometimes Lin would hold my gaze as I sang, and I'd forget what verse I had been singing. His eyes would laugh at me without bringing his face along, and he would keep them locked on mine for one verse or more. Was he starting to trust me? Or something more?

Then one foggy night during our most requested song—"Lila and the Moons" — a brilliant glow burst out of Lin's heart, and his emotions rolled over me like a summer breeze before pummeling me like an attack.

Hope. Sorrow. Fear. Desire. Jealousy. Love. I stumbled on the lyrics of "Lila" for the first time. The others laughed, seemingly unaware of this new stream of emotions. Lin's eyes met mine with his final chord, and the flow of emotions stopped as quickly as if it had slammed into a stone wall.

I felt Roni staring at me, but I couldn't tear my eyes from Lin's. *Was he —*

Except Lin had already launched into another song. The chords were stark and violent, which disoriented me. It took a moment for me to recognize the introduction to "The Death of Puika," the tune I'd refused to sing that first night. Lin had never suggested it again, and I had brushed it off as an impulsive moment on his part to try to get me to sing something that would make the sailors fear me even more. "The Death of Puika" was one of the saddest songs I knew, even though it was such a classic since it was impossible to get through any musical training without learning it.

Well, these men may or may not have liked me, but they didn't seem afraid of me at that moment. Surely some sorrowful emotions over an old story wouldn't change that, so I sang.

The legend of Puika was far older than the Great War and was about a young man cast out by his family and his betrothed after doing some unnamed horrible thing. He spent the next ten years proving his worth through heroic deeds—slaying monsters, discovering lost islands, rescuing children—and returned to find his family dead and his betrothed married to another. In his grief, he set off to stop an approaching supernatural storm and sacrificed himself to the sea demon to save the people who hated him.

I hadn't sung the ballad since my mother required me to learn it years ago. Nonetheless, I remembered every powerful word that fit beautifully with the mournful melody. By the end of the first verse, drunken Mo actually wiped a tear from his cheek.

It was during the chorus that I faltered. I'd never really thought about the words beyond the surface level, but now, every line was like a slap in the face.

> To be ripped asunder, simply for knowing
> For seeing through souls to the heart of the truth.
> To find darkness and hate where love should be growing
> The knowing has robbed me of joy and of youth.

Puika was a Knower. His horrible deed was being who he was, and no amount of heroism could save him from the hatred and fear of his people.

What was Lin trying to tell me? That I was as doomed as Puika? I knew that wasn't true. Some may have feared or even hated me, but others, like Roni and Flick, accepted and cared about me.

Lin stared at me until I recovered my composure, then scowled at his *lele* as we finished the song. Every word was painful now that I realized the truth behind the story, and the men felt it too. Heads drooped, and more tears fell as Puika asked the sea demon to take his life in exchange for the safety of the people who'd abandoned him.

The deck was silent as the last notes faded too quickly into the mist. Finally, Lin stood and stomped off into the darkness. I gaped at the spot where he'd been sitting, unsure of what had just happened, until Roni touched my arm and thought, *Are you all right?*

I wanted to follow Lin, but some of the sailors' sadness turned to crankiness, which never ended well. So, I nodded to Roni and smiled at the rest. I launched into a silly folk song where the singer couldn't find anything appealing to eat and ended up dining on clouds and stars. Soon the men were laughing and clapping along.

It was so easy to change their mood. So easy to manipulate them.

For a moment, I hated myself.

Roni gave me a look of concern, and I did my best to project happiness toward him, trying not to think of Lin. When I finished, I coughed slightly and excused myself, pleading that I had a sore throat. I gave Roni a reassuring smile and walked in the direction Lin had gone.

I found him alone in the dark near the stern, standing at the railing and looking out to sea. Sadness rolled off him in waves stronger than the ocean. He looked like a child, then, alone and lost. For the first time, I noticed the slight fuzz on his cheeks and neck and the gangliness of his limbs. Lin must have been younger than Roni, even.

He hadn't turned me away yet. I lay my hand on his arm.

His emotions shifted. Threads of wariness hit me like sparks from a fire, but he still didn't close himself off. And there was something else there, too, something tender and longing.

"What happened, Lin?" My whisper produced nothing, so I kept my hand on his arm and tried again. "Puika was a Knower, wasn't he? Would you believe I never noticed that?"

Lin's exasperated snort wasn't what I'd call encouraging, but at least it was a response.

"You tried to make me sing it that first night, and I thought it was because you hated me. I thought you wanted me to scare the crew even more than I already had, but now I'm not sure."

Silence.

"Were you trying to tell me something? Are you—"

The sorrow hit me again like he'd thrown it at me on purpose—like an answer.

"You're a Knower too."

Lin finally turned to me and spoke, his voice hoarse with emotion. "I thought it was obvious."

I shook my head. "I knew you could close off your emotions, but... I've only ever known one other Knower. Before the Solstice, I didn't even think they existed anymore."

Lin's smile was bitter. "That's no surprise. You flaunt it, and somehow they still accept you. Some of them practically worship you!"

I recoiled like he'd hit me and pulled my hand from his arm. "What? Flaunt it? I'm trying to control it so badly! I never asked to be a Knower!"

"And did your family cast you out? Did your village curse you, despite all your good deeds?"

Anger flared inside me. "My family didn't get a chance to cast me out. They were stolen. Enslaved. Remember?" Memories flashed across my mind, unbidden. "And no one would help me, only Roni because he felt guilty, and the head Kokkan elder called me a 'filthy Knower' and tried to stop us from saving them. Is that good enough for you?"

I gasped as the most complex storm of emotions bombarded all my senses. Anger melted to regret, mingled with profound grief, and my anger melted away too.

"I'm sorry." Lin's gentle words accompanied the laying of his hand on mine.

I liked the way that felt. I liked his growing emotion even more: *Hope.*

"So... why *did* you make me sing 'Puika'?"

Lin didn't answer for a long time, though his emotions continued to mellow into something nearly resembling contentment, and my hand tingled at the connection. "I guess I wanted you to know. I wanted to know *you* too. You're so... but I couldn't make myself tell you. You had so little control."

This time I laughed, choosing not to take it as an insult. "Maybe you could teach me some."

"Maybe I can." He looked at me and quirked his eyebrows playfully, his mood shifted entirely.

"Really?" I squeezed his hand, then let go, my face burning unexpectedly. "Please, do."

He turned toward me, propping one arm on the rail and looking more relaxed than I'd seen him. I noticed with shock that he had dimples when he smiled so widely. "Well, then. You asked so nicely, so I suppose I'd better." He reached up and tucked a wayward lock of hair behind my ear, which made my face even hotter, and my stomach uneasy. I knew my feelings couldn't be a secret to him, but he pretended not to notice even as his fingers lingered on my hair. "Just keep your voice down."

"Does anyone on the *Phoemek* know you're a Knower?"

"Only you."

I listened to the water splashing against the hull, wishing he would find another reason to touch me, but he'd looked back to sea. "The thing is, I taught myself control. I don't really know how I do it, just that I had to if I wanted to avoid a beating."

I shuddered. "I'm so sorry." Once more, without thinking, I laid my hand on his and felt the thrill of the secret conversation under our spoken one. "Do you meditate?" I covered my mouth, realizing I had spoken louder than I should have.

"Sort of, but my family wasn't really *A'lodi* devotees. So I had to pick it up from other places. One elder in my village—she tried to help me. She had known another Triple years earlier."

A Triple. It rang in my head like a Great Hall bell. I had a name, a race. "And?"

A bubble of laughter. "I was a stubborn bastard. I should've listened more." He looked at my hand over his, then flipped his over to interlace his fingers with mine. "By the time my Pa started beating me, she'd passed on."

"I'm sorry." It came out as a whisper. His hand was so warm.

"So it goes." He fell into silence, and all I could pay attention to was the connection between our hands, practically sparking with energy. *Say something, say something...* "You said I was so... What were you going to say?"

Something changed in Lin's energy. The melancholy of talking about his past evaporated with the sea mist, and I felt something new — *Was he nervous, too?*

"You were so different. Fierce, but innocent." Then, so softly I may have imagined it, "Beautiful."

His nerves set mine trembling even more than his words, so much I was sure he could feel my hand shaking. "So, controlling my emotions?" I remembered to keep my voice low.

He glanced at me, then jerked his eyes away as if I'd burned him, but he didn't release my hand. He cleared his throat. "Try imagining whatever you feel as if it's something solid. A rock or a ball."

"Okay." I blinked fast, trying to comprehend his words through the emotional currents overwhelming my senses.

"Then, imagine putting that object in a cage. A strong one, without a key or even a door."

"A cage."

"Sounds stupid, doesn't it?"

"No! Not at all. I—" A memory came over me: shaping my anger into arrows and throwing them at the people of Ana. "I think I've done that. At least the first part."

"Hmm." The corners of his mouth quirked up, and he looked at me again, skeptical.

"I know, I know, I'm a total failure." I grinned. "I forgot the cage. I think I had more of a... a catapult."

Lin laughed outright. "Sounds about right." He pulled me in closer, so I was nearly leaning on him.

My emotions fluttered in my belly like a swarm of butterflies or maybe wasps. *A cage, make a cage...*

Except it was too late. Lin looked into my eyes in a way I hadn't seen before. Like he...

"A cage." All I could do was release a whisper as Lin's gaze captured my eyes, mind, and body.

He smiled, showing me his dimples again, and leaned his face closer, so close I could feel the heat from his forehead on mine.

I wanted so badly for him to close that small distance, but part of me also wanted to run away, terrified of the chaos of emotions swirling through the air: Lin, my own body. So I kept babbling. "Do... have you ever talked with anyone with your mind?"

"What?" There was that adorable eyebrow quirk, and he backed up just a little.

"Without talking out loud. I... Roni... I have to hold his hand."

Lin looked down at our hands, where I was squeezing his too hard. "Then what?"

"I just..." I closed my eyes, willing my distracted mind back to attention. *I just think it at him,* I thought.

Lin gasped, and I kept my eyes squeezed shut, sure I'd made a horrible mistake, but then I felt his warm fingers on my cheek, and his breath so warm and close...

Oh, moons and stars, Alesea, he thought through our connection, then he kissed me.

I reveled in the waves of joy he radiated for the first time since I'd known him. The first real joy I'd felt in ages. I wrapped one of his coarse braids around my wrist and pressed my body against his as I let myself forget the horrors of the last months and experience Lin, only Lin. He let out a stifled moan and kissed back even harder.

When he pulled away, he breathed hard, his emotions wild with no cage in sight. "Alesea."

No one had ever said my name so perfectly and musically without singing.

"Lin." I hoped I said his name the same way, and I pressed my lips to his.

CHAPTER 25

Men's shouts startled me awake. The boat lurched, then banged against something hard. Had we already docked in Fa'ad, and why the shouting?

I hurried up the stairs to the deck to see sailors running about, their panicked emotions flying in every direction. It seemed like far too many sails billowed beyond them.

A man with dozens of braids and a yellow beard leaped onto the deck, wielding a curved sword and shouting unintelligible words at more yellow-haired men who seemed to materialize out of nowhere.

Pirates.

"On yer knees!" A half dozen others obeyed the man's command and joined him to swarm around Flick and the shorthanded crew of the *Phoemek*.

They hadn't spotted me yet. I forgot every promise I'd made after Ana. I gathered up my fear and anger and shaped them into a weapon in my mind, but before I could let it fly, the man I aimed at spun around and stared straight at me, sword raised and shouting.

"S'another 'en, a gull!"

What did he say? *A girl?* He grabbed my arm in a bruising grip and dragged me to the others, his sword waving dangerously close to my face. I then realized I'd lost my opportunity to act as he shoved me between Roni and Lin.

I wished I could melt into the deck and disappear. Every time I thought I understood how much more horrible the world was than I'd ever imagined, something happened to prove it was even worse.

"Who are they? What's happening?"

"Hush!" Lin replied to my whisper without moving his lips. A strangely-accented voice interrupted us.

"Ye'll be inspected. Don' stand till we tell ya!"

Inspected? For what? My knees were already aching as a tall, thin man approached me and circled, examining every inch of my body with pale blue eyes. My skin recoiled as he took in my warm-weather clothing, my island braids, and my ridiculously small stature.

"What right have you to board our ship?" Flick's voice was soft but menacing. "We have no quarrel with Fa'ad. We're simply traders."

The burly man squatting down to examine the folds of Flick's linen pants growled at him. "Ye should be thankin' us. We're warnin' folks ta stay away from Mata an' the Paav." He stood and faced Mir, the biggest of our group. "We're comin' back from the west villages, recruitin' fer our army."

"Army!" My exclamation came without thinking.

The man whipped his face toward me, giving me a look another might save for a revolting slug, then turned back to Mir. "An' if ye turn out ta' be spies, yer dead as dead can be, I tell ya. So tell me why yer here, headed ta Fa'ad 'stead of Mata City."

"We're headed to Fa'ad because we heard rumors of unrest in Mata City," Flick answered. "We've had some run-ins with the Paav, ourselves. We thought it wiser to avoid the place, though we're losing gold over it."

I kept my breathing slow and listened to the conversation, trying to ignore the thin man's closeness and pungent body odor that I couldn't block out.

A cage. Put my feelings in a cage. I knew down to my bones that these people wouldn't appreciate being surprised by a Knower.

With a smirk, the smelly man crouched and began patting my body, starting with my feet and working his way up.

Breathe. I could *not* let this man hear my thoughts. *A'lodi sahm.*

"Watch your hands!" Lin snapped, but no one had been touching him.

"I'm fine." I hoped my calm whisper would take the edge off Lin's rising anger, but it didn't.

Lin ignored me as the man's inspection moved to my belly and up. "Don't touch her there!"

I collected myself — *Breathe, breathe* — as the man spun to face Lin to speak to him in the same thick accent as the others.

"I'm not going to hurt your girl. She's not to my tastes."

I breathed some more, disgusted by his comment, and focused on the accent. It had sounded more like, "*Shiz nut ta my tests.*" I forced myself to imagine what kind of nut a 'shiz nut' might be.

I breathed a sigh of relief as he finally moved on to Roni.

"He's Paav!" the man cried, holding up a patterned scrap of cloth that had once been part of Abel's clothing but now served as Roni's handkerchief.

All the others stopped their inspections to scrutinize Roni with their swords raised and fists clenched. No one spoke up to defend my friend, who knelt there, frowning.

After everything Roni'd been through—after all *I'd* put him through—how could they just stand there? I crept on my knees toward the vile man who'd made the accusation, ignoring Lin's hissed warning, and released a shout I'd regret.

"He's no more Paav than the rest of us. Does he look Paav to you?"

Every eye shifted away from Roni onto me. With growing horror, I realized what I'd done. My emotions had come completely uncaged, with anger, repulsion, and frustration pouring onto these already-suspicious men. Now fear spilled into the mix as two more pirates stalked toward our group.

"Whassat? Ya' feel it, Dar?"

Make a cage, a cage, A'lodi sahm... It was no use.

"Sa' girl!" The second pirate grabbed me and wrenched me around by one arm. "Knower!"

"No!" Lin stood and shoved between the man who held me and myself. "It's me! I'm the Knower."

It was as if the ocean itself froze at Lin's proclamation. All was an eerie silence for a long moment.

"Feels like th' girl." The man who'd grabbed me looked between my face and Lin's as if choosing which of us he should cook first.

"How ya no' tell us you'd got Knowers!" As another yelled at Flick, he made a gesture similar to the Kokkan sign against evil.

Flick sputtered, but Lin answered calmly. "We didn't know how you'd respond, and I obviously won't hurt you."

What did he think he was doing? He'd been hiding his Knowing successfully for years. I couldn't let him ruin that now, just for me. Besides, I didn't need anyone to protect me. I was dangerous enough on my own.

"He's lying!" I pointed to Lin as I raised my voice loud enough for everyone to hear. "It's me."

"Bind the demon girl!" The man holding my arm was quick enough to believe me. He pulled a dirty cloth out of his pocket and tied my wrists behind my back. He jerked so hard I feared he would dislocate my shoulders.

Lin's body clenched, his face reddening, but as usual, I couldn't feel a hint of his emotions. He stared death at the man binding me.

Mir, flanked by men as large as him, watched with concern. "She hasn't hurt us yet, and she's had plenty o' chances. We share a common enemy—the Paav. She doesn't stand to make ya' enemies, too."

The man who bound me released a growl. "Knowers're everyone's enemy. How'd we know she's nah controllin' you?"

Flick let out a forced laugh. "Don't be stupid! Knowers can't control anyone. That's just a myth."

Mir nodded at his captain. "An' the Paav hate Knowers more'n anyone. Fear 'em more too."

My captor furrowed his weathered, ruddy brow. "Yah, so?"

"So, you're building an army. Maybe we could help each other."

The man harrumphed, clearly unconvinced. I tried to pull against my bonds, but my wrists were bound tight. What was Mir trying to do? Hadn't these men just attacked our ship?

Mir, standing, took a step toward me, giving me a strange look. Almost apologetic. "I saw 'er fight off two dozen men, just with 'er mind. Like th' Knowers of old."

Was he insane? "Mir! I can't—"

Lin lost his balance, or pretended to, and caught himself on my arm. *Shut up and go with it*, he thought to me through our link. Then he righted himself. "Sorry."

"Les' take 'er ta Arne. He'll know what ta do."

It would be my luck that my captor would believe an outlandish lie. I lurched as he pushed me forward. None of my friends objected as he guided me to a ramp between our ships, a makeshift thing of thin boards and rope. My shoulders and wrists smarted, and I feared what awaited me on the other ship but thought with some satisfaction they at least forgot all about Roni.

The other boat didn't look much different from the *Phoemek*, but it was far more crowded. Pale men were everywhere, rapidly talking in their strange accents I could barely understand, leering at me as my captor forced me past them to the cabin door and handed me off to someone else before disappearing inside.

"Wha's a lil gull like ye tied up fer?" This new one whispered into my ear, his putrid breath hot on my face and neck.

A'lodi sahm, I thought, struggling to keep my disgust caged.

The cabin door burst open, revealing yet another burly, pale man. His near-white hair was long and tangled, blowing about in the ocean breeze, and he had food caught in his overlarge teeth.

"Bern!" he barked at the man holding me. "Untie the girl. Surely we needn't be afraid of such a slight one." His accent was light enough that I could understand him clearly.

He grinned as Bern untied me, his frighteningly pale eyes boring into mine like a predator's. One hand toyed with an ugly knife lashed to his belt.

"Nothing to be afraid of, girl. My name's Arne, and I'm the captain of the *Ocean's Fire* and, I suppose, this growing army."

I remained silent as he freed my hands and gestured for me to follow him into his cabin.

He turned, looking surprised I hadn't moved. "Come ahead, girl. I have no dishonorable intentions."

"Does your knife have dishonorable intentions?" I stared at it warily.

Arne laughed at that—a humorless, mocking laugh. "I only want to talk, and perhaps, we can work together against our common enemy. So, come in."

I didn't see any other choice. I walked into the cabin, where Arne shooed my original captor out, closed the door, and we were alone.

"Have a seat." Arne motioned to his bed.

"No, thank you."

He sneered and sat where he'd gestured. "Have it your way, but like it or not, you're with us now. Dar told me your sailors have some fighting experience, and they'll be in the army. We'll find out just what you can do, how you can help."

My voice came out steady despite the increasingly hard pounding in my chest. "Our world no longer needs armies. My people refuse to use violence, and I will never help you. I am here to find them and go back home."

"So who are your 'people?'" He spat the last word like a curse.

Mama. Itu. Konu. Brahn. Just thinking about their names filled me with courage.

"The Paav stole my family and my island, and I have come to get them back."

"Without fighting? You're insane!" His eyes narrowed. "Unless you're as powerful as your companion claims. In which case, you're a danger to everyone."

"It has nothing to do with power. *To kill another is to destroy one's own soul, thrice over!* We can't—"

"Ha! So tell me, how did an island demon like you come to control an Anan traders' ship, spouting the *A'lodi* like some devotee?"

"I'm not —"

Arne punched me hard in the face. I staggered backward against the wall, shocked. My vision blurred, and my stomach heaved, but I caught my balance, hands pressed to my knees.

I chose not to show weakness in front of this awful man. I stared straight into his eyes. *A'lodi sahm.*

His projected emotions were cruel curiosity combined with a thread of fear. I could see that he wanted to break me, to have me react and ensure I wasn't too much for him to handle.

Well. I was Alesea of Akila, Maia's daughter, and "filthy" Knower, and I would not be broken.

"*A part of the* A'lodi *resides in everything living thing,*" I quoted, ignoring the pain in my cheekbone. "*And to destroy it is to destroy yourself. Even your cowardly soul.*"

Arne laughed as if I'd told a wonderful joke, but his eyes were dangerous. He stood over me and stroked my cheek with the back of his pale hand.

"What if I take it right out of you?"

I glared into his eyes, caging my disgust, even when his other hand reached for my breast as he drew nearer. I could feel his body's heat and smell his sour breath.

"*A'lodi sahm,*" I said aloud.

He punched me in the stomach. I doubled over, gasping for air, struggling not to vomit, but still, I controlled my anger. Once I caught my breath, I stood tall despite the room spinning around me. Blood trickled from my nose and dripped on the floor.

My voice came out in pained gasps as I quoted, "*If the A'lodi resides in us all, how can one seeker hurt another?*"

Arne laughed, but he projected fear and fury. "The good news is, you passed the test."

"What test?" I swallowed down another wave of nausea.

"If you were really as powerful as your bodyguards said, you would've shown it." He made a nasty hocking sound, then spit on my feet.

Anger immediately filled me, but I didn't let it spill over. *Make a cage.* "Or maybe I don't hurt people who are weaker than me."

Arne's face turned redder than I'd imagined it could, as if his anger burned him from the inside out.

I would not let him hit me again. I sent the tiniest bit of my anger flying at him on purpose just as he opened his mouth to speak.

He flinched, then laughed before his face paled to its previous shade. "You really *are* a Knower, little girl, but with control. What a weapon you will make against the Paav!"

"*A'lodi sahm,*" I said again, threw the door open, and walked away. Men watched me pass in astonishment, but no one stopped me as I headed for the ramp that would take me back to the *Phoemek.* Arne called after me.

"You'll understand when we get you to Mata City. That'll wash the *A'lodi* right outta you."

CHAPTER 26

My triumphant departure from Arne's cabin only lasted for a few seconds. The man called Dar caught me at the ramp.

"Oh, nay ye don't!" He grabbed my already bruised arm. "None o' ye back on yer ship, no' yet, 'til after dinner. This a'way."

He dragged me to an open area at the stern of the *Ocean's Fire*. All the sailors from the *Phoemek* sat in a circle with a few of Arne's men as Dar shoved me toward them, and I fell to my knees next to Roni.

Lin, across from me, growled as he started to rise and glared at Dar. "What did you do to her?"

"I didn't—"

"It wasn't Dar! Sit down, Lin." The last thing I wanted was a fight over me, and Dar looked ready to draw his sword and slice Lin down. "I'm fine. Let it go."

Lin was so angry that tiny threads of it seeped out of his mind, but he sat back down. "Who hurt you, then?"

I could only shake my head. *I'm okay, I'm okay,* I thought as hard as I could, but I couldn't tell if he heard me.

I adjusted myself to sit cross-legged, my knee touching Roni's. *What's happening?* I asked in his mind.

Something about sharing a meal before we join their army. What happened to you? I can feel your pain.

Roni's gentle thought voice nearly undid me. It took a moment for me to form an answer. *Their leader wanted to find out how dangerous I really was.* An image of Arne fondling me and punching me in the stomach flickered across my mind.

Roni physically flinched at my thoughts, projecting as much anger as Lin. *How could he do that to you? And how do we get away? I think the others are actually considering fighting, for real.*

I'm working on it.

Arne appeared then, holding two steaming bowls that he handed to Flick and Mir. "The meal of peace, my friends." His announcement came with a hearty, welcoming voice as if he hadn't just hit me minutes before. "After we eat, we will discuss our path from here."

No one spoke as men brought bowls of hot stew to each of us. It was as foul-smelling as my mood. The silence broke only because of the ship creaking and the sailors slurping. I could only manage a few sips, though it tasted a little better than it smelled. The seafood bits were too chewy, and my stomach still churned. Lin got his emotions back into their cage, even though he scowled at his stew as if offended.

I felt Arne watching me from his seat next to Flick, but I refused to look up. I told myself I was defiant, but my burning cheeks reflected pathetic weakness.

Finally, a man collected our bowls, and Arne stood up. "Now we have shared a meal and made our commitments to one another. Let's see what these Islanders can do."

Our commitments? Had my friends, my sailors, already agreed to fight alongside these men without even asking me? I went to stand, but Roni stopped me with a hand on my leg. *Not now, Alesea,* he thought. *We're too vulnerable here.*

Fine. The confusion and Arne's blow made my head spin, and my mind refused to come up with a plan. Regardless, Roni and I wouldn't be joining these men, not even if they took all the rest of our allies with them.

Arne held up two swords, both curved. He tossed one to a bearded man who'd been laughing with Mir. I flinched, but the man caught it by the handle like a child's toy.

"All right!" Mir rose to his feet and towered over Arne. "I'll spar. But I don't use that kind of blade."

Arne laughed and gestured at one of his men, who sprinted away and came back with a long, straight sword, its sheath decorated in patterns that reminded me horribly of Paav tattoos.

Didn't they want our help? *Why are they going to fight?* I thought to Roni.

Just practice fighting, Roni thought back. *To see if we're worthy of their army.*

I struggled to cage my emotions, appalled. *How barbaric.*

"Flick, how 'bout you help me show these cold-weather men how they do it on Ana?"

Flick didn't look up. "You're good as three men, Mir. You show 'em."

Mir shrugged and drew the Paav sword. It glowed an ominous orange in the dying sunset.

Arne glared at Flick, then at me. "What, you let that *A'lodi* child control you? What kind of captain doesn't fight for his honor?"

"A tired one, Arne," Flick sounded jovial, but his face displayed the opposite. "It's been a long journey here."

Arne gave a cruel laugh and turned back to Mir. "Fine, then. To the first blood?"

"Aye!"

The two faced one another a few paces apart as they held their weapons in front of their bodies.

Then, all was a blur of blades, arms, and swinging hair, punctuated by grunts and the clash of metal. The sailors around me cheered, but I sat straight up, alarmed. Surely they would kill one another! Sweat glistened on their faces, and at one point, their weapons locked in a battle of pure strength.

The sailors—even Lin!—laughed as if they watched a dance at a Great Feast, not a violent battle.

"Ah!" Arne cried, and I caught a bit of his pain as the curved sword clattered onto the deck. Then he laughed, despite the crimson blossoming through the sleeve of his gray tunic. "The sailor has some bite with that straight sword, eh? Good fight." He bumped Mir's chest with his fist. "You'll do."

Mir grinned and bowed to Arne, then swept his gaze around the fire. "Any other takers?"

The man who'd caught Arne's other sword moved to stand, but Arne stilled him with a hand on his shoulder. "Nay, save it for the Paav. We'll discuss our plans afore sleeping. These fine sailors are free to sleep on their own ship after."

Mir looked to his captain, whose face was nothing but glum.

"Aye, Mir, Arne. We've much to do."

"Come, Bern, we'll get our maps." Arne headed toward his cabin.

My thoughts swirled, my head aching. I had to stop this, but how? Flick was acting like I wasn't even here anymore. Arne certainly didn't see me as any leader. How could I get them to listen to me?

Lin glanced around, then scooted across the circle to squeeze between Roni and me and put his arm around my shoulders. He examined my beaten-up face but couldn't see the annoyed glare Roni shot at his back.

Alesea, Lin thought to me, *I know it's hard to accept. But these men... they're good sword fighters. Really good.*

So what? Killing Paav makes us just as bad as them! An unbidden image of Abel entered my mind, terrified and stumbling over the railing of the *Phoemek.*

A'lodi sahm, A'lodi sahm, I thought desperately, but it was too late. He'd already seen it.

He pulled me close. *Is that what this is about?* he asked. *You should be proud of that! If I'd known – if we'd told the sailors – even Uri might've come around!*

I stiffened. *I am* not *proud of it. I'm ashamed, as I should be.*

What if some people deserve to die? Lin asked, not noticing – or ignoring – the regret and guilt I sent through our link. *Maybe the* A'lodi *isn't inside everyone. Maybe the Paav killed theirs.*

The A'lodi *is in everyone,* I thought. *You can't kill it. And I never meant to kill Abel.*

Lin held me tight. For a moment, I almost relaxed and cleared my mind of everything but that comfort. How easy it would be to go along with all this. I could stay by Lin's side, cooperate with these men as we fought our way to our families, and punish those who'd stolen them from us. I wouldn't have to worry about it as my fault if forced into it.

It would be so easy.

"All right, sailors." Arne returned to our circle with a bundle of papers under his arm. Then to me, with a sneer, "Knower, you go ahead to your bed. This isn't talk for a little girl."

"What? I'm part of this group too! I'm the only reason –"

"Alesea!" Flick interrupted, finally looking straight at me. "You'd best go. I'll brief you in the morning."

"Fine!" I shouted like the child Arne thought I was. I flung off Lin's arm and stomped away toward the darkness of the *Phoemek.*

***

All alone in my hammock, despair pressed against me until I feared I would suffocate. I was cold despite the three blankets I'd wrapped around myself, and I was struck again by how easy it would be to give up to follow these men, take their orders, and forget about the *A'lodi.*

"No!" I said aloud. My voice died in the mountain of blankets.

What if Lin was right? Maybe murderers did deserve to die, which meant *I* deserved to die, along with Sinon, Abel, and all the others who hurt my people.

THE WATCHERS

Except the Paav were only part of Mata City. If we fought, what about innocent Matans — maybe even innocent Paav, for all I knew — who tried to defend themselves, their own families, and their homes? How could we guarantee that everyone killed on our swords deserved to die?

Lin had gone along with them so easily. He'd laughed when Mir struck Arne with his sword. He seemed almost as comfortable as he'd ever appeared on the *Phoemek*. He was only upset that I'd been hurt.

And what about Roni? Once he'd heard their plans and had time to think away from me, would he decide it was easier to go along with these people too? How much did he really believe in the *A'lodi*, and how much was just a debt he felt he owed me? I imagined him joking with Lin and Arne about my naivety, my faithful adherence to the *A'lodi* against all sense.

Maybe they were right.

"What a weapon you will make against the Paav," Arne had told me.

At least twenty men were at the dock when we escaped Ana. I bet I could handle twice that or even more. I'd be practically invincible, surrounded by a dozen armed men. Yet how many people would we have to kill to get my family back? Who were we to decide the worth of strangers' lives?

I felt so tiny. Smaller than nothing — a speck, an irritating piece of dirt in someone's shoe as my thoughts swirled: *What did I think I could do against a world that wanted to ruin everything my people held dear? How could I stop all these grown men who wanted to go in with swords and violence, just as bad as the people who'd started it? Who was I to judge?*

My face throbbed, and the small bit of stew I'd eaten churned in my stomach. *Oh, goddesses. How do I decide what to do?*

***

I woke in total darkness, too cold to move. I must have thrown my blanket pile onto the floor. The only one I could reach was the thinnest, full of holes, so I wrapped it around my shivering body and curled up into as tight a ball as I could manage.

I shook too hard to sleep, so I tried to meditate. *One. Two.* I used my most basic technique, counting breaths to ten and starting over again and again.

Except Arne's men loomed in my mind, mocking my practice with curved swords, leering eyes, bloodied fists, and condescending sneers. Lin, Mir, Flick — even Roni — brandished swords dripping Paav blood.

The decision tormenting me was hardly a decision at all. Arne would never let me go alive, not after what he'd done to me, what he knew I could do.

The numbers morphed into words. *Please,* I chanted inside my head. *Please. I'm weak. I'm small. I'm powerless. Homeless. Lost.*

Help.

Warmth flooded my skin, light burning through my eyelids, even with the blanket over my face. I pushed it away, startled, opened my eyes, then shut them against the light, feeling I'd stared directly into the sun.

Not the sun. The moons. Lily-white but a thousand times brighter than even the fullest Solstice double-moon. I took a deep, shuddering breath and dared to squint toward the source.

An impossibly beautiful, smiling young woman—skin black as night, sleek white hair flowing over glistening white robes. My tiny part of the *Phoemek* seemed to grow with the glowing sphere of light that surrounded the two of us, its source indiscernible, no wall or stairway visible beyond the radiant visitor.

She was like nothing I had ever laid my eyes upon, yet familiar as my beloved *lele*. "Luna."

Her smile grew, dimpling her perfectly round cheeks, and someone giggled behind her.

A child—a miniature version of the magnificent figure she had hidden behind—stepped out on glorious bare feet and bowed. "Alesea."

Her voice was ageless, indescribable. It was the wind, the stars, and the ocean.

"Phoemek." My voice was but a grain of sand.

She laughed again and looked to her older sister, who still gazed upon me, smiling as a mother would at a beloved child.

As my own mother would if I ever found her.

"Alesea." Luna's voice was a matured version of Phoemek's, deep water and ancient treetops. "You are lost only if you cease searching for the truth." She stepped toward my hammock and raised a perfect eyebrow over an eye that pierced my mind and soul.

Phoemek did the same, only exaggerated, as if to tease.

One step closer, they waited. Luna had quoted the *Book of* A'lodi. Was I to continue the quote?

"You are homeless only if you fear the truth of your own soul." My voice trembled, so small and faint.

Phoemek giggled again. "You are powerless only if you deny the truth of your heart." The words pounded into my chest like a mallet trying to break it open.

The two goddesses took another step each, closing the distance between us. I threw my face into my blanket, awed and terrified, wanting to wake from this dream or for it never to end.

A rustle of fabric, a warm hand laid on my head, and the constant swinging of my hammock stilled. Heat flowed from my scalp to my toes. My breathing slowed, even as my eyes poured tears of awe, pain, and joy into the bedclothes.

"Say the rest of the words, Alesea." Luna hovered close to my ear.

"Say them." Phoemek stood on my other side. "Mean them."

"They are written for you. Say them now."

I said them with my forehead pressed into the rough cloth of my hammock. As if they really were written for me and as if my life depended on them.

"Like every being, I am nothing. I am the whole universe. My deepest truth is at the heart of this paradox."

"Go on," Phoemek's whisper was a thousand island sunsets.

"When I find that truth, my path will be clear, and I will despair no longer."

"Be blessed, Alesea." The words swirled around me like the warmest of sea breezes before the heartless cold of the northern night enveloped me again.

CHAPTER 27

Light poured into my tiny window when someone's sandals clomping down my stairs startled me awake. I threw my legs over my hammock and tried to gather enough emotions to keep Arne and his men away, but sleep clouded my mind.

I needn't have worried. As soon as I saw dark legs and a ratty tunic hem, I recognized Flick. The pounding in my chest slowed, and the previous day's events washed over me. Pain returned to my face, ribs, and heart as I whispered, "Luna, Phoemek."

"What's that?" Flick knocked his head on a beam, cursed, and sat down in a hammock so hard the bolts creaked in the walls.

"Nothing. What's the plan?"

"Demons, Alesea, you look worse than yesterday."

"You know how to charm a girl." I forced a smile, making my cheekbone throb. "So, what's the plan—are you really going to join this army?"

Flick scowled. "We aren't exactly being given a choice. They may be acting friendly now, but I've no doubt they'd kill us all if we refused."

Was the situation that dire? "So you'll go kill other people instead."

"Stars, girl, it's not like the Paav're innocent! Your village isn't the only one they've pillaged, and Arne says the Paav have been breaking their treaty with Fa'ad for at least two years now by paying traders half what their goods are worth and threatening to make slaves of them if they refuse."

"That still doesn't make it right. You nearly joined an *A'lodi* monastery, right? So how could you even think about joining an army?"

Flick slumped in his hammock. "I wish it were that simple. But I don't know if anything but force can stop these people. Is it right to stand by peacefully while they slaughter innocents?"

"Of course not. I don't plan just to stand by."

"What *do* you plan to do, then?"

I didn't know. Not yet. Something swirled through my mind, but it was more of a feeling, a conviction than a plan, and I didn't want to tell Flick that because I wanted him to believe in me.

"What made the Paav start hurting people, anyway? What are they thinking?"

"I'm not sure if it's true." Flick scratched the thickening beard he'd grown on this journey. "I've heard some folks claim they're trying to reestablish the ancient Watcher monarchy."

"That's crazy!" My forceful response caused a jolt of pain in my sore ribs. "That's what led to the Great War! What about the *A'lodi*?"

"It hasn't stuck so well, especially not in the cities. The Paav never stopped believing they've got some sort of blood right to rule, passed down from the Matan Watchers of old, and after five hundred years of peace, the rest of the people, well, they weren't willing to see what was happening right in front of 'em, especially during the plague."

It was too much, and I could barely make sense of it. Yet I couldn't let my desperation — or Flick's — win. I tried to keep my voice strong. "So what's your army going to do about it?"

Flick winced. "We're docking the *Phoemek* in the Fa'ad village we're heading to because it's too conspicuous to go close to Mata City."

"We are already doing that."

"Yes, but then we'll board the *Ocean's Fire* and sail to a new port the Fa'ad have set up just a few miles from the Matan border. We'll have to be careful so the Matans don't suspect Fa'ad building forces, but the Paav haven't been bold enough to invade Fa'ad. We'll stay in hiding while we wait for all the recruiting ships to return. Arne expects two, three thousand-odd men. Once we're all gathered, it's only a short march along the border and a few miles into Mata to get to the city."

"And once you're there?"

Flick gazed at my bruised face, then his own hands. "Fight through to the Paav district, rescue all the slaves and prisoners, and restore order to the city. Something like that."

Something like that. "Arne can't make me use my Knowing to help him. Nobody can."

Flick met my eyes. "I know, Alesea. Thank the goddesses."

"I'm going to escape."

"I'll bet you are. I'd expect nothing less, but watch out. Arne's men will consider that an act of war for sure."

***

I stayed isolated in my cramped quarters for a full day until we landed at a dock in a tiny Fa'ad village. One of Arne's men escorted me directly onto the *Ocean's Fire,* and as I crossed the plank, I saw the continent for the first time.

It was beautiful and terrifying. The forest near the dock blazed with strange colors—orange, red, and yellow like the trees thought they were a sunset. The other trees weren't much more than oversized sticks without a single leaf. Above the forest loomed the mountains—imposing grey rock—and on their impossibly tall peaks, pure whiteness glared in the sun. *Snow.*

My gaping lasted only a moment before rough hands thrust me down a ladder into a hold even tinier than my quarters on the *Phoemek.* There was barely room for the bedroll laid out on the damp floor. I had no view outside the ship, only a tiny grate that allowed me to peer into the next hold, apparently a storage area.

Above me, the hatch banged closed, and something scraped across the top. I panicked, climbed the ladder, and pushed up with all my strength.

Nothing happened.

This hold was a prison cell, not "quarters."

"Let me out!"

No one answered my incessant screams.

I didn't know how many hours had passed in the near darkness when a shout far too close to my ear startled me.

"Knower girl!"

I breathed hard as I turned to the voice.

Pale eyes peered through the grate, visible even in the low light. "I've got food. Dunna try anythin'."

What did these people think I could do—shrink myself to escape out a hole through which I couldn't even fit my head? "I won't."

The man messed with the grate until it came off the wall, then passed me a stinking bowl of the stew we'd had the previous day. He reattached the grate and left without another word.

The food was awful, but I forced it all down because I felt faint from hunger. With my head a bit clearer, I thought to cast my awareness around the ship to see if I could find my friends.

It's impossible to put into words, but as I explored, I found that each person's feelings had a unique accent—more distinct even than their voices. The first few minds I touched were all wrong to be my friends.

Then, I bumped against a blank space—I could sense a mind, but nothing came out of it. That had to be Lin, his mind fully caged, unless there was yet another Knower on the ship. Near him, I found more minds I knew. One was either Flick or Mir, then a less familiar sailor, then the mind I sought—Roni's.

I concentrated hard on his feelings, trying to find a way to communicate without touching. I separated fear from worry and anxiety from heartache, but I couldn't change any of them. So, I focused on his position and projected my worry and need.

Something changed in Roni's mind. A new kind of alertness and a thread of hope crowded out the other emotions.

I pictured my tiny cell and the grate on the wall. I couldn't tell if the image got through, but I kept sending everything I could to help Roni find me.

He wandered around the deck, interrupted for a long moment while projecting anger and disgust—*had he been stopped by one of Arne's men?*—but finally, I felt him above me.

Yes. Since Roni and I were so close, I projected my excitement at him, then sent another image of the grate.

It took another painfully long search on Roni's part, but light finally appeared beyond the grate, and Roni came down the ladder I hadn't been able to make out in the dark.

I stuck my fingers through the metal bars, and Roni grabbed them. *Alesea.* His mind was full of worry for me. *Are you hurt?*

Not any more than I already was, but I'm locked in here.

He squeezed my fingers. *How are we going to escape?*

While relief filled me, a jolt of hurt came from Roni.

You thought I would abandon you? he thought.

I hoped he could feel my regret. *No, not really.* I added to his skepticism, *A little, but only because everyone else has.*

His emotions calmed as he thought, *We'll arrive at the port in another day. Then they'll take us to our camp, where we'll stay for at least a week. It sounds like there are lots of guards to keep anyone from escaping. We aren't the only unwilling soldiers, not even on this boat.*

Then why am I the only one locked down here?

Roni laughed internally—a strange sensation. *They think you have to make eye contact to kill them.*

What? I nearly laughed out loud. *Kill them? Eye contact?*

Oddly, Roni radiated pride. *They're absolutely terrified of you. And they don't realize I can read lips. Both of these should be useful.*

Definitely.
So what now?
I'll figure something out.
Of course, you will.
I smiled at my friend. *Thank you, Roni. I'm sorry I doubted you.*
Roni smiled back — a wide, open-mouthed smile, nothing like a Paav.
I'll come back when I can.

***

After one more visit from Roni and two more smelly bowls of stew, they released me from my cell. As soon as my shaky legs had made it up the ladder, Dar held my arm in his iron grip and led me straight off the *Ocean's Fire* onto the dock and then land.

"Keep yer head down," he growled as I gaped at the scenery.

I obeyed Dar's command long enough to see that even the ground was different from home. It was muddy and rocky, without a trace of sand. Thick blades of grass-like plants poked out of the mud as if waiting to cut someone.

When I looked up, the view was similar to the one I'd glimpsed when I changed ships, though now the mountains were on the opposite side. Here, at least, some of the trees were green, and the air was warmer and muggy.

Then we turned to the right, and my breath caught in my throat. In the distance, a mess of gray fog hung above an impossibly large city. Buildings tiny as children's blocks stacked in endless rows led uphill from the sea, and dozens of tall ships waited in the bay.

Mata City.

"Stop yer gawkin', gull!" Dar pulled me hard along a dirt path into the woods. After a short walk, we arrived at a large clearing and waited for everyone else to disembark from the *Ocean's Fire*. All the crew of the *Phoemek* arrived at once, carrying large packs, and I realized with a pang of loss that the pack containing my father's letters and Konu's blanket had never left the *Phoemek*.

I told myself I'd have Konu before long, but I still felt sick.

I didn't have a chance to talk with my friends before the pirate crew forced us to march to our assigned camp. Arne's men, who seemed to have multiplied ten-fold — there must have been far more people on that ship than I'd realized — surrounded me.

Having to walk immediately after so much time at sea made me unstable and nauseous. To top things off, I was so much shorter than the men that the dirt beneath my sandals was all I could see of Fa'ad. I watched for the slightest opening to sneak toward the side of the group but was constantly shoved back to the middle, harder than necessary, and my captors looked away whenever I tried to communicate with one of them.

The sun was high when we arrived at our campground, and finally, the men spread apart enough for me to see dozens of canvas tents set up among the trees and a single small wooden shed standing in the middle with a heavy metal latch on the door.

Dar's sour breath hit my face as he snickered. "Hope ye like yer accommodations, gull. Got ta keep ye safe among all these soldiers."

Dread filled me as he forced me toward the tiny building, barely bigger than me. How long would I be locked in there? Would they ever let me free, or would Arne change his mind and leave me to die there?

I wasn't caging my emotions. Dar had noticed.

"Ye stop that Knowin'. Makes 'em angry, see?"

Sure enough, a dozen men settling into tents stopped to watch me. None of their eyes looked the slightest bit friendly.

"Dun' look at 'er eyes, men."

One complained to Dar. "I kin feel 'er."

When Dar turned to respond, I wrenched my arm out of his grasp and ran.

The men must've been shocked by my sudden escape because none of them were quick enough to grab me. Dar shouted a string of curses, but I was already in the woods.

I ran until my lungs were on fire, which was not very far after all that time at sea. Yet I put enough trees between me and the camp to be well out of sight, and I didn't hear anyone following me. I paused, panting, trying to clear my panicked mind.

What the demons was I thinking? I didn't know where to go. I didn't have anything but the clothes on my back. I didn't know what plants were edible here or how I might get food or even water. What would happen to Roni? I'd left him with those people, which was horrible, but I would not allow myself to be imprisoned again. *I'll rescue him later.* More slowly this time, I continued away from the camp.

Something went *schwing-thump.* A stick lodged itself in the tree trunk I'd been leaning on seconds earlier. Another one hit the tree just beyond me.

Arrows, I realized, with a new surge of terror. They were shooting at me like a hunted deer. *Trying to kill me!* I took off again, and two more arrows flew past my head as I sprinted.

"Stop, gull, get down an' we won't hurt ye!" Dar's shout sounded alarmingly close. How had he been so quiet?

Something knocked me to the ground. At first, I thought Dar had pushed me, but a moment later, I succumbed to a sharp, fiery pain that quickly spread from my right shoulder blade to my upper body.

"Gods, gull, why'd ye have ta run?" Dar and another man knelt on either side of me. "This'll hurt." He jerked the arrow out of my shoulder.

I screamed, and the men jumped away from me. I retched, unable to control my pain. Dar sat in the dirt, eyes wide and fearful, refusing to look at me as I forced myself to my knees.

I couldn't just let them take me back to that cage.

Then half a dozen more men surrounded me, swords raised and bows cocked, not a single one meeting my eyes.

I swayed, breathing too fast, my shirt hot with fresh blood. Everything grew darker.

Mama. Konu. Itu. Brahn.

"Luna," More bile rose in my throat as I whimpered. "Phoemek." My lips could barely form the words.

Terror seeped from the minds around me as I tried and failed to suppress my pain and hopelessness.

Dar visibly trembled, his voice cracking as he spoke. "Ye coulda done that ta us the whole time! Why din't ye?"

I knew what to do in a flash. The *A'lodi* was inside Dar, whether he knew it or not. It was inside all these men. I just had to show them somehow. Show them we were all parts of the same whole, why they needed to stop fighting, and let me go.

The influx of hope pushed aside some of the fog in my mind. I filled myself with as much compassion for these men as I could muster. "You don't really want to hurt me." My words slurred barely. "I don't want to hurt you either."

Each of their chests began to glow with soft light.

I gasped with astonishment. How could I not have realized? The light I'd seen since the Solstice *was* the A'lodi, the spark of truth inside us all, and it offered proof that it really did live inside everyone—even the vilest and most violent of men—and evidence that I was doing the right thing.

I focused on that *A'lodi* light and sent out love, pure love.

Arms dropped, swords and bows falling harmlessly to the ground. The men looked into my face, eyes full of wonder, for the first time. Dar was no longer shaking.

"The *A'lodi* within me sees the *A'lodi* within you." I said. My head dangerously spun as I stood, saying those words, but I held my chin up and staggered through the stunned men to return to the camp. I lurched from tree to tree, out of their sight and disoriented. *Goddesses, please help me, help...* I needed Roni and anyone else who would choose to come with me, and now I knew I could free them if only I could make it there.

I followed the crescendoing buzz of angry voices, then flecks of white through the trees that I hoped were the tops of tents. I collapsed against a tree at the edge of the camp, too lightheaded to walk another step. Then, they spotted me.

Arne himself was leading a dozen men in my direction. What did he think I'd done to his men? He certainly wouldn't have guessed I'd filled them with love and compassion.

Luna, Phoemek, give me strength. Despite my pain, I willed myself upright one more time. "I will not stay with you." My performer's voice was loud but slurred, a thick fog descending over my thoughts and vision.

Arne's arrogance mixed with confusion. "So where are my men?"

As if in answer, two of them emerged from the woods, bemused but content, weapons hanging by their sides.

"Gareth! Vane! What's going on?"

One answered with, "She was shot," while the other apologized to me, saying that they'd get help as both men walked past Arne into the camp.

Arne sputtered like an angry tea kettle as the rest of the men from the woods followed. Dar turned to me and gingerly placed a hand on my non-injured shoulder.

"Be well."

Though Dar barely touched me, I fell back against my tree. I could hardly feel my body anymore. I had to finish this quickly, so I yelled with my last bits of strength.

"Lin! Flick! Tell Roni I'm ready."

"Aye!" Thankfully, Flick's voice was nearer than I expected.

"Ha!" Arne looked around at his men, scoffing, since they appeared reluctant to defend their leader against a small wounded girl. "So, you'll go tell 'em about us, is that it? Sell our location to get back your families? You think the Paav'll let you leave alive?"

That's what Arne was afraid of? "No! S'the *A'lodi* ..." I was so dizzy, I wasn't sure I made any sense. "Wouldn't betray... wouldn't hurt you or a Paav."

Arne sneered at me, then snapped his fingers. The men on either side of him raised their curved swords to block me from the camp.

"This is your last chance to halt," Arne growled.

"Your las' chance... let me go," I slurred against his growling, but since I was so weak, I wasn't sure he heard me.

Arne screamed an ancient and horrible scream. A war cry. His blade *snicked* out of its sheath, and he raised it to slice me in two. The men holding their swords between us were confused, their weapons faltering.

Now. Even half-conscious, it was easy to feel compassion toward Arne's puppets. I imagined he'd forced them just like he'd forced my friends, and I saw their A'lodi glow.

We are the same, I thought, fighting back the fog. *I see the A'lodi within you.*

They dropped their swords onto the ground, and I expanded my love to the rest of the group. Finally, Arne's chest began to glow. I felt his anger, his fear, then something else—something softer, buried deep in his soul.

"The A'lodi in me sees the A'lodi in you." I felt my knees buckle as I whispered.

"Demon," Arne lowered his sword as his whisper radiated utter bewilderment.

Roni rushed past all of Arne's men, projecting painful horror at my blood-soaked tunic. He scooped me up in his arms like a child and ran toward the road.

The last thing I remembered was how good it was to bury my face into Roni's warm chest before all went dark.

PART FOUR - TREKANA

One blessed with the strongest gift of Knowing, who has chosen the most difficult path of non-harming, is a rare flower to be treasured. These few souls will be called to be leaders among the people, and their journey must be to find the A'lodi within all the world. This treacherous path of greatest power must not be traveled without guidance and contemplation, lest the gifts be poisoned and corrupted.

~ The Book of the A'lodi

CHAPTER 28

I slipped in and out of consciousness as Roni carried me through the flatlands of eastern Fa'ad for the rest of the day, most of that journey lost to me. Yet I remember waking once and telling Roni to let me walk. He kissed my forehead and kept going. *Hold on, Alesea,* he said in my mind. *You have to hold on. Your family needs you.*

Thoughts smeared together into crazy, frightening dreams. Roni turned into Lin, then to Sinon. *I need you, Alesea,* he thought as my mind faded, *I love you,* he thought, but I didn't know if it was a dream.

I woke face down on a bed of blankets on the forest floor as someone pulled — ripped? — my tunic and touched my shoulder. Searing pain shot through my arm and torso.

"Stop, it hurts!"

"I know. I'm sorry."

But Roni can't talk, I thought before passing out again.

It was light out when I fully woke. I lay on my stomach, afraid to move. Although the pain was marginally bearable, my shoulder throbbed.

"Roni?" I switched to thinking it as hard as I could. *Roni!*

"You're awake!" Lin squatted next to me and laid a gentle hand on my forehead. "Oh, thank the goddesses."

"How'd you —"

"Alesea?" Flick's voice rumbled from somewhere nearby. "She's awake?"

"What? I thought Roni... I thought..."

Lin smiled his wonderful dimpled smile, seemingly just for me. "You didn't think we'd let you go without us, did you? Me and Flick followed you two, and we were right there the whole time." His smile dropped. "Roni insisted on carrying you all the way here, though."

Roni's leather sandals stepped into my field of vision.

Roni. He'd saved me. Again. "I'm hungry, and thirsty."

"Thank the goddesses!" Lin kissed my cheek, then jumped to his task. "Be right back, my lady."

Roni knelt and laid his hand over mine as I'd hoped.

Thank you for saving my life, I thought.

Any of us would have. Even Arne's men. And Dar! He would've cut off his hand if you'd asked him.

I suppressed a shudder. *I don't think that will last very long. You were so brave to walk right past Arne's sword.*

Not half as brave as you, he thought, though he felt a burst of pride. Or was he proud of me?

It wasn't until I'd finally but painfully made my way to sit to devour all of Flick's dried meat and an entire canteen of water that I learned I'd been unconscious for two days. As my head cleared, I also began to sense anxiety coming from the others.

"Do you think I'm going to die, or are you worried Arne will come after us?"

"You're *not* going to die, Alesea." Lin spoke while Roni signed simultaneously.

"So, Arne?"

The three of us looked at each other awkwardly before I spoke and signed.

"For Luna's sake! Thank you for taking care of me while I needed it, but I'm an equal part of this. It's my fault we're all here, alone."

She's right, Roni signed, looking sheepish. Then, to me, *You're in charge now, anyway.*

Flick looked startled at that, but after a moment, he nodded.

Lin frowned, opened his mouth as if to speak, then shut it again.

Thank you, I signed to Roni. "Where are we, anyway?"

"We're a day's walk from Arne's camp," Flick answered. "From what Arne told me, we're another day from the border crossing at the Black River. From there, it's only a two-hour walk to the Listener monastery."

We were so, so close. "Let's go, then, Flick!"

"Not yet!" Lin jumped forward to stop me from standing, and I sat down hard. It felt like someone stabbed me through the back. Tears sprung to my eyes—half touched, half annoyed by his overprotectiveness. Either way, my shoulder throbbed even worse than before.

"I'm sorry!" Lin let his concern spill out. "I didn't... you just need another day to rest."

Roni glared at Lin, but he added, *We have to figure out how to disguise ourselves, too.*

The tension between Roni and Lin was palpable as we discussed our cover story for Mata. Lin suggested I should be a Watcher and partner with him, making us the reverse of the fugitive pair. Roni argued — with an apologetic look in my direction — that I couldn't possibly disguise myself as a Watcher in a city full of them. I suggested a Listener, but Flick broke in to remind us that Listeners, outside the monasteries, were nearly in as much danger from the Paav as Knowers.

So, I would have to stay a Double... with a condition, and one that would keep men away.

A *"condition."* That's how I tried to think of it. I was going to pretend to be pregnant.

Roni and Lin refused to make eye contact with me as we debated who should play my husband. We eventually settled on Lin. If anyone were looking for Akilan fugitives in Mata, pairing me with Roni would be too dangerous. Though the idea that I would have to pretend to be married to Lin with a baby on the way — mere days into our relationship — made me sick to my stomach, like a little kid playing house, taking it too far.

Miraculously, Flick found an old, dull needle at the bottom of his bag, and he set to sewing one of our blankets into Lin's extra tunic. I doubted it would look compelling, but how much time did anyone spend staring at pregnant women's bellies? It would have to do.

Lin brought me more food when Flick held up the finished tunic for our inspection.

Lin grinned. "Ready to get pregnant, little wife?"

Flick snickered.

Roni didn't look.

"Please don't call me that! I mean. unless you have to."

Lin's face fell, and I immediately regretted my words. Flick went back to rearranging his pack.

"Sorry." I leaned my head on Lin's shoulder. "It's just... it's so much, all at once."

"You're right." He kissed the top of my head. "Also, I keep forgetting you're younger than me, so I won't joke about it anymore."

"Thanks." I let the warmth from his body spread into mine for a moment, replacing my pain with something much more pleasant.

Roni stood and kicked dirt over our dying campfire. His kick was hard enough to send some right onto Lin's legs.

"Hey!"

Sorry, Roni signed, not even looking at him. He stalked over to where he'd set up his sleeping things.

My heart hurt for Roni, but there was nothing I could do about it. I pushed him from my mind and snuggled up against Lin, marveling that we were finally about to enter Mata City.

***

The following morning I was incredibly stiff, but the pain lessened to a dull throb, except when I stupidly tried to pick up a bag. At my cry, all three men lunged to grab it—even Roni, who I suspected felt my projected pain the most. I carried nothing in the end, and Lin tied a sling to support my right arm.

Despite my injury, we kept a decent pace. The land was mostly flat, with no one else on the freshly smoothed dirt road. Perhaps this whole route, like the port, had only recently been created for Arne's army. By midday, we could already make out the sound of rushing water—the Black River—and by evening, it was so close and constant I felt it would jump out and drown us at any moment.

Then, we reached a row of stones blocking the end of the path, and beyond that, nothing but dark forest. For a moment, we stood in silence, staring at the woods.

"Uh, Flick?" My voice emitted a croak, probably because I was weak from walking for so long, so injured. "Did Arne mention—"

"No." Flick's abrupt response accompanied a grumble.

Roni turned to us. *Arne couldn't connect to the other roads, or he'd give away his camps. We've got to be close.*

We decided to stop for the night at the dead end—the men said we wouldn't have enough light to continue, but when I saw the way they looked at my shoulder, I noticed blood seeping through my bandages, soaking the thin cloth of Lin's tunic that had replaced my shredded one. I fell asleep sitting up while Lin cleaned my wounds.

At dawn, sharp-eyed Roni led us through the woods. It wasn't as easy as I'd hoped. We came close to the river four times, but thorny thickets and impassable underbrush always concealed it. Roni would shove a hole through the greenery as we listened to the watery roar, and each time he returned with a few more scratches and a disappointed shake of his head.

I started to think I wouldn't be able to walk a step further when Roni stopped so abruptly that Lin ran into his pack and cursed. Roni held up a finger — *wait* — and carefully set his pack on the ground. He tied Abel's treacherous handkerchief over his head to hide his ears and signed, *Stay here. I'll check if it's clear.*

Flick handed me the doctored tunic as we waited, and I barely suppressed a curse. At that moment, I wanted nothing more than a soft bed — even a soft pile of leaves would do — and uninterrupted sleep.

No. *Mama. Konu. Itu. Brahn.* I had to be strong for them.

I let Lin help me put the too-large tunic over my stained one. The weight of the blanket pulled dangerously on my shoulder. There was no way to get my injured arm through the sleeve without removing the sling, so it rested atop my fake belly. At least the injury wasn't anything the Paav could use to recognize me.

By the time I was ready, Roni had returned. He stared at me in my pregnant disguise, his expression unreadable, then signed, *It's clear. Let's hurry.*

He led us through the densest bit of forest yet. Thorny vines and tangled clumps of branches scratched our bare arms and faces, and we tripped over treacherous roots riddled beneath the layers of dead leaves. As I shoved aside the thousandth branch, blessed sunshine hit my face. I blinked at the wide-open road before me, paved with millions of tiny rocks and edged with colorful stone tiles. On the other side of the road was a farm that looked as large as the whole island of Akila. Neat rows of unfamiliar plants stretched for acres, and an impossibly fluffy, white creature looked up from its grazing long enough to bleat at me.

A burst of shouts sent me scuttling back into the woods. The animal so entranced me that I hadn't noticed the group of men on the road close to where we'd emerged.

One of them, a Double wearing a ragged brown robe and abundant black hair piled atop his head, said something to us, his accent even stronger than Arne's men. As my panic settled, I was able to translate. "We have nothing to give you! We carry only the clothes on our backs and food."

One of his companions frantically translated into Watcher-speak, but a glint of metal behind him told me at least one of them had a weapon in addition to their clothes and food.

"Flick, he's got a knife!"

Flick held his hands in the air and stepped towards the men. "We have no ill intentions, men. We are only travelers."

Stay back, the group's Watcher signed. *Only bandits come out of the woods here.*

"Bandits!" Flick harrumphed, translating as he spoke. "Surely there aren't any bandits so close to the Matan border?"

I risked a few steps forward to join Flick. Lin and Roni did, too, and held up their hands to show they had no weapons.

"This road is cursed, now." The man with the knife nodded to his companions, who relaxed slightly. "Been attacked here thrice by those stinkin' Fa'ad mountain folk." We watched his well-practiced movement as he turned and smoothly slipped his weapon into its sheath on his belt.

I exchanged a look with Lin. Had Arne's men come this way to steal goods for their army?

The one who spoke first turned his attention to my fake pregnant belly. "Ah, miss, this is no place for an expectin' lady."

So, at least one person was taken in by my disguise. Not trusting myself to speak, I nodded shyly and took Lin's hand.

The man who'd held the knife approached us, almost friendly. "Ye don' look Fa'ad. More like for'ners."

"Islanders."

"Ay! Ye picked a bad time to visit."

Flick nodded to the man's response, and we all stood silent for an awkward moment.

"Thing is, there are those we'd rather not let know we've left Mata. We've got Listeners, you see." The man jerked his head toward two men at the back of his group—the two with the most tattered clothing, one with horrible black-and-red bruises on his forehead and cheek—who'd turned their heads to the side to hear our conversation better.

"I see... And there are those we'd rather not let know we've left Fa'ad."

Flick's dragged-out remark had both men release forced laughs. "So I'm glad we didn't make your acquaintance."

We parted in opposite directions with friendly waves and didn't look back.

***

"More trouble's brewing than we thought. Listeners actually having to flee the city?"

Lin glanced around in all directions before adding to Flick's observation. "And Arne's army is bold enough to raid the main road."

I didn't respond, too distracted, caging off the pain that expanded down my back and into my head.

Are you all right? Roni signed.

I'll survive, I managed.

I did survive, but I had to walk ever so slowly that it took us more than an hour to traverse the easy two miles to the border crossing. When we crested the last hill, my breath caught finally to see the Black River. It was wider than I'd ever imagined a river could be and violent as a hurricane goddess. A lone traveler led a horse over the massive stone bridge to Mata. Less than halfway across, they already appeared tiny.

Then I saw a group of men blocking the road directly in front of the bridge. They wore belted blue pants and shirts with shiny buttons down the front, large enough for me to count even at a distance. Their tattooed heads and necks emphasized their lack of ears, and each had a long, thick metal piece hanging from their belt, which I quickly recognized as a scabbard housing a sword.

CHAPTER 29

"They'll never let us by." My forehead pounded, and my face broke out in a sweat. It was one thing to use my Knowing to influence people and another entirely to hide it while in horrible pain in front of tattooed Watchers with swords.

"Just stay calm." Lin was clearly not in pain. "Meditate. Make a cage. Breathe deep, and don't let your fear show."

I repeatedly counted to ten to the rhythm of my steps until something creaked and groaned behind me. I looked over my shoulder to see four enormous black and brown beasts—two pulling wagons and two piled with bags—and twice as many colorfully-dressed men and women.

"Traders. Good news for us! Maybe the extra traffic will keep the guards from asking too many questions." Flick seemed optimistic.

Lin squeezed my hand. *See? We'll be fine.*

I went back to counting, anyway.

Minutes later, we reached the guards. The six of them moved to block the bridge in a synchronized maneuver. The one whose shirt bore an extra row of buttons took a step forward and signed *Halt*.

I wondered why someone would waste metal to put a non-functional row of buttons on a shirt. If they wanted decoration, some embroidery would look much nicer—and certainly friendlier.

Welcome to the Matan border, he signed, scowling. *In the name of the First House of Paav, please show us your papers.*

Papers? I struggled to suppress a new wave of panic as Flick, being the eldest and most traveled of our group, approached the guard. I lost track of what was going on as his body blocked half the conversation.

The traders caught up with us then, and their beasts—horses, I realized—blessedly distracted me. They were more massive than a child's nightmare yet gentle as chicks, with velvety snouts and gorgeous brown eyes. One nudged me with her warm nose, and I reached up to stroke it, trying to absorb some of the animal's natural calm.

A Watcher—earless but not tattooed—held the horse's reins. *Sorry,* he signed with a sheepish grin.

I smiled back. *She's beautiful.*

We require you to fill out these forms and register at the Anan embassy within two days, the guard signed when I turned back. Another guard reached into his bag and produced a stack of papers. *We will need full names and backgrounds for each of you and the names and addresses of the family you are visiting. Also, we must search your party for weapons or illegal items.*

I wished I hadn't stopped petting the horse. Did we even know any names and addresses that these guards would believe? Would they pat me down like Arne's men and discover my pregnancy to be a fake? What would happen then?

Lin placed his hand on my back. *Calm down,* he thought.

I closed my eyes and caged my panic until Lin pressed me forward. A guard led us off the roadside to a clearing with a small stone building. He handed Flick a board and pen for writing and gestured for the rest of us to line up in front of him. Flick's eyes filled with worry.

Let me do the talking, Lin spoke in my mind. *I have an idea. I'll need you to pretend to faint right after I let go of your hand.*

All right.

The guard patted down Flick, then signed for him to move aside. Roni was next.

Lin let go.

"Oh!" I rolled back my eyes as I sighed and pitched sideways to fall on my uninjured left side. Lin caught me, somehow avoiding my right side, gently lowered me to the ground, and yelled to Flick.

"Flick, my wife!"

Since I closed my eyes, I couldn't see the communication between Lin, Flick, and the guards. Nevertheless, Lin sent me messages as I lay there.

Nice faint. Wait a minute to wake up. Act like you think you're going to have the baby.

Yes was all I could manage, still counting to keep my pain and panic from hitting the guards. I heard heavy footsteps approaching.

Now, Lin sent.

I fluttered my eyelids and groaned. "What happened?" I wondered if the guard who loomed above us read lips.

"You fainted." Lin's answer, laced with worry, convinced even me.

"I think the baby's coming." The guard couldn't hear me moaning, but it would look right.

I writhed on the ground as I'd seen Akilan women do in childbirth, careful not to jar my injured side. That stage could go on for hours, so hopefully, their expectation of me producing a baby wouldn't happen anytime soon. Lin stood and signed, and I couldn't make out his words or see the guard's response. I rested as if the labor pains had paused, as they do.

My most recent involvement in childbirth flooded my memory: Konu's, over three years ago. Mama insisted that I attend her, partly because she wanted me to be the first to hold my baby brother, and partly—as she admitted later—because she wanted me to witness the pain and gore of childbirth, to ward off any too-soon desire for my *own* babies.

Now I lay on the cold ground of a faraway land, pretending to have a baby much too young. I faked another labor pain by placing my hand over my mouth as if I might hurl.

The timing was good. The guard looked over at me again with a face full of alarm. *Can you sit?* he signed.

I held up a finger to sign *Wait* and kept the act going for a bit longer. *Now.*

He stooped on my side opposite Lin, and the two hefted me up to a sitting position. I cried out when the guard caught my shoulder, but he didn't realize it. *We'll try to make this fast,* he signed. *I know a midwife close to the border. I will give your husband directions.*

Despite his tattoos and sword, this man was kind. I felt oddly guilty for deceiving him. *Thank you for your help* I signed.

He smiled at me, then walked over to Flick—who furiously scribbled on the papers—and tapped his shoulder. I couldn't see their conversation, but the guard took half the papers and disappeared into the little building for a moment. He came back out with a second pen, writing.

Probably time for another, Lin sent. *Lean back onto me.*

I leaned into Lin's lap and moaned some more. Flick shot me appropriately worried looks. The guard wrote even faster.

I never did get searched. I'm not even sure the men searched all our bags in their urgency to get us across the bridge before my pretend baby would be born.

The traders behind us were halfway across the bridge by the time we were allowed to cross. Though some of the guards still looked suspicious, the one who'd helped me gave us a closed-mouth smile and signed *Good luck, and your child be blessed.*

Thank you, Lin and I both signed.

The bridge was solid and wide with wooden guardrails along both sides, but I found it terrifying, nonetheless. I leaned against Lin and distracted myself by wondering about the guards. Did they live in the city or a village? Did they also keep crops and animals, or was guarding their only job? Did they have families?

What would happen to the friendly guard if the authorities discovered him as the one to let me into Mata?

That thought hadn't even crossed my mind as I'd pretended to be in labor. I'd endangered that man simply by lying to him, maybe as much as if I'd stabbed him with one of Arne's swords. Guilt ate at my heart. Did he have children? Was he tricked into working for the Paav, or did he believe in their cause?

We were nearly across. Green fields dotted with small houses stretched on either side of the road past the bridge. In the distance, the buildings grew denser, a layer of fog, or perhaps smoke, hanging over them.

"Mata City." I was awed by the immensity of it all.

Flick laughed. "Oh, no. That's just the bigger villages."

Roni turned to me and signed. *We made it, Alesea. We're almost there.*

Though guilt, fear, and pain loomed beneath it, a goofy smile rose to my face. *I can't believe it.*

Roni smiled — the real smile that I'd been so sorely missing. *I can believe it. You...* He paused, glancing at Lin. *You did a great job back there.*

Thank you, I signed, but he'd already turned around.

***

Though Lin and Flick assured me these villages were tiny compared to the city, I already longed for the comfortable quiet of the Islands or even the *Phoemek*. All these people heading in so many directions made me claustrophobic. Worse, so many emotions clashing together hurt the insides of my head. Everyone rushed, worried about something or somebody. Were they all that unhappy, or did I feel those emotions more strongly?

A'lodi sahm. I searched for hope in my heart and, as an experiment, directed it to a pair of Double women whose voices rose in a frustrated argument as they struggled with a cart laden with unfamiliar red, round fruit.

One woman smiled and jerked the cart forward, and gave a triumphant laugh as it cleared the rut in the road.

"Sorry, my fault!" The other touched her companion's shoulder.

"What are you doing?" Lin snapped.

My face burned as I looked away. "Sorry."

Lin's emotions, of course, were once again perfectly hidden from my Knowing. "You have no idea what people will do to you... to us... if they find you out!"

"It doesn't make any sense."

His eyes softened, and he touched my hand. "I know. Just stop trying to help people because it never turns out well."

I wondered if Lin had ever tried to help people with his Knowing because how else would he know not to? My gut told me he was wrong. How could making people feel happier be a bad thing? I would have to trust his experience, though, if I wanted this mission to succeed.

***

The following morning, I caught sight of the ocean. My breath stuck in my throat, and Lin tensed at my uncontrolled burst of emotion. Miles away, the sea sparkled in the sunlight, making the land between appear dark and foreboding.

That land in between was Mata City, at last. The incomprehensible sea of rooftops and winding streets appeared, even through a looming gray fog was insurmountable compared to the tallest of Fa'ad's mountains. The temptation to cast my mind out and search for my family was so strong I wanted to run the other way.

"Mata City," Flick announced as we stopped at an overlook.

Roni watched me as I gulped down the rising lump in my throat. He looked as overwhelmed as I felt. I walked over to him, taking his hand, though Lin's eyes bored into the back of my head.

It's so big, I thought.

Enormous, he agreed. *Why would anyone want to live that way?*

I thought you wanted to... I stopped at Roni's internal flinch.

I never wanted a big city. I just wanted to be accepted. Not always have to wish I was a Double.

Love and acceptance had always been a part of my experience. Only recently had I developed the talent that Lin claimed would make me an outcast, and people were right to fear me for it.

Not Roni.

I'm sorry, I thought.

For what?

I just am.

Flick beckoned to us, and we gathered around him. He spoke quietly and signed in tiny gestures. "We'll take the second left. I don't see any guards, but I don't know what to expect at the monastery. Stay alert, and Alesea, keep up that pregnant act. You may need to pretend the baby's coming again."

I caged my anxiety and gave Flick a sharp nod. "Let's go."

There weren't any guards—no one at all— traveling on the narrow road to the monastery, so once we were past the village, our path was as deserted as Arne's road.

"Where're all the people?" Lin spoke what I was thinking, his voice sounding too loud in the quiet forest.

Why is it so overgrown? Roni signed.

"Last I was here, this road was just for the monastery. It doesn't get much traffic, and the Listeners hardly ever leave."

"That must be it." Lin's response to Flick lacked confidence.

We fell into an uneasy silence. It took another two hours to reach the monastery gates, much longer than Flick estimated. I barely kept up, dragging myself along the way.

The only other monastery gates I'd ever seen—on the island of Kuul—were largely symbolic, never locked, and easily scaled. They represented the monastic community's solitude, not a barrier to the outside world.

These Matan monastery gates were tall, solid, and functionally built, with a single entrance through the heavy fencing stretching into the forest on either side of the road. Yet they gaped open, with a fancy locking mechanism dangling from the right gate like someone had hacked at it with an axe. A crooked, weathered board containing a single unfamiliar symbol—a red hexagon inside a yellow circle—hung on the left. The paint, unlike the board, looked fresh.

Flick sucked air through his teeth. "That's not good."

"What is it?"

Flick met each of our eyes in turn. Roni and Lin looked as clueless as I felt.

"An ancient symbol. I saw it in books, on Kuul."

He forgot to translate, so I did.

What does it mean? Roni signed.

"I didn't think it'd been used since the Great War. It's a sign from the old worshippers of the Sun-goddess, the one who supposedly created Watchers. It means 'blasphemy.' "

The *A'lodi* didn't have much of a concept of blasphemy, but I knew from history books that it was a big deal in the ancient religions.

"Why is it here?" I wasn't sure I wanted to know.

Flick blinked fast and turned back to the sign. When he answered, his voice was gruffer than usual. "In the Great War, coming home to that sign on your door meant your worst nightmare awaited you inside."

CHAPTER 30

"I'll go in. Stay here, and if ya' hear anything bad, run." We stood in stunned silence with Flick's announcement.

Lin finally stepped forward. "Let me go first, but I wish I had a sword."

I gave Lin a sharp look and steeled my nerves. "I'll go."

"No."

I caged my anxiety and projected courage to the three men who spoke in unison, one in Watcher-speak. "I won't stand here while you put yourselves in danger because I wouldn't let you bring weapons. I'll go." I met Flick's eyes. "I'm my own weapon, remember?"

Without waiting for an answer, I marched through the open gate. A large, round stone building with big windows stood at the end of an overgrown cobblestone path. That would be the *meditasi*, the main gathering place for the monastery. Smaller buildings dotted the landscape on either side.

Behind me, Flick cursed, but no one stopped me.

There were windows all around the *meditasi*, many of them cracked open. I crept off the path toward one away from the door, but before I could reach it, the breeze shifted, and the stench of decay overcame me. I slapped my hands over my nose and mouth and turned to the gate where my friends watched.

I shook my head, tears already coming. There would be no one here to confront us.

***

With rags over our noses and mouths, we stood inside the doorway of the *meditasi*. For several minutes, we stared, weighted down by sorrow and fear.

Blood was everywhere—on the walls, the benches, in dried puddles in the center of the sparsely furnished room. Trails of it led to the far side, where individual blankets dark with fluids covered a dozen human-sized lumps.

My stomach heaved, and I stumbled outside, landing on my knees in the tall grass as I took great gulps of the fresh air. Lin retched behind me. Tears wet my cheeks as I looked up into Flick's kindly, weathered face, his eyes spilling over. He angrily batted at his nose and offered me a hand to stand up, but I didn't take it.

I felt as if I would drown in the sorrow and hopelessness of my friends, my heart, and those poor people who dedicated their lives to the A'lodi and helping others. What would it mean for us? We counted on these Listeners to get us into Mata City. If the Paav murdered A'lodi devotees in cold blood, what would they do to us who were trying to take back the people they'd stolen?

I curled up on my good side in the weeds, my breaths coming faster and faster, my senses sucked into the dark whirlpool of my thoughts. I grasped for hope, for the love that had brought me here, but all I could find was death and cruelty. I hugged my blanketed belly, shaking, sobbing, in pain, and half-wishing to die.

I was dimly aware of someone crouching beside me, then two warm hands cradling my face.

Alesea, Roni thought to me. *Alesea. Come back.*

I can't. My breath escaped in tortured gasps.

I felt Roni enveloping me in the calm of the island Shallows, but it was too distant, too unobtainable. I started to black out.

Then he sent a different image—one of me singing a funeral song in the moonlight over Sasha's body on Akila. I couldn't hear it, but I could feel it—peaceful, sad, and strong, a song to help the deceased on their journey between worlds, to give the living the strength to continue.

I clung to the memory like a life raft, forcing myself to hum along though my throat was so tight my voice was a tiny muffled creak. Roni took my hand and squeezed it, encouraging me. With the memory of music and Roni's deep calm, my breath slowed, and my senses cleared enough to open my eyes and look into his familiar, worried face.

He helped me to sit up, and I looked around at my tattered, loyal friends. Flick openly cried while Lin stared into the woods, shaking. As my gaze rested on each, I found myself able to detach their emotions from mine. My sorrow and fear were still heavy weights but no longer posed a threat to suffocate me.

What did you do? I thought to Roni.

He shrugged and let go of my hand.

I gave it back and held on tight for courage. I began the song aloud and allowed myself to feel the words that had comforted countless generations of my people lost to the violence of the Great War, sickness, injury, or simply old age. They were all part of the *A'lodi* — beloved, remembered, and mourned.

My friends placed their palms together, thumbs to their foreheads, in a gesture of respect for the departed.

We soaked in the silence for several minutes after I finished, our sniffling and the chirping birds in the woods the only occasional sounds. Then the breeze shifted and reminded us of the horrors inside the *meditasi*, and Lin glared at Roni's hand, again holding mine.

Thank you, I thought to Roni, and let go.

Flick cleared his throat. "I suppose we need to find another way into—"

"Shhh!" I held up my hand, and Flick's eyes went wide with surprise. "Listen."

It wasn't a sound but a feeling—a feeling of the life of another human, which meant someone else was here.

"This way." I limped toward one of the huts on the edge of the woods to the right of the *meditasi*. The feeling pulled me there in a way I couldn't explain. I could only follow, trembling with nerves but unable to stop walking.

I was only a few feet from the little hut's wooden door when it cracked open to reveal a tiny old man in monk's robes. He had no eyes in his ridged face, wrinkled and drooping with sorrow.

Someone behind me gasped in astonishment, but I kept my eyes on the man.

"Papan, we come in peace."

"You sang the ancient funeral song of the Listeners." He answered with a gravelly voice, one not used for a long time. "You *Knew* the song."

"Yes, Papan. I am so sorry for your loss."

"Who are you, who dares bring hope to an old man?" He gave a few Listener clicks as he waited for my response.

I looked to my companions, but they only offered encouraging nods. "I... we are also ones who have lost much. I am Alesea of Akila, and I bring greetings from Sofi of Kuul."

The deep grooves in his face lightened the tiniest bit. "Sofi, child? A name that is known well to me, though I've not seen her in double your lifetime. So, you are from the Islands?"

"Yes, Papan."

"You have journeyed far. Please, come sit, though there is little room for all four of you. My name is Aanuman."

We followed him into the single-room hut furnished with only a bed, a desk, a wood stove, and a stack of cushions. Flick handed us each a cushion, and we squeezed together to sit against the wall, me between Lin and Roni.

I pulled too hard on my shoulder, trying to adjust my overlarge tunic with one arm, and my suppressed pain shot down my back and all around the room.

"Ah, my child, you are hurt. What— "

"I'm fine, Papan." I slowed my breathing to offset his shock. *A'lodi sahm.* "It's nothing."

He must have believed me. He dropped the subject and lowered himself with ease to sit cross-legged on the hard floor, facing us. "I am sorry not to offer you tea, but we have been afraid to light a fire since..." He trailed off, the lines above his forehead ridge becoming deeper still.

"Papan, what has happened here?"

Aanuman clicked and sighed to Flick's query. "The darkness of men. Please, tell me your story. You must have had quite an adventure, coming here all the way from the Islands and ending up at my sad door."

So, we told him—mostly Flick and I spoke—with Lin occasionally adding a word or two. I held Roni's hand to translate the conversation in his mind.

"So," Flick ended our story with our arrival at the opened monastery gates. "The Paav are even eviler than we thought."

"Cold-blooded murderers." Lin spat in disgust.

"Ah, young men, have you strayed so far from the *A'lodi?* There are no evil men, only choices that lead to suffering and sorrow."

Aanuman's comment made Flick's brown face take on a reddish tinge, but Lin sat straight, and I felt his burst of anger before he closed it off as if snapping on a lid.

"How can you say these men aren't evil? They slaughtered your friends! They stole Alesea's family! They—"

Aanuman held up his hand, a gesture learned for communicating with a Double. "Some choices lead to evil actions, and weapons make it all the more easy to act impulsively. But the men who killed us—they were likely threatened themselves. And when my people would not follow their orders to go with them..."

"Go with them where?" Flick looked between Lin and Aanuman, clearly trying to defuse the tension.

"To the city to work, or be held captive."

"Why not leave them alone? What kind of threat could the monastery possibly pose to them?"

Aanuman folded his slim fingers and straightened his back as if preparing to teach a lesson. "Alesea, the *A'lodi* teaches that Watcher and Listener, beggar and rich man, child and elder, are all beings of the same One, filled with the same universal light, but those who torment us now have given into greed and the words of old gods. They feel threatened by anyone who sees them as equals. They would divide us as in the ancient times, ruling over those who need no ruler."

"And so they play on divisions that already exist." Lin gave a humorless laugh. "Because anyone with eyes to see knows we aren't really equal."

I shot Lin a warning look.

Aanuman chuckled. "Ah, to be young and feisty, and a Triple, at that."

Lin stiffened. "I am sorry, Papan, I didn't mean–"

"No offense taken, child. But I do hope you search your own heart. Just because you have been hurt does not mean you must continue the cycle."

Lin's nostrils flared, but he breathed deeply and remained silent. I couldn't feel his emotions, but his arm was extremely tense against mine. How had Aamuman known he was a Triple?

"Papan, Can you give us guidance?" I asked.

"If you mean advice, little one, no, but I can give you literal guidance into the tunnels under Mata."

"Tunnels!" Hope bloomed in my heart.

Lin sat forward on his cushion. "We can get into the city without passing through the gates?"

"Yes, although you must be extremely careful to keep your way secret. The other survivors now live in the tunnels, along with Listeners from around the city."

"Other survivors?" Flick sounded as if he had regained a bit of hope, too.

"Yes." Aanuman dropped his hands to his lap. "There are quite a few of us still. I'm not sure if the Watchers who killed so many last moon were unaware of our numbers or if they chose to turn a deaf ear to those not yet gathered for meditation that evening. I was one behind the *meditasi*, tending the garden."

"Are all of them in the tunnels?" I asked.

"Most are, though some are risking the city. I insisted on staying in my home. I have lived here for almost my entire life. And someone needed to watch over..." For the first time he became overcome with emotion, eye-ridge dipping toward the floor. He gulped and wiped his nose. "The lost ones."

His sorrow hit me, and I leaned toward him, dropping Roni's hand to take his. "I am so sorry, Papan." I felt for the hope he'd given me when he'd mentioned the tunnels and gently sent it his way.

Aanuman smiled. "You have a gift, child. More than I've ever felt in this lifetime. You remind me of someone."

"*This* lifetime?" Lin grunted. Of course, he was angry I'd given out my emotions.

"Who?"

Aanuman smiled at me. "A Listener, who came from Kuul to stay with us many moons past. He blessed us with his strong gift of Knowing, but yours is stronger still."

My heart skipped a beat. "Was his name Alok?"

"You know him." Aanuman beamed. "Tell me, is he well?"

I squeezed Aanuman's hand much too tightly, then I let it go. "I don't have any idea, and I don't even know him, but he's my father."

CHAPTER 31

No matter how many questions I asked, the only information Aanuman could remember about my father was that he had headed north to follow rumors of Knowers in the Matan mountains. The conversation soon turned to the logistics of our entry into the city. Aanuman fetched clean water for Lin to clean my injuries and change my bandages, then laid out a light evening meal of bread and cold lentils despite our objections that we should eat from the meager leftovers in our packs.

We waited until twilight to explore the empty huts around the monastery, taking with Aanuman's blessing anything we thought could be useful. It wasn't much, but everyone found some clothes that Flick assured us would blend into the crowd in Mata, and at the bottom of a dresser drawer, Roni found a handful of golden coins stamped *Paav*.

Guilt gnawed at us as we looted the humble rooms—I could feel it even from Lin—but Aanuman insisted that it was his gift to our mission. Regardless, I said a blessing of love and forgiveness for each unfortunate, unknown soul.

"At least keep the coins, Papan," I said when we gathered back in his hut, holding them out near his hand.

"And what would an old man who never leaves the monastery do with those?"

"Give them to the others in the tunnels? Buy food?"

Aanuman clicked and reached to close my fingers over the coins. "The others would do the same. You will need them in the city. Only Paav currency is allowed these days."

Reluctantly, I dropped the coins in my new bag, scavenged from a monk's room and small enough to hang from my left shoulder without putting any pressure on my injuries. "We will repay you and your people, Papan."

Aanuman smiled. "I do not doubt that, my child. You have already brought a wealth of hope and kindness to this old man's heart."

***

We split into the huts to get a few hours of sleep—Aanuman would lead us to the tunnel entrance just before daybreak. Despite my exhaustion, sleep would not come. Images of the bodies in the *meditasi* haunted my thoughts. Was I in a dead person's bed? I couldn't stop my imagination from creating brightly-clothed men with cruel swords and crueler eyes slicing down the peaceful monks. Whenever I started to drift off, the bodies became those of my family, and the attackers became Sinon and his crew. Sinon gripped Konu with one arm and came at me with his sword in the other, grinning a horrible close-mouthed sneer. I jerked awake and kept my eyes open until Flick knocked on the door to wake me.

"Come in."

Flick opened the door, letting in cold air and a whiff of terrible decay. He carried a dim oil lamp, which he sat on the bedside table. "Alesea, I've made a decision." He ducked his head as if embarrassed.

"What?"

"I feel the *A'lodi* has called me to help Aanuman, to bury the dead and start to rebuild the monastery."

My first feeling was one of relief. "So, he won't be alone. That's a perfect idea, Flick." Growing panic came next. Yes, Flick had been deferring to my decisions since we escaped Arne, but he was still the elder on our journey. Leaving him here meant leaving the last person I could pretend was taking care of me and that I really was in charge.

"You don't look like you think it.

I swallowed hard at Flick's candid reaction. "I do think it. It's the right thing to do."

"Well." Flick cleared his throat and kept standing there.

"I'm awake now." I stretched my good arm and found I was stiff and achy but in significantly less pain than the previous day. I swung my legs off the bed to stand, startled when I nearly stepped on Lin, who lay on the floor, blinking sleep from his eyes. I hadn't even realized he was in the room. *Hadn't he been in a hut with Roni?*

Flick cleared his throat.

"Was there something else?" I asked, pulling my eyes back to the captain.

He shook his head, then embraced me in a fierce, one-armed hug, somehow missing all my injured parts. We stood that way for a long moment. I felt Flick gifting me some of his strength and courage, and maybe I was doing the same for him.

"Alesea," He stepped back, his voice thick with sadness, "you come back. You come back, and bring Roni and Lin back too."

I stepped back and gave him the salute I'd seen his sailors use to greet him aboard the *Phoemek*. "I will, Captain. I will."

I sat back down on the bed as Flick shut the door. "I thought you were with Roni. Are you all right?"

I couldn't hide my surprise when Lin sat up. His eyes were puffy, and his cheeks streaked as if he'd been crying. Lin—the expert at caging his emotions inside and out.

I reached out to him. "Come up, Lin."

Instead, he took my hand with both of his, then pressed his forehead to my palm. His sadness and regret overcame me as he shook with sobs.

"Lin!" I tried to pull him up, but he wouldn't budge. *Lin,* I thought to him. *What can I do?* I eased myself off the bed to sit in his lap, freeing my hand to embrace him. We rocked back and forth until his shaking subsided, and he buried his face in my hair.

Aanuman could tell Lin was a Triple and possibly not as guarded as I thought. Was he caught up in all our grieving like me?

It's not that, Lin thought, hearing my mind even in his distress. *It's... I'm so sorry, Alesea. It should've been me. I just can't... I couldn't...* His thoughts broke up into a stream of emotions.

You couldn't what? Why are you sorry?

I'm sorry I'm so weak, he finally answered. *It should've been me helping you yesterday. It should've been me who rescued you from Arne. I'm not good enough for you.*

What? I didn't know what to think. *It was horrible for all of us, Lin. We all did the best we could.*

I should've followed you the moment you ran. Instead, you got shot.

But I'm fine. At least, I will be. I pulled away to look into Lin's caoro-brown eyes, still beautiful, red-rimmed, and wet. *We all did the best we could. And you came.*

I almost didn't, though, he thought. *Roni came without even thinking about it.*

But you did *come.* I brushed a loose strand of hair out of his face then because he needed to hear it even if it wasn't entirely true, *I knew you would.*

Lin's emotions were still uncaged, fluctuating wildly between confusion, regret, sadness, fear..., but as he gazed into my eyes, a stronger feeling pushed those aside. "Oh, Alesea, I don't deserve to be with you."

He kissed me as passionately as if he needed to tell me everything in the world with that kiss. As if he would never have another chance.

***

Lin, Roni, and I followed Aanuman's clicks and pops to a woodshed along the overgrown monastery wall in the near darkness. Inside was pitch-black.

"Here is the trapdoor." The creaking of rusty hinges followed Aanuman when he opened it. "The stairs are sturdy, and the first right turn will lead you to friends. I have marked this token. Give it to them, and they will know your story is true."

I made my way toward Aanuman's voice, and the old man caught my wrist and pressed a small, cool object in my hand. It felt like polished stone, marred by a series of bumps that might have been Listener-script.

"Thank you, Papan. May you be safe."

"Do not worry for me, child, but please be careful." With a click, he gripped my uninjured shoulder. "And know that the *A'lodi* is always with you."

My emotions spilled through the link created by Aanuman's hand. Hope, fear, sadness. He sucked in a breath. "Ah."

I backed away, pulling myself out of his grasp. "I'm sorry! I didn't mean to..."

Aanuman grabbed my hand. "Such a gift. Never apologize for your true self."

"Alesea!" I heard Lin hiss from somewhere below, and I wondered if he had heard Aanuman and guessed what had happened. I wasn't sure he would ever approve of a Knower sharing their "true self" with anyone but fellow Knowers.

"Be well, Papan."

I shuffled my way to the first step, and the three of us went down, down, down with painstaking slowness and no visible light. Aanuman warned us that torches were signs of enemies in the tunnels, so I kept my hand on the walls of the narrow stairwell. I cringed at the cold dampness and the bugs that skittered away when I brushed them with my fingertips. I wondered how much worse it must be for Roni. There couldn't be enough light for even a sharp-eyed Watcher. I wished I could hold his hand and talk to him, but Lin was between us.

Finally, my thin soles hit a rock as solid as the walls I touched. We made it down.

"We're here. Let's go!" Lin sounded less steady than usual.

Let's go, let's go, rang through the tunnel, and my focus returned to feeling my way further into the earth. The darkness played with my sense of space — making me claustrophobic for one moment and afraid I would drop into a vast void the next. Pressure built up in my ears, and I started to hum, stopping when I heard the shakiness in my voice.

As we continued in that black, timeless hall, something strange started happening to my Knowing as if it were growing, perhaps in response to my lost vision. I felt a pang of hunger from Roni's stomach and a burst of fear and revulsion from closed-off Lin, followed by the sound of a skittering creature. When I focused on a feeling, I heard pieces of thoughts and caught images of people and places I'd never seen.

I paused on an image from Lin's mind, fascinated. He was sitting on a stool inside some tiny building, dark but for a few thin sunbeams emerging from the cracked boards. His bare toes scratched meaningless symbols on the dirt floor.

Lin coughed, which startled me out of his mind. *Had he noticed?* He said nothing, plodding along the damp corridor.

Stop, I told myself, knowing I was treading dangerously on the edge of that which I'd promised never to do.

My curiosity won out. *Roni.* Could I reach him without touching him, with Lin in between us? My friend, deprived of his sight with no hearing to fill the void? I rationalized that he must be afraid and lonely, so I tried.

It was easy. I already knew what Roni's mind felt like, more intimately than anyone else's but mine, and found myself filled with warmth at the familiarity of it, surprised because instead of seeing Roni's thoughts, I saw through his eyes — and he *could* see a little. Moisture on the tunnel walls shone with a faint greenish light, like the glowing algae that washed up on Akilan beaches on moonless nights. Crawly things, fleeing from our footsteps, were yellow streaks, and when Roni glanced back from his position at the front of the line, our exposed faces and hands glowed red.

I don't know how long I watched through Roni's eyes, awed at the transformation of our surroundings, but the longer we walked, the more my control wavered, and my mind wandered. Soon I replayed Lin's desperate, breathtaking kiss while seeing the tunnel through Roni's eyes.

A word broke into my consciousness. *Alesea.*

Roni! I'm sorry, I...

I felt uncharacteristic anger rising in his mind, shoving against my thoughts. *Couldn't help yourself?*

No, I just...

Wanted me to know how you really felt?

No! I... I stopped, filled with guilt. I'd been too afraid to let Lin know I was in his mind—Lin, who had shown his passion for me so clearly. I contemplated why I would think it was more acceptable to intrude into Roni's mind by taking advantage of his eyesight to show him my kiss with Lin in great detail, of all things.

Something was wrong with me. No matter how much I promised to, I couldn't keep myself out of other people's most private space. Plus, I couldn't control my thoughts, which were as likely to hurt as to heal.

Maybe I should go away—far away from anyone I might hurt with my Knowing, find my father in the northern mountains, and live the rest of my life—

Something flashed red far ahead of us, bright enough to briefly light the tunnel. I couldn't tell if it was real or if I still saw through Roni's eyes. Listener clicks echoed all around me until we heard a woman's voice.

"Who goes there? Come no further without an answer!"

"Alesea, say something."

I responded to Lin's urging, my voice wavering weakly down the tunnel. "We are friends."

A cacophony of clicks. "Three of you? And your voice is unfamiliar. Explain."

"I am sorry to alarm you. I am Alesea of Akila, and Aanuman sent us. I have a token."

Multiple voices murmured before the original one rose in response. "Alesea of Akila, please approach alone, and hold out the token."

Lin squeezed my good arm as I passed, and I tripped over his foot and whispered, "sorry." Without my friends in the way, my word bounced down the tunnels—*sorry... sorry... sorry... sorry.*

I crept along the moist wall toward the voices, exposed and completely blind, not daring to reach out with my mind.

"We are here." The woman spoke so closely to me I could feel her breath on my face. I jumped, and pain stabbed through my shoulder.

I held out one shaking hand, offering the token.

She took a shuddering breath and a loud step back.

"Are you all right?" I didn't know how to address her.

"*Trekana* of the *A'lodi*." The woman spoke in a low voice.

Someone behind her, another woman, repeated the strange word, *Trekana*, as if awed by it.

"*A'lodi* bless us all," came from a male voice.

Some will think of you not as an enemy but a savior, Sofi had said.

I felt sick.

Hands grasped both of my shoulders, then released as I gasped in pain. "Alesea of Akila, *Trekana* of the *A'lodi*, you and your friends are welcome here. I am Goshi. Come, all of you come, and tell us how we can be of service."

***

The Listeners led us to a room a few minutes walk down the hall, which was quite large, judging by the echoes and Goshi's claim that over thirty Listeners made their homes in it.

As soon as I could, I took Roni's hand, careful not to probe into his mind. *Do you want me to translate?*

The pause was so long I thought he'd somehow broken the connection completely.

Yes, he finally answered.

Goshi ignored my companions and pulled me to sit on a cushion facing her. Roni and Lin sat on either side of me on the hard floor. I squirmed when Goshi called me *Mamani*, a title for the wisest female elder. I summarized the last months of my life for her and told her our mission to find my family, friends, and others stolen by the Paav.

"*Trekana*, we will help you gather more people. If we start with the outer districts, find sympathizers —"

Lin sat up a little straighter next to me, leaking a tiny bit of excitement out of his mental cage, and I knew I had to cut off the idea before it took hold and added months to our plan.

"Thank you, truly, Goshi, but we need to get to the Fisher district right away. We have an urgent message for our friends there." I hoped it was true that they were our friends. Who knew how Sasha's family would receive us, carrying tidings of her murder?

Goshi grabbed my hand in hers, tearing it out of Roni's. "*Trekana*. You will bring so much hope to my people, and all those the Paav have mistreated. We can deliver the message for you. Please, reconsider. You must stay safe."

I pulled my hand away as gently as possible, though her grip was firm. I did not want to share my thoughts with this confusing woman. "What is it you keep calling me?"

"You do not know? But Aanuman..."

"Um..." I took back Roni's hand. *They think I'm somebody else.*

"Alesea, we should consider it. If we had support in the city, we could start an uprising, defeat the Paav and get everyone back!"

"No, Lin!" I tightened my grip on Roni, hoping he at least would support me, despite my latest violation of his trust. My voice rose to a high pitch, and I didn't push it back down. "Every day without my family is a day they might suffer even more. If we start an uprising, *A'lodi* knows what the Paav will do to them before we even find them. We have to rescue them, and we have to rescue them now!"

Thankfully, Roni sent his agreement through our link. Lin sighed but said nothing.

I broke the awkward silence. "What's a *Trekana*?"

"A Triple." Lin answered quickly.

"No, not a Triple." Goshi sounded offended. "Most Triples only have the smallest amount of Knowing. A *Trekana* need not even be a Triple at all. They could be a Listener or even a..." she paused, then spat out, "a Watcher. A *Trekana* is a Knower blessed by Donya herself."

"Donya?" The goddess of the earth and of the ancient Knowers? I thought of Sofi and her fish people. Did she believe I was a *Trekana*? Surely not!

Goshi must have felt the disbelief drifting off me in uncomfortable waves. "You don't need to believe it to be true. All the Listeners and many others of the *A'lodi* will feel it and be drawn to you wherever you go. Your powers will bring us peace and freedom."

"But there are other Knowers. What makes you think I'm the *Trekana*, instead of somebody older, wiser? Someone with more control?"

I could hear the smile in Goshi's voice. "Aanuman would not have named you the *Trekana* had he not been sure of your purity of heart. The *Trekana* must have the Knowing powers of old, but even more importantly, she must have decided never to use them for harm. Control can be learned."

Lin cleared his throat, tentative this time. Something strange showed through his emotion-cloak. Fear, yes, but what else... jealousy? Of me? "It would be best not to let the Paav know you're here, then. Go to the outer districts first, like Goshi said."

I bristled and didn't try to hide it. "No! Our plan was for *me* to go, and Roni. You don't even know them! And what about that healer's daughter I promised to find as soon as I got here?"

I agree, Roni spoke in my mind.

"Thank you." I forgot myself, speaking aloud. Lin let out a soft sound between a sigh and a growl.

I didn't wait for any more arguments. "How do we get to the Fisher district from here?" I stood, pulling Roni up with me. "Or do I need to find it myself?"

CHAPTER 32

Goshi led us through tunnel after tunnel, mumbling complaints about my rash behavior between her navigating clicks as if she didn't realize I could hear her. Lin didn't speak at all.

Twice, the tunnels opened into larger spaces marked by cooler air and sounds of human activity. Each came with the waves of emotion and the strange tickle in my mind I was learning to recognize as the sensation of nearby living beings, with an occasional glow of emotion. At that moment, I wished I knew how to make it stop.

Both times, Goshi called out a strange word—perhaps a passphrase—then announced she was leading the *Trekana* into the city. Gasps and dozens of overlapping conversations joined the rising emotions, nearly suffocating me.

Breathe. A'lodi sahm, I thought over and over until we were again alone in the tunnels.

I had no sense of how much time had passed by the time a beam of light appeared through a crack far above.

I stopped, causing Lin to bump into me. He turned the collision into a careful, one-sided hug, and we stood like that for a moment, transfixed by the dust motes dancing in the light ahead.

Thank you for coming with me, I thought to him. I flashed back to the early morning. *And for kissing me like that,* I added with a spark of embarrassment.

Not like I could help it now that you're some sort of hero. He planted a kiss on the top of my head. Maybe I had only imagined that jealousy earlier. *And I could kiss you all day, every day if you wanted.*

I smiled. *You could be a hero to them, too,* I thought.

He let go.

"We have arrived. *Trekana*, you still have time to reconsider. Please."

"No, Goshi." I took a step toward the light. "Thank you for your help."

She sighed. I could finally see her outline—a woman as small as me, with a voluminous cloud of hair and a Listener's eyeless ridge in her round face. "We will be ready to help when you return. There is plenty of room in the tunnels." Then, almost reluctantly, "Please do everything in your power to keep the entrance a secret. My people depend upon it."

"I will." I rested my hand on her shoulder for a moment. She was so thin that sharp bones poked through her clothing. "Thank you."

"Bless you, *Trekana*."

Lin held up the awful fake-pregnant tunic he'd been carrying in his pack. "Time for disguises."

A'lodi sahm, I thought as he pulled it over my head. I desperately wished I could use my right arm, but nothing could be done about that. It would all be worth it. It had to be.

"Do you have your *ratina*?"

"My what?"

"You must cover your ears, now, in Mata City." Goshi's previously excited voice became flat. "Even Listeners. It's the law."

"All of us?" I had a moment of panic, wondering if we had enough spare cloth.

"No, only women."

I waited, irritated, as Lin rummaged through his bag and came up with a rag-like piece of cloth that would have to do.

I tapped Roni's arm. *Help me?* He'd been the first to ever tie one of the hateful things onto my head during my brief stint as a Watcher on the *Phoemek*.

Roni nodded and took the cloth.

I'm sorry, I sent to him as he touched my head. *Truly.*

I forgive you, he thought, though if a thought could be stiff, his was.

While Roni tied the *ratina*, Goshi told Lin the passphrases he'd need when we came out of the tunnel. A woman speaking for her husband apparently would attract too much attention in Mata City, so Lin should do all the talking. That angered me as much as the *ratina*.

Goshi led us to a narrow, twisted staircase so steep I had to keep my balance by holding the higher stairs with my good hand. We wound our way up to the source of the light, where according to Goshi, a trapdoor led to a tavern in the Fisher district. Lin went first, with me behind him— an obedient Matan wife. Roni waited for our signal.

Lin opened the trapdoor, and light flooded the stairwell. He grinned down at me before climbing the rest of the way, then extended his hand to help me up. I emerged into a dusty storeroom, little more than a closet, the light coming through a narrow window near the ceiling. I blinked at the feet, walking past the warped glass—some bare, some sandaled, in all shades of flesh. Shelves full of bottles and glasses lined the walls below the window. Deep voices rumbled somewhere nearby.

Lin lifted and lowered the trapdoor three times—the signal for Roni. Roni would come up in ten minutes and take a different route to the address where we hoped to find Sasha's family so that no one would connect us.

I squinted at the scratched but clean wooden floorboards, waiting for my eyes to adjust.

"C'mon, Alesea." Lin already had his hand on the storeroom's doorknob. "What's wrong?"

What a ridiculous question. I managed a smile, though it must have looked like a wince because he asked if I was in pain.

I shrugged stupidly, then winced for real. "Nothing I can't handle." I adjusted my blanketed belly and nodded at Lin. He creaked open the door, and we emerged into a dark corner of a nearly empty tavern.

Among the smattering of lonely customers lost in their drinks, only a grizzled older man serving ale from a barrel spared us a glance.

"How're the rooms?"

"Too small and smell like horse manure." Lin followed everything according to the script. Goshi said they rotated the answers to keep regulars at the tavern from getting suspicious, though most of the regulars were in the know anyway or too drunk to care.

The old man flung his hand out in a dismissive gesture. "Well, y'aren't goin' ta find better. You'll come back beggin' ta stay here. Hmph."

He was so convincing I nearly apologized. Fortunately, Lin grabbed my hand and steered me toward the exit. "Likely as that manure turning to roses." Lin stayed perfectly in character as he threw open the paneled door, and we walked out onto the streets of Mata City.

It was all I could do to keep myself from turning around and running straight back to the tunnels. Now I understood why Flick and Lin laughed at how overwhelmed I was in the villages.

I could barely see the sky. Every building was multiple stories, with clothing lines and other contraptions stretched between them, high above the narrow street. A huge gray horse pulled a wagon towards us. Crowds of hunched and bedraggled people scurried out of its way, their bright clothing belying their defeated posture. Even the children kept their eyes on the street as they walked, dragged along behind women carrying heavy loads and wearing *ratinas*. The air stank of urine and rotting garbage, and a quartet of crows screamed from a single scraggly tree. Someone shouted nearby, but hardly anyone spoke or looked at anyone else.

Look down! Lin spoke into my mind, linked through our joined hands.

This is horrible! Look at those people, I thought, looking down to find myself standing in a brownish puddle. Other people's emotions—exhaustion, hopelessness, fear—were descending on me like a dense fog.

Just close yourself off and walk, he said. *We don't have far to go.* He put his arm around my shoulders, taking care not to put any weight on my injured one, and led me away from the horse and wagon down the street that appeared to stretch forever.

Somehow, Goshi's muddled directions led Lin through several zig-zagging turns to a splintery sign that read "Thera St. Apartments." We turned into the little alley by the aging wooden building and found the third door.

"Here we are. Go ahead, knock."

My whole body shook. I couldn't remember feeling so nervous the entire journey—our whole mission could fail right now if Sasha's family decided to report us instead of helping us. I'd never had to deliver such bad news in my life, but we owed it to Sasha. Without her help, we wouldn't have made it at all, and without local guides, we might never find my family.

"Hurry up, Alesea. There are guards everywhere!"

Lin's warning sent me into a new wave of trembling. There were? How did he know, or had I walked right past them without recognizing them?

Lin reached past me and tugged the Watcher flag string twice.

"I was about to." My words came out childish.

With barely a pause, the door opened a crack, a metal chain pulling tight at eye level to keep it from opening further. A man's weathered brown face peered at me from far above the chain. He was earless though he didn't have tattoos or the enormously wide eyes of the Paav.

We are friends, I signed. *Sasha told us to come here.* I spelled out the name, having no idea what Sasha's personal name sign might be, even though I realized it made me seem like a liar. I had to take the risk.

The man made a choking sound and took a step back. *Sasha?* he signed what I assumed was her name sign. *Where is she? She's alive?*

Why hadn't I planned this out better? *I'm sorry,* I replied. *She died near my home months ago. But she...* Someone shouted near our alley, and I jumped. *May we come in?*

His face went blank, and he stared at us for a long moment, taking in our worn sandals, mismatched clothing, and ears. Then, he nodded.

The door closed, the chain rattled, and the man let us in. He calmly closed the door behind us, fell to a nearby cushion on the floor, put his face in his hands, and wept.

A tall girl dressed in sunny yellow rushed into the room. "Who are you? Papa!" She knelt beside the man, shoving away books and papers that littered the floor, and pulled one hand away from his face. *What happened?* she signed.

He gestured at the two of us, then again covered his tear-streaked face.

The girl pulled herself up to her full height — the braided pile of sleek black hair on top of her head making her seem even taller — and glared at us. She looked me up and down, forehead crinkling when her eyes reached my fake-pregnant belly. "Who are you, and what have you done?"

I pressed my palms together and gave a shallow bow as if addressing an adult, though she didn't look any older than me. "I am sorry. I bring news of Sasha, whose last instructions sent us to you."

The girl's eyes widened. "Last? Is she... gone?"

I bowed my head. "I am sorry. She is."

When no answer came, I lifted my head. Her wide brown eyes filled with tears, but she remained standing, tall and calm. "Tell me what happened."

Her father lifted his head and wiped away the tears. *Please, sit,* he gestured. He faced the girl and made a gesture I didn't recognize — perhaps her name — followed by, *Bring some tea.*

"Oh, there's no need —" The girl left before I finished what I had to say.

Lin and I found cushions between the books scattered all about the floor and stacked against the walls, most looking like histories — some of the Great War, others of the old religions. A well-worn copy of *The Book of the A'lodi* rested on a small table between two candles in the center of the room. It was hard to drag my eyes away from the titles to look at the sad man across from me.

My daughter is stronger than me he signed when I met his eyes. *She never expected to see her mother again. But I...* His hands fell in his lap.

Is your daughter Yalene? I signed, spelling out the name.

Yes. She is Yalene, he said, showing us her name sign. *I am Juhani.* He glanced around the room at all the books. *I am sorry for the mess. Sasha would never have let my research take over the house like this.*

Yalene returned with a stack of cups and teapot and served each of us a steaming cup of tea, dark and full of unfamiliar scents, then took a cushion.

"How did you know my mother?" she asked, translating for her father. "Did she escape from prison, or did you?"

I shook my head and sat down my tea. I spoke out loud and awkwardly translated with my free hand, following Yalene's lead. "The Paav were using her as a translator. I am from Akila of the Village Islands, and she saved my life."

Yalene gasped. "The Village Islands! Mama had never even been so far as Ana!"

And the boy? Juhani signed, looking at Lin. *How did you know her?*

"I did not, Papan," he spoke politely, translating as we had. "I met Alesea after she left the Islands."

Yalene raised an eyebrow and gave a pointed look at my belly. "What, the next day?"

Lin, to my surprise, laughed. "It's only a disguise." He must have already decided to trust her. In what, five minutes? It took him weeks to trust me.

Oh, please, Lin spoke in my mind. I hadn't even noticed his hand on my arm. Would I ever be able to keep my thoughts secret as he did?

I covered my embarrassment by launching into the story of the Paav coming to my island, telling them how Sasha had slipped me the sharp seashell that allowed me to escape. I spoke of the note Sasha had left for Roni, telling us that Juhani and Yalene would help us if we ever reached Mata City. I didn't mention finding Sasha's body, the glassy opened eyes, and the pool of blood that sent me retching.

The first murdered person I'd ever seen, but not the last.

All because of the Paav.

I stopped and reined in my anger, counting my breaths. *A'lodi sahm.* Fortunately, Juhani and Yalene didn't seem to have noticed as they exchanged a lightning-fast conversation in Watcher-speak.

"Did anyone follow you here?" The sharpness had returned to Yalene's voice. "You should've told us you were fugitives right away!"

"I don't think so."

"Definitely not." Lin confirmed my answer.

Yalene didn't look convinced, but Juhani gave her a warning glance. *Why did they come all the way to the islands?* Juhani signed. *Why would they travel so far for slaves?*

"They certainly have no trouble kidnapping their pick of workers from the outer districts," Yalene agreed, "and here they can keep them from running away by threatening their families."

I took a sip of tea to quell my growing nausea. It was sweet and spicy and more delicious than it smelled. My stomach still twisted into a ball. "Our forest." I sat the cup back down so I could translate. "They wanted the *kreo* wood. So they took my people, and now they're taking the forest."

"*Kreo* wood! That's where it came from?" Yalene reached into the folds of her tunic and produced a tiny wooden bird.

I lurched forward at the sight of the deep red, polished *kreo*. "Where did you get that?"

Yalene seemed taken aback by my strong reaction. "In the market, near the Paav district. They were practically giving these away, trying to get the rich Watchers to make orders for *kreo* furniture." She passed me the figurine from her slender, long-fingered hand.

It was beautifully carved, with feathery details on its open wings and a wide tail. I held it to my nose and inhaled the scent of my island — the scent that never should have left it.

I squeezed my lips together, trying not to cry.

"You can keep it."

Thank you, I signed to Yalene, though I could feel her reluctance.

Someone knocked on the door, and all but Juhani jumped, though he did look up at the feathered Watcher flag as it started to swing.

"It's probably Roni, our friend."

"There's another one?" Yalene snapped at me.

Hide, just in case, Juhani signed.

Yalene gestured for Lin and me to follow her to the back of the apartment. We crouched behind cabinets in the tiny kitchen, and Juhani answered the door.

I strained my ears toward the front room but could hear nothing except for my breathing. Footsteps approached our hiding spot after an eternity.

Yalene peeked over the counter. "It's okay. It's your friend."

I stood too quickly, jolting my shoulder and knocking my head against the edge of the countertop.

I let out a yelp, and at Yalene's dramatic cringe, I realized I'd let my pain overflow from my mind. If she hadn't already figured out that I was a Knower, she had now.

Roni stood just inside the door, his usual steady expression replaced with a worried frown. I ran to him but stopped short of grabbing his hand. *What's wrong?* I signed.

I found Itu.

CHAPTER 33

With all the air knocked out of me, my emotions flew around the room. Yalene and Juhani backed away, looking terrified.

Right then, I didn't care. *What? Where? What's he —*

Itu's being forced to work as a street messenger, running their errands. He couldn't stop for long. He called me 'Sir' like I was a cursed Paav. Then Roni inexplicably smiled, throwing my emotions into even more turmoil.

What is it?

He was on a bicycle! He'd always wanted to try one.

I couldn't remember how to sign Watcher-speak, baffled at the thought of my brother on a bicycle.

Lin looked between the two of us. "So, he's just... biking around Mata City?"

"Why doesn't he run away?" I wondered if Itu could have been in a position to save my family all along.

Roni shook his head. *They've threatened to hurt people if he runs away. Brahn and Lori are working in the fields. Your mother... your mother is in jail, and Sinon has Konu.*

"Mama is in jail? And wait... *Sinon* has Konu? Here, in Mata?"

Itu said so. I didn't have time to ask.

It made no sense, yet my brothers were all here! *Where is he now? When can I see him?*

A guard was coming, and he raced off. I didn't even get to tell him you were here. But he said he's with the violet house, wherever that is.

Someone's name?

"That's a Paav family house." Yalene looked uncomfortably between us when she spoke. "The pure families each have a color. You know, they always wear the same color robes."

I didn't know, but now I had another clue about finding Sinon. Blood red.

Who's violet? Yalene signed to her father.

Juhani made an unfamiliar name-sign, and Yalene winced. "Bannen. They're really into Paav 'purity.' I'm not surprised they've started keeping slaves. They're some of the wealthiest merchants, so they can afford it. And bicycles."

Itu, on a bicycle, here. At that moment, I realized something I hadn't even admitted to myself—I'd half-thought my family would all be dead by now, but no.

Itu, Konu, Brahn, Lori, Mama—even if she was in jail—they were all alive. They were here, in the same city as me.

"I wonder why your mother's in jail instead of working the fields," said Yalene.

I pictured my mother as I'd last seen her, radiant in her Solstice clothes and strong as anyone I knew. "She probably said no, or maybe they thought she was too famous for putting in the fields. Everybody loves her. Why was your mother in jail?" I regretted the question before it was out of my mouth, knowing what had happened to Yalene's mother, but she didn't seem bothered. Instead, she gave a little smile.

"She danced with music in the Paav district." Yalene proudly translated for Roni. Juhani looked away.

"What?" I must have misheard her.

"My mother was famous, too. A dancer. She had the audacity to bring a musician with her to perform in a Paav house instead of coming alone."

"That's it?"

Yalene nodded. "She knew it was against their laws. But she wanted to make a statement, and I was supposed to go with her."

I've never been so grateful for a sprained ankle, Juhani signed.

"Are you a dancer too?"

Yalene glanced at her father, then became suddenly interested in her feet. "I was. Now Papa will barely let me out of the house. Technically, we're in hiding, but it must not be very good if Mama gave you our address."

Her sadness reached me then, but a complex mix of pride and anger, wistfulness and determination mingled with her sorrow.

"I'm a musician. Maybe we can be rebels together."

***

I wanted to run straight to the Paav district and find my brothers that instant, but even I recognized how foolish that would be, starving and exhausted, and I imagined Lin and Roni were too. Juhani was dead set on feeding and hosting us overnight. As little as I wanted to admit it, it took all my willpower to cage the pain in my shoulder.

We spent the rest of the day in the little living room, learning more about Juhani's and Yalene's lives, the current state of Mata City, and the Paav takeover.

I can't even imagine living through that Roni signed after Juhani reeled off the statistics from the plague—one in four Matan citizens dead in a matter of months, the vast majority from the farming community and the poorer city districts. *No wonder the Paav took over so easily.*

Juhani nodded sadly. *The Paavden family—the one that claims the monarchy—spread rumors that the Listeners had brought the plague. They covered up any Paav deaths and claimed that 'Thera's bloodline' was immune, proof of their divine right to rule.* He shook his head in disgust. *By then, most of the city would've done anything for clean water and a loaf of bread.*

In the silence that followed, I scanned the titles of Juhani's books. Many were about religion and history while others were collections of folk tales and works of art. "Did you say you were a scholar?"

Juhani perked up immediately. *Yes,* he signed. *I don't want to bother you with too many questions about the Islands and the A'lodi as it is practiced there, but I do study the history of religion, how the stories of the old gods intersect with the practices of—*

Yalene interrupted the pending lecture. "Papa was one of the most popular professors at the university. Last year, the Paav forbade the study of religions other than the old gods, and they disbanded his department."

Juhani looked so sad and wistful after Yalene's explanation that I couldn't help myself. "I'd be happy to tell you anything you'd like to know, Papan, though I'm probably not the best source."

Yalene rolled her eyes, but the corners of her mouth also quirked up a little when she met my eyes.

Lin laughed. "Not the best source? Alesea is practically made of the A'lodi. She wouldn't let us fight back against armed soldiers, for Luna's sake."

She didn't 'not let' us do anything, Roni signed sharply. *She was right to refuse weapons.*

I hope you will allow me to write these things down, Juhani signed, looking excited by every one of our words. *I've never met anyone from the Village Islands, at least not anyone I could talk to about the A'lodi.*

Of course, Papan, I signed.

"How did you get hurt? By not fighting back?"

Yalene's questions made Lin snort with laughter or maybe exasperation.

"By running away, actually." I glared at Lin halfheartedly. "I got shot in the back."

Yalene's skepticism neared anger. "And *still* you won't fight back?"

Papan. I turned to Juhani, desperately trying to change the course of our conversation. *Have you ever heard of a* Trekana? I finger spelled the word, not knowing its Watcher-sign.

"A what?" Yalene asked, but Juhani's eyes grew even brighter.

Yes, where is it... He turned to a stack of books behind his cushion, skillfully pulled a book from the center of the pile—*The Listener Diaspora*—and thumbed through it.

Ah, here. Juhani sat the book on his lap to sign with both hands. *A Trekana is a rare person of any race with a deep devotion to the A'lodi, a commitment to love and peace at all costs, and a sense of Knowing strong enough to provide hope, love, and protection to all his or her people. Some groups of Matan Listeners have developed the belief that a* Trekana *is a person sent to them by the moon goddesses in times of greatest need.*

I shuddered, wishing I had kept my mouth shut. Everyone stared at me.

Why do you ask? Juhani finally signed.

Roni watched me with neutral curiosity, but Lin shot me a sharp warning. He was right—I wanted to trust these people, but I had to stop acting so naive. "Just something I heard."

Except it was too late.

"You're a Knower?"

I gulped hard at Yalene's accusation. "Yes."

"And you said the fugitive Listeners somehow helped you into the city?"

Yalene, Juhani signed, but she ignored him.

"And you wouldn't fight back, even when they attacked you?" Her voice rose with emotion. "You wouldn't let your friends use weapons, even in self-defense? You're not just a Knower. You're a *Trekana*, aren't you?"

"I don't know. I..."

Yalene, Juhani signed again, but this time reaching his hands out in front of her face so she couldn't ignore him, *these three have been through so much to get here. At least allow them a meal before your interrogation.*

That did not appease Yalene, however. "What if the Listeners are telling everyone their *Trekana* has arrived? What if someone saw her come here?"

"They didn't, and the Listeners are more scared of discovery than anyone else." Lin's assurance restored a bit of calm to the room.

We are all safe here, for now, Juhani signed after a few moments. *The Listeners would never give away their* Trekana *if that's what she is. The guards will not come.*

The guards who had taken away Sasha and had driven Juhani away from his university job? I felt stupid. Of course, Yalene wouldn't be happy hosting a wanted fugitive, even if we were on the same side.

"But—"

Yalene! Juhani's sign was like a punch in the air.

"I'd better start some dinner."

I felt the pain leaking from her defeated statement and wished I had never put her in this danger. "I'm so sorry about your mother, Yalene."

She nodded, blinking back tears.

***

It was still dark when I woke to someone tapping a rhythm on my head. *Yalene.* I painfully jolted upright on the sleeping mat she had set up for me in her room.

"What is it?" I wondered if she had come to kick me out while her father was asleep?

She held a finger to her lips. "I have an idea for getting close to the Paav district without catching anyone's attention, but it has to be this morning."

"What? Why?"

"It's the double new moon."

"Huh?" I rubbed the sleep from my eyes with my right hand, my arm unbound for sleeping. Pain sparked through my back like lightning.

Yalene sucked in air as she felt it, too, but she didn't back away. "You're too hurt."

"No! I'm not. It's because I just woke up." I had not come all this way to fail my brothers because of a stupid man with a sharp arrow. *Why are you suddenly helping me,* I wanted to ask but thought better of it. "What's your idea?"

I couldn't make out her expression in the dark. "The Paav have started this ritual. They claim it's an ancient celebration of Thera defeating the two moons. It's only three times a year, and I think it's this morning."

"How does that help us?"

"Women and children run around throwing flower petals on everyone's doorstep. They started that in the Paav district, but last spring, they spread out all over the city and made all their slaves throw the petals, too, trying to convert everybody to Thera worship."

"And it could help me into the Paav district?"

"If you dress like a slave and we find some flower petals for you to throw, I think it would work."

"What about Roni and Lin? How will I get them in?"

She glanced towards her shut bedroom door. "You won't, not now. Men with ears, like your friends, attract too much attention." She paused as if waiting for me to picture Roni and Lin. "But a small girl with braids and a *ratina*, and especially if you keep that pregnant belly on, they won't bother you. They'll assume you're some high-ranking Paav's little plaything, throwing flowers as he told you to."

I cringed at her frank explanation but found myself nodding. "I hope they believe that. They won't want me to go alone."

"They can't stop you if you don't wake them up."

I wavered for a moment between relief and suspicion. Was Yalene trying to get rid of me? No. This was Sasha's daughter, and I may have never made it off Akila without Sasha. I had to trust her.

"All right."

Yalene proclaimed the clothing I already had as slave-worthy and took the risk of loaning me a violet *ratina* out of her large collection, hoping I could get close to the violet house with that on my head. Minutes later, we snuck out her window into the extra-dark alley behind her apartment.

I breathed deeply and caged my pain as I maneuvered through the small opening, feet first, but with my right arm tied up again, I couldn't quite grip the windowsill as I came out the other side. I fell onto the ground with an agonizing bump. Yalene squeaked, and this time I was sure I knew why.

"I'm sorry. I'm learning to control it, but sometimes I just can't."

"Hush! Don't speak of it!" She reached a hand down and pulled me up by my good side. Her beautiful face looked like a bare skull in the light from a single, dim street lamp.

"Why can't I? It's who I am."

"Why don't you just read my thoughts to find out?"

"I can't read your thoughts. Even if I could, I wouldn't." I snapped at her too loudly, jerking my hand out of hers.

"Are you sure?"

"Yes!" I hoped it was true.

Yalene's face fell. "I'm sorry. I've never met a real Knower. I've been taught all my life not to trust..."

"Don't worry about it. Let's go!"

She didn't move. "I don't really think you're like that. And... and I don't know if I agree with you about not fighting back, but it should never have made me so angry. You're right, it's who you are. I spent all night trying to get up the courage to wake you for this."

I felt the sincerity in her words. "I really am sorry for putting you in danger, and thank you for helping me."

"My mother trusted you, and you were right to come here." Yalene straightened her dull grey *ratina*, then handed me an empty shallow basket. "For the flowers. Let's go."

CHAPTER 34

Fear melted to wonder as Yalene led me out of her overcrowded, stinking neighborhood onto a wide road cutting straight downhill to the docks. The salty ocean breeze cleared the stench and gave me the courage to raise my eyes and soak in the view, the yellow street lamps giving way to a grey light spreading across the cloudy sky. In the distance, I could make out the silhouettes of dozens of fishing boats dwarfed by several tall ships to the west.

"Stop gawking!" She kept her voice low as she took my hand and pulled me along the road until I reluctantly ducked my chin and watched my boots plod along the cobblestone. I gritted my teeth and did my best to cage my emotions, afraid of how she might react if I accidentally spoke to her through our linked hands.

Fortunately, she let go as we passed a slow-moving procession of women chattering in a mix of spoken words and Watcher-speak. I was relieved to see she'd been right—looped around most of their arms were baskets like mine, full of flower petals.

Yalene gathered a handful of petals that had dropped out of their baskets and dropped them into mine. "The Paav district is where the tall ships are." She barely moved her lips. "The most important people, the actual Paav families, live right in the center near the water. It's all gated off. Look, you can see the violet house from here because it's huge."

I dared to stop for a moment to see. I couldn't make out colors in the dimness, but I saw a sprawling house twice as big as its neighbors, standing in the middle of a huge grassy lawn. *Was Itu there, right now?* My heart raced at the thought.

She urged me forward. "Your Sinon is probably somewhere in there too. What's his color?"

"Red."

"Hmm. Not sure I've seen the house." We walked for a few minutes in silence before she spoke again. "We'll look least suspicious for now heading to the markets down by the water, but there will be more guards there, too."

Yalene pointed out a few other landmarks—the university, the newly restored ancient temple to Thera, the tailors' district—until I jerked my head up to a popping sound in the distance. Red sparks danced in the sky near the docks with the tall ships.

I gasped. "Fireworks!" I'd seen pictures of them in a book about the innovations of the great cities, along with bicycles and plumbing.

Yalene burst my wonder bubble. "Don't let on you can hear them! It's how the Watcher guards call for help. They're not a good thing, not anymore."

Had the Paav ruined all the wonders of the world?

"We're about to pass some guards now. Don't look."

I looked. Two head-tattooed men—one showered with flower petals sticking in his hair and shoulders—stood across the road from us, nodding at the few passersby. They almost looked friendly, but scabbards hung on their belts, and both had those useless metal buttons on their jackets. I lowered my gaze.

"Oh, good people, please have mercy on an old woman." The creaky voice, so close, nearly made me jump out of my skin. A shadowy lump of cloth inches from my feet shifted, revealing the forehead ridge and oversized ears of an elderly Listener.

"Maman." I leaned toward her with opened palm to give the touch-gesture of welcome.

"Stop it!" Yalene jerked my arm away so hard my good shoulder nearly popped out of its socket. She dragged me away, grumbling. "Don't talk to Listeners! Especially crazy ones!"

"I'm sorry, Maman." I sent the happiest thoughts I could muster her way.

"*Trekana! Trekana!* You are here, here at last." The woman's voice rose to a high-pitched shriek, and I glanced back to see her throwing off her blankets and groping around as if to find me in the air. "*Trekana*, come back!"

A Paav guard standing at the next lower street corner marched toward the woman. He couldn't have heard her, but now she was making a spectacle.

A'lodi sahm, I thought, swallowing down my fear. Would the guard help her, or was she in trouble?

Yalene's whisper was pure ice. "How did you even make it off your island without getting killed?"

"I was trying to help an old woman." I risked a glance back and wished I hadn't. The flower-covered guard held the Listener's arm with one hand, and a big stick—a club—in his other. My stomach dropped. "What's he doing? What crime did she commit?"

"The crime of being homeless and a Listener." Yalene's eyes sparkled with tears behind her fierce expression. "It used to be different, before the plague."

Behind us, the old woman wailed, and it took every ounce of willpower to keep my anger under control. I couldn't look up, certainly not at Yalene.

What had I done? Hot tears spilled down my cheeks onto my fake belly and to the pristine road beyond—a road free of poverty and illness and marred only by the occasional dropped flower petal.

I hated that road, and I hated Mata City. I also hated those guards for being so cruel. I could still hear the old woman's screams of pain from two blocks downhill.

A *Trekana* was no blessing on the people like Goshi had claimed. I was nothing but a curse.

***

"Grouper, just caught!" "Codfish, fresh or pickled!" "Shrimp, a bucket for two silver coins, going fast!"

The fish market, already crowded at the break of dawn, felt more like home than anywhere I'd been in moons. I'd helped my brothers at the fish market on Kokka a few times when their catch had exceeded the needs of our little village, and despite the strange accents and the booths that seemed to sprawl for miles, this place seemed familiar and safe.

A pair of bicycles paused at the next stall as Yalene bargained for a bag of shellfish. *Itu!* One rider was a boy as blonde as the Fa'ad—a light Watcher with half-formed ears—and the other was a dark-skinned girl with a bright blue *ratina*. She met my eyes, and I jerked my chin down.

"Let's get you some more petals." Yalene led me west into a still-waking section of the market. Two booths selling flowers, however, were swarming with dully-dressed women and children carrying baskets like mine. She handed me a small coin and pushed me forward.

Everyone seemed to be buying the same thing—a single bunch of yellow flowers—so I pointed at one and completed the transaction with the Watcher flower vendor without a word spoken or signed.

Yalene whispered to me as she helped me pick apart the flowers. "From here, walk straight along the market all the way to the Paav district. You'll be able to see the gates around the family houses from the road. You already know where the violet house is, and it can't be that hard to find red in there. Good luck." She turned as if to leave me there.

"Wait!"

She stopped walking, but kept her back to me as she pretended to examine the vegetables at a just-opened produce booth.

I messed with the petals in my basket until all eyes had turned away, then slowly approached Yalene. "You aren't coming with me?"

She shook her head, almost imperceptibly. "I can't do that to my father. Losing Mama nearly broke him. Besides, there are people who might recognize me."

"But what about Roni and..." I trailed off, feeling ashamed. Yalene had brought me here, which was already a big risk.

"Your boyfriends will be fine. I'll look out for them. Go find your brothers."

My boyfriends. I'd felt no malice in her words, only sadness. "You're right. Thank you for helping me."

We faced each other awkwardly. "Alesea?" It was the first time she had said my name. I looked into her *caoro*-brown eyes, so similar to Lin's.

She smiled, just a little. "I'm sorry I... judged you so much. Good luck. I hope you find them."

I smiled back. "Thank you, Yalene. I will, and I'll be back before you know it."

***

Blending in with the slaves was disturbingly easy. I tagged along with a group of brown and grey-clad women with flower baskets, walking in the direction Yalene had indicated. No one questioned my presence. They didn't speak a word, aloud or in Watcher-speak, as we walked a dozen blocks through deserted market stalls. I didn't dare reach out too strongly with my Knowing, but I couldn't help taking in their feelings of sullen resignation.

I kept my eyes downcast, only risking occasional glances up to get my bearings. Finally, we turned right and walked uphill until we reached a massive iron gate set in an extravagant tall fence that seemed to go for blocks in either direction.

A tattooed guard with a many-buttoned jacket nodded at us and opened the gate from the inside. Just like that, I was in the Paav district.

So far, it was the most beautiful place I'd seen in Mata City. The road turned to smooth white stone, sparkling even in the early dawn light. Meticulously landscaped paths branched off either side of the road, meandering over grassy lawns to reach opulent homes of every color, and on every doorstep, flower petals.

People started breaking off from my group onto the small paths. I slowed my pace to watch one of them scatter a handful of petals in front of a door, then disappear around the corner of the house.

All I had to do was find the violet house, scatter petals, and locate Itu, or at least a sign of him. I had to. I walked and walked, sweaty and short of breath from the continuous incline.

As my last companion turned off the road, I saw another enormous gate looming. I'd gone all the way to the far end of the Paav district and missed the violet house. I turned right and tossed a handful of petals toward the nearest door as I followed a path along the north side of the barrier.

I was almost out of petals. I glanced around, then crouched and ripped a handful of small white flowers out of the dirt next to the path. It wasn't enough to refill my basket, but at least it was something.

Now I was only miming throwing petals at each home, feeling increasingly desperate as the sky brightened to full daylight, and I still saw no trace of the violet house. The houses weren't as large here, though their colorful paint was just as bright and fresh as the bigger homes to the south. Trees towered higher over the roofs with a stone wall that held remnants of an ancient-looking one. Perhaps this was an older part of the district.

The eastern fence glinted ahead of me—it seemed this path would take me straight to it. How large was this place? I had no idea how long the slaves would be expected to keep tossing petals at doorsteps instead of doing their usual work, but it couldn't be for much longer. Paav families were starting to come out of homes, clad in colors that matched the paint on their walls. Not far away, two children grabbed handfuls of petals from their porch and threw them at their parents, who started laughing in that strange, close-mouthed way of the Paav.

I swallowed down my rising anxiety. How long did I have before I would have to hide, or leave?

With only two small houses between me and the fence, I paused and rested my hand on my fake belly to give myself an excuse for catching my breath.

The sprawling house Yalene had pointed out from so far away had been near the eastern part of the district. If I continued south from here, I should run into it or close, and that enormous grassy lawn would be hard to miss.

I continued toward the eastern fence, heartened, and reached into my basket for petals for the last house on this path, the one in the farthest northeast corner.

I froze and suppressed a burst of excitement and fear. Aside from a pristine white front door, solid blood-red paint covered the walls.

CHAPTER 35

Don't be stupid! Don't be stupid! I forced my feet to keep walking and threw a few real petals at the front steps of the red house. No wonder Yalene hadn't known where it was. It was one of the smallest I'd seen in the district, and shade trees towered over it from all sides except for the one I faced.

Besides the blood-red color, the house looked sweet and inviting. Plus, it looked very easy to climb over the fence using one of those trees.

I couldn't go after Konu now, not without finding Itu first. Even though it was horribly wrong, Konu had seemed safe—even happy— with the blue-eyed man in Ana. Surely he would be all right for a few more hours or even days.

I did the responsible thing for once and kept walking.

Halfway down the long hill and the sun well above the horizon, I found the huge lawn Yalene and I had seen from the road. Part of it seemed to be a public park, with several families walking along paths through the greenery. Men and women in the brownish-gray slave clothing swept sidewalks and trimmed hedges. Two guards signed to one another near the road on the far side. No one held flower baskets anymore, but I had to risk crossing that wide-open space anyway because the back of the violet house loomed on the other side.

I slumped over my blanketed belly like a defeated slave and shuffled along a rocky path that cut through the park. I didn't dare turn to look at the guards, but no one stopped me.

The violet house dwarfed even the most ostentatious elders' houses on Kokka. Trying to enter it directly seemed like a terrible idea since it probably was full of family and servants. *Slaves.* So, I plodded along until I reached a path that would take me around the side of the house, hoping for a miracle.

As I turned onto the new path, I heard male voices coming from what I'd thought was a storage shed — a small building painted the same violet as the mansion. Leaning next to its door were two bicycles.

Of course! They wouldn't put their messenger boys in the main house, which filled me with triumph.

A'lodi sahm, don't be stupid, A'lodi sahm... I couldn't ruin this now with my uncontrolled emotions. I scanned the area for any sign of observers, caged my nerves, then crept to the shed's single little window.

Two men sat on cushions, eating. The one closest to me had an unfamiliar profile, but the one with his back to me had a single, sleek black braid — an Islander's braid.

It was Itu, I was sure of it. My excitement flared, and I stepped away from the window to take deep breaths until I could cage it.

I knocked on the door.

The man who opened it looked to be about Itu's age, with a stubbly beard, squinty eyes, and long, loose hair that was either wet or very greasy. "Who're you?" he spoke and signed, eyes wandering up and down my body, taking in my pregnant belly and dirty *ratina* with obvious disgust.

"Is Itu here?"

"Really?" He showed no signs of moving.

"Yes. Really!"

He laughed — a teasing laugh. "Island boy!" he called loudly, though he didn't need to, given the size of the space. "Your whore is here!"

Enough. I shoved past him just in time to see Itu rising from his cushion.

Itu. All the breath left my body at the sight of my brother's face, different yet still so familiar. He'd grown a beard fuller than his scruffy roommate's. He seemed an inch or two taller and had more angles and more muscles.

The color drained from his cheeks, and he blinked and blinked as if I might be a vision or a ghost. "Laysi," he whispered.

"Itu, it's me!" My heart started beating again, and I rushed forward to embrace him with my one good arm.

"Laysi!" He opened his arms wide and then stopped short, his eyes on my belly. "What... Who did that to you? And your face!" His voice rose to a shout. "What happened to your arm?"

"Shush, *Pipan!*" The other man's warning came with a jerk of a ratty curtain over the window.

"It's a disguise!" I half-laughed, half-cried. "A blanket." I closed the distance between us and threw my arm around him. "But watch my right side, that's real."

Itu squeezed my left half so hard I could barely breathe.

It was the best feeling ever, despite my throbbing shoulder and ribs and the heat spreading down my back. Tears poured from my eyes; Itu sobbed into my hair as he held me.

My brother was here, safe, healthy, and whole. I'd made it halfway around the world and found my brother.

I wanted to stay like that forever, but my emotions struggled to escape like wasps from a crushed hive. It wasn't fair. Why did I have to be so dangerous, even when I was so happy?

"You were dead, Laysi. Dead!" Itu pushed me away to examine my face as if looking for signs of resurrection.

"Turns out I'm hard to kill." I felt myself grinning like a madwoman. "I missed you so much, Itu. I thought you might be dead, too."

"I can't believe you're here." He kissed the top of my head and hugged me some more. "Oh, Laysi, I thought I'd never see you again."

For just a moment, I could pretend we had never left Akila, that as long as I kept holding onto my brother, the world would be right again.

Just then, the greasy roommate butted in. "Well, this is very sweet, but we need to figure out what to do with her."

"Oh, shut it, Hector!" Itu switched from crying to giddy laughter. "This is my baby sister. My sister! She's here, she's alive!" He didn't let go, but he loosened his grip enough for me to glare at Hector.

"The Knower, yeah." Hector finally smiled a real smile, though his eyes were wary. "I wouldn't believe it if I couldn't feel her from over here, ever since she saw you."

So, Itu had told Hector that I was a Knower. Had I been the last person on Akila to find out?

Itu motioned to a stained cushion. "Sit and tell me everything, Laysi. Did Roni get you here somehow?"

I felt a stab of resentment at the assumption. After all I'd been through to find him, how could he think I would still be that naive Island girl, singing and weaving seagrass mats all day? "We worked together, and I brought myself. It's a long story."

Itu smiled. "Roni, of all people. He'd have given anything to—"

Hector lifted the curtain to peek out a corner of the window."The Captain's got to be by any second now, *Pipan*. It's only the holiday making him late."

"The Captain?" I had a brief, ridiculous vision of Flick.

"The slave driver!" Hector spat the words. "To give us our impossible list of deliveries for the day."

"Where can I hide?" I scanned the little house, seeing no closets or nooks. "And the red house—I found it in the northeast corner. Is it really Sinon's?"

"Uh-oh," said Hector, flashing a crooked smile at my brother. "She's worse than you, *Pipan*."

Itu glared at him. "It's not funny, Hector. You know he's got my little brother there."

"Spoiled rotten and living the life of a wealthy Paav. He's probably better off there."

"No, he's not." Itu and I snapped at Hector in one voice.

Oh, how I had missed Itu. Hector threw his hands in the air, then sat back down on his cushion, returning to his meal.

"But you're hurt, Alesea," Itu said. "We've got time—they don't know you're alive, and they certainly don't know you're here, and as much as I hate to admit it, Hector's right about Konu. I don't think he's in any danger right now."

"What are you saying?" My emotions welled up dangerously, even though I'd gone through the same thought process walking around the Paav district. "I shouldn't rescue Konu?"

"Of course, we'll rescue Konu." Itu took my hand.

"Try not to get anyone killed." Hector had a mouthful of bread, which muffled his voice .

"Yes, Hector, that would be the idea."

"Why does Sinon have Konu, anyway? I saw Konu with somebody else, another Paav, in Ana."

"Ana? I don't know what you're talking about, Alesea. I saw him, four days ago, with Sinon and some other Paav idiot."

Could the "other Paav idiot" be the blue-eyed man from Ana? "So, have you made any plans for getting him back?"

Itu looked at his feet. "A thousand, at least, but not one of them feasible. Before he let the Bannens have me, Sinon told me if I stepped out of line, he'd take it out on Brahn, Mama, or Lori." Hector scowled at that, but Itu brightened, his smile revealing a glimpse of the carefree Island boy he'd so recently been. "But he thinks you're dead, right? That's how we'll do it."

I hated to squash his hope, but he had to know. "He probably doesn't think I'm dead anymore, not after I tried to get Konu back in Ana."

"What? What happened —"

"I'll tell you later. Please, not now, but is it true Mama's in jail?" A painful weight grew in my stomach.

Sadness crossed Itu's face. "You should've seen her. She screamed something awful at the inspectors, saying she wouldn't work for the Paav for anything, especially after they murdered her daughter and kidnapped her son. They almost killed her on the spot."

A bell rang nearby, making me jump, and Hector leaped up from his cushion, scattering breadcrumbs in all directions. "It's too late!" He panicked. "Hide her somewhere!"

Itu looked nearly as worried as Hector. "Quick, Laysi, get on my bedroll. I've got an idea." He gestured at a bundle of blankets in the far corner. Hector nodded and gathered blankets from what must've been his bed, a few feet away.

I did as Itu said, pulling aside his blankets and lying face-down on the thin pad. I shoved my blanket-belly to the side, suppressing a yelp at the painful pull on my shoulder, and flattened myself as much as I could. Itu pulled the blankets over me then more weight landed atop me. *Hector's blankets?*

I could barely make out what was happening through the heavy layers of cloth, and the heat made me sick. Hector and Itu started arguing about something — I caught the words "blankets" and "that's mine" and then there was a banging on the door.

Three raised voices. The new, deeper voice yelled something about "quiet" and "madhouse," and then the talking fell away to a level I couldn't distinguish any words. One person stuck out — the Captain — and if that was him, he must be a Double, and if he'd heard me, it could all be over.

A'lodi sahm, A'lodi sahm. I focused on caging my anxiety and lay there for what seemed like hours. The blankets grew unbearably hot, and my back was on fire with pain. My whole body itched as if stinging ants swarmed me.

Finally, the door slammed, but I didn't dare move until Itu returned. *A'lodi sahm...*

Finally, sweet air on my face as Itu lifted blanket after blanket, smiling down at me. "All good!"

I was suddenly too exhausted to get up. "Captain's a Double? Why?"

Except no one heard me. Hector sounded utterly exasperated. "I can't believe he fell for that. Arguing over blankets?"

Itu laughed, and from the corner of my vision, I saw him give Hector's hand an affectionate squeeze before pulling off the last blanket. "Well, we probably won't get away with—"

Hector gasped and dropped his stack of blankets on the floor with a *whomp* before leaning over me. He sucked air through his teeth. "What exactly happened to you? There's blood everywhere."

"That's a lot of blood loss." Itu knelt by my head. "How long ago was that injury, exactly?"

My bandages must've come loose when I'd shoved my padded tunic aside to hide. Now that a pile of blankets didn't smother me, I felt fresh blood trickling down my side.

"A few days. It's a long story." I rolled onto my good side to look up at my brother. "I got shot."

Itu let out a curse I was sure he hadn't learned on Akila. "You'll have to tell me later, all right? Hector, can you help?"

"Of course, *Pipan*."

"What? Why Hector?"

Hector grunted, or maybe laughed, and started ripping apart one of the thinner blankets into strips.

Itu explained. "He was training to be a doctor on Ana when he was forced here. He'll have you fixed up in no time." His voice was light, but he couldn't hide his worry from me.

"I'm sorry." I tried to project some calm reassurance and gratitude into his mind.

"What the demons..." Hector paused his shredding and looked at Itu. "Is that... *her*?"

"Told you she was a Knower, but I thought it was just when she made music or got mad at me."

I tried to explain, but my brain was already half-asleep, and the words didn't want to come out. "Gotten worse. Stronger. They... the Listeners called me something..."

Hector sat on his knees by my side. "It's okay, Alesea, you can sleep." His voice was different now, smooth and kind. "Just roll onto your stomach, okay?"

I did, and with Hector's gentle hands working on my injury, I drifted into the most peaceful sleep I'd had in weeks.

CHAPTER 36

I woke in the dark, hot and disoriented, my body again covered in too many blankets. I tried to peel myself out from under them but stopped at the sound of a hushed voice.

"I can't lose her again, Hector. Maybe I should send her to—"

"Itu." An orange light flared, then flickered as Hector lit a candle at their small table. It was nighttime. I must have slept all day.

Hector leaned close to my brother from his cushion at the table. "Itu, you'll never be happy... or whole... without your family. Even I know that."

"Will you come?"

Hector waited a long time to answer. He took one of Itu's hands, and suddenly I felt I was eavesdropping on something very private. "I want to, but your family..."

"They won't care, Hector, I told you. On the Islands—"

"Sun and moons, I have got to go to those Islands." Hector pressed his face to Itu's, and they kissed. Passionately. For a very long time.

I didn't know whether to laugh or cry. So, now this rude, greasy-haired almost-doctor was part of my family, too? The last thing I needed was another person to worry about, to grow to love, to feel obligated to protect.

The happiness rolling off of Itu at that moment was pure as dew on a *kreo* leaf. My brother needed Hector, and that was obvious.

I finally managed to wriggle out of the triple layer of blankets they'd buried me under, and Hector jerked away from Itu, shocked.

"Forget I was here?" My query came out harsher than I meant.

"I... I..." Hector looked about to burst into tears.

I smiled. "Itu's right. Islanders don't care if your lover's a boy or a girl." My brother relaxed into his cushion with a relieved sigh.

Hector blinked furiously, eyes wet.

I couldn't stand any more sadness just then, so I pretended sternness. "But if you want to join our family, you have *got* to wash your hair."

Hector let out a surprised bark of a laugh, then collapsed into himself, shaking with what I hoped was more laughter.

Itu laughed too. "I'm sorry I didn't tell you, Laysi. There was just so much, and Hector was being such a jerk this morning because he was so nervous—"

"It's fine." I meant it. "And I'm happy for you. Really. How long have you been..."

Itu rubbed Hector's back—he was still doubled over. "Two moons, now. I got placed here right away, and Hector was all alone..." His eyes went dreamy.

Did I ever look all gooey-eyed like that at Lin? Surely not. "So, what does *Pipan* mean?"

Itu blushed. "It's... kind of a secret between us. On Ana they use it to mean 'brother,' but in Old Anak it means more like... well, 'dearest.' "

"I've met someone too."

"Roni." Itu guessed. "I figure I can't complain about that anymore."

Hector sat up, wiping tears from his cheeks but smiling wide. "Was he the one who knocked you up with that blanket?"

"Not Roni." I gave Hector a half-hearted glare. "A sailor named Lin. He's from a little island near Ana."

"Huh. I always figured it would be Roni."

"What do you mean, always, Itu? You didn't even know I'd been with him all this time until yesterday."

Itu opened his mouth as if to speak, then shut it again, thinking. "How're you feeling now? Hector sewed up that gap next to your shoulder blade. He told me it wouldn't hurt much, but it looked terrible."

"Really? I didn't even wake up."

"You were starting to get a fever from infection, but I think I caught it in time. You're lucky I'd just found a patch of halder-root in the Tailor District. I had enough to knock it out."

"Thank you, Hector." I smiled at him. If I ignored the hair, I could imagine him in a doctor's tunic. "I'm even more lucky that you were here at all."

The three of us talked through half the night. Itu bombarded me with questions as I told him everything that had happened to me since the Solstice. He seemed annoyingly dubious about some parts, especially my escapes from Ana and from Arne's army, despite the gory proof on my back.

Itu raised his eyebrows skeptically at my description of Dar's transformation from captor to admirer.

"Do you not believe me?" My question came laced with some indignation.

Hector gave Itu a light punch on the arm. "Are you serious, *Pipan*? You said your sister was a Knower and tough as nails in the forest, and everybody loved her to boot."

"Yeah, climbing *kreo* trees and singing like a moon goddess, not fighting off armies! Besides, I thought she was dead."

"Ha!" I liked Hector more every second. "I think you underestimated her. A lot."

"I think you're right. Sorry, sis."

"Your turn now." I sunk into the cushion Hector had brought me halfway through my story. "Start with leaving Akila."

It was hard to hear, and parts were hard for Itu to tell. For weeks, he and all the men of Akila had been stuffed into the Paav ship's hold and fed just enough to survive and forced to relieve themselves in buckets that spilled more often than not. The whole time, he and Brahn worried about the others—Konu, who was with Mama because of his age, and pregnant Lori. It wasn't until they arrived in Mata City that my older brothers found out Konu had been ripped from Mama's arms when they docked for an hour in Ana, and Lori had given birth too early to a baby girl who'd only lived for a few minutes.

"Mama was beside herself." Itu batted at his tears with one hand as Hector held the other. "She'd lost you, Konu, her first grandchild... She refused to walk when they brought us off the ship, so they carried her, kicking and screaming curses at them the whole time."

"Oh, poor Mama."

Hector dug a handkerchief out of his clothes and handed it to Itu.

"They finally held a knife to Lori's throat to make Mama stop." Itu's voice cracked. "So, she cooperated the rest of the way to the slave market, but when we got there, one of the guards kept walking with her and saying she had to go to jail."

"How do you know they really took her there? They might have killed her."

"Because I have to believe it, Laysi." Itu wasn't even trying to stop the tears anymore. "Like I had to believe you were some sort of storybook hero, which turned out to be true, didn't it?"

It wasn't until Hector's chin hit his chest that I realized it must be the middle of the night. Itu insisted I use his bed again, and before I could argue, he curled up next to Hector, but after sleeping all day, and with my shoulder feeling so much better, I wasn't tired anymore. I thought through a thousand possible plans for the following day and beyond. I meditated. I tested moving my arm, gingerly, and found that it stretched a little further than it had the previous day.

I explored the tiny house by candlelight out of boredom. A meager store of food filled a single cabinet next to a wood stove. A shelf in the corner served as a wardrobe, with a few drab tunics and pairs of linen pants scattered. A fat book stuck out from underneath one of the tunics. I pulled it off the shelf and opened it to find page after page of Itu's sketches.

A memory flashed across my mind—Itu's sketchbook, abandoned in the dirt, as he ran off to tell Uma about the tall boats. Where was that sketchbook now? Had it been destroyed, or was it still somewhere on Akila?

The book I held now—oddly bound together with little metal rings—showed me how much Itu had grown as an artist. Instead of rough sketches of wildlife or boats, he'd been drawing people. Interspersed with dozens of portraits, often several to a page, were complex scenes from life in Mata City. Hector appeared around the halfway point—on his bicycle, laughing, sleeping. Only a few pages from the end, I found the final, presumably most recent drawing—a family portrait. Mama and I stood, holding Konu's hands, with Lori and Brahn smiling down at a bundle in Lori's arms—their baby—and Itu stood with Hector, beaming.

Already the beautiful, happy picture was a lie—the baby hadn't survived. Would any of it ever come true? I carefully returned the sketchbook and went back to bed for a few short hours of sleep.

***

I snuck out of the Paav district the way I'd come in—pretending to be someone's slave. Before I left, Itu and I set up a meeting place in the Fisher District to try at dusk each day. If, after three days time, we'd failed to meet, I would come back to him among the slaves. I promised to sequester myself in the apartment to learn everything I could from Juhani and Yalene and let Lin and Roni explore. Though I bristled at the order to stay hidden, I did need time to heal. Plus, the Paav now had too many people they could use against me—not only my scattered family but all the refugees beneath Mata City.

As I went through the market, my stomach grumbled, and my mouth watered. At full light, all the vendors were out, and now that my pain was only a dull throb, I realized how little I had eaten in the past several days. As I passed stalls full of hot bread, steaming meat pies, puddings, custards, fresh fruits, and vegetables, I wished for even a single coin. I'd left the Paav-stamped coins with Lin. I had nothing but the clothes on my back until I made it back to my friends—if I ever found them.

I recognized the road leading up from the fish market into the Fisher District, but as the streets to either side grew narrower and noisier, the buildings grew taller and less well maintained, and the smell turned from enticing to repulsive, I realized I was lost. *Thera Street, Thera Street,* I repeated to myself, but without a sign of Thera Street, the opulent road Yalene and I had taken out of the district turned to rocky dirt and pathetic lumps of people resting in the muck on every corner.

The temptation to help these people paled to busily suppressing my panic. I turned around, recognizing nothing, and walked back to the place where the road transitioned to dirt. A pale-skinned woman with an even paler *ratina* hung an "Open" sign over a nondescript doorway.

Excuse me, I signed when she turned my way.

She narrowed her eyes and snapped aloud. "Whadya want?"

"I'm lost."

"That's obvious. Lookin' fer your brothel?"

"No!" I glanced around, hoping no one was listening, but I couldn't even tell if the nearest lumps were people or trash. "Thera Street. I'm looking for Thera Street."

She rolled her eyes. "Everythin's called 'Thera Street' 'round here, haven't you noticed? T'ain't even a proper street name anymore."

"Um..."

She continued her rant as if venting to the whole neighborhood. "Everybody jes' wants to get on them Paav's good side, stay outta th' prisons. Thera Street Grocer. Thera Street Pottery. Thera Street Apartments. What next, Thera Street Outhouses? Serve 'em right." She threw her hands in the air, grumbling, and turned to go back in her store.

"Wait!" I winced as a nearby heap of trash groaned and turned at my shout, but fortunately, the woman stopped. "Thera Street Apartments. Where's that?"

She shrugged. "Nah, too many ta keep track." She paused a moment, frowning. "Come ta think of it, might be that way," she pointed vaguely down the street, "two east, three south. Eh, might not."

"Thank you, thank you, *Mamani,*" I gushed, relieved even to get questionable information.

Her eyes widened—at the Island honorific or because I'd let my thanks out too carelessly, I didn't know which—and she slowly backed into her shop and shut the door.

CHAPTER 37

Fortunately, the strange shopkeeper had been almost right. It was two blocks south, not three, but I immediately recognized the little hand-painted sign. This time, I knocked on door number three and pulled the flag without hesitation.

Like when I'd first arrived at the apartment, the door cracked open and caught on the chain, but this time, Yalene's eyes peered down at me. She let out a little squeak, shut the door to detach the chain, then opened it wide.

"You made it back!" Yalene—gorgeous in her bright yellow dress and no *ratina*—ushered me in, then leaned in as if to hug me. At the last second, she seemed to think better of it and rested a hand on my good shoulder. "What happened?"

Before I could answer, Juhani waved at me, widely grinning as he extracted himself from piles of books. *My A'lodi friend has returned! Lin and Roni will be so happy to see you.*

"Where are they?" I asked, translating for Juhani, but Yalene answered.

"They're looking for more of your people and for supporters around the city."

They were very upset you left without telling them, Juhani signed happily.

"Upset with *me*." Yalene gestured to the only cushion not surrounded by books, and I gratefully sank into it. "They were sure I'd made you leave."

"They'll get over it. They should know better than to blame anybody but me by now."

Yalene smiled. "Are you hungry? We've got plenty of breakfast—your boys were so eager to leave us this morning that they barely ate a thing."

- 235 -

"Famished."

Between bites of boiled egg, muffins, and sweet fruit, I told Yalene and Juhani everything I'd learned in the Paav district. I told them about the blood-red house I was sure was Sinon's, the sad story of Brahn's and Lori's baby girl, and how frighteningly easy it was for me to blend in with the slaves. I ended by asking for clarification on something Yalene mentioned earlier.

"What did you mean, Roni and Lin are looking for supporters?"

"For the revolution."

It took a moment for me to process Yalene's answer. "Revolution? We're here to rescue my people, not to fight."

Yalene frowned. "What do you think you're going to do, then? Find your people and go back to your island like none of this ever happened?"

"No, I—"

"How will you even leave Mata? As long as the Paav are in charge, you'll never be free again. Do you remember what they did to that Listener woman? You'll—"

Juhani put his hands in front of his daughter's face. *Yalene. Stop.*

It didn't matter because she was right.

"I won't fight, and I won't support anyone who does fight." I felt sick. "I can't hurt anyone else. I won't. It's against everything my people believe."

"So tell me how this peaceful revolution will work. What about all the people getting hurt because you won't act?" Yalene's eyes bored into mine, as if she were the Knower and could read my most shameful thoughts.

What would she think if I told her how many people I'd already hurt to make it this far?

"Maybe no one would have to fight. The Paav are completely outnumbered. If everyone stopped doing what they said, all at the same time—"

"It would be a massacre," Yalene finished.

"I made the people who wanted to kill me love me instead."

"What?" Yalene looked confused as her father signed, *How?*

"I... I used my Knowing. I sent them love, and the man who shot me ended up helping me. These violent men all dropped their weapons and let me escape because of love, not violence."

"So, you *can* control people?" Yalene appeared both disgusted and fascinated.

"No! No, I just... I saw the *A'lodi* in them and showed it to them. I didn't control them."

No wonder they call you the Trekana, Juhani signed.

Yalene looked between me and her father and projected a complex mix of emotions—fear, confusion, exasperation. "Fine, but there's only one of you. Let's say everybody really thinks you are the *Trekana*. If you tell them not to fight, they'll do what you say. Can you protect them all with your Knowing?"

"I don't know, but I have some ideas. What if we overwhelm the Paav so much—with art, dancing, kindness, even sheer numbers—that they can't help but listen? What if we show them love instead of—"

"And will love dull the Paav swords? If all these people you're leading are killed because they refused to fight back while they were making art and dancing and being kind, will your conscience still be clear?"

Hot tears spilled down my cheeks. I felt helpless, stupid, and naive. I couldn't look at Yalene. Instead, I distracted myself by reading titles of the books stacked all around the floor.

The well-worn *Book of* A'lodi was there, along with several histories of the A'lodi. *War: Never Again* was one title.

Then I shifted my eyes to the next stack. These books were different. *The Ancient Martial Art of* I'kaan. *Basic Swordsmanship. The Case for War.* My stomach twisted.

A knock on the door saved me from answering Yalene. Three quick knocks, three slower. "Lin." Yalene went to open the door.

"We couldn't find—" Lin said as he walked into the door, then he saw me. "Alesea!" He knelt by my cushion, taking me into his arms. "Oh, Alesea! We thought you... We..."

He let out an uncharacteristic burst of emotion—relief, mostly, with a hint of fear, and desire. "I'm fine, I'm fine!" I suddenly felt smothered. I kissed him on the cheek, then looked up to see Roni standing in front of us, stony-faced.

I smiled at him. *I'm okay,* I signed as Lin turned to sit next to me. *I'm sorry I left like that.*

You could have told me, Roni signed. *I... we were worried sick.*

I didn't know what to say to that. Roni was right. Lin might have tried to stop or follow me, but I should have told Roni. Instead, I'd left him without a word again. I cast my eyes down at his feet, ashamed. *I'm sorry.*

"You're here now." Lin rested his hand on my knee. "Did you find your brother?"

"Yes. He's—"

The Watcher flag on the door swung wildly, and someone pounded on the door—hard enough to rattle the window.

"Hide!"

Go, Juhani signed with Yalene's command and gestured to the back rooms as he stood. *Take this,* he said, tossing his copy of the *Book of* A'lodi at me. *Now!*

Our collective fear made me dizzy as we crammed into Yalene's room. "Stay here." Yalene crept into the kitchen and left her door ajar.

I crouched with Juhani's *Book of* A'lodi hugged to my chest and peered out the crack in the door, but I could only see an empty sliver of the living room. All was silent, which made sense if it were Watchers at the door. Surely, it was only a friend of Juhani's or someone with the wrong address.

Then something flew across my view and landed with a bang, followed by others. Juhani's books.

"Run!" Yalene called. "Go!"

I looked around frantically. "The window!" Thank goodness I'd climbed out of it once already.

Lin shoved it open, and Roni gave me a boost. In seconds, all three of us were in the alley. I stuffed Juhani's book into my waistband just as something banged against the wall from the inside.

"We have to do something! What about Yalene?"

Lin grabbed my hand. "No. We planned for this while you were gone. They have other help. We run."

To the inn, Roni signed, and Lin nodded. *Walk fast, but don't run.*

I focused on stilling my pounding heart as we walked through the narrow streets. We took turn after turn—which disoriented me—presumably to throw off anyone following us, but I was too busy caging my emotions to ask.

We turned the last corner, and I recognized the first block of Mata City I'd ever seen. It had only been days ago, but it felt like moons had passed since we'd emerged from the tunnels into that dusty storeroom.

"I'll give the passphrase." Lin discreetly signed for Roni.

Then it hit me what we were about to do. We were going back into the tunnels filled with people who thought I was a savior who came to start a revolution. I didn't want to hide or start a revolution. I wanted to know who was raiding Juhani's apartment. Were they after Juhani? Yalene? Me? And if they were looking for me, was my family in danger? I couldn't disappear into the tunnels without finding out. And I had to warn Itu.

"No." I took a step back from Lin and Roni.

Lin turned to face me. "I know, it's dumb, but they said if there's a man in the group, he should say the passphrase."

It took me a moment to understand what he meant. "No, not the passphrase, Lin. I'm not going. I have to meet Itu."

"No!" Lin forgot to sign. "It's too dangerous. What if they know it's you?"

We're attracting attention, Roni signed, small and in front of his body so only we could see.

"You go in. I know how to blend in now. I'll find Itu, and we'll all come to the tunnels."

I could find Itu, Roni signed, but I shook my head.

"I know where Konu is, and if they're onto us, I need to rescue him soon. Now."

Lin bit his lower lip, looking exasperated. "You won't listen to us anyway, will you?"

"No."

Roni nearly smiled. *Alesea, you go find Itu. I'll stay nearby. As soon as you've done what you can, come back here, and we'll go into the tunnels together.*

Can you find out where Brahn and Lori are working the fields? I signed. *We won't have long to get them once Itu and Konu are out.*

I'll try.

Lin scowled. "I'll find out what happened to Juhani and Yalene and make sure they're all right. If I can, I'll bring them to the tunnels, too."

I squeezed Lin's hand and smiled at Roni. "Let's do this." Before any of us could change our minds, I disappeared into a crowd of Doubles and began the long walk to the Paav district.

CHAPTER 38

My confidence wavered as I realized I'd left my fake-pregnant tunic in the corner of Juhani's living room. Juhani's *Book of* A'lodi now pressed uncomfortably on my belly, but I feared I'd look even more suspicious carrying the book outright. Were slaves allowed to have books? I had no idea. At least I was still wearing a *ratina*, though it was Yalene's violet one. My drab old cloth would've blended into the crowd much better.

Fortunately, finding the Paav district was much easier than finding Yalene's apartment or the tavern. All I had to do was walk downhill, then west. I stuck to the back streets, and keeping my head down, I tried to look despondent yet purposeful simultaneously.

My heart cracked a little more each time I passed a homeless beggar—there were so many more on these streets than the main road, both Doubles and Listeners—but I pretended to ignore their pleas and kept my emotions to myself. *Itu,* I thought whenever my resolve started to waver. *Konu.*

It was midday by the time I arrived at the gates of the Paav district. Two armed guards stood at the gate—one inside, one out. I paced for as long as I dared, but I saw no opportunities to blend in with groups of slaves. Worse, while I was pretending to examine vegetables at a market stall, I watched a slave-garbed woman show some paper to the guards before they let her in—papers, like at the border.

I hadn't seen anyone in my group of flower-basket slaves offer identification, but it had been a holiday. I'd never get in that way if they required it now.

The vegetable merchant eyed me suspiciously, so I started walking again, away from the Paav district. I needed a new plan.

I wanted to sit on one of the many benches near the water to rest and think. My shoulder ached, the sewn-up skin extremely itchy under the layers of bandages and tunic. Still it seemed the only ones allowed to relax were Watchers and occasional Doubles in colorful, expensive-looking clothing. The slaves and other drably-dressed people rushed from place to place, rarely communicating or even looking up.

I didn't hear the first bicycle coming until it blew past me fast enough to send a wayward lock of my hair flying into my mouth. I stepped off the road to make room for the next one. Dozens of market-goers did the same—glancing up for a moment, stepping toward the stalls, then resuming their sullen activities.

I watched the bicycles race into the distance and understood why Itu had always wanted to try one. How freeing it must feel traveling faster than anything else on the land, flying past slaves and slave traders alike. How ironic that Itu experienced that freedom and felt completely trapped simultaneously.

Close behind me, something made a strange screeching sound, and a bicycle slowed beside me.

"Laysi! What're you doing out here?"

"The guards—"

"Stop!" Itu pedaled alongside me to whisper. "Up two blocks, east one. Door three-oh-one." Then he sped away, standing over his seat until he was going fast enough to catch up with the rest of the bicycles.

Up two blocks, east one. Three-oh-one. I chanted it to myself as I resumed my slow, slave-like pace. I walked an extra block in each direction, watching for guards. I doubled back, convinced no one noticed me, and found the door marked 301. Two steps down from the road, it had no sign or indication of its purpose, just the street number.

Itu wouldn't lead me wrong. I descended the two stairs and, seeing no Watcher-flag pull, I knocked.

"Who is it?"

I had no idea how to answer the hoarse voice that called through the closed door. I settled on, "Itu sent me."

"What island is two south of Itu's?"

"A'shindo," I answered quickly.

The door swung open to reveal a stocky, middle-aged Listener woman a head taller than me. She wore blue clothes and a matching head cloth tucked above her large ears, half-covering her generous forehead ridge. Her skin was dark as Tika's at the Kuul monastery, and her hair hung in two neat braids on either side of her round face.

"Come in quickly, child," she said, stepping back and closing the door behind me. She clicked her tongue and led me to a shabby but clean sitting room lit by a single oil lamp. A Listener child played in one corner, humming and clicking to herself. Scents of baking wafted in through another opened door. "Please have a seat," the woman said.

"Thank you, *Maman.*" I sat in a narrow, wicker chair opposite the child's corner. "I think Itu will be here soon."

"And how did Itu happen to send you here?" She took a seat next to me.

"I'm his sister."

The woman's sharp intake of breath belied her calm tone. "How wonderful that you found each other. Your name?"

"Alesea, *Maman.*"

"Alesea of Akila, I am Driki of Mata City, born of generations of Listener and Double fisherpeople, now driven into hiding by the Paav."

"I'm sorry." What else was there to say? I didn't know how this woman had suffered, who she'd lost, what she knew of Itu, the Listeners in the tunnels, the *Trekana.* I didn't know how any of it fit together. The only thing I knew was I had to cage my emotions, or somebody would get hurt.

A clatter at the door rescued me from speaking. Driki popped and clicked as she jumped up to answer the vigorous knocking.

I thanked the goddesses, it was Itu. He burst into the sitting room with his bicycle, out of breath, face red from exertion. "Laysi!" He leaned it against the wall and threw his arms around me, letting go of my right side when I squeaked. "What happened? Why were you in the market? You were supposed to stay in until tonight!"

I explained everything to him and Driki. I figured Itu wouldn't have asked me in front of the woman if I couldn't fully trust her.

"So, we need to rescue Konu as soon as possible. Then Brahn, Lori, and we can all go in the tunnels."

Itu whistled. "That's a lot, but you're right—if there's any chance they know you're here, we don't have any time to lose."

"It seems likely it was a simple Paav raid at Juhani's." Driki spoke for the first time since Itu arrived. "Sasha's arrest has become quite a legend, and now Juhani in his own right. They'd probably been planning to raid his home for some time."

"Wait, Juhani?" Itu looked shocked. "*That* Juhani? I didn't realize... *That's* who's been helping you?"

"Uh..."

"He's some kind of hero to the locals, the slaves from the other districts. He's been organizing them, teaching classes..."

"What? He didn't say anything—"

"Of course not because he just met you, and you're all about the *A'lodi*. I bet he could tell right away you wouldn't approve of his teaching people to fight."

"Fight?" Were we talking about the same person? Yet there had been those books—martial arts, swordsmanship... did I really know anything about Juhani or Yalene at all? I suddenly felt the press of Juhani's *Book of A'lodi* in my waistband. Why had he given it to me?

"It was a raid." Driki kept her voice firm. "The wrong person found out about his lessons."

The thought of his "lessons" made me feel sick, tricked, and more naive than ever, but it didn't matter. It was time to act. I felt it in my gut. "What were the chances they would raid today, of all days? It could have been any day in the last several moons, but it wasn't until after we arrived. Someone could've seen me leaving his apartment. And I... I talked to a woman for directions, and I think she might have reported me." I didn't really believe my own words—how could the Paav know I was in Mata City? Why would that woman have reported me, and for what?—but Itu nodded his agreement. Any excuse allowing me to get the rest of my family back right now would do.

"Tonight. We'll get Konu tonight and send Roni to get Brahn and Lori. He'll be the best at blending in with the Paav."

I shuddered at Itu. "How will I get into the Paav district, though? I watched for an hour, and everyone had some papers they showed the guards to get in."

"Yeah, they're tightening up again." Itu's nose twisted to one side— his thinking gesture since childhood. "It's too risky. I'll get Konu myself and meet you somewhere."

"No!" I half-stood out of my wicker chair. "Konu won't know you. It's been months! You're taller, and you have a beard..."

"And he'll recognize you better?"

"Yes, because..." I glanced at Driki, but I had to say it. "He can feel me. He did in Ana."

Driki didn't react. Maybe she didn't know what I meant.

Itu ran one hand through his hair, over and over, mussing up his braid. "Demons, you're probably right. I don't know if I could get him out of that house fast enough if he doesn't want to come with me."

"I'll use the trees to get over the fence. There are a bunch of tall ones around the red house."

"You're in no condition for that. You could barely stand me hugging you, Laysi. What if you get stuck or too hurt to get Konu back out?"

"There's a furniture delivery this evening," Driki said. "We could smuggle her in."

"Smuggle me?"

"Perfect, Driki! Who's doing it?"

"Pol's crew. None of them are in the know, but they're not the sharpest, either. We've used them before with no problem."

"I don't know —"

"Once you're in, Laysi," Itu spoke over my objection, "come straight to my place as long as you're not being followed. We'll get Konu from there, and my life as a slave will be over."

It seemed impulsive, even for me. I didn't like the idea of being smuggled, and un-smuggling myself once inside the Paav district sounded even worse, but what other choice did I have? "How will we get back out?"

"With the trees. It's easier from the inside, and I'll be there to help you."

"You're sure we can get to Brahn and Lori in time? And what about Mama?"

"I'll find Roni as soon as I finish my deliveries — he's watching for you near that tavern, right? He'll be to Brahn before the Paav even figure out what's happening. We know exactly where they're assigned, down to their barracks. How hard could it be to find them?"

Driki added her agreement. "It is a rather rash plan, but it could work."

"And Mama?"

Itu met my eyes, then looked down. "We haven't heard any news since they took her away, Alesea. I... I don't think we can count on her being... well..."

"You think she's dead."

Itu didn't answer. Driki clicked her tongue.

"All right." I tried not to think about Mama. "I don't know what other choice we have. Let's go ahead with it."

CHAPTER 39

"We have to take these all the way to the Minister's house? He's crazy!"

"It's straight uphill. Why'd he said no animals, that idiot Paav?"

"Shush! You know they can read your lips."

Squeezed between two dressers in a rickety donkey cart, I listened to the furniture makers bicker with one another for what felt like hours. At every bump in the road, sawdust and straw showered me, and I had to grab my nose to keep from sneezing. I'd counted to a hundred at least seven times when we jolted to a stop.

"Pol, you idiot!"

"Did he just go in that tavern?"

"What the demons?"

The men erupted into exasperated groans.

"You watch the dressers, I'll drag 'im out."

To my dismay, the front of the cart dropped to the ground, and I couldn't suppress an agonized yelp as the dressers shifted and squished me between them. I nearly vomited with pain and motion sickness as they stabilized, upright again. Fortunately, the noise of the tavern was loud even through the dressers and heavy blankets covering the cart, so my cry went unnoticed.

I worked to cage my panic as long minutes passed. Sweat streamed from my forehead into my eyes and dripped into the straw. *Breathe. Breathe.*

"Dammit, Pol, next time you're doin' all the heavy lifting," someone finally complained, close to my hiding spot. "Now it's goin' ta' be dark 'fore we get to his haughtiness' place."

Pol's voice was the deepest of the bunch. "Aww, I got ya' all a pint, no charge. Ya' should be thankin' me."

I nearly shouted again when the cart tipped upright, jolted into motion, and banged my bandaged shoulder again. I spent the whole rest of the journey trying to cage my pain and growing terror—that the dressers would crush me, that the men would discover me before we made it into the Paav district, that I'd be rammed through by one of the guards' swords the second they spotted me, but none of those things happened. Instead, we finally stopped. My teeth felt rattled loose, and my ears rang louder than a great feast gong. I could tell from the cracks in the cart that the complainers had been right—it was dark outside.

"All right, Pol, you get to interrupt his dinner."

"Aww." Pol whined, but he didn't argue.

After a moment of stillness, another person spoke. "We'll probably take 'em through the back door."

"Right. Let's go ahead that way. Less complaining, then."

The cart lurched forward, and with panic, I realized the men wouldn't leave until the dressers were in the house. I'd been counting on them to leave the carts by the house, but why would they? Why hadn't I asked Driki how I was supposed to safely get out of the cart she'd had her furniture-making contact construct to keep me concealed? Stupid, stupid, stupid!

My panic rose, and I knew I had to act before everyone felt it. The cart banged to another stop, and I burst out of the back of it covered in straw and so stiff from the awful ride I fell right to my knees on the hard pavement.

"By the demons!" cursed one of the men.

"Who're you?" said another.

"Guards!"

"Shush! It's us'll get it!"

I didn't wait to hear how the argument turned out. I fought the pain and half-limped, half-ran into the shadows of the great Paav houses.

They won't report me. They won't report me. I repeated it as a mantra from inside a trio of lush bushes outside a windowless wall of a house. They would get in as much trouble as me, wouldn't they?

I was ashamed as I realized I'd once again put innocent people at risk. What if they did get in trouble? Would they be sent to prison, beaten like that poor old Listener woman, or just reprimanded?

No. I couldn't think about it, not now. *A'lodi sahm. Itu. Konu.*

I had to move. If Itu thought I wasn't coming, would he wait, or would he act alone? I couldn't risk that. Driki's friend had said the furniture delivery was three blocks west of the violet house. So all I had to do was walk three blocks.

I brushed the last pieces of straw from my hair, checked that no one was within view, then stepped out of the bushes onto the nearest sidewalk. Without the weight of my fake-pregnant belly, I felt even more exposed, but I forced myself to hunch like a slave and walk slowly.

Fireworks burst above me, close. *A'lodi sahm. A'lodi sahm.* A Paav woman walking toward me stopped and stared, perhaps feeling my panic. I kept walking, head down, as if it had nothing to do with me until I passed her and sped up to almost running.

There. The side of the huge violet house was on the next block. I veered left toward the back as another firework crackled somewhere above me. Every step felt dangerous. I imagined guards surrounding me, preparing to attack, but I didn't dare move my head to look.

Then, I was at Itu's door. I pounded on it.

"Laysi!" Itu threw open the door and caught me as I fell into his tiny house.

"What's wrong?" Hector was right behind Itu, wearing his concerned doctor's face. "Did you hurt yourself?"

I held my hand up, afraid to speak, until I calmed my nerves down. I heard more fireworks. *Please, let those not be about me. Please.*

I waited until my heart finally slowed to a relatively normal pace before I told Itu and Hector what had happened. "Those fireworks — they might be looking for me."

Hector's eyes widened and his face paled, but Itu only looked excited. "Then we have no choice but to move right now, Laysi. We'll ride my bike and be out of their range fast."

Hector looked like he might be sick. "I don't know —"

"Remember our plan. Here's the fake message to show the guards." Itu handed Hector a folded paper. "We'll meet you in the alley by the tavern. Roni's friends are expecting us." He turned to me. "Roni's already left for Brahn and Lori."

"So, we have to go now." Itu nodded to my response.

Hector pressed his forehead to Itu's. "I love you, Island boy."

Itu's eyes revealed the slightest bit of fear for the first time. "I love you too, little doctor. See you before you know it."

Hector's eyes watered, but he gave a single nod and left, clutching his fake message like the ticket to freedom it was.

Itu tried to smile at me. "Ready, sis?"

"No."

"Well, it's almost curfew, so we're going anyway."

"I know."

I rode on the back of Itu's bicycle, which wasn't freeing at all. It was horrible. I held my feet off the ground, squeezed Itu around the middle with one arm, and felt my bottom bruising over and over as it hit the narrow rack meant for tying packages. How could anyone get used to this? At least I was too busy clinging to my brother to notice if there were more fireworks.

Itu was fast even with me weighing him down—so fast my *ratina* nearly ripped off my head in the fierce wind. We swerved from alley to alley and raced past colorful house after colorful house, all lit by the district's abundant street lamps. I imagined the entire district had seen us by now.

"Almost there." Itu grunted as he pumped his legs hard to get us over the steep top of a hill. "One more house... here's the back gate."

We stopped so quickly my nose smacked into Itu's back. I nearly fell off the bike as he tilted it to put one foot on the ground.

"What're you doing?"

"Get off." Itu slurred the way Doubles spoke to keep Watchers from reading their lips.

I swung my leg over just as Itu let the bike drop. I stumbled sideways and saw what had stopped us.

A Paav guard, shirt lined with at least twenty buttons, stood in the middle of the path, not ten yards from the red house. My insides sank.

It is curfew, he signed slowly, probably because we were Doubles and slaves. *Show me your papers.*

Papers? Not again. Itu squatted down and fumbled with the small bag tied to his handlebars. I hoped he had something that would cover both of us. My knees started to tremble. I suddenly noticed my *ratina* hanging loose against my face, my hair's tangles keeping it from falling. One ear was exposed, but I didn't dare attract more attention by adjusting it.

The guard turned his attention to me anyway, and his wide Watcher eyes went even wider as he took in my mussed *ratina*, my wild hair, and eyes. *What house do you belong to?*

Amon, I signed, randomly making up a name, but I was in the Paav district, and Paav families were few and large. Stupid, again.

I don't know any Amon, he signed, *but I do know some deliverymen reported an undersized female stowaway with a violet ratina not long ago.*

Now my whole body shook. *A'lodi sahm, A'lodi sahm...* I couldn't find my cage.

Itu stood up, blocking me so I couldn't see what he signed to the guard—but he hadn't been holding any papers. He took a step back, nearly knocking me over.

Fireworks exploded directly overhead.

I exploded into a panic. It sparked out of me as uncontrollably as the flaring fireworks, my mind struggling in vain to rein it in.

Itu gasped, and I knew he had felt it. "Run, Laysi!" he cried.

He lurched forward as one guard's muscled arms snaked around his neck and threw him to the ground, the guard holding up a thick, rough wooden club in his other hand—a club like the one used to beat that poor Listener woman.

Itu kicked and struggled, but it was no use—the guard held him with a vice-like grip. Footsteps approached from at least two directions.

Not my brother. Not Itu! I gathered up my anger like I had when I left Ana. Like I swore I would never do again.

"No, Laysi, run!" Itu screamed, and somehow he squirmed his way out of the guard's grip.

"Itu!" I couldn't hold it in. The fear and anger spun out in all directions, striking everyone around me.

The guard who'd held Itu flinched and jerked as if Itu had hit him. *Knower,* he signed frantically to the one who'd just arrived.

The new guard lunged for Itu, perhaps thinking he was the Knower, wildly swinging his club.

"No! It's me!" In my attempt to ball up my wild waves of emotions, spots danced in front of my eyes, and the whole scene swerved and swayed.

Time slowed as I watched the club arc through the air, Itu stumbling and falling onto the sidewalk and the club making contact with Itu's head.

That sound, that sickening sound. Blood everywhere, on me, on the guards, on Itu, *oh Itu...* I couldn't breathe, couldn't do anything. Itu's pain washed over me, my skull crushing in on itself...

And then nothing.

The pain was gone. Itu was gone.

"Itu, Itu!" I threw myself into his bloodied arms one last time, sobbing and breathing in his sweet island smell and feeling the scratch of his beard. I wouldn't let go. I couldn't.

Someone grabbed my hair, someone else my arms, jolting my injured shoulder so hard I almost passed out. I screamed curses at the guards, at the Paav, at the goddesses themselves as they jerked me upright and pulled me away from my brother's broken body, half-carrying, half-pushing me through the cruel iron gates of the Paav district.

CHAPTER 40

There was no light in the Paav prison. There was cold stone, soft weeping, and the smell of death.

Once an hour or a day or a month, guards would pace the corridor, their torches so blinding I barely glimpsed my surroundings through squinted eyes.

I didn't need to. I was never leaving this place of frozen stone and metal bars.

Sometimes the guards would leave a hunk of stale bread, nearly too hard to eat, and a cup of water that tasted like the Fisher district smelled. I hated myself for eating and drinking anyway. I wished they had killed me. Why hadn't they?

I quickly learned how dangerous it could be to try to communicate with my fellow prisoners. Maybe the spies were Watchers who could see in the dark or Doubles who'd joined the Paav, but the only two times I heard another prisoner make more than a cough—once, a man wailed, "Is there anyone there?" over and over, and once, a woman let loose with a string of curses—the guards came. Metal clanged and squeaked. Something whistled through the air and hit its target with a sickening smack.

When the screaming stopped, my ears ached from the silence.

I thought of Roni and how I'd left him all alone in a cruel city so far from everything he'd always known. He nearly gave his life to help me and stood by me even when I hated him—maybe he even loved me—and I'd abandoned him.

I thought of Lin and wondered if he would find someone else to love or if he would die alone and recklessly like Puika. I thought of how I'd briefly been his fake wife as I wrapped myself in a rough blanket that could have been the twin of my false pregnant belly, but I didn't think of Itu.

I could not think of Itu.

Instead, I pictured Brahn and Lori. Would they be punished for what I'd done, or did Roni get to them in time? How closely did the Paav keep track of the relationships between their slaves anyway?

Mama. Could she have been held in this very prison?

Surely, Konu was safe. No matter how horrible the Paav were, the blue-eyed man in Ana did seem to care for him. Hector had said Sinon spoiled Konu, so Sinon wouldn't hurt Konu. Would he?

Once while I lay on my stomach on the floor, the only position in which my battered body would cooperate with my wish to drift off into nothingness, a light glared through my eyelids and wouldn't go away.

I didn't even have the energy to feel angry.

When the light refused to dim and a foot stamped near my head, I looked up.

Red, red, red. Red as Itu's blood, red as the rage still simmering deep inside me under suffocating mounds of hopelessness and despair.

Sinon squatted down with his lamp and dared to put his face near mine. I could have reached through the bars and poked out his eyes if only I had the will.

Who are you? he signed.

I didn't respond.

They said you were babbling about me the night they found you outside my house, babbling about my nephew. He shoved the lamp against the bars and stared. *Who are you?*

All he had done to me, my family, my island, and he didn't even recognize me?

I took my time sitting up, shoulder smarting, stiff joints cracking with the effort. I gathered my revulsion to let it fly as I signed at Sinon's sneering mouth and nasty tattoos.

I am Akila. I am the people you destroyed.

No expression crossed his face, but Sinon couldn't hide his burst of shock and recognition from me. *How did you get here?* His fingers were like shriveled claws in the harsh lamplight. *Why aren't you dead?*

I refused to give him the satisfaction of a response, even as he rose to his full height and loomed above me.

What do you want? I signed with fingers that were frail feathers to his talons.

If you use your Knowing again, I will kill you, he signed, and I believed him. I was mildly surprised to discover that there was still a little will to live left inside me.

What do you want? I repeated.

I want to know who's helping you. If you tell me now, they won't be harmed.

I stared at him.

I will have you executed if you don't tell me.

So?

Sinon smiled dangerously. *I will have your mother executed if you don't tell me.*

My stomach dropped because he *did* know who my family was.

My mother was alive, unless he was bluffing.

I waited until I had caged my surprise and anger, then signed calmly, *Why do you think I had help?*

Sinon's smile grew wider and his body shook. A Paav's laugh. *No Knower is powerful enough to control people, like in the stories. Somebody had to help you. You're just a little girl.*

And I suppose the friend you sent to kill me back on Akila just lost track of his knife and forgot to slit my throat?

Sinon took a step back as if reconsidering how dangerous I might be. *The only reason you are still alive is that I know you have information about other traitors in our empire, but our ruling family has little patience for threats and lies and even less for Knowers. Your execution – and your mother's – can be ordered at any moment.*

I have no information about any traitors.

Don't be so stupid. He flexed his hands, knuckles cracking. *There are many ways to coax that information out of you. Believe me, this is by far the most pleasant.*

I told you, I signed, *I have nothing to say. I had no help.*

Did you swim here, then?

I made myself smile, though every part of me fought it. *There are many places for a 'little girl' to hide in a trade ship.*

Sinon's unnaturally round eyes seemed to actually grow. *It was you, wasn't it? In Ana? You tried to kidnap Konu. and the* Phoemek *– that was your ship!*

I had to tread so carefully at that moment, but not because I cared for my own life. *Roni. Flick. Lin. My family.* I had caused them enough harm already, a hundred times over. I signed more and more slowly, as if I were growing tired. *I have no idea what you're talking about. Besides, it wouldn't be kidnapping if I was rescuing my own brother, would it?*

Sinon dropped his sneer, and I thought I caught a whiff of worry from his mind, but his signs were forceful as ever. *He is not your brother. He is Berik's son, my nephew.*

Berik. Your brother? How could this monster have a brother? How could he have anything in common with me at all? *Does he have blue eyes?* I signed stupidly.

He is a good father. Konu wants for nothing.

My anger simmered. I swallowed it down. *Konu wants for his real family.*

Sinon shrugged. *He's already forgotten you. You frightened Berik with your act in Ana, but they'll leave here soon, and you'll never need to worry about Konu again.*

I waited until I could stop my hands from trembling. *Where does Berik think Konu came from?*

He knows where he came from. He thinks he is an orphan, which is as good as true.

The simmer threatened to boil over. *I'm done talking,* I signed.

The sneer was back. *You have one week to tell me who's helping you. Then we resort to other methods.*

I laid back down on my stomach, wishing I could melt into the stone and disappear. Sinon walked away, his footsteps fading into hated memories.

***

In the endless dark, I prayed to the goddesses I'd always believed looked after me. Luna. Phoemek, Thera, and now, Donya of the earth and the Knowers. *Is Itu with you? Are you even real?*

There was no answer.

I imagined the fish-people from Sofi's stories on Kuul. I thought I knew what they must have felt like, pulling themselves out of the safe, warm water onto cold and heartless stone.

Itu, Itu, Itu... His name was a weight, pushing me back into that water but finding it was no longer safe. I couldn't breathe. I was drowning.

The only hint that time had passed came in the guards' movements — the bread shoved through the bars and the glaring light in my dark-weakened eyes. Three times, four, then Sinon, to whom I told nothing, five, six...

The seventh time, though, was different. A thought intruded into my half-waking nightmare, only striking in its blandness, its distance from anything I was feeling—the thought of looking forward to a bowl of noodle soup, a glass of sweet wine, and a comfortable bed in a house I'd never seen.

My bars rattled, and the bread dropped through. The guard walked on, and the thought faded.

I remembered then how I'd been so overwhelmed by everyone's grief when we found the slaughtered monks outside Mata City. Roni had helped me out of that—helped me separate the world's grief from my own.

Roni wasn't here to help this time, but maybe I didn't need him to be.

I'd experienced horrible, awful things. I'd watched Itu brutally murdered when it should have been me. I ached for Konu, for Brahn, for my mother, for my island and the life I would never lead. That was all real, terribly real, but giving up—that wasn't real. That wasn't me.

I am Alesea of Akila, daughter of Maia and protector of my people, I told myself. *I will not give up.*

Emotions that weren't my own trickled into my consciousness. How had I missed them before, so intense and sorrowful? That weeping woman mourned her lost son. A man across from my cell—a Watcher—was near-paralyzed with fear. I reached into myself and found a little of the hope I'd felt when we made it to Mata, when Sasha's family let us in, when I found out Konu was alive and well. I took that tiny hope and nurtured it as best as I could. Then, I spread it as far as I could over the sad and frightened prisoners, until it met something it recognized, something more potent—a hope mixed with a love so fierce it hurt.

Mama.

Of course! How many Paav prisons could there be?

Mama, I'm here. Could she hear me? Sense the love I poured into every word? *I'm here, I'm alive!*

Alesea?

Mama, I'm really here! I'm a Knower... I—

Alesea, are you talking to me?

It's me, Mama. I am.

Am I dying? You're dead! They told me you were dead, but I felt... I felt something so familiar. As Mama spoke to me through our mind connection, her emotions grew more complex. Joy—finding out I was alive. Deep sorrow—having lost me before, having lost Konu. Hope and love, and then pain. Agonizing, physical pain.

Mama, I sent, having lost track of her words. *Are you hurt?*

There it was again, a throbbing pain I couldn't localize. *I'm all right, Alesea. How did you get here, if this is real? Have you found your brothers?*

She wasn't all right, it was apparent now. I couldn't tell her about Itu. I could only tell her Konu was safe, and Brahn and Lori as far as I knew. I felt for her with my mind and tried to hold some of her pain like I'd done for Roni on the *Phoemek*. Without physical touch, it was too exhausting. The words got harder to project as I went on, like they had to pass through a thickening sludge.

Mama was silent when I finished. Maybe she couldn't hear me anymore, but having told her about Konu, the question I'd been waiting to ask burned inside me. I forced my mind out and tried again. *Mama, why did you tell me my father was dead?*

I had to strain my mind to catch her thoughts. *He... it was best. He loves you.* Her presence continued to fade, and I felt guilty for wasting our conversation on blame. A neighbor's fear butt into my thoughts, like someone running into me in the marketplace.

Mama! I thrust into the thought-sludge. *I love you so much.*

Alesea. The love I felt in return was enough to warm my bones, lift my heart, and give me the strength to plan a way out of that hell.

***

I felt like I'd finally woken up from a long, drugged sleep. I couldn't waste any more time getting out of this cell, couldn't wait for Sinon's "other methods." And that meant preparing my body for action, keeping my mind controlled and my purpose clear.

So, I swallowed every crumb of stale bread and drank all the musty water. I made myself do one-armed push-ups and paced around my tiny cell until I was too dizzy to continue. I meditated for hours. When Sinon visited again, I turned my back to him and lay down, pretending to be the harmless, destroyed girl he wanted me to be.

With my renewed vigor, I could no longer numb my thoughts to the memories of Itu's murder. I watched it in my mind, over and over, and every time I came to the same conclusion: if I hadn't let my panic spill over, the guard wouldn't have been so alarmed and killed Itu, at least not so quickly.

I hated myself for it, but I knew it was true. Every time I used my Knowing as a weapon—on purpose or not—people got hurt. Sometimes it had saved my friends and me like leaving Ana, but there were too many outcomes I couldn't predict. Despite all that had happened since that vision on the *Phoemek*, I didn't intend to renege on my vow of non-violence, and I wouldn't.

To escape the Fa'ad army, I had used my Knowing differently—and it had worked. I didn't control anyone, did I? No matter what Yalene thought, I hadn't read their thoughts or made their choices—I had just shown them love as best I could. No one got hurt.

Aanuman and the Listeners in the tunnels had found something in my heart, something deeper than a freakishly strong Knowing power. They didn't call me *Trekana* because of my power alone, but because of the choices I'd made in how to use it.

What if I *was* meant to use my Knowing, but only for good? If that meant accepting my role as *Trekana*, and whatever responsibilities came with it, so be it.

So, I practiced reaching out with my mind, sending little bits of hope and comfort to the depressed souls close to my cell, and occasionally glimpsing Mama further away. *Love will win,* I told myself and the minds around me. *Love has to win.*

Every time a guard passed, I pushed a little harder with my Knowing. *We are innocent,* I sent, keeping my projections as subtle as possible, but real. I gathered up my neighbors' sorrow and let it spill gently into the hall as guards passed my cell, and my next hunk of bread was a little larger. I sent hope, and a guard's hand lingered by my bars as his round eyes glinted in his torchlight, studying me. *Let us go,* I sent. *Set us free.*

Soon, the guards shone their lights into my cell to look me in the face. *Do you need anything else?* one of them signed.

I reached out and nearby felt sharp hunger pangs. *No, but my neighbor needs more bread,* I signed back, smiling sweetly.

The guard nodded and pulled an extra chunk from his loaf.

The next time that kind guard came by, I was ready.

Do you need anything else? he signed.

My heart pounded so loudly he must have seen my tunic trembling. *Now,* I thought. It was time.

I need to get out, please, I signed. At the same time, I gathered up all my courage—nothing subtle about it—and sent it to him. *Let the girl out,* I thought at him. *She's innocent. She's not dangerous. Let her out.*

The guard stood there, frozen, for a long time. I did my best to radiate love, innocence, and the need to be free.

Exit's that way, he finally signed, jerking his head to my left. *You've got two minutes, no more.*

I held my breath as he pulled out the silver hoop that held a dozen or more little keys. His hands shook as he fumbled for the right key.

He turned it in the lock, then walked away in the opposite direction he'd told me to go for the exit.

I kicked my discarded blanket into a heap, hoping it would look like I was still sleeping there. Then I pushed on the door.

With a tiny squeak, it swung open. I suppressed my rising excitement, trying to project calm and contentment, and reached out to my mother.

Mama, I thought. *Mama, where are you?*

I couldn't find her, couldn't feel her anywhere. I crept down the hallway, thinking her name, daring to whisper it out loud. Every cell was pitch black without a lamp or a Watcher's eyes.

A door slammed shut somewhere behind me. Footsteps approached, and a glance back revealed a fast-growing point of light.

I ran. I ran until I smacked straight into a wall. Or was it a door? I felt up and down and sideways, ignoring the pain in my nose and forehead until I found a handle. It pushed down to open quickly, while the dimmest light revealed a long, straight stone staircase heading up.

I closed the door behind me and took the stairs two at a time, my leg muscles screaming at the effort after so many days or weeks in that tiny cell. At the top, I found the light source—a few horizontal slats high up in a solid iron door. Was it sunlight? I grabbed the wrought iron lever handle and pressed down.

It didn't move.

Before I could decide what to do next the door swung into me, hard, whacking my nose a second time. This time I heard it crack. Blood trickled, then poured down my face. I struggled not to sniffle as I stood trapped between the wall and door, dripping.

A leather boot stomped into view and paused. A gloved hand appeared and started to push the door closed.

No! I struggled out of my corner, slipping once in my own blood, then ducked under the person's outstretched arm to flee onto the twilit street.

CHAPTER 41

I must've looked like a wild drunk—I nearly collided with a bicycle, and in avoiding it I leaped in front of an oncoming horse and carriage, which missed me by an inch. Something boomed, and the sky lit up with red fireworks.

I had no idea where I was. My memory of the night I'd been captured was foggy at best, and I was reasonably certain it had involved a wagon at some point, my mind too clouded with grief and shame over my brother's senseless death.

Move. I randomly picked a direction and ran along the sidewalk, then dashed into an alley between two pubs. I pictured a cage in my mind, the best I could do, and hoped it would keep my emotions from driving everyone into a frenzy.

I took another random turn and, running down a crowded street, I barreled straight into a hooded man whose Watcher tattoos extended onto his face and neck.

I nearly collapsed to the ground. It would be the shortest escape ever. I jerked from side to side, trying to escape his grip on my arms until relief and love flooded me.

Alesea. Alesea. Alesea.

I stopped struggling, shocked, and looked up at what I thought to be the Paav man.

Roni! How did—

He loosened his hold on my arms, and I looked closer. The hood covered his ears, and whoever drew the fake tattoos did it with much more skill than me back when Roni was dying on the *Phoemek*.

Yalene drew them, Roni thought. *She's very good.*

I fought an unexpected, misplaced pang of jealousy, and Roni's mouth turned up for just a moment.

Roni, Itu — he's —

More fireworks exploded, nearly straight above us.

Roni swept me inside his cloak, putting his arm over my shoulders, and I suddenly realized how much my injury had healed, thanks to Hector.

What had happened to Hector?

I clung to Roni's cloak like a life preserver.

Try to look like a woman of the night, Roni thought, his voice tinged with the humor that was so familiar and so... Roni. How was it possible, after everything that had happened?

I'm bleeding all over your cloak.

It's okay, pretend I punched you. He guided me past a group of loudly arguing Doubles and turned us onto the next street.

I could barely see a thing, but I didn't really care — it was a relief to let Roni steer me to wherever we were going. *How did you find me so quickly?*

Ever since we got word you were in the prison we've been watching it, trying to get on the good side of the neighbors and find a way in. He smiled, at least in his mind. *Then I saw you bolt out of there all by yourself, and I had to catch you.*

Roni's pride in me made me feel even more ashamed of all my horrible mistakes. I didn't know what to say. Instead, an image of a club descending over Itu's head flashed across my mind, and I couldn't make it stop.

Roni flinched. *Oh, Alesea.*

It was my fault.

None of this is your fault, Roni insisted, and I could tell he believed it, but I would never forgive myself, not for Itu.

Brahn and Lori are safe in the tunnels. You'll see them soon.

Oh! The tiniest bit of weight lifted from my heart. *Oh, thank you.*

Stupid little words. I didn't deserve Roni.

I cleared my mind and tried to focus on keeping my steps steady over what now felt like cobblestones. *Where are we going?*

Safety. Without warning, Roni veered through a narrow doorway into a room crowded with bodies and smoke.

Fire! I thought, alarmed.

It's just smoke. They set these herb sticks on fire then they breathe it.

What? Why?

Except Roni didn't answer, because suddenly I flew. Someone grabbed me around the waist and swung me around in the air.

Alesea.

Lin!

He set me on the ground and gave me a long kiss, bloody nose and all, right in front of Roni. Pain stabbed through my face, but I kissed back.

You rescued her! Lin signed excitedly when he finally let go. It was so loud in the pub from shouted conversations and out-of-tune music that I wouldn't have heard him talk, anyway.

I turned to see Roni's reaction. No one else even spared us a glance as they held those flaming sticks, and some swayed like they were in a trance.

She escaped, Roni signed. *I just caught her.*

I can't believe it! To me, *How did you do it?*

I shook my head. *No time.* I took both of my friends' hands and thought-spoke. *I've got to get Konu, now. Before Sinon finds out I've escaped, before Sinon's brother takes Konu back to Ana.*

Sinon's brother? Roni thought, then Lin just after, like an echo.

Yes. That's who Konu is really with right now, at Sinon's house. Once Sinon finds out I've escaped, he'll hide them, or send them away. Let's go!

Wait! One of them thought, but I let go of their hands and headed towards the door.

Which way to the Paav district? I signed to my side.

Roni grabbed my arm, turned me around, and spoke through contact. *We should at least take the back door.*

***

We found a coat rack with a few items of clothing hanging on it in the back room of the pub. I silently begged forgiveness from whoever would be missing their clothes as I selected a dark blue cloak with a hood like Roni's. It was way too big for me, but it was worth it for the complete coverage, especially with my bloody face and exposed ears.

Lin had found a rag and dumped someone's drink onto it and used it to wash the worst off my face. When he touched my swelling nose, I stifled a cry, and he stopped with a sympathetic wince.

Roni and Lin held my hands as we headed out the back door into a seedy alley and the blessed, double-mooned night.

***

I became even more disoriented as we walked through the dark city streets, but Roni and Lin seemed to know exactly where we were going.

We spoke in our thoughts, convenient but awkward as Roni and Lin couldn't hear each other, only me. They chattered simultaneously, and my already aching head felt like it might burst. Once I fed them all the information I'd learned about Sinon and the Paav district, Roni and Lin came up with a plan to get into Sinon's house with all the enthusiasm of two boys planning a treehouse raid.

The closer we got to the Paav district, the more carefully we walked. I pretended to be drunk, which wasn't difficult in my condition, and Lin and Roni put their arms around me as if holding me up.

I didn't care as long as it got me to Konu.

Two more zig-zagging blocks downhill, and we arrived at the dark barrier fence of the Paav inner district.

We kept to the shadows and scouted out the area around the northeast wall. At least something was in our favor. A light went out in the back window as we passed the red house a third time, so someone was home and going to bed.

We settled on a huge, leafless tree that had been allowed to grow branches over the Paav fence. There were a couple of similar trees on the other side for our return trip.

The only problem was the street lights. One of them cast its glow into the middle branches and was just a few feet from the tree I needed to climb.

You two hide over there, Roni thought to me, jerking his head toward a shadowy area next to a storage building. *I'll take care of the light.*

I repeated the instructions for Lin. We kept up our drunk act until a young Watcher couple passed out of view, then Lin and I hid in the darkness.

Roni picked something up off the ground and straightened to his full height, somehow transforming into a real Paav right in front of our eyes. He walked — no, strutted — along the sidewalk as if he was patrolling it. He disappeared around a corner as a group of older Double men passed by, slumped and dragging from a long day's work or maybe the pub, but once they were out of sight, he reappeared and walked in our direction.

He approached the offending streetlight and made a lightning-quick motion with one arm.

The glass globe shattered. The light sputtered and went out.

Roni acted like nothing had happened, still strutting toward us.

Lin and I crept along the now-darkened fence until we reached our tree. Roni faced away from us and stayed there as a lookout. No one would dare to question a regal Paav man standing in the dark, glaring at strangers. Or so we hoped.

The bare branches, so different from those of my beloved *kreo* trees, still held something of the comforting feeling of home. I was up above the fence so quickly I caught a whiff of surprise from Lin before he caged it off. I swung myself around and slid down one of the iron posts. My knees buckled at the impact as I fell into the inner Paav district.

Lin whispered from above me. "Go ahead. I'll be right there."

I crept around the corner of the red house to find the window we'd seen from outside the fence. I pushed branches of shrubs aside and carefully peered through. The room was dark, but from the outline of an armchair and table, I guessed it wasn't a bedroom. The "family" would be asleep in other rooms, hopefully.

I winced at the thud that was Lin dropping over the fence. A moment later, he was behind me, breathing fast.

"Will it open?"

There was nothing to hold onto, so I pressed my hands hard against the glass and pushed up. Something cracked, and I grasped at the air as the entire pane of glass fell into the house with a deafening crash. I glanced back at Lin, frozen behind me like a mouse run into a predator, fear seeping out of his emotional shield.

I kept focused. "C'mon, they can't hear us. Boost me up."

Except one of them could hear us.

Konu's cry spilled out of the house into the night. Oh, those familiar little gulps and whimpers.

All I had to do was follow that sound and finally hold my baby brother again.

I stepped onto Lin's joined hands and thrust myself through the window, stupidly landing on my side on the broken glass. Konu sobbed louder as I lay there, gasping with pain.

Lin hadn't come through the window yet, but I knew I had to hurry with Konu crying. How did Watcher parents know their children were crying, anyway? I'd never thought of it.

I struggled to my feet, creating a new cascade of tinkling glass shards, and followed the sound of Konu's cries down a short hall to the open doorway of a bedroom.

Oh, goddess. A lamp flared to life on the far wall, lit by the round-faced man. Berik. He picked Konu up off a little bed, piled with pillows and red blankets, and hugged him tight.

Berik hadn't seen me yet, and I backed further into the shadows. He wouldn't have heard the glass. Should I risk hiding until they all went back to sleep or rush in and grab Konu? Berik gently bounced my baby brother, patting his back until the sobs slowed.

Lin's feet crunched in the broken glass, and I signed *wait* behind my back.

Then, Konu's head lifted and turned enough toward me that I could see him smile at something in the hall.

Sinon stepped into the lit room. Even his nightclothes were red. He tousled Konu's hair then signed something. Berik signed back, and I made out a couple of words. *Cold air.*

Sinon nodded and turned toward the broken window. He would see me any second — as soon as he stepped out of the light to investigate the source of the draft. I balled up my anger in my mind, ready to cast it towards him, Berik, whoever got in my way.

Sinon turned back to sign something else to Berik, and I released the breath I didn't even realize I'd been holding.

What the demons was I doing? Hadn't I just renewed my vow, in that horrible prison cell, that I would never hurt anyone with my Knowing again?

What if all I did was make Konu terrified of me, again? What if I lost him forever?

Sinon turned back around, and Berik walked with him toward the doorway. They spotted me at the same time, their already-large eyes growing wider in unison.

Konu squeaked — perhaps Berik had squeezed him too hard. *Please,* Berik signed with one hand, *take what you want and leave.*

Sinon stepped forward, a look of astonishment plastered on his too-long face.

"I want my brother!" I spoke aloud and signed every word, forcefully spelling out his name. "Konu."

At his name, Konu lifted his head from Berik's shoulder and peered at me, sniffling.

He looked so much older, bigger. His long hair flew around his head in wild wisps.

"Laysi?" he said, but he shrunk back into Berik as he spoke, squinting at me like I might be a ghost, a vision. "Laysi?"

Berik looked between Konu and me, Konu and me. I heard Lin approach behind me, but I kept my eyes locked on Konu's.

"I love you." I imagined his little arms around my neck and me burying my face in his soft curly hair. I took that love and sent it straight to him.

"*Konu, Konu-lala Ko Ko.*" I sang his personal lullaby.

"Laysi!" Konu struggled to come to me, but Berik held tight. Simon took another step toward me.

Berik grabbed Sinon's shoulder to stop him, then signed, *Who are you?*

I'm his sister, I signed, keeping my eyes locked on Konu as I continued to pour love on him. *He's not an orphan.*

I could feel fear and anger radiating off Sinon, but Berik's emotion was open bewilderment. He sat Konu on his bed and squatted down to face him. *Sister?* Berik signed.

Yes, signed Konu. He looked nervously into Berik's face, his eyes darting between us.

Berik stood and turned to his brother, and now the strongest anger in the house came from him. *How could you?* he signed furiously. *I never believed them that you had become a monster. But...*

Sinon turned his back on Berik. I couldn't read his profile, couldn't separate his emotions from Berik's at that moment. Instead, I sent more love to Konu.

"Laysi?" Konu stood and pulled on Berik's hand, but when the man didn't budge, he let go and ran to me.

My brother leaped into my arms. He had grown heavier and taller. His head knocked my chin, hard. Before I understood what was happening, my swollen nose was in his hair, smelling his sweetness, his arms encircled my neck, and my love poured through the two of us. "Oh, Konu. I've missed you so much."

Berik backed away from Sinon and stood frozen in the center of the room, tears running freely from his strange blue Watcher eyes.

"Let's go." I directed that command to Lin, who was still silent behind me.

"And just leave them here?"

I realized with a shock that much of the fury I felt was Lin's. It rolled off him in hot waves, his emotional shield broken.

"I have Konu now." I turned to look directly into Lin's eyes. "We're leaving." I started toward the window and then thought better of it and looked around for a door.

Lin growled low in his throat and stomped past me. He grabbed Sinon's arm and spun him around, forcing him to look at us. Sinon lost his balance and landed on his knees.

"*You* are the monster!" Lin roared and didn't bother translating into Watcher-speak.

Lin fumbled with his pants leg before producing a knife, then stood over Sinon with the evil thing pointed at his heart, its blade reflecting yellow in the lamplight.

"Lin, no! You promised."

Lin glanced at me as Sinon kneeled calmly, expressionless.

Berik stared at his brother, weeping.

"He killed Yalene's mother! He kidnapped all your people, stole your brother, and tried to kill you." Lin's voice cracked. "He deserves to die!"

"Laysi, Laysi," Konu whimpered.

"Lin, stop." Somehow my voice held steady. "He may deserve to die, but you don't deserve to be a murderer."

"I'm not a murderer if it's justice." Furious determination took over Lin's uncaged emotions as he raised the knife to strike. He really planned to kill Sinon, and maybe Berik, too.

"No!" I focused all the rage I'd shoved to the back of my mind and threw it out to stop that knife and Lin.

The weapon dropped harmlessly on the floor, and Lin grabbed his head with both hands, falling backward until he sat rocking on the floor. Blood poured from his nose, and a horrible groaning sound emerged from his throat.

Sinon and Berik flinched away, too, but it was Lin I'd hit directly and whose mind I'd attacked.

His eyes meeting mine were so much worse than the sound. The face I'd kissed and caressed now contorted with pain, confusion, and utter betrayal.

Hatred.

"Lin, I'm so sorry, Lin."

CHAPTER 42

As I stared at Lin, horrified at what I'd done, Sinon spun on his heel and fled down the hall. A door slammed.

Go, Berik signed. *Leave.* He turned back into the bedroom and sat down hard on Konu's little bed. I almost felt sorry for him.

I love you, Konu, I sent to my brother. "Lin," I projected my regret as hard as I could. "Come on, let's go."

No response.

"Lin, come on. Sinon's probably gone to get help. Hurry!"

Lin pulled himself to his feet, but something was terribly wrong. He slouched oddly. His features were stuck in an expression of agony, or disgust.

"Lin, I'm so sorry. I didn't mean —"

"Go away. And don't follow me." His voice was hoarse, broken. "Ever."

He turned and half-ran, half-limped in the direction Sinon had left.

"Lin!" I rushed after him, holding Konu tight. The front door at the end of the hall was left wide open, with no sign of Lin anywhere.

"Lin!" I dared to whisper, then softly call, into the darkness. "Lin, come back!"

Nothing.

Then, marching footsteps — heavy ones, not far away. I had to get Konu out of there.

I plunged through the bushes toward the perimeter fence, pushing Konu's face into my shoulder so only my face got scratched. Roni stood next to the tree we'd come in on, waiting.

His face lit up with a broad, open-mouthed smile, ruining his Paav disguise. *Konu! I saw the light, I was worried —*

Quick, I signed with one hand. *I'll need help.*

We rushed on opposite sides of the fence to the far end of the house, where a tree on my side stood close enough to climb over.

"Konu, baby, remember climbing trees?" I tried to keep my love flowing and my panic caged. "I'll lift you up on a branch and then you need to climb up one more so I can come up. Then we'll be safe."

Konu turned his head, looked at the tree, and then buried his head in my shoulder.

"Konu, please, I know you're scared. Please." I peeled him off me and turned him back toward the tree. He sniffled.

Konu. Roni leaned down and signed through the fence at Konu's level, smiling nervously. *It's me, Roni! I'll catch you.*

I lifted Konu onto the lowest branch, grateful that my right arm cooperated with my left, even though it was weak. "Just one, KoKo. Climb to the next one." I struggled to keep my voice as cheerful as if we were playing a game.

He climbed, and I swung myself up into the tree. I helped Konu to the edge of the iron fence, balancing between the tightly spaced branches. He whimpered. *Go back,* he signed with one hand.

I'll catch you, Konu. Roni lifted his arms high.

Footsteps echoed from all directions. Somewhere nearby a door slammed. Konu squeaked as fireworks exploded nearby.

"It's okay, KoKo," I said. "Roni's got you." Steady on my branch, I lifted Konu over the edge and dropped him into Roni's waiting arms.

***

We ran through pitch-black alleys, our footsteps far too loud, fear and desperation forcing my exhausted legs to take one more step, just one more step.

Where's Lin? Roni signed as a single-lit window gave me enough light to make out his hands.

I shook my head. Someone might take Konu if I let go of him to sign, even with one hand. I would lose him again, and I would die.

So I clung to him, his hair blowing into my face and his fingers digging into my back. How did he still smell like the southern sea?

Once he realized I'd taken away his new father, would he hate me more than Lin now did?

Roni slowed and turned to face me. *I can feel your mind,* he signed. *I don't know how far it goes.*

I glanced around the empty street, wondering if my Knowing was reaching into buildings, influencing strangers' dreams. I turned my mind to chanting and counting. *A'lodi sahm, A'lodi sahm.*

Lin, my mind whispered again and again, but I built a cage just for his name and stuffed it inside. *A'lodi sahm.*

We slowed our pace close to the Fisher district. I hoped we were far enough to be safe in our disguise — a hooded, head-down girl with a small child and a hooded, tattooed Watcher leading her.

I couldn't make my body run for another second as I dragged behind Roni. He tried to take Konu from me. A growl like a scared animal came out of my throat along with an uncontrolled burst of emotion. Roni flinched.

Sorry, I signed with two fingers.

He didn't try again, even though our pace grew slower and slower.

We passed a pair of Watcher guards. Roni nodded to them as if he belonged among their ranks, despite the revulsion I felt coming from his mind. They nodded back.

Thank the moons. By morning, they would all be hunting us.

The first dull grey of dawn seeped into the filthy cracks of the Fisher district as we finally reached the *Fisher's Rest,* our entrance to the tunnels. Roni knocked a pattern on the locked door, and as we waited, I wondered who had taught it to him.

The same grizzled man who'd recited the passphrases to Lin answered the door, blinking sleep from his squinted eyes.

"Lookin' for a room?" His eyes opened a little more as they scanned Roni's fake tattoos, then lowered to meet mine.

I nodded, unsure of the correct answer. The man's eyes returned to Roni, who must have signed it because the man opened the door the rest of the way to let us in.

"Donya be with you." He kept his voice low as we made our way to the storeroom and the entrance to the tunnels.

***

Down, down, down. My eyes longed to stay and watch the sunrise. Just the thought of going back underground for goddess knew how long made them water with frustration, but Konu slept on my shoulder, and though my muscles trembled, my injuries throbbed, and my stomach cramped, I would not let go.

Roni stopped at the bottom of the stairs. He put his arms around me, squeezing Konu between us, and I reached out for the comfort of his mind.

Are you all right? he asked.

I have Konu. That will have to do for now.

And Lin?

The flood within me burst to the surface, and I sank to the bottom stair, heaving with sobs. Konu mumbled and shifted, half-asleep, and I cradled him in my arms as I had when he was a baby and life was easy. Would he be happy to see me when he woke? Or would he want to return to his new Paav home and the man he called Daddy? Would he see me at all down here in the oppressive darkness of the tunnels?

I felt Roni's warmth as he knelt in front of me. He touched my hand.

You rescued Konu, he thought. *He's safe here.*

I gulped down another sob and wiped my nose on my shoulder.

I broke people to do it. I broke Lin.

I cried and rocked Konu as he finally slept. It felt like hours before the sobs subsided, and I was able to absorb some of Roni's ever-present calm. Roni never took his hand from mine.

We should go, I finally thought, and rearranged Konu to rest again on my shoulder. I considered asking Roni to carry him, but I still couldn't bear to let him go. I might hold him forever.

I fell into a trance as we walked that endless pitch-black tunnel. I didn't count, I didn't chant my mantra, my thoughts didn't stray to the night's events. I simply walked, Roni's and my footsteps making dull echoes down the tunnel. *Ka-chunk-a-pop. Ka-chunk-a-pop.*

"Halt!" This time the voice that shook me into awareness was male, low, and gruff. "Who approaches?"

I touched Roni's arm to stop him as the man's clicks and pops resounded down the corridor. "We are friends." Konu jerked awake with a tiny whimper. "Shhh, Konu, you're with Laysi now, Go back to sleep."

"Name yourselves!" The man sounded closer.

The tunnel was wide enough for me to step up alongside Roni. He put his arm around my shoulder.

"Alesea of Akila, with Roni and Konu of Akila." I searched my mind for the name I'd learned before my imprisonment. "Friends of Goshi."

"The *Trekana?*" Skepticism laced the man's voice. Another voice spoke, muffled, then another. How many people had we alerted?

The murmuring died down as a familiar voice rang joyfully from further down the tunnel. Goshi. "*Trekana,* you have returned!"

I stepped back at the wave of reverence that hit me like a physical force – full of joy, but joy that burned with a religious fervor that terrified me.

I pressed into Roni's side, solid as a hundred-year *kreo* tree. *What do they want from me?* I asked.

Hope.

Bodies shuffled and Goshi's voice came closer. "Come, *Trekana*. We are prepared for you."

I couldn't make my feet move. Then something rushed at me—something I couldn't see, but it was big, fast, and full of life. I shrank back, trying to shield Konu from this new threat, but it wasn't a thing.

It was a *who*.

Brahn threw his burly arms around me, squishing Konu between us. "Alesea! Oh, Alesea, Konu, we thought you were dead... we couldn't believe..."

I squeezed back. "I'm okay, Brahn, I'm okay." Brahn cried, but I had no tears left. "Itu... your baby... I'm so sorry."

"I know. Me, too, but you're here. You're here!"

"Bahn?" Konu's little voice came out muffled against my shoulder.

"Oh, Konu!" Brahn reached out for my baby brother, and I finally released him into Brahn's arms. "I missed you so much."

"Laysi came."

"She did." Brahn agreed. "Now that we're together again, let's go find Lori."

"Lori!" Konu chirped as Brahn started walking back the way he'd come.

Roni gave me a gentle push, and I could walk again, following my brothers. We took a sharp left turn and heard the sound of swishing cloth, followed by an orange-yellow illumination of the damp walls of the tunnel. I caught a glimpse of Brahn—remarkably unchanged despite everything he'd been through—before he disappeared around the corner with a happily chattering Konu.

The Listeners who'd welcomed us stood in the glow, clad in dull robes, barefoot, and their arms and faces streaked with dirt. All but one of the half-dozen we'd followed had ridges instead of eyes. A short woman, curly hair matted into tufts around her eyeless face, held back a thick brown curtain. Goshi.

"There's light." I couldn't believe I sounded so stupid.

"We have changed our ways for the newcomers." The man with closed eyes helped the woman pull the curtain further aside for us to pass. Roaches scuttled away from our feet into the shadows, and before us stood a huge chamber filled with hundreds of people.

Some slept on blankets against the walls, while others sat on the bare floor or cushions, talking, laughing, and eating from crude wooden bowls. Brahn and Konu sat with Lori in front of another curtain not ten steps away. She smiled with that familiar mischievous glint in her eyes despite her sunken-in cheeks and overall thinness.

The conversation came to a halt as far too many pairs of eyes swiveled toward me, and a chorus of Listener clicks resounded like a forest full of crickets. Konu let out a tiny giggle—a sound that at any other time would've filled me with joy, rather than trepidation.

"The *Trekana* has come back to us!"

The crowd burst into whispers with Goshi's announcement, my pulse racing at their rising emotions as some repeated "*Trekana*," while many bowed their heads and placed their palms on their chests in a gesture of respect. Even a few Watchers—one of them tattooed—made the gesture.

Was someone translating, or had they been expecting me? Sleepers woke and whispered or signed to their neighbors, then joined in the show of adoration.

Roni, I thought to my friend. *What do I do?*

Roni didn't answer. I felt a gentle sense of awe even from him. Was it at the unexpected crowd or at me?

I cleared my throat. Anyone in the room with eyes to see locked them on mine. I translated my words into Watcher-speak for those without ears.

"Thank you for providing a safe space." My voice rose to fill the chamber. It wasn't so hard to look at their admiring faces if I thought of it as a performance. "You should know, I do not know what it means to be a *Trekana*. My people have never spoken of it, and I only came into my Knowing when the Paav stole my family."

The silence was palpable—not a single whisper or click, no help from the Listeners who'd brought me here or from Brahn and Lori, who looked at me as if I were a fascinating stranger.

"I don't know what I can do. I don't know if I can save the rest of my family, much less the others I've promised to help. I've hurt people with my Knowing without meaning to. I don't want to ever do that again."

They kept watching me as if waiting to hear the words that would change their lives, fix everything, and get them out of these depressing tunnels. I didn't even know what they wanted. For all I knew, maybe they liked the tunnels.

A leader. I didn't know if it was my own thought or someone else's, but it was right, all the same.

"What I do know is that what the Paav are doing is wrong. My people gave up violence five hundred years ago and slavery even longer ago than that. The Paav have no right to force you underground, just as they had no right to claim my brother was an orphan and take him from his family, to murder my older brother..." My voice cracked, but I did not stop. I could not stop. "To imprison my mother and force my people to work the fields." Some people nodded, and others whispered or spoke in rapid Watcher-speak to their neighbors.

I turned to meet Roni's eyes. *I believe in you*, they said.

It was all I needed to find enough hope to share.

I gathered strand after strand of it in my mind, naming each as I went. *Konu. Brahn. Lori. Flick. Aanuman.*

Roni. At his thought-name, Roni sent me his hope, too, and an inexplicable joy at being there with me in the bowels of Mata City.

I saw it all in my mind as clear as the Shallows on a calm, sunny day—sparkling and full of promise. Then I let it rush over the impossibly large and desperate crowd.

People gasped, laughed, and burst into sobs. *Trekana* they breathed, signed, or thought. *Alesea, Alesea,* they called.

"We will take back our people, your city, and my island," I hardly knew what I said, compelled by all their overcome minds to say what they needed to hear. Regardless, I let the words come out. "We will do it with love and peace, not killing and prisons, because we are right and the Paav are wrong. The goddesses shine down upon us. *A'lodi* bless."

A'lodi bless they murmured. Someone shifted along the back wall, drawing stares as she stood up from the piles of awed refugees. She glided through the maze of bodies—tall, thin, and dressed in a brilliant yellow dancer's costume of flowing pants and cropped tunic—until she stood in front of me, proud and arrestingly beautiful. Her abundant black hair was piled atop her head without a *ratina* in sight, just like when I'd first met her.

"I think I believe you," said Yalene. "Welcome to your revolution, *Trekana.*"

THE END

acknowledgements

When I started writing, acknowledgment sections were a source of wonder: how could so many people be involved in a book written by a solitary author? Now I understand, and I truly hope I'm not leaving anyone out!

First, thank you to Dave Lane (AKA Lane Diamond) and Evolved Publishing for taking a chance on Alesea's story and helping me through the publication process. Thank you to my editor Anita Lock, whose eye for the big picture and tiny details was invaluable during the editing process. I'm looking forward to working with you on the next book and beyond! To Melissa Craib Dombrowski, thank you for jumping in with your expertise to help with the launch and for being an awesome friend (and director!). I never would have finished this novel, and certainly not seen it published, without my critique group extraordinaire: Laurie Zuckerman, Bonnie Olsen, and Leslie Selbst, as well as Jeanne Fischer, many friends at Scribophile.com, and beta readers Natalie Prado, Lydia Netzer, Juliann Dean, and much of my extended family (you get the last paragraph)!

I am forever grateful to my colleagues, students, and families at Carolina Friends School, who not only tolerate but encourage my writing, even though I am technically paid to be a music teacher. Special thanks to Lisa Carboni, Ida Trisolini, Katherine Scott, and Ruffin Powell. Thanks to my Middle School advisees past and present, who've provided more inspiration and support than they know—and especially Ori Sandler, who helped me brainstorm early in the process and gets credit for the book's title.

As any author knows, a "debut" is rarely a writer's first book, and there are many people without whom I never would've made it to novel number four. Thank you to Allison Freeman, my very first beta reader for my very first novel; Lonnie Plecha and *Cricket Magazine*, the first to publish my stories; the many beta readers for my previous novels; all the wonderful folks at the Society for Children's Book Writers and

Illustrators (especially SCBWI-Carolinas); Flyleaf Books and the Root Cellar (check them out if you're ever in Chapel Hill, NC!); and the kind and creative souls at NaNoWriMo.

Most of all, I could not have done this without my family. My parents, Pat and Mike Sisk, never doubted for a moment that if I wanted to write novels, I would eventually be published. My brilliant sisters, Martha Wheeler and Stephanie Sisk Hilton, are a constant inspiration, support, and shoulder to cry on—or complain to! Thanks to my brothers-in-law Dan and Phil and nieces and nephews Erin, Kelly, Hannah, Max, and Juliet, most of whom beta-read this book. And, of course, to my wildly creative children who are my greatest cheerleaders and inspiration: Wednesday, Finn, and Davey, and my husband Jos—brainstorm partner, pet wrangler, and emergency comedian. I love you forever.

about the author

Jo Sisk-Purvis is an eclectic, enthusiastic, jump-in-feet-first creator, which means "scattered," but sounds more impressive. Her STEM-rich childhood led to a sensible three degrees in flute performance, with sides of composition, piano, and conducting. Jo has been a storyteller since she first learned that "Quack Quack knows that he's in luck, for he's a very special duck." For many years, she told her stories through music, but in 2010 decided that maternity leave was the perfect time to start writing novels (and adopt a puppy), and has been hooked ever since (on writing. Also puppies).

Jo's short stories have been published in Cricket Magazine, and she is excited to share her "The Trekana" series through Evolved Publishing. She teaches music at a wonderful Friends school that not only allows, but encourages, her quirky detours (they call them "diverse talents"). She music-directs for several theatre companies in central North Carolina, where she lives with her husband, three children, and a menagerie of pets from Captain the Cockatiel to her two sheep, Phineas and Ferb.

For more, please visit Jo Sisk-Purvis online at:
Website: www.JoSiskPurvis.com
Facebook: @JoSiskPurvis
Twitter: @Jo_Sisk

wHaT's next?

Watch for the second book in "The Trekana" series to release in late 2023: **THE KNOWERS**.

Teenage musician Alesea has become the reluctant leader of the Matan People's Revolution, as thousands find refuge in the tunnels under Mata City.

Alesea has found her surviving family, but it's a hollow victory, as the Paav still control Mata, the Islanders are homeless and grieving, and everyone is looking to Alesea as a miracle worker. Everyone, that is, except for Matan-born Yalene, whose mother died to save Alesea.

Yalene knows the Paav won't be overcome without violence, not after all they've done. She throws herself into teaching the refugees the ancient martial art of *I'kaan*, hoping they'll be able to defend themselves when Alesea's nonviolent movement fails.

When the tunnels are breeched, Alesea has to launch her plan before it's ready, and dozens of refugees are slaughtered. Torn by grief and indecision, she flees the city to find her Knower father, and Yalene leads the evacuation of the tunnels to find a new home—with the Paav hot on their trail.

MORE FROM
EVOLVED PUBLISHING

We offer great books across multiple genres, featuring high-quality editing (which we believe is second-to-none) and fantastic covers.

As a hybrid small press, your support as loyal readers is so important to us, and we have strived, with tireless dedication and sheer determination, to deliver on the promise of our motto:
QUALITY IS PRIORITY #1!

Please check out all of our great books,
which you can find at this link:
www.EvolvedPub.com/Catalog/

Thank you!

9 781622 530359